HER LIVING IMAGE

Jane Rogers was born in London in 1952. Her family moved frequently, so she attended eight different schools, including two in New York state. She read English at Cambridge, and trained to be a teacher at Leicester University. She has worked in a children's home, for a housing association, and as a teacher in comprehensive schools and further education. Her first novel, *Separate Tracks*, was published in 1983, her second, *Her Living Image* (winner of the Somerset Maugham Award), in 1984, and her third, *The Ice is Singing*, in 1987. She has also written a play, *Dawn and the Candidate*, for Channel 4.

Since 1980 she has lived in Lancashire with her husband and two children, and combines writing with childcare and occasional teaching of creative writing. She has paid several extended visits to Australia, where her family now live. In 1985–6 she was Arts Council writer-in-residence at Northern College, Barnsley, and in 1987–8, writing fellow at Sheffield Polytechnic.

By the same author

JANE ROGERS

Her Living
Image

faber and faber
LONDON · BOSTON

First published in 1984
by Faber and Faber Limited
3 Queen Square London WC1N 3AU
This paperback edition
first published in 1990

Filmset by Wilmaset, Birkenhead, Wirral
Printed in Great Britain by
Richard Clay Ltd, Bungay, Suffolk

British Library Cataloguing in Publication Data

Rogers, Jane, 1952–
Her living image.
I. Title
823'.914[F]   PR6068.03/

ISBN 0–571–13611–7

To Mick

Part One

Chapter 1

At eighteen, Carolyn Tanner was as thin as a stick, with lank no-colour hair which filled her mother with despair. She had the sort of face you wouldn't notice in a crowd; especially when she had carefully applied her make-up. The effect of the pearl-grey eye-shadow, blue-black mascara and black eye-liner which she favoured at that age was to make her look even more ghostly than nature intended. Without a crowd – or the make-up – you would notice her eyes. Not the eyes themselves, which were a pleasant if fairly ordinary clear grey, but the eyelids. Her eyelids were fuller than is common, framing her eyes with a thick, almost puffy-looking, curve of flesh. That fullness above the eyes was capable of curious effects, making her look at times as if her eyes were swollen with tears, at other times giving her plain face an exotic sensuality. She was never beautiful, but the combination of small regular features, clear pale complexion, and that soft vulnerable fleshy roll of eyelid, made up a face that people warmed to.

The day before her accident was a beautiful one. It was June 3, 1972.

Carolyn liked coming home in the afternoons. In summer she was often early, especially once exams started. The estate was quiet, its raw little gardens lying tranquil in the sun, the grass rectangles with curling-cornered turves and neat snapdragon borders basking purposefully as though they were the only reasons for the existence of the houses.

That summer the heat stood on the pavements and drooped in shimmering layers over the boiled new red-brick houses of the estate. Teachers wryly called it exam weather and claimed that May was always like this; it did not seem so, to Carolyn. The heat was exceptional, and so was everything else. Everywhere, suddenly, freedom was showing, like light in cracks behind heavy curtains, shining under doors, showing in pinpoints through keyholes – and brightening, intensifying like the warmth of the sun. Here she was coming home from school at two-thirty on a Thursday afternoon, and in another month it would be over entirely, exams and all. School would be over.

As she walked up the heat-shiny hill she was happy. In all directions: Alan (still greatly flattered, she was astonished and, yes, delighted); the luxury of coming home alone instead of in a yowling fighting four o'clock mob; the empty house ahead (which would smell of hot stuffiness, her nostrils tested the air for it already and touched on scents of hot tar, dry earth, cut and drying grass). Most of all, the English lesson made her almost bounce with glee. She used the word to herself, savouring her feeling; it was glee. How pathetic they were!

In the hot classroom the venetian blinds had made horizontal stripes which flowed up and down over desks and chairs like contour lines on a map. Lumps was talking about *Persuasion*.

"What about Anne then? What do you think of her, finally?" Carolyn felt she was a tiger, camouflaged by the stripes of shade, crouching ready to pounce.

"She's a wet!" said Katie Lawton, in the way that she did, looking round for appreciation of her biting wit.

And then they all chipped in, "Yes, she *is*, it's sickening the way she lets them push her around . . . she never does what she wants – how can she pretend she loves him when she just gives him up? She's pathetic. . . ."

Carolyn bided her time, waiting, listening.

At last Lumps said ruefully, "Does *any*one like her?"

Carolyn the tiger pounced.

"I – I – I – she *is* likeable. And good." She felt her red-hot blush spreading up her face as everyone's eyes were on her. "Because – she – she isn't wet at all, she does exactly what she thinks is right – and everyone else – in the book – does what they think they ought to do. At the beginning she does what they say – yes, that's why it's called *Persuasion*, but she does because she thinks they must be right and that's how she ought to behave. And then as

14

she gets older she manages – as she gets older – she thinks for herself what's right and wrong – she trusts herself more than what they think –'' Out of breath. Lumps grinning, everyone else still staring at her in surprise. *I did it. I told them!* Sitting back like a purring cat she only half listened while Lumps went rambling on about Romantic influences on Jane Austen. *I told them. So there!*

Arriving home she unlocked the door and pushed it open, standing still on the step to feel the stuffy heat expanding out, and to breathe in the lovely baked atmosphere of empty house. She went into the lounge, inhaling deeply the airless mix of undisturbed smells: Palmolive washing-up liquid, her father's pipe, and the simple smell of hot wood and fabric, like ironing. Then she opened the windows wide and stood waiting for the outside air to flow in, feeling the house air diluting, cooling slightly, its smells fading. That smell guaranteed emptiness. It was the greatest luxury of all, to come home before her mother.

Carolyn was happy. She had reached a peak of almost-confidence, both in her thin pale looks, which Alan liked, and in her own intellect. She could do it. She was as good as them. She felt the dizzy excitement of a diver on the highest board, facing the plunge – and the sense that (this was a secret which no one else knew) her own life was special, and would be somehow more important, more real, than anyone else's. When she was younger she had thought the same thing about her handwriting, which made her smile now. She used to think it amazing that of all the styles of handwriting (even in her class in Juniors where they were all taught the same kind of round joined-up writing by Mr Maples) only her own was instantly clear; everyone else's presented that momentary obstacle, of looking strange, of being handwriting instead of instant words.

Meg Tanner, walking home from work at the woolshop with her bag full of lunch-hour shopping, tasted like a sweet the image of Carolyn at home studying her books in the nice airy lounge.

Her bag was heavy and her varicose veins ached with a dull pressure on her shins and the back of her calves. She'd tried it with no tights today but it wasn't worth it, not by the end of the day. It may be very nice in the morning, but really you need support more than you need the cool. The cool is a luxury, put it that way, the support's a necessity. Jean said she wasn't keen on this heat either, well where's the pleasure in it when your feet swell up and your corset's wringing with sweat, where's the pleasure in that? You wouldn't catch me paying to lie and cook like meat in rows on the beach, they've got more money than sense.

Nearly five pounds for that wool, it's daylight robbery. Oh, go on – it'll suit her down to the ground, you knew that as soon as you saw it in the box, it's the colour of her eyes. Sea mist. Nice name too. It'll look a treat with that flared skirt.

Hearing the sound of a train from down the valley, she faltered in her step, then swapped the shopping bag to the other hand, straightened her shoulders and went on more quickly up the hill. Crawling along like an old woman, I bet you look a sight. My God though, my blouse is sticking right across my shoulders, it must be in the nineties. Have a bath when I get home. At least you can breathe up here, a bit. Get the breeze if there's any going. I'd be going mad down there and that's the truth – I would.

The Tanners had moved to one of the first houses on the new estate, from Railway Street, three years ago. They had started their married life in a council house, and it had taken them nine years to get to Railway Street. Railway Street was their own, paid for by Arthur's hours of filthy silent wrestling with recalcitrant engines, in the small garage that Charlie Watson owned but where Arthur did all the work. It was their own – but that was about all there was to be said for it. When a train passed every spoon and fork in the drawer had clattered up and down, separately and together, even after she'd lined the drawer with felt. Sometimes she'd got so she felt like screaming when the trains were coming. It's no good giving in to it, we can all be neurotic I always say, but it's enough to drive you round the twist when they're every half-hour and you're waiting for it and expecting it if it's a minute late, waiting to be rattled and joggled till your dentures click in your mouth.

Mrs Bateman and Angela coming. She's a tarty-looking thing, that girl, with her hair frizzed out like that.

"Warm enough for you? It is, isn't it? We should all go on strike, I say. I like your new hairdo, Angela love, it does suit you." As she walked on she considered Carolyn's hair, which was one of the major problems of her life. Would a light perm

16

help?

Regularly she ransacked the shelves of Boots the Chemist for new varieties of shampoo for her daughter, and the bathroom cabinet was stuffed with half-used bottles, discarded temporarily in favour of the latest seductive purchase: Silvikrin lemon and lime for greasy hair, Vosene medicated for dull lifeless hair, Sunsilk conditioner for light flyaway hair, Wella herbal cream rinse (to add body), Johnson's baby shampoo for frequently washed hair, and Bristow's Free and Lovely (for any sort of hair that wasn't). You name it, it's wrong with my Carolyn's hair. Always thought she'd grow out of it, but no, eighteen and she's still got hair like a baby, too fine to hold a curl or style at all. It wouldn't be so bad if it didn't get so greasy. She smiled to see in her mind's eye Carolyn's despairing demonstration of what it was like when she put on her new synthetic jumper. One side of her hair stuck flat to her head with static, the other stood on end and waved slowly up and down like a dishcloth boiling in the pan.

She noticed the new paint at number fourteen – like a sore thumb, bright orange. It's time Arthur gave that back door another coat. I'll have to remind him. He can give his blessed allotment a miss for once. Get that shawl finished tonight, Jean can put it in the window tomorrow and take the fisherman's rib out. Never sell a thing like that this weather, stands to sense. As she thought of Jean she remembered with disproportionate anger Jean's remark that afternoon. Meg had said something about Carolyn being good – in the house, or something, being helpful.

"She is, isn't she?" Jean said. "She's nearly too good to be true, your Carolyn."

Stupidly, Meg had fallen into the trap of defending Carolyn. "Well she is, though I say so myself. *I*'ve never had to lie awake at nights wondering where she is or what she's up to, she's always in bed by ten-thirty, and I've never had the cheek from her that some people have to put up with. She's not one for having lots of noisy friends in to mess up the place, either – she can amuse herself, thankyou. When I look at other people's kids I thank my stars, I do really." She wished she'd bitten off her tongue first. Spiteful bitch, saying things like that. Oh yes, Meg knew it was only jealousy, because Jean's Lizzie was such a little tramp, and she'd told herself again and again not to blow her own trumpet about Carolyn. But it's only natural, isn't it, to take a pride. Jean shouldn't have said that.

What Meg feared was that Carolyn really was too good to be true. It seemed to her to be quite likely. She had lost her first baby at birth; complications in a long slow labour, followed by the use of forceps, had injured it – killed it, she believed, although they told her its heart had already stopped. The second, Darren Philip, was born by Caesarean section. He died for no reason at two months. A cot death, the doctor said. And Carolyn June was the third. A beautiful baby, a good girl, watched like a hawk by her mother. For the eighteen years of Carolyn's life, Meg had held at bay the horrible diseases, the debilitating accidents, the rapists and murderers, snakes and spiders, hot kettles and irons, sharp knives and scissors, soft smothering pillows, electric sockets, steep stairs, chewing gum, plate glass and fumes from gas fires which daily, minutely, threatened her daughter. Behind every kindly daily surface lurked death, black jaws agape. And Meg was brisk and sensible and said cheerily, "Well, you can't let it get you down, can you?" and was better in herself and happier than ever now, since they'd moved from Railway Street.

But her enduring secret terror was that the black jaws would catch up with her Carolyn – and Carolyn's perfection made it all the more likely. Jean's remark made her want to cry.

And of course she remembered it afterwards – luridly, hideously, knew it had been a warning and hated Jean. Only many months later did she remind Jean of her remark, and Jean, horrified, cried, "But you know I didn't mean – I never meant – you know how I go on. Oh Meg, I am sorry!"

The young couple on the corner were out doing their garden. Meg smiled and nodded at them and wondered how they felt about number four? That garden's never been done since they moved in, it's a bit much when you try to keep the place nice and there's weeds and rubbish spreading like wildfire from next door. Spoils the whole row, it does. She saw the front room windows open and thought with pleasure of seeing Carolyn through the window – which she did as she turned in at the gate, Carolyn with her fair head down over her books. Meg turned her key in the Yale, plumped the shopping down in the kitchen and went and collapsed on the sofa.

"This heat takes it out of me – it really does."

18

Carolyn nodded without looking up. "Want some tea?"

"Please. Oh, Carolyn love, can you put that butter in my bag in the fridge? It'll be running away."

"Yup." Standing up, Carolyn glanced at her mother, who had just prised her feet out of her shoes. The shoes had left red indented rims around the flesh, so the feet looked like cakes newly turned out of tins.

After she had washed the tea things Carolyn went to her room to work, as she always did. Her Dad went out to the allotment as he always did, and her Mum sat watching telly, knitting, as she always did.

Carolyn liked her room, even though it was small. It was pink and white and clean. There was appleblossom on the wallpaper which she had chosen, and she had made two patchwork cushions for her bed, from pink and white flowered remnants. On the shelf above the bed were her foreign-costume dolls, each in its shiny Cellophane tube, and by the bed the poster of a baby polar bear and the one of Cliff Richard that Mandy had given her. The carpet, from the old house, was beige and faded, but by her bed she had a white (washable) long-haired rug. Her Dad had made her a work top, out of plastic wood, so she could study in her room. Opening her file, she bent her head over the intricate doodle on the inside cover, and started to add fine heart-shaped curlicues to the letters A–L–A–N which were drawn in stars at the bottom of the page.

Chapter 2

June 4 dawned hot again, but with a change, a closing in, of atmosphere. The sky at noon was metallic, and people felt in their heads a mounting pressure like rising irritation. The sky had turned into a great hot mouth which closed down over them, exhaling stale used air, came closer as if to suffocate and swallow them. Finally, in the afternoon, the first full hot drops fell from the sky – as if the sky itself was yielding to the great heat, and melting.

The first drips made big individual splotches on the school drive, and released smells of soil and cement. Then came lightning and very close thunder, and the rain began to fall more quickly, no longer in drips but in lines, pelting down, drilling into the ground. Where they drove down on to concrete or tarmac they bounced up again, to a height of six inches. Through every window in the school, children were looking out at the rain, transfixed. Carolyn, making Art History notes in the library, found her gaze irresistibly drawn to the window. Her friend Mandy was sitting beside her. Mandy was plump, energetic and unafraid. She knew a lot about things that Carolyn didn't, like religion and sex. She had been Born Again last year and it had weakened their friendship. Mandy had gone all the way, and told Carolyn about johnnys. ("They sell them in Boots. You go and have a look – on the medicine counter, near the aspirins – anyone can buy them!") Where Mandy led, Carolyn sometimes followed, although she was becoming increasingly stubborn and at times dug her heels in and refused to listen to reason at all. She had done this, to Mandy's regret, over Jesus. They did not see much of each other outside school, since Mandy's time was much absorbed by Jesus and her boyfriend George, and Carolyn's mother thought Mandy, with her tight jeans and loud voice, rather common.

"Coming out?" asked Mandy.

"In this?"

"Yes – it's amazing in a storm, it's like being under a really strong shower, it won't be cold –"

"But we'll get wet."

Mandy pulled a face.

Carolyn hesitated. "Well – what are you doing – are you going home after?"

"'Spect so. Yeah. Come on."

"Um – I'll ruin my sandals."

"Don't be so pathetic. You can dry them can't you?"

"But my Mum –"

"Oh for God's sake –"

Subdued, Carolyn neatly began to pack away her books. "Have you got a coat?"

"No, you berk, that's the point."

Carolyn nodded. Carefully she folded her mauve cardigan and tucked it away in her bag. 'OK."

Mandy led the way through the empty library, the quiet mid-lesson corridors, to B block door. They went through the first set of swing doors and stood staring through the second, listening to the roar of the rain.

"You going to run?" asked Carolyn.

Mandy shrugged and laughed. "Come on." She pushed the door and ran out into the rain. Carolyn watched her curly hair suddenly flatten to her head. Then she went out. It took your breath away – not because it was cold, but because it fell so hard, stinging your bare skin, falling like blows on your head. Gasping and laughing, she and Mandy ran down the drive, half blinded by the streams of water running down their faces. When Mandy cut off along the path home, Carolyn settled into a more carefully paced run, head down, mouth half open to breathe through. The rain was running down her neck, inside her blouse, making her shudder. She looked up quickly, blinking, when she had to cross the road. At Leap Lane, which was one-way, she glanced only to the left. As she jumped the flooded swirling gutter a noise made her swivel her head to the right where she took in instantaneously a red coming-closer wheel-splashing

21

van

and in mid-air time faltered, hesitated long enough for her to see herself and the red van hurtling forwards in a mad race to occupy the same spot of road, and herself still in mid-air suddenly reversing her pumping legs like a cartoon character who's run off a cliff and backpedals desperately – and all the revolving world of mother father Alan school Mandy all stopped still like a frozen film, broken down oh no

and she landed, stumbled – here

no – not –

> me.

The lad driving the red Post Office van was in a state. It was the first time he'd done the collections on his own, and this bloody weather had fouled everything up. Visibility was awful, he'd driven right past two boxes and had to go back for them, although he knew where they were. He was soaked to the skin and shivering, from fiddling with keys and heaving sacks of letters out. He'd even dropped one and been scrabbling in the gutter for pale sodden envelopes, hoping no one had seen. He was very late. And all the roads looked different in the rain – what you could see of them through this bloody windscreen, whose wipers moved at one sweep per minute. At a familiar junction he peered through the underwater screen and managed to glimpse the main road, away up there to the left. So he turned left into the narrow empty lane and accelerated thankfully towards it. As he touched the brake to slow down, a thing jumped out of the air from the left – and hit the van. Like lightning he hurled the van to the right, foot flat on the brake. When the van had slithered slowly across the road and stalled in a final juddering jump, he could almost pretend he'd been quick enough – in minus timing – not to have hit it. Let it not be a person. Sitting in the blind streaming steamed-up van he was oddly unable to move – got his right hand on to the door lever but couldn't seem – didn't seem to have any – force. He gave up after a bit and sat with his head resting against the wheel, weak as water.

At last a policeman opened the door, asked if he was all right and pulled him out. An ambulance moved straight across in front of his eyes with blue lights flashing and a crowd of people's heads moved round towards him so it seemed everything was moving, slipping, sideways and he had to lean forward, supported by the policeman, to be sick which slipped away quickly too carried in lumps by the swirling rain. When he was sitting down he said to the policeman, "Are they – are they –"

"What, are they what?" said the policeman patiently.

"Dead?"

"I don't know sir," said the policeman.

After the ambulances and crowd had gone, a policeman got into the red van and carefully wiped the steamy windows. He drove slowly the right way back down the street, muttering to himself, "Bloody hell" at the slowness of the windscreen wipers.

The rain, driving down on to the convex gritty surface of the little lane, washed out and swirled away the last traces of the spreading red stain which Carolyn Tanner had made on the road.

Chapter 3

Coming towards and from behind too is darkness pressing up against pressing hard hard I can see you blackness my eyes are wide open. It presses like a weight against the wide open eyes hurting me, pressing till the eyes don't take it in

not the sight of blackness extending in through the eye from outside to inside the head, not the eye a channel a hole for blackness to flow through no more

because pressed and squashed by insistent blackness it bursts to colours, each melting and oozing, flowing to the next, under the constant black pressure on the liquid film of the eyeball. It shows purple with yellow glowing bars and flickers of red, pressing harder shows stars which melt to dribble down midnight blue with coloured shooting pains.

Carolyn found herself in a desert. It was breathtakingly beautiful. Bare sands stretched away to the far horizons, and the sky above was so pure that she looked straight through it to outer space, to stars and planets and deep space beyond them. Everywhere was open and led the eye on. The air, she noticed with pleasure but without surprise, was fresh and cool. People pretended deserts were hot. The flat sands were yellow as children's seaside beaches. She saw that the desert was perfectly clean, as if it were new. Like a million sheets of blank white paper, or a country covered by fresh snow, without a mark. But as she turned slowly around to take in the perfect remote circle of the horizon, she thought to herself that this was better than paper, or snow. Paper would be written on, filled with words, each of which was one choice among thousands, and the combination of whose singular choices made one meaning among hundreds, specific and limited. The writing would confine the blank paper, narrow all its possibilities down to one. And in the country where snow fell, children would rush out with boots and sledges and criss-cross the white with tracks. Men, women and children, all of whom delight in making marks on white snow, in making their mark, would score and scar the snow, and desecrate its clean white face. At least, she thought, the snow will melt.

But here in the desert the firm sand holds no marks. She imagined that she stood on the spot where the stone had proclaimed, "My name is Ozymandias, king of kings." And all around the lone and level sands stretch far away. Even his stumps of stone have gone.

She was happier than she had ever been, with a feeling of exultation like something growing and swelling inside her, joy, wanting to burst out, of her throat in singing, of her eyes in light, of her body in dancing. Alone in the desert, she danced.

When she was tired she sat on the sand, which was firm and warm, like the reassuring touch of a friend's hand. She was thirsty. Looking around she could see nothing to drink, and so she started to walk. When she had walked for a while across the unmarked sand, she stopped and laughed. "You're walking through a desert looking for water! What are you doing?"

And her own sensible head replied, "There is no water in deserts. You'll die."

"Ah no, not now I'm here, now I have arrived here at this perfect place. Don't let me die." She was scared, the change from joy came cold over all her flesh.

"This is where there are no marks. Boundless and bare the lone and level sands stretch far away."

"But," she cried like a child in a tantrum, "I'm not going to leave any marks. I don't *want* any marks."

The sand led her eye away across its emptiness, its perfect cleanness, and the wind scoured in her ears, "You are a mark. You. You."

She looked down at her body, and the squat black shadow it made on the sand, and she thought that it needed food and water, and shelter from the sun and wind. She was pierced by prescient disappointment. "Can't I stay here then?"

If you die. Boundless and bare, you can join the lone and level sands, stretch far away.

Stretching her with impossible longing to stay forever in that pure and empty place, stretching her taut as a bird-pulled worm, her body called her back to its living, moving, hurting, drinking, eating, excreting needs.

Chapter 4

It called her back to a world of horrors. Of random senseless pains and a rain of things which hurtled down upon her, determined to crush and confine. She saw the wet red metal charging at her, dark ceiling coming down on her, hands briefly winding a bandage which blinded her. People – shapes moved above, between her and the light, hovering like birds of prey. Once as she lay half drugged, floating on the surface of pain, a dark shape interposed itself between her and the light and fell right down on her blackly, smothering her with its hot breath, awakening pains that shrieked like alarm bells.

Meg, who'd just been told that they'd taken Carolyn off the critical list, had gone into the room weak with relief. When she saw her daughter's lips move, knew that she would live, she couldn't help but embrace her, trying to hold in the sobs that were choking her.

All the time, it seemed, they were tormenting Carolyn. They would never leave her in peace. One after another they grabbed and pushed and pulled, pierced her skin with needles and her throat with tubes, bound her down with tight white blankets like bandages to the bed so she could not escape. They moved near her, spoke, clanked instruments. She could get no peace.

In between waves of panic she was floating, still and lethargic. Heavy timelessness and helplessness, nothing to be done. No energy to burn, just keep still, hold together. The blank peace was interrupted by pain, or an insistent voice requesting – requesting something, God knows what –

"Do what you want!" Her first feeble querulous words in response to her mother's daily greeting. The nurse had told Meg that Carolyn had been more wakeful this afternoon.

"Carolyn! Oh Carolyn!" Meg burst into tears and Carolyn closed her eyes again.

While she was critical, and for a time afterwards, she was kept in an ante-room on her own. Once it was clear she would live, and that healing would take a painfully slow time, she was transferred to the end bed on Women's Surgical. It was a long dim high-ceilinged ward with two large windows at the opposite end. She did not ask what was wrong with her until so many days after it had happened that her mother couldn't believe she didn't know. The whole hideous sequence was etched vividly in her own brain, and repeated so often to friends and relatives, that it had become a chant:

"In a coma for two days, fractured skull, broken ribs (five), fractured right femur, severe bruising and laceration to right side of body, twenty-seven stitches –" and, most poignantly horrible to one who remembered playing "This little piggy went to market" with Carolyn the baby's tiny perfect toes, "three crushed toes on the right foot." The doctor had said, "I doubt if we can do much for them. We'll probably have to amputate. But it's not the end of the world – after a few months, she won't even notice. Just a question of adjusting her balance slightly. They're not enormously useful things, toes."

Carolyn spent a short time absorbing the information, then said, "I could be dead." She thought about the toes when Meg had gone. It seemed to her that she could feel them, that they were all right. The van must have run over them. She remembered quite clearly the sudden closeness of the hot engine, and thinking (or had she thought it since?), "It's going to run over my head." But it had only run over three toes. Idly she considered which bit of your body could you most easily do without? Apart from inaccessible bits like tonsils and appendix, toes came top of the list. She supposed she must be very lucky.

The toes were amputated later that week. It made no difference at all to the way she felt, or to the pain. She wanted to see them, but refrained from asking out of a sense of embarrassment. The doctors would think she was peculiar. But they are my toes. Were. She wanted desperately to see them and worked herself up into a state of sweaty frenzy to ask, never mind what they thought, as the anaesthetist bent over her. She heard the doctor laugh. "We'll have to see," he said. She realized that her embarrassment had been pointless because of course he wouldn't show her them. When she woke up in her own bed again she didn't even bother to ask, though her memory later cradled the pathetic image of three squashed little toes in a sauce of blood in a kidney-shaped bowl as tenderly as if they had been a stillborn child.

She was more and more awake, lying still and dull-headed, not in control of her body. All she could do was stare. She could half turn her head and stare through lowered lashes at the thing in the next bed. She watched it without interest, just as she would have watched a tree or dog or anything else that happened to be there. It was soothing to watch because it lay quite still. There was a metal thing over its face, a sort of cage stuck on to its head. It was rather horrible, but so inhuman that it didn't matter. Its hands were bound round and round with bandages. It was always propped up on its pillows and had a contraption like a music stand across its bed, upon which rested a book. Clumsily yet delicately, with its bound paw the monster turned the pages of the book. Carolyn watched it sometimes succeeding easily, sometimes having to move both stiff paws to the elusive page, turning its caged head to left and right as it started and finished each line of print.

One day as she lay staring at the paws she noticed them become still around a half-turned page, and moving her eyes on up, saw that the thing was facing her.

"Hello." The voice was muffled. Carolyn realized that it could not open its mouth properly. Its cage was stuck into its teeth.

"Hello."

"How're you feeling?" asked the voice kindly.

There was no point in replying. Instead Carolyn said, "What happened to you?"

"I had an accident." The voice was very dry, the accent peculiar. Carolyn stared at the metal contraption – it looked like nothing so much as scaffolding – and began to laugh. She stopped straight away because it sent fire through her ribs. The monster seemed to snort.

"Me too," said Carolyn.

The thing nodded. "Clare," it said, using a paw to point at itself. "Does it hurt?"

"When I laugh," Carolyn whispered helplessly.

29

"I had two hundred and thirty-five stitches," pursued the disembodied voice.

"Poor you –" Carolyn started to giggle again. "Don't make me laugh –"

"I'm not." The thing's voice was indignant but still humorous. "Two hundred and thirty-five stitches isn't my idea of a joke."

"Why?" said Carolyn.

"The stitches?"

"Mmn."

"Cut. All over."

Carolyn spat out "Why?" again.

"Glass." The monster nodded sagely. "Sharp glass."

Carolyn in control now; "Where?"

"Well, everywhere, really. I walked on to a roof of it, fell through it, smashed my face on a ledge and landed on a broken heap of it. Silly really," it said reflectively. As Carolyn continued not to be able to speak, it added, "It was a conservatory. I was trying to repair the roof." Then it asked Carolyn for the details of her accident. "Less ridiculous. Less messy. You should have seen me when the ambulance came. I was coated in blood – like a used Tampax."

Carolyn's weak hilarity was checked by this image, which she found shocking. The funny accent, she realized, was American. The acquaintance developed in little hysterical bursts, from which each sank back into her book or helpless weakness respectively.

Carolyn's mother visited her every day. Arthur came with her on Wednesdays and Saturdays. Meg brought grapes, oranges, chocolates, peppermint creams, magazines, freesias, fruit cordial, knitting, books of puzzles, talcum powder, Carolyn's old teddybear, a transistor radio, a little photo of herself and Arthur, and a new turquoise blue bedjacket which she had crotcheted. Carolyn seemed so weak and weepy that Meg didn't know how to treat her and tried anxiously to think of things that would amuse or console.

"You *will* be all right, love, and that's the main thing, isn't it? In a few months time this'll just be past history. When you come home we'll go for a little holiday somewhere nice and restful, by the sea for a few days. Whitby or Scarborough. That'll be a tonic,

30

won't it?" And "Father and I are thinking of getting a new carpet for your room for when you come home. Would you like that, love? I went down to Whitefields and that nice woman, you know the one with the grey strcak in her hair, well I told her what I was looking for and how you were you know, in hospital, and she said, 'Well you take the sample book to her, Mrs Tanner,' she said. 'I'm not supposed to let it out the shop but if you promise to get it back first thing on Friday why don't you take it and let her choose herself.' It was nice of her wasn't it, thoughtful, people often are you know when you have trouble. So here it is, careful, it's a weight, I've lugged it all down Plantain Street off the bus – but anyway, let me show you. This is the one I was thinking about, but what do you –?"

Carolyn turned her heavy-as-lead head sideways and let her sight fall on the thick rectangles of carpet. Buttermilk. Mushroom. Sahara. She couldn't care less. "Yes," she said. "Sahara." She could feel her mother looking at her, and feel the oppressive weight of her anxiety. Sound more – enthusiastic. "Yes, it's nice. Thank you." She watched her mother purse her lips, close the heavy carpet book and wrestle to get it into her bag again. Her mother looked up brightly.

"Well. What've you been up to since yesterday?"

Carolyn felt terribly miserable. She felt like crying. She wished her Mum would go away. "Nothing much. I had some ice-cream at dinner time."

"That's nice. The food's not really so bad is it, not compared to what it used to be. They've got it quite nice in here really. There's a good view you know, from that window down there – when you get up and about."

Pause.

"You don't mind your Dad not coming with me today, do you love? He sends you his love and everything, but he's not too good in hospitals, he really isn't, they get him all jittery. Men, eh? And there's not that much room for two visitors anyway, is there? We can make it nice and cosy with just the two of us, and have a bit of a natter. No point everyone sitting round like lemons with nothing to say, is there?"

Pause.

"Anything else you'd like me to bring, Carolyn? The sister says

you can read if you like, they'll do you one of those frames –
you know, like –"

Carolyn moved her head once to the side, shorthand for
shaking it, and tears started to roll down her face.

"What is it? Carolyn? What's the matter? Does it hurt?
Where does it hurt you?"

She was miserably hopelessly alone and afraid, and her
mother's worried face and kind offers were so far away they
seemed like mockery. Her mother couldn't help her, couldn't
touch her. Would go home and leave her here. Her mother
didn't know what it was like.

As Meg came day after day trying more and more anxiously
to cheer Carolyn up and get her out of herself, with news of
the outside world and comings and goings at the woolshop,
Carolyn became more and more unresponsive, sullen or
weepy. She didn't want her mother to come. Obscurely, she
blamed her. Carolyn had never been away from Meg so much
as a night, before.

She had other visitors. Alan came with a great bunch of
roses. He sat by the bed and smiled at her and held her hand.
The A levels were in full swing, but once he had told her about
the questions there wasn't much to say. His roses wilted
overnight and died without opening. It was the same with
Mandy. She came full of gossip about who was going out with
who and what so-and-so said they'd put in the such-and-such
exam, and it was all tiny and quite unreal to Carolyn. She
couldn't be bothered with it, they seemed like small yacketing
dolls. She had missed her exams, school was over, their lives
were all going on and she was stuck here. None of them knew
what it was like. She didn't care what they were doing. She felt
that she would never escape from the hospital. They were
doing different things to her all the time. They put her leg in
traction then they took it out. They operated again on her foot.
They gave her different drugs. They were going to do a skin
graft. She didn't want them to keep chopping and changing
her, she wanted to be left alone. No one ever seemed to tell her
what they were doing, they were evasive and in a hurry when
she plucked up the courage to ask. It was nothing to do with
her, her body. Once when she and Clare were discussing their
respective injuries she confessed how much she wanted to see

her foot. "I feel as if I don't know what's there – I don't know what I'm like any more."

Clare snorted. "Miracles of modern medicine. You can come in here a human being, and go out as Frankenstein's monster. No –" she corrected herself, "You do come in as a squashed human being –"

"And get remade into a monster," repeated Carolyn. "Sewn together with new bits."

"Well look at me," said Clare.

"I can't. What will – what's that for?"

"This?" Clare raised a paw towards her cage.

"Yes."

"It's for a fractured middle third of maxilla, so they tell me."

"But what does it do?"

"Sort of external splint, I suppose. Screws into the bone – keeps it in place."

Carolyn looked at Clare with real horror. She had thought the cage rested on her face – although clearly that was silly. It had such nice neat white little bandages on its ends. But it went through her flesh – through two holes in her forehead.

"It's all right," said Clare. "It looks worse than it is, I think. But I've got an awful craving for real food." She had to drink mush through a straw because her teeth were fixed together with metal. Carolyn was suddenly conscious of her own good fortune.

Often she had trouble sleeping, and at night she was more frightened and lonely than ever. Once she woke suddenly in the small hours of the morning, sick with fear. She lay, as she had woken, flat on her back and looked at the ceiling. It was dim and shadowy, but it was slowly lowering itself towards her. Breaking out in sweat she turned her head to the left, to the mustard painted wall which gleamed dully in the shine of the safety lights. It took a step towards her. Turning her head back she saw that the ceiling was lower again, already her body could sense the pressure it would inflict on her, the way it would close and crush –

Panting with fear she tried to roll over in the bed, but the tight blankets held her pinned in position. She could not move. She could only lie and watch, in the shadowy artificial light, the ceiling and wall creeping noiselessly closer and closer. Into the horror of her helpless solitude came a voice.

"Sssh. What's the matter?"

She couldn't take her eyes off the ceiling which moved more quickly when she looked away. "The ceiling."

"What's wrong with it?" said the muffled voice.

"It's coming down – oh – it's coming–"

"Hush, hush it's all right."

"No–" sobbing now, "no – no–" The room was closing the walls coming in, she couldn't breathe, already she was choking, gasping, there was no air no light no space – "No!"

"All right. It's all right." Clare leaned helplessly over her for a moment, then moved to the head of Carolyn's bed and wound the handle, as she had seen nurses doing. Gradually the wheels came down, lifting the bed silently off its feet. She moved to the other end and pulled the bed out into the centre of the ward, then manoeuvred it down towards the window at the opposite end. "Look," she whispered. "Look out the window, it's all right. See the streetlights. See the stars." Carolyn looked. "Can you see the line of the hills against the sky?"

Carolyn, whose heart and breath were racing and body shaking with helpless fear, gazed out of the window and saw street, house, star, lamppost, hill, and tried to attach her spinning fear to these stationary things. The quiet night, the shapes of houses, the world and sky asleep. Staring at them, she began to calm, and her breathing to quieten.

After a while, when Carolyn's breathing was regular, Clare wheeled the bed about.

"No – no –" Carolyn's voice was panic-edged already, at turning in to face those dark gleaming walls. "No!"

Clare turned her again so that she could anchor her fleeting sight safely out there in the still night streets. Clare stood by her stiffly, watching, until dawn began to make pale the sky, and a nurse walking quietly down the early ward spotted them and hurried them crossly back to their places. Carolyn laid hold of the grey gleam of dawning light on the ceiling as a drowning person grasps a lifebelt. Testing the dark, she closed her eyes –opened them to see that safe morning light – closed, tried again, opened. At last she was able to trust it to stay, and so sleep.

She remembered her terror vividly in the morning, it was still too real for her to feel embarrassed about it. After the nurse had set up Clare's reading frame for her, Clare said, "Sleep well?" in her dry voice.

"Thank you," said Carolyn awkwardly. "I don't know what I would have done – I was –"

"It's OK," said Clare. "All part of the fun. What day is it today?"

"Thursday."

"Thursday? Oh Lord, it's God's gift today."

"What?"

"The consultant. Young and handsome. Thinks he's God's gift. You watch him with the nurses. Acts as if it's as big as the Eiffel Tower."

Carolyn was embarrassed. Later in the morning the consultant appeared at the end of the ward, accompanied by a flutter of nurses, and strode along bestowing a word or smile on the more likely-looking of his patients.

"How're we doing today?" he said blandly to Clare's bed.

"Don't know about you, but I'm great, never felt better," came the dry voice from behind the scaffolding.

Carolyn wriggled down under her sheet, blushing for Clare's daring and trying not to laugh. He blinked at Clare's bed then smiled.

"I see. Nurse –" He turned with some technical request about changing Clare's dressings, and Carolyn saw that he did stare shamelessly at the nurse, so that a faint pink flush came up on her cheekbones.

He walked on and Clare said softly, 'Bet it's wearing a hole in his pants."

The nursing staff, who had been no more than a faceless army who irritated, interrupted, hurt, or occasionally brought relief, were sharply defined by Clare's distant voice. There was Come Hither, Martinet, the Hairdresser and Vile Chops. "Vile Chops" was an unfair name, and reduced both of them to mild hysteria. She had a way of pressing her lips together and grimacing, which made a slight sucking noise, when agreeing with someone. They both lay rigid, straining their ears, as Martinet gave her instructions for the morning, and tried to stifle their delighted squeaks as she nodded gravely and lisp-sucked her lips.

Clare was taken away frequently to be X-rayed, and to have her screws tightened and loosened, like a faulty robot. One day she returned and told Carolyn that they were going to take the cage off next week.

"What then?"

"Christ knows. Buy a mask, I should think."

"Oh, it'll be all right. It'll be funny so see your face."

"I'm sure it will. I'll probably die laughing."

It had not occurred to Carolyn that she might be serious.

When Clare was brought back from having her cage removed, Carolyn lay with her eyes ostentatiously closed. She heard the nurses fussing, then going away, and finally Clare's two-edged voice, "Well, all is revealed."

Carolyn opened her eyes. The woman in the next bed looked odd. Her face was white with several fine scratchy scars across it, as if fragments of her face had been sewn together. Two little pieces of gauze were attached to her forehead, as if she were just sprouting antlers.

"Neat, eh?" said the woman with Clare's voice, and tears began to run down her face.

"Don't Clare – don't cry –" Carolyn moved ineffectually. She couldn't get out of bed on her own yet. "Don't. It's silly, you'll be fine, in a bit. You'll look fine."

Despite the tears the voice remained brittle and distant. "Sure. I'll be fine. A new thatch and you won't know the difference."

Carolyn realized then that the hairstyle was adding to the bizarre effect. She had never noticed it, while the cage was over Clare's face. Two big patches of Clare's thick black hair had been shaved around cuts. One was just above her forehead. There was a fuzz of new hair growing there now, but the effect was to make her look as if she had a receding hairline.

Clare suffered Carolyn's scrutiny. "I'll get a mask to go home in," she said. "Something more attractive – Dracula, or a werewolf, perhaps."

"Your hair won't take long to grow," said Carolyn gently. "It's like being a baby again, isn't it?"

"Goo goo," said Clare.

Chapter 5

Visiting Carolyn was hard work for Meg. She had to rush back from the shop, grab a bite to eat and put something out for Arthur's tea, pack her bag with whatever she was taking to the hospital, and get down to the High Street to catch the 344 at six-fifteen. On the bus she had time to remember what Carolyn had said and how she had looked yesterday, and to be filled with miserable apprehension about how she would be today. She didn't seem to be interested in anything. It was awful, as if the accident had knocked all the life out of her. It's early days yet, she told herself bravely, but it made the visiting hour into something she looked forward to and dreaded all day long, a twisted choked-up feeling, of loving someone and wanting to please, and them acting as if they don't want to know you. She tried to explain it to Arthur. "You should ask that doctor," he said. "Stands to sense, all those drugs and what-have-you they're pumping into her, she's bound to be a bit dopey-like." Meg said she would ask the doctor. She hoped that was it, but she didn't think it was. When she got home at eight-forty-five she'd have a cup of tea and a sandwich and watch telly for a bit then put herself to bed, and lie awake half the night staring at Carolyn's sullen shut face, looming out of the darkness. She wanted to hug her and love her and tell her it was all right, and make her laugh. And Carolyn had that horrible distant look on her face, as if she couldn't be bothered with you, and then sometimes she'd cry and not want you to comfort her – as if you couldn't comfort her, as if she was beyond it.

"I said it when she was little and I'll say it again now," Meg told Jean. "I remember when she was so poorly with the measles, I said to Arthur, I wish to God I could have it for her – and I feel the same now, I do. I wish that bloody idiot in his van had hit me instead – twice over, instead of her."

She asked the sister if she could talk to the doctor, and Martinet said, "Well, what do you want to know? Can't I help you?" standing there by the end of the bed where Carolyn could hear every word.

"I'll leave it for tonight, there's no hurry," said Meg, and the woman looked at her as if she was odd and went off to boss someone else about. They treat you like dirt, the snooty bitches. They're no better than they ought to be, most of them; half of them can't even bloody well speak English.

"It's a bit much, isn't it?" she said to Carolyn's averted face. "They've not got many manners. And how d'you get on with all these Coloureds? It doesn't make you feel any better, does it, when you're poorly, to have someone who can't even speak English mucking you about."

Carolyn didn't say anything. Meg told herself she should be more cheerful.

"Well, Carolyn, and what are you going to do with yourself when you come home, eh? Time we started making plans, isn't it, love? I saw your Miss Lomas from school, you know, in the post office, and she said you could go back and do your exams again next summer. Would you like that? I said, well, she'll be nineteen you know. Carolyn? are you listening?"

Carolyn nodded.

I'm going on too much, Meg thought. "Carolyn love – please –"

"I'm all right," snapped Carolyn. "Go on."

Meg swallowed and went on. "Or you could always go to those evening classes, you know, at the technical college and do . . ."

The bossy sister was in her little office by the door as visiting hour ended. Meg summoned her courage and went in.

"I just wanted to ask – to know if it's normal – you know –for her to be so – depressed. I mean, she's so miserable, she's like a different girl."

The nurse pulled a face and fidgeted with some papers as if she was busy. "It's a shock to the system, Mrs –"

"Tanner."

"Mrs Tanner. Isn't it, an accident like that. It can affect people in all sorts of ways. Upset them. I expect she gets a bit fed up lying there all day, but she's just got to put up with it, I'm afraid. She'll be all right."

"But those – the medicine, the drugs she's having, could they make her – you know, sort of lose interest in life?"

"She needs a lot of rest, Mrs Tanner. Nurse!" – as a nurse walked past the door. "Excuse me, Mrs Tanner." And she rushed after the nurse.

Meg set off on the walk to the bus stop. They treat you like dirt.

She slept very badly at nights, imagining Carolyn lying in the hospital. The thought of Carolyn being hurt made her cry. And she was powerless to help. Arthur woke up and comforted her. "Come on lass. She'll be all right. She'll be home soon." Meg turned her thoughts to Carolyn coming home. She'd make her room really nice, with that new carpet and a new bedspread; and take some holiday off work and bake some nice food to fatten her up again. It would be all right when she came home. It was being in that awful hospital made her like that. Not that Meg wasn't grateful for what they'd done for her, it was a matter of life and death when she'd gone in – but now, she was like a different girl. A different girl.

When her mother left at the end of visiting hour, Carolyn would lie still staring at the ceiling, listening to her heavy tread moving away down the ward and round the corner. Straining her ears she listened for the yielding swish of the swing door, followed by three gentle thuds as it swung back past its closed position, back again, and finally blessedly shut. Her mother was always the last to leave, after they'd rung the bell. Carolyn knew that everyone must stare at her as she left. She wished she would leave on time. Or early, for that matter.

"Your mother comes every single day," marvelled Clare.

"Yes."

"Do you like it?"

"It's wonderful," said Carolyn, copying Clare's dry tone. After Clare's expected laugh, Carolyn was lost for words. "I – she comes because she wants to. She's my mother."

"So?"

"So – what? Wouldn't your mother visit, if she lived near?"

"Not every day she wouldn't. We'd both go up the wall."

"Well she doesn't drive me up the wall."

39

"No – obviously. With those riveting tales of life in the carpet shop–"

"Woolshop," corrected Carolyn.

"– and what colour Nellie's woolly combinations are going to be, I'm not surprised. I can hardly wait for the next instalment."

Carolyn was almost offended. "That's just the way she talks. It doesn't matter. You let it wash over you."

"Well there you are. Your poor old Mum, rushes home from work, gobbles her tea, huffs and puffs down to catch the bus and then when she gets here dashes down miles of faceless corridors to get to you for seven on the dot, so she can sit next to your bed and not be listened to for an hour. You should give her an evening off."

Carolyn shrugged. "She enjoys it."

Carolyn couldn't tell if Clare was serious. It would be impossible to ask her mother not to come, although she did occasionally go on about what a scramble it was to get here on time (she was always on time, waiting there when the doors opened) and how nice it would be when Carolyn was home and there were evenings again. Her mother's conversation didn't wash over her any more. It tormented her. It went on and on like a dripping tap, from one inconsequential boring subject to the next. And there was no escape, she couldn't walk into the other room or pick up her schoolbooks or start to make the tea. She was captive, here.

Her Mum harped incessantly on what Carolyn would do when she came home. She brought a prospectus from the technical college, and a pamphlet about adult education evening classes, and another about courses run by the WEA. Then she started bringing the evening paper, and pointing out the Classified Employment columns.

"There might just be something that takes your fancy – I thought, since you've got all day lying here, you could have a look. It might give you an idea, that's all."

Pause.

"Look Carolyn, you've got to pull yourself together you know. There's nothing worse than self-pity. You can't lie moping here, just think of all the poor people who're worse off than you. You're nearly better now. You're lucky to be able to think about a job and what you're going to do. I bet there's plenty of people in this hospital would give their eye-teeth to be going home soon. Come on now, love, make a bit of an effort for goodness' sake."

Lying there, Carolyn hated her. She didn't want to look at the prospectuses and papers. When her mother left she shoved them in her locker and slammed the door, and they piled up on top of her clothes in a slippery heap and shot out all over the floor every time the door was opened. Meg opened it to put in some biscuits she'd brought her, and was shocked by the mess. "That's not like you Carolyn, my goodness, fancy letting your things get in such a state."

Listening for her coming down the ward, the first and quickest set of footsteps, always, Carolyn told herself, I'm not going to listen. I'm not going to talk to her, I'm not. And when she saw her mother's bright hopeful smile and eager-to-please presents and heard her first cheery comments about what so-and-so had said to her and what a funny little boy she'd sat next to on the bus, she was filled with a stifling guilt and tried to smile. But her face was as stiff as cardboard. She could hardly bear to see her mother, couldn't meet her eyes to say hello. And the less she could say, the more Meg persecuted her with "What's wrong?" and "What have you been up to today, then?" and "Have you lost your tongue, Carolyn?"

When the swing door gave its final thud after she had left (sometimes she came back even then, with some vital message like "I met your friend Mandy in the Co-op and she sent you her love, I nearly forgot. She's coming to visit you soon. That'll be nice won't it?") there was peace. Carolyn lay with her eyes fixed on whatever spot their gaze had fallen on, and let her head gradually fill up with silence. She didn't think – couldn't concentrate, didn't want to think about what would happen when she got out. They still didn't know when it would be. She didn't know how long she'd been here, it was interminable. Partly she didn't dare believe she would get out, and felt superstitiously that the more she handled the idea and imagined and planned, the less likely it would be to happen. Which made her mother's insistence on jobs and courses and pulling herself together all the worse. It was calling for trouble.

I don't have to think about it, she told herself. I could be dead. I could easily have died, and then I wouldn't have to think about it

41

at all. Or it could have not happened. It could have simply not happened.

The idea dawned on her gradually, filling out and getting clearer over days. The imagining of it was an escape from pressure like a hole punched to let out steam. If. If it hadn't rained. If I hadn't gone out with Mandy. If I hadn't run so fast. Or if I'd run faster . . . If I'd had an errand at the shops. If.

She tried it again and again in her head, cranking and rewinding the jerky film, making cuts and substitutions. If. With concentration, with sheer mind-force, she could push it through until she was there, on the kerb at Leap Lane in the pouring rain, glancing left and running over

and hearing startlingly close behind her the whoosh and splash of a vehicle from the wrong direction. It scared her. She turned and screamed, "One-way!" at the idiot red van, but she couldn't see the driver through the streaming steamy windows. Stupid pillock.

When she got home she was soaked to the skin and shivering, partly cold and partly shock from the near miss. God, it was a near miss too. That maniac could have killed her. She ran a hot bath. Climbing into it was exquisite pain, once her icy feet were in she crouched slowly, allowing the hot water to creep inch by inch up her body. The room filled with steam. Her mother always insisted on the window being opened to stop condensation ruining the wallpaper. Carolyn relished not opening it when her mother was out.

After her bath she wrung out her blouse and put it in the dirty-clothes, and hung her skirt over the bath to drip-dry. She stuffed her sandals with newspaper and hid them in her room. Her mother would be cross if she saw them. Her skin was glowing all over from the heat of the water, it felt wonderful. She sat on her bed, facing the mirror, and started to comb out her wet hair.

It was perfectly convincing. At nights Carolyn touched it with her thoughts, gently, testing it for durability.

One day they told Clare that she'd be going home that week. The possibility had not entered Carolyn's head, although Clare had been up and about for several days.

"What about me?" she asked Martinet.

"You'll have to ask Doctor," said Martinet. "But it'll be a couple of weeks yet, I should think."

Clare, who was only too obviously delighted, said "Come on, smile! At least you can, without danger of your face splitting at the seams." She touched her cheek scar gingerly. "Shall I come and visit you?"

Carolyn hesitated, then said, "Yes please." She knew it would be awful. Clare in the next bed was an ally, her only friend. Clare the visitor would be someone strange and difficult to talk to. Probably she'd look like those women who came to visit her.

She had studied Clare's visitors many times, as she nodded and half listened to Meg. No one came regularly, but there were quite a few who came more than once. They were all young. She had asked Clare where her parents were. "My father's in Edinburgh. And my mother in California. I think." Clare didn't seem inclined to talk about them. The two who visited most regularly were the women Clare lived with, Carolyn knew. Both were vaguely scruffy, one with long red hair and the other with a wide jack-o'-lantern face and such short hair it bristled. She didn't much like the look of them. Student types.

Now she wanted to know more about what Clare was going back to. "Is it just you three who share your house?" She thought it odd that none of them was married.

"There's Sue's kids, Robin and Sylvia."

Carolyn didn't like to ask what had happened to their father. "Are you a student?" It was absurd that she didn't know, after lying next to Clare for all these weeks. But it had been completely irrelevant.

Clare laughed. "I wish I bloody was! No, me dear, my student days are over. I have to work for my living."

Carolyn was pleased. "What d'you do?"

"Refuge for Battered Women."

"Oh." Carolyn was baffled. She could think of nothing to do with battered but fish or Yorkshire pudding. And Refuge Assurance. She felt so stupid she didn't dare ask anything more.

Already conversation between them was awkward. Clare seemed to become short and brisk. She was moving away, back to the real world. Back to her complicated grown-up life that Carolyn didn't understand; leaving Carolyn behind. On the last day she watched in miserable silence as Clare dressed.

"Shall I leave you my books?"

"OK."

43

Clare transferred a heap of unglossy, boring-looking magazines and five or six books on to Carolyn's locker, and packed the rest of her stuff into a big canvas bag.

"Well." Carolyn was going to cry.

"Well, how do I look? Fancy me, do you darlin'?"

Carolyn laughed.

"I'll see you. I'll come back and tell you what it's like out there – whether the natives are friendly. Take care." Clare pecked her on the cheek and left.

Chapter 6

Once Clare had gone Carolyn spoke to no one. She simply lay and stared. She liked the first part of the night, when people stopped walking about. They turned off the fluorescent lights between ten-thirty and eleven, and then the ward was dimly lit by a small safety light over each bed. They were yellow electric bulbs, their wattage so low that their light seemed thick and dusky, full of texture and shadow. It did not shine, it seemed almost to be dark light, at which you could stare and stare without dazzling your eyes, but rather as if it was pulling your sight into it, by its soft luminous attraction. She heard the sounds of the building vibrating around her: footsteps in corridors, doors swinging and thudding, clink of glass or metal, the swishing wheels of a trolley. They were all sounds of quiet, contained efficiency.

She remembered the times when her Dad had taken them out in Harry's car, when he'd serviced it for him – when she was little. It was a big old-fashioned square black car, like a taxi or a hearse. On nice days you could roll back part of the roof to reveal a rectangle of sky framed by black. If you sat with your head back, staring up, you saw a strange moving picture above you: clouds, sometimes blue sky, and sudden intrusions of branches and leaves and lampposts, as if they were on the same plane as the sky – the black edges of the picture cut them off from earthly contact. She remembered the ache in her stiffening neck, and not wanting to turn her head down even for half a minute. It was too hypnotic.

Now she only wanted to stare. Stare and stare and not think. Everything was too much effort. Nod and smile at them if they ask something, because then they'll go away sooner and leave you in peace, to lie still and blank, watching without seeing, sunk down deep inside yourself, wrapped and wrapped inside curling layers of tight wordless thoughts, like the tightly enfolded petals of a bud.

And when it was completely peaceful, sometimes if she lay very still and empty-headed, the film would begin to run again. It stuck and jerked a few times when it started up, or went too slowly, making those dreadful groaning noises. But if she held herself right back (it was like not frightening away a wild animal) it would get going, and once it was well-started it carried on of its own accord. She could not interfere with it. It told its own story. If she was quiet, it let her watch.

Once school was over, Meg fixed Carolyn up with a job at Jean's friend's shop, the 'Craft Basket'. "You might as well be earning money while you decide what you're going to do with yourself," she pointed out. "Any experience is good experience, when it comes to looking for work."

Carolyn was pleased to be earning money, and quite happy to postpone decisions about greater things, at least until the results were out. Although when they came (two Cs and an E) she still didn't know what to do. She and Alan saw each other nearly every day over the summer.

Before Alan left for university at the end of September, Carolyn slept with him. Her reasons for doing so were complicated and made her feel bad, because, romantically, she wanted it to be simple. It should be because she loved him enough. She argued miserably with herself that she did love him enough. But she was afraid of him meeting someone else at university. If she slept with him, he wouldn't have the excuse that she hadn't done. He would also, she knew, feel a lot worse about dropping her. She coldly analysed her motives, and called one of them emotional blackmail, and felt then that she was glad she'd done it because now she knew that if he did do anything nasty (meaning go out with someone else) she deserved it.

Sunday morning in November, seven o'clock. The house is quiet and will be for an hour or two, while Meg and Arthur lie in. Carolyn finds that she isn't going to burrow down into bed and sleep again, she's going to lie quite still on her back with her eyes open. It's dark outside and the street is quiet. It could be much earlier. There's a train going by all in a rush, in this house they always make her want to poke her finger in her ear to clear it, because they are so quiet and faraway. She is going to be sick. Perhaps

46

not, if she lies completely still, it might fade away. She lies completely still, and feels the sweat prickling her armpits, and her throat trying to flex itself in readiness. No. Slowly and cautiously she sits up, her stomach gives the first spasmodic heave, and she presses her lips together and runs to the bathroom.

It was very easy to forget after it had happened. She felt fine. She felt like curling up and going back to sleep in the still-warm bed. It was nothing. And although it occurred to her to mention it when her mother asked the regulation "Sleep well?" at breakfast, for some reason she didn't.

On Monday morning at seven o'clock she was woken by her parents' alarm, and knew as soon as she woke, I'm going to be sick again I'm pregnant Oh God. And she ran to the bathroom and was.

Her mind ferreted at it all day as she sold embroidery silks and painting-by-numbers sets. It was impermeable and immovable, like a meteorite that had landed in her head. Pregnant. Not me. I'm not that sort of girl. Pregnant at eighteen. Not me. Why not? Look at Libby and Sue, and Tracy at fifteen. Yes, not eighteen. No one is at eighteen. It's impossible. He used those things every time. What will he say? He'll go mad. We'll have to get married. I'll be fat. What will Mum? What will I? Pregnant. I don't believe it. Not me. There was nothing she could do. She went on being sick quietly every morning and flushing the toilet as she was, and she opened the new packet of Tampax on the bathroom shelf and took out a handful to throw away. It was all she could think of.

Her mother's conversation became more and more surreal. She found it impossible not to listen to her. Everything that Meg said dropped in vivid disconnected pictures into the blank space of her head. Purple was going to be in, this autumn, and they'd already sold a lot of that lovely heather-mix wool. She'd taken some steak back to the butcher's because it was so tough, and she'd paid nearly a pound a pound for it, they thought they could get away with murder. Next door had used some chemical weedkiller on the path, the idle devils, and some of it had blown over on to the garden so Arthur thought, because there was a nasty yellow stripe right down their side of the front lawn. Some people had no respect for other people's property. Words and phrases rang in Carolyn's ears when she had gone. "They think they can get away with murder." What did it mean? The idle devils. Id–dle–dev–vils. I–dledev–ils. She saw the letters which spelt the words, but little glowing devils too, with pronged forks and forked tails. A fork like that isn't that sort of fork though, she thought.

Clare came to visit. Although she had outdoor clothes on, her patchy hair and her scratched white face made her welcome and familiar to Carolyn. She came in the afternoon. "Hope you don't mind – but I can't compete with your Mum. I told Martinet I work evenings." She pulled a chair up to the bedside and sat down. "God you look awful," she said cheerfully. "I've brought you some dried apricots to chew."

Carolyn laughed.

"When're you going home?"

"I don't know. I don't want to." Carolyn was interested to hear herself say that.

"Don't want to go home?"

"No. Not really."

There was a pause. "Well don't," said Clare briskly. "We've got a spare room. Come and stay with us if you like."

Carolyn stared at her.

"You can – if you want. That's what you meant, isn't it? Or d'you mean you like it so much here you want to stay for the rest of your life?"

Carolyn laughed weakly. "Could I?"

"Sure. No problem."

With a great effort Carolyn visualized her room at home, with its new carpet and new bedspread. It belonged to a different life.

"Ring me, when they give you a date, and I'll come and get you."

As if there was nothing simpler or more ordinary, than that Carolyn should go and stay in their spare room. Carolyn stared at her.

"All right? It's a nice room too, it's got a sloping roof. On the top floor."

"Good."

"Well." Clare looked round. "I can see it's as jolly as ever in here. Have you read my books?"

"No. Some. No." Carolyn admitted.

"You should try this," said Clare, and pulled a paperback from the pile. "I've just reread it. It's wonderful."

The book looked boring. The cover was black, and the author's

48

name in big letters was DORIS LESSING. Carolyn was surprised that Clare read books by someone called Doris. It sounded like the Archers. "OK." She wanted Clare to go so she could think.

"Getting you down?" said Clare.

She nodded.

"Want me to go?"

In relief, Carolyn smiled.

"All right, I know when I'm not wanted. Look Caro, I'll write my number in the front of this book. OK? Give me a ring when you know when they'll let you out."

Halfway through writing she turned with her pen in her hand. "What about your Mum?"

Carolyn stared at her dumbly.

"You'll have to tell her."

Carolyn nodded.

"OK?"

Clare was staring at her worriedly. With a great effort Carolyn smiled. "Yes. It's OK. Bye-bye."

Alan came home the following weekend. After the pub on Friday night they stopped his father's car in a lane. Carolyn got out of the passenger seat and stood shivering in the dark while he spread the blanket over the back seat. He was always rather embarrassed to do this, and turned around with a foolish laugh saying, "Well—" He put out his arms to her. She had spent the evening in a glaze, because she was trapped (trapped, yes, she remembered Libby saying that Jenny was only a year old when she caught with the next one and thinking what a funny word, caught, did she catch it like a disease or does she mean she was caught in a trap? Now she knew) and had no choice but to tell him. But the inevitable moment which after all had to come at some point in the next nine months wasn't presenting itself from minute to minute. She couldn't really concentrate on anything else for fear of it springing up on her and her not being ready. He clasped her cold hands and pulled her to him. Lightly, he kissed her face, just brushing her skin with his lips. Tell him now. I can't. Say it now. The little brushing kisses were as irritating as a moth that flaps about in your face when you turn the light out. She would burst if she didn't tell him. It was unbearable. The moth kisses moved brushing lightly down her neck. She shivered. Please stop. Tell him. I can't. Please. All her tension was in her skin, and he was irritating her, tickling her, making her want to scream. Her body was seized by rage. "Stop it. Kiss me." Turning her mouth abruptly up to his she met his lips hard, butted against his gentleness and bit at his mouth. He half drew his head back in surprise. "Come on," she said, and climbed quickly into the back seat. It was warm and dark in there, she didn't want to see his face or his surprise. She didn't want him to see her. She was full of harsh energy. Too bad. It was too bad. She didn't care what he thought of her, as she normally did, waiting and wondering (what's he doing, shall I touch him where shall I? What does he expect me to do, is that right or does it hurt when he sighs like that?). She was so angry and tightly coiled that it didn't matter. She wanted to grip him hard and hurt him.

For the first time, she made love to him, blindly, fighting him, as if driven by a rage that had to burst out of her body somewhere; using him to find relief.

Afterwards they lay silent, uncomfortably cramped and sealed together with sweat, both shocked by the force of what had happened. At last Alan wriggled and shifted slightly. "There's somethig biting into my bum. A zip, I think," and Carolyn raised herself up from him and began the furtive scramble for clothes. Not until they were fully dressed and sitting in the front seats again did they look at one another properly, for a moment with absolute curiosity, as if at strangers. Then Alan smiled at her broadly, and Carolyn felt her surprised face grinning back. Their grins widened into giggles, and then into open-mouthed laughter, as if some huge joke had suddenly been revealed to both. It was minutes before Alan leaned forward and started the car.

On Saturday Alan borrowed his father's car to go on a day trip, and they made love all afternoon, drugged with it, unable to stop. In the evening they drove to a pub for food and drink, and as she tidied herself in the Ladies and distantly admired the way her skin was glowing and her eyes sparkling, and thought that everyone who saw them would be sure to know what they'd been doing, Carolyn suddenly remembered she was pregnant. It was an extraordinary thing. But it wouldn't matter. She could tell him easily now. As she slid into her seat next to him and picked up her half of lager she said quietly, "I think I'm pregnant."

He looked at her and laughed.

"No. I mean I am. From before."

Alan hesitated, and put his glass down. "You are or you think you are?"

"I am."

"Have you seen a doctor?"

"I'm sick every morning."

"And how late?"

She shrugged. "They're never very regular, but usually five to six weeks. Now it's been eight."

"Eight weeks?"

"Since my last period."

Alan scratched his face. "Why didn't you tell me before?"

She was remembering how she'd felt, now. In fact she felt like it again. Completely. Pregnant? Not me. It was impossible and awful. She shook her head. "I couldn't. I don't know. I couldn't believe it."

"You knew yesterday?" he said, and then, flatly, "—last night. Today."

She nodded.

"That's why it was different."

"I don't know. I don't think so. I forgot it. I don't know."

"Why do you think it was?"

"We just — I wasn't afraid any more — and — we — fitted together—" Talking about it made her terrified and doubt it, that it had been so much. Talking might reveal it not to have been, or to be just something you can talk about. He bent his head over the table, staring at the wood grain. There was a very long silence. She watched the barman reading the evening paper at the quiet bar, holding each page half open as he read it, tilting his head to scan the columns. Perhaps he was reading the advertisements. Looking for a used car or a lawnmower. Perhaps he had a wife and children and didn't have to worry, perhaps if she stared hard enough she could turn herself into him and be standing there peacefully propped against the bar, half-open paper lying there, pint of bitter in arm's reach and the pub cat rubbing warm against her leg.

Alan moved. He raised his head and said, "Well."

"Well," she said.

"What d'you want to do?"

"I don't know."

He put his arm around her awkwardly, making her want to flinch away and snap despite herself, *"I'm not ill."*

"No." Humbly he took his arm away, and then said grudgingly, picking at the edge of the table, *"I love you, I suppose."*

"I suppose," she said. *"What's that supposed to mean?"*

"Oh fuck off!" He jumped up and ran out of the room, leaving her open-mouthed and horrified.

Pretending for the barman's sake that nothing had happened, she sipped her drink slowly, anxiously replaying the conversation in her

mind's ear and unable to make any sense of his reaction. Would he leave
her here? Was that it? How would she get home? Did he hate her? She felt
she had not understood anything, ever, that had happened between them.
Last night – Misunderstood everything, taken bad for good, no for yes,
not understood, got it all wrong like someone speaking another language
got it wrong.

With icy dignity at last she took her empty glass to the bar, put on her
jacket and went out. The car was in the car park. As she walked towards it
she realized Alan was slumped over the steering wheel, and that he was
crying.

He drove her home in complete silence, drawing up outside her house
and sitting still, the engine racing, eyes staring ahead through the
windscreen. She got out without saying anything and he drove away
before she had got her key out.

Next day it made a great pressure in Carolyn's head, thinking
about not going home, and about going home. She didn't want
to. She felt as if she'd never believed that she would. It all seemed
impossible – going home with her Mum to her room, and all the
things she kept asking her to do and the way her Mum looked at
her and was upset. She couldn't stand it. She couldn't. The only
way she could stand to be was if they left her alone, gave her
some space. Then things would come right. Life would begin
again. She needed the space. She allowed the difficulty to
mushroom in her head till its physical pressure made her
nauseous. All the time she knew, though. I'm not going home.
OK. Not going home.

Gradually it subsided. The decision had made itself. Things
began to change in the hospital. The physiotherapist came and
gave her leg and foot exercises. She had a walking frame, then
crutches. She put on real clothes and sat in the day room. She
could walk to the window and look out at the little toy cars and
houses. No sounds of outside came through the thick glass.
Finally they told her she could go home next week. She was miles
away from them; calm, polite, with a little smile on her face she
nodded as her Mum talked, God's Gift talked, Vile Chops and
Martinet came and went: far, far away, like the Snow Queen with
the ice splinter in her eye, deep frozen in her own winter.

When at last she walked down the ward without a stick,
walking slowly and holding herself very erect, her whole body

was glassy ice, brittle and thin so she must not jolt or bump or stumble, she must move as smoothly as if she was on wheels.

Then it was going to be tomorrow – tomorrow – and her Mum brought her a suitcase to clear out her locker into and her anorak to keep out the cold. She looked down without interest or pity on this confusion. Her Mum brought her a new jumper to go home in. Harebell blue with a flower in little pearls stitched above the chest. It was the sort of jumper they have in expensive shop windows, but Meg had made it. "They're machine-washable!" she exclaimed, brushing the pearls reverently with her fingertips. "Jean put some round the neck of Lizzie's cardigan and she just pops it in the wash. They come up lovely, every time. I was afraid they might chip or flake – hmmn?"

"It's very nice," said Carolyn. "Thankyou."

"Aren't you going to try it on?"

Carolyn tried it on, pulling it down over her dressing gown. It was very tight.

"You should have taken that off first – you're going to ruin the shape – Carolyn! What are you doing?"

Carolyn took it off, and undid her dressing gown. She put the jumper on again and Meg stood back to admire her.

"It's lovely. It really suits you, that colour, it's lovely and dainty – it really is. Oh love, you look like a different girl!"

Carolyn smiled and nodded. Looking down she saw a woolly blue torso with two small pointed breasts and a sprinkling of pearls resting above them, like a first layer of snow. She thought, it must be funny to look like that.

She took off the jumper again, her Mum told her what they were having for tea tomorrow, and asked her what she'd had for lunch today. At last her Mum went away. Carolyn went to the phone and telephoned Clare. When she came back she picked up the jumper again from her locker, and spread it on her knees. It was not her jumper. She did not look like that. She took the letter she had been writing and rewriting all week, and propped it up on top of her locker. It was addressed to Meg Tanner.

Dear Mum,

Please don't be upset. As you know I'm feeling a bit mixed up at the moment. I need some time on my own to think things over. So I am going to stay with a friend for a bit. It's Clare, the girl from the next bed. She's said I can stay in their spare room. She shares a nice house with two other girls so don't worry. I hope you and Dad don't mind. I think I'll be better at deciding what to do, on my own. So don't worry about me, and I'll come and see you soon. Thank you for visiting me every day and for everything.

    Lots of love,
    Carolyn xxxxxxxxxxxx

Meg was given the letter by Martinet when she arrived at two o'clock to take Carolyn home. She had taken the afternoon off work. But Clare had been and collected Carolyn that morning.

Part Two

Chapter 7

Clare had led Carolyn along endless humming corridors, whose walls were punctuated by closed doors. Fluorescent lights shone down on dull red rubbery floors, making a pinkish reflection on the walls, and at intervals the passages were interrupted by semitransparent plastic flapping doors, like valves in a vein. At last they emerged into a wide entrance hall, where a porter was loading a trolley, and two receptionists sat like bottled specimens in glass cages by the wall. On the opposite side, daylight shone through glass doors. Clare, who was carrying Carolyn's suitcase, leaned against a door to hold it open for her. Carolyn rushed out, almost falling down a flight of stone steps.

The sharpness of the cold made her cough and brought tears to her eyes. It took a long time to focus and get rid of the swimming water. The light. It was so bright and sharp. It was spiky as spilt pins. And the cold air – like getting a different substance into your lungs, water or another element. She could feel it, thick and cold in her chest, like something she'd swallowed; as if before she hadn't been breathing air at all. The atmosphere was still and very quiet. Sounds from specific distances moved across the silence, footsteps in the gravel, voices, traffic. But the clog of sound she had never noticed in hospital was removed, as if a plug of cotton wool had been taken out; that constant humming buzz of the working building like a machine or a living body around her. Now she was outside.

Clare was staring at her. She propelled her to a low wall and sat her down beside her suitcase.

"I'm going to get a taxi. You don't look fit to walk. Wait here. OK? Just sit here till I come back."

Crunch crunch Clare walked quickly over the gravel. Carolyn

stirred it with her foot. She could feel the separate movements of hundreds of small pointed stones through the sole of her shoe. Now the patch she had stirred was darker grey. The gravel was damp underneath. Beneath her bottom the brick wall was hard and penetratingly cold, with a sharp edge that cut into her thighs. On the other side of the path stood a sapling. It was bare, its straight grey branches raised like arms to the cloudy heavens. It was as simple as a naked body. Above the tree, about a quarter of the way up the sky, the sun was an opaque light behind layers of grey cloud, eye-wateringly white.

She stood up carefully, feeling the cold air move across her exposed face and hands, and turned around. Behind her, beyond a patch of raw dug earth, was a car park full of brilliantly coloured cars, red yellow and blue. Their shapes seemed as dear and familiar as friends' faces, she wanted to pat their cold metal bonnets.

Then Clare took her by the elbow and led her along the path which suddenly went through a gate and stopped. There was a lot of noise. The road. Clare helped her into a black car that stood by the kerb with its door open.

Meg returned to the hospital early next morning. It had been Arthur's brainwave in the night; they must know Clare's second name, and address. Meg went up to the familiar ward hoping against hope to find Carolyn back in her bed again. She walked past the nurses' cubicle unchecked. There didn't seem to be anyone around. It wasn't visiting time. She walked in and around the corner, and her heart leapt to see someone in Carolyn's bed. But it wasn't her, she realized, as she stepped nearer and faltered. It was a little grey-haired old lady, propped up on cushions and staring intently at something Meg couldn't see. Meg hesitated and turned round, searching for a nurse. She spotted one just going into the cubicle.

"It isn't visiting time, you know," she told Meg as Meg knocked on the open door.

"No, I'm sorry, I just wanted to see a nurse. I'm Mrs Tanner, Carolyn's mother."

"Oh yes Mrs Tanner. How is she? Getting along all right now?"

"I – I don't know. I need – she went – another girl took her home. Called Clare. She was in the bed next to her. Can you tell me, what's her address? I don't know where she's taken Carolyn."

The nurse made a funny sucking noise with her lips and stared at Meg. "Um, I don't think I can, really. I mean, a patient's address is confidential."

"But –" Meg was speechless.

The nurse continued to stare disapprovingly.

"But my daughter's gone. I don't know where she is. She could have been kidnapped for all I know. She didn't even tell me herself – just left a note – anything could've happened to her."

"I'm sorry Mrs Tanner. I don't know what to do. We're not supposed to give patients' addresses. It's confidential – I mean, you wouldn't like it if we gave out your address would you?"

"But it's my daughter –!"

"Yes, I know. Look, let me ask Sister. Can you wait here? No, sorry, you'd better wait outside." She took Meg out into the ward, and to Meg's humiliation locked the little cubicle before disappearing.

The bossy sister confirmed that it wasn't possible to give an address. Meg realized she'd been a complete fool. She could have said it differently. If she'd said Carolyn had borrowed a book from Clare and wanted to return it, they'd have given her the address. It was only because they saw how much she wanted it that they weren't telling her. It had been the hope which had kept her going through the dawn and early morning. Falling heavily into the one chair in the cubicle she began to cry hopelessly.

The sister watched her for a while, then sent the nurse on an errand.

"Mrs Tanner – Mrs Tanner, please –" Sister crouched beside her. "We really can't give you her address. But I'll tell you what I could do, if you like."

Meg paused in her sobbing.

"If you wanted to write a letter to your daughter and give it to me, I could address it to Miss – to Clare for you. How would that be?"

Meg nodded. She couldn't stop crying now to save her life. It had been like this last night. She thought she'd cried herself out. It was the sense of dread, the awful dropping away with fear of her stomach, that was worst. It had happened, something terrible. After all her vigilance, all her care, still, it had happened. "I was always meant to lose her," she had sobbed to Arthur, who tried to comfort her with cups of tea and brief, common-sense reassurances. The chink in the sister's armour now made her cry the more.

Half an hour later the sister had her organized at a table in the day room, with writing paper and pen and a cup of sugary tea. Meg sat over her letter for nearly an hour, crossing out line after line, and neatly copying her final version like a schoolchild. The sister wasn't in her office when she went back, so she left it in the middle of the desk: "Miss Carolyn Tanner, care of Clare". I won't hear from her until the day after tomorrow, she told herself. Even if she is all right. She doubted her own ability to survive that long.

The house was an awful place, Carolyn thought. It was huge and bare and dirty, and smelt of damp plaster and old food. They all stood around staring at her and smiling awkwardly, as if she was embarrassing. She asked Clare if she could go to her room. It was at the top of the house, and very big. At first she thought it was like a watch-tower, because the roof sloped down to the tops of the two windows, making them the most important things. If she looked down she could see the wilderness that was this house's garden. There was a high brick wall around it. It backed on to a big grey building like an overgrown garden shed, with no windows. A factory, she supposed. To the right was a road which she couldn't see because of the height of the wall, but she could see the tops of buses and lorries, travelling along it. Over the road were roofs – endless rows of them. Above them, like low cloud, she could see far away, an outline of hills. She could see for miles.

In the room each bit of furniture seemed to be too far away from the others, as if they had been dropped there as markers, but the space was eroding them. The bed, tucked in under the corner where the roof sloped down, looked small and safe. But there was a huge old-fashioned wardrobe marooned against the back wall, and an old armchair with square arms and greyish padding showing through the brown cloth, in the exact middle of the floor. That was all, except for a little box by the bed covered with a beautiful silky blue and green scarf with long black fringes. Carolyn sat on the bed, which she noticed was low and very soft, and fingered the silk. The room made her think of the children's game where the floor is the sea and full of sharks, and you are only safe on the furniture. In her Mum and Dad's house you were so safe there wasn't much point in playing – there were so many bits of furniture crammed into the room. Here the game would be terrifying. The carpet itself, old and threadbare with strange geometric patterns on it (like the flying carpet in one of her childhood story books) floated like an uneven raft on the knobbly floorboards, which it was too small to cover. The rough boards and window-frames were painted dark blue, and the long walls were clean and white and empty.

It took away her breath, a little. But the windows were the main thing. She sat in the armchair and looked out of the window. She didn't know what. But it was all right sitting here. She wanted to sit here, and stare at this view, which was much better than hospital. She was pleased not to have to do anything. She didn't have anything to do. At home – her mother would –

She concentrated on the clouds, which moved quickly and smoothly as a train across the top of the hills. She wanted to sit here all day. She didn't want Clare or those others to come in. She wanted to be left alone.

As it got dark in the evening she became scared. There was something by the shady side of the wardrobe that made a noise. As darkness intensified it seemed to grow. It leaned forward to try to reach her. She had to stay on the chair, to be safe. If she sat very very still, it would forget she was there, and recede. But if she got pins and needles and had to move, it woke with a jump and crept forwards again. There were other things in the room too. Something under the bed moved softly, rustling like a woman walking past in long skirts – or a soft breeze in high trees. It wasn't unfriendly. But it was better not to anger it by sleeping on the bed. And a more frantic presence was trapped behind the skirting board. Suddenly in the silence of the small hours its patience would break and she listened rigidly to its scrabbling attempts to break out. It had claws like an eagle – talons; she could hear them shredding and splintering the wood. The only defence was to sit very still, to be invisible; to fade right into the shadow between the arms of the big square armchair.

As the dawn came she was weak with exhaustion and relief, watching and willing the first barely perceptible lightening of the sky.

But then a different kind of terror came in daytime, starting on the second day. It was worse. She could not glare at it or protect herself by clutching at the chair's arms. She could not hold in a corner of her mind the rational knowledge that this was purely childish. It was a terror that started in herself, instead of attacking from outside. It was as if, somehow, she became a telescope. At first she was closed, then gradually she was pulled open, extended to a great length, leaving an awful hollow giddy sensation in her stomach. Once extended her own eye was pressed to the lens of the telescope that was herself (was it her own eye's lens she was looking through the wrong way?) and she saw herself at the other end. But not only did she see herself, small, sitting there; she also saw through herself (because the telescope, with its hollow inside, was her) and she saw that she was hollow. She was terrified by her own existence.

In a way she saw quite objectively, a person sitting on a chair, afraid of shadows – someone who was probably mental. "Get on, get up! Stop moping! Get on with something!" cried the Meg in her. But it was equally obvious, to the impartial eye at the lens, that there was nothing else to do. What shall I do? Here I am, replied the person she could see in the chair. There she was. What was she to do?

She was scared. When it happened, when she was pulled out like this, she felt sick, giddy and unbalanced. She might even fall into the telescope lens and go crashing down upon herself. What would happen then? She tried to think of things to do. She didn't know what. She didn't want to meet any of those people. Wait till they're out. Go and make a cup of tea. Look in the paper for a job. Wash some knickers. But it didn't seem as if doing any of these things would help.

Clare thought Caro didn't look fit to come out of hospital. She was pale and unsteady, and moved maddeningly slowly. Clare got her back to the house, and introduced her to Bryony, Sue, and the kids. They made her a cup of coffee.

"Sit down, make yourself at home." But Caro stood by the table and didn't move. She seemed terrified.

"How do you feel? It's good to get out, isn't it?"

"Yes–" Carolyn's frozen face became animated. "It all looks so brilliant – so – like everything's deadened, in there. Muffled. It's really – I really–"

"Yup," said Clare. "Brave new world. It's funny how quickly you forget what it's like out here."

Carolyn nodded but she seemed to have lost interest already.

"How d'you feel?"

"OK," she said quickly.

"Do you–"
"Can I–"   }They both stopped.

Clare smiled. "Go on."

"Can I see my room please?"

"Yes – yes, OK. Now?"

"Yes, please."

Clare got up and went to the door. She noticed that Caro's coffee was untouched. "Don't you want that? It'll warm you up."

Carolyn picked it up unsteadily, slopping a pool of coffee across the table.

"Oh, sorry," she said, and put the mug down. Clare waited, but Carolyn did not pick it up again.

She seemed pleased with the room. As Clare went out Carolyn quickly and unexpectedly closed the door behind her and said "Thankyou," as if she'd been shown her hotel room by a maid.

And there she stayed. When they asked her down for meals she didn't come. Clare took snacks up to her – poached eggs, milky drinks – thinking she was probably exhausted by the change, and needed a couple of days in bed to recover. She looked shocking: absolutely white, with huge purple bags under her eyes. She said nothing, and replied to questions monosyllabically or not at all. It was impossible to find any pretext for remaining in her company. She very obviously wanted to be left alone.

But after a few days Clare began to worry. Carolyn looked no better. Sue (who was at home most of the day) confirmed her suspicion that Carolyn never came out of her room. She was hardly eating anything. Bryony attacked on the third night.

"What are you going to do about her?"

"Caro?"

"This is a communal house. It's ridiculous, we can't have someone like that here. No wonder you didn't bother to ask us, you know what we'd have said. We have to live with her as well as you. She's hopeless – she doesn't do anything. She doesn't speak to anyone. She can't take a share in child-care. She's a nervous wreck. Didn't you ask her anything before she came? Didn't you tell her it was a shared house?"

Bryony, on occasions like this, was always self-righteous: the problem and answers were obvious, why hadn't she been consulted?

"For God's sake, the girl's ill. She's just come out of hospital."

"Well it's deeply wonderful of you to offer this as a convalescent home – but you've got no right to do it without consulting me and Sue. You're not the only person who lives here. Have you considered the kids? Has it occurred to you that she might disturb or upset them? She doesn't even bring her dirty cups down. Does she think it's a hotel? Why doesn't she go home to her Mum?"

Clare did think it odd that Carolyn's Mum hadn't been. Ironic that that was originally the reason she'd hesitated to invite Carolyn: fear of her Mum hovering round the house all the time. She went up and knocked on Caro's door. There was no reply. She looked at her watch, it was nearly ten o'clock. Would she be asleep already? Clare opened the door quietly and looked in. Carolyn was sitting in the dark looking out the window.

"Shall I put the light on?"

She didn't reply. Clare switched it on. The room looked uninhabited.

"You all right?"

Carolyn nodded.

"Why don't you unpack? D'you want some help?"

Carolyn shook her head.

"Caro, does your Mum know where you are?"

"No."

Despite herself, Clare was shocked. "Where does she think you are?"

"I told her I was coming here. But I didn't know the address."

Instinctively, Clare glanced out of the window. It was amazing they hadn't been invaded by detectives and policemen already.

64

Carolyn's Mum wouldn't leave a stone unturned. "Look, shall I tell her? Shall I ring her up for you?"

"No." The voice was the same tight voice that had told Clare the hospital ceiling was coming down.

"Can I – why don't–" Clare stopped. "She'll be terribly worried – frantic."

Carolyn continued to stare rigidly through the window.

"I think we should tell your Mum where you are," said Clare firmly.

"No."

"Why not?"

"She'll come and get me."

Clare thought this was probably true. She also quite hoped it would happen. She had thought Carolyn needed a space in which to pull herself together, not to crack up. Jesus Christ, she told herself angrily, the hospital's discharged her. There can't be that much wrong with her. "Look, Caro, if you want to stay here, you've got to make a bit of an effort to fit in. The others aren't very happy about you."

"Why? What have I done?" For the first time, Carolyn looked away from the window and at Clare, an expression of anxiety on her white face.

"Nothing. It's just – well, it's a shared house, we all do things like cooking and cleaning, you know – and usually we eat together. They just think it's a bit odd because you hide in your room all the time." She hesitated. "I mean, there's no need for you to bother with cooking or anything, yet. But I don't think it's doing you any good, sitting up here on your own. I just think you'll get depressed. I think you should come down for meals."

There was a silence.

"OK," said Carolyn.

Clare waited to see if she would say anything else. She felt clumsy and awkward; but irritated too. Carolyn was ignoring her like a sulky child. She's so young, that's the trouble, Clare told herself. Basically, this is a teenage crisis. Well, I'm not her mother.

Carolyn came down to tea next day. She grimaced a smile at each of them, and nodded hurriedly at any remark directed at her. She radiated tension and embarrassment, so that after the meal Clare

65

went immediately to watch TV in the sitting room, Sue took the children to bed and Bryony went out to a meeting. Carolyn cleared the table, washed up, dried up, took everything out of the cutlery drawer and cleaned and tidied it, cleaned the cooker and swept the floor. She was about to start washing the floor at five to ten when Clare went back into the kitchen to get her cigarettes.

"What on earth are you doing?"

"Just cleaning up."

"Well look – that's splendid – there's no need to go mad. Stop, for heaven's sake. D'you fancy a quick drink?"

Carolyn shook her head and continued to squeeze and soak the dried, shrivelled mop.

"Caro, when I said about helping – I didn't mean –" Carolyn ignored her. Clare shrugged and left the kitchen. She felt very angry. She had tried to help Carolyn, and now the bloody girl was acting as if Clare was a bossy teacher. Damn her.

Next day, a white-faced Carolyn with horrible silent determination dusted and vacuumed the landings, stairs and hallway, washed down the woodwork in the kitchen, and cleaned out the fridge and food cupboards. Bryony and Sue were appalled.

"Can't you stop her?" Sue asked Clare when she got home. "She'll have to go. It's impossible to live in the house."

"D'you want me to tell her to go?" asked Bryony. "Why don't we phone her Mum?"

Reluctantly, after supper, Clare mounted the extra six stairs to Carolyn's room. She knocked and there was no reply. So she opened the door cautiously. It was dark. She made out the shape of Caro squatting in the armchair, rigidly still.

"Caro?"

The figure didn't move.

"You all right?"

Carolyn appeared to be staring at something horrible in the corner.

"What is it?" Clare stepped into the room, and some of Carolyn's terror communicated itself to her. Quickly she stepped back and switched on the light. She couldn't see anything in the corner.

Carolyn shifted abruptly on her seat, turning her head away.

66

"What is it? What did you see?" Clare ran round the chair to face her.

Carolyn lifted her head sightlessly, tears and snot streaming down her face.

Much later that night, Clare lay in her bed staring at the ceiling. They should never have let Carolyn out of hospital like that. She was settled for the night; Clare had put her to bed and given her a mug of warm milk and two sleeping tablets. But tomorrow? She wasn't in a fit state to be on her own.

Before she finally fell asleep, Clare decided to contact the mother. It wasn't fair not to. They couldn't handle a nervous breakdown.

After she had swallowed the sleeping tablets, Carolyn slept for fourteen hours. Her sleep was black and absolute, as if she had been dropped into a bottomless pit. Waking meant rising, as a diver surfaces from deep water, to a lightening of colours, navy blue, aqua blue, turquoise, pale blue, clear light – day light! with a shocked gasp at the change. It was the first time she had escaped consciousness properly for days.

She lay relaxed and dizzy on the bed, with the lingering sense of floating on top of the depths she had plumbed in her sleep. Her white room was full of light. Through the open window came a breeze which separated and fluttered the curtains, which in turn made moving watery patterns of light and shadow on the white ceiling. She felt peaceful. She remembered . . . different feelings and flavours. Memory was a great open channel she could float down. Had it been blocked before this morning? Had she forgotten it? She remembered going to the seaside. They had gone once with school. She remembered the coach ride, and having no one to sit next to because Mandy was ill. They went to a strange place, with no piers or fun-fairs or candy floss. By the sea the empty beach was wide, and the dunes were dotted with bristly little bushes. Then the sand dunes flattened out and there were pine trees. They were quite far apart, it was light but still felt enclosed: you could look up and see the high tops of the pines swaying in a wind that you couldn't feel down on the ground. The air smelt sweet and sticky, and there were those big wide-open pine cones lying on the sand, with their little woody layers peeled back like petticoats. Mr Marshall told them you could forecast the weather with pine cones. After lunch they all trooped back down to the beach with plastic bags and jars for specimens, and Carolyn lagged behind. Following the tidy path through the pines, past a picnic site with slatted wooden tables and large litter bins, she was soon out of sight of any other people. There was the sound of the sea, at a distance, like regular quiet breathing. There was the secretive rustling of the wind in the tops of the pines. There were sudden sharp sounds, a fir cone dropping to the ground, a seagull. Mainly there was silence, in still greenish light, as if she were at the bottom of a pool. She sat and held her breath, and felt that she could hear the trees growing around her and that she was part of the same quiet measured progress, in a world devoid of people.

Carolyn began to get better. Although Clare had decided to call in Meg, she didn't; at first because in the morning things weren't so pressing as they had been at night, and then because she was too busy at the Refuge, and then because it really didn't seem fair. She could see that Caro was trying very hard.

Gradually these impressions, and the passing of time, merged with her observation of Caro's improvement to wipe all thought of Meg from her mind.

Chapter 8

As Carolyn got better, she stopped hearing her other story. She no longer needed it; didn't have time for it.

The story, once started, continued though, as stories will – quite unknown to Carolyn. It featured a Carolyn no less real than herself: her double, her living image, separated from her only by a second's timing in a rainsoaked dash across Leap Lane. A Carolyn who led another life, with no more than the ghost of a thought that things could have been different.

Carolyn never really understood Alan's reaction to her being pregnant. Two days after the scene in the pub, he rang her up. His voice sounded forced and sulky, as if someone was telling him what to say.

"I'm sorry if I upset you. Let's get married."

There was a silence. She couldn't think of any reply.

"All right? Carolyn? We'll get married at Christmas. I'll come back again next weekend and we can plan it."

When she had put the phone down she went and sat in her bedroom. She was very relieved, so much so that she felt weak. It would be all right at the weekend. They would be able to talk and explain.

But she was disappointed. Alan remained distant and slightly sullen. He insisted on discussing practical details, as if they were planning a sale of work or an expedition. At last she lost patience.

"You don't have to marry me."

"I know," he said evenly.

"Well why are you?"

"Because I want to."

"Well why are you being so horrible about it?"

"I'm not."

"You are. Why are you being so distant and unfriendly? Anyone

would think someone was standing behind you with a gun."

"It is a shot-gun wedding," he said and grinned, making it, briefly, all right.

"No one is. We don't have to."

"Look I'm OK. I've decided — unless you don't want to?"

She hesitated. "I don't want you to do me a favour."

"Well I'm not. Now let it drop."

Carolyn knew that he was angry with her, for some reason which she couldn't fathom, and that the more she pressed him for an explanation the more he clammed up over it. She knew that it was to do with her being pregnant, but that it wasn't the simple fact of her pregnancy. She remembered vividly the sight of him crying in the car that night, and she still didn't understand what that had been about. But he refused to let her get near the subject.

"Forget it. I don't want to discuss it."

She could see that he would lose his temper if she pressed him any further, and so she left it. But it made her miserable that they were not open with one another. Her position in relation to him had slipped. He was forcing her to be careful of what she said; setting up areas which were not to be talked about. It made her feel that he wanted her to be grateful to him for marrying her. But confusingly, he seemed sincere enough in wanting to (almost the more sincere, because of his grimness about it).

His mood wasn't consistent. Often they were just on the edge of being happy. She thought it would come right when they were married.

Alan was very unhappy. He hadn't imagined being married, or having children, for years. It was like discovering you have a disease; something permanent but liveable-with, like diabetes. It altered the shape of his life.

He liked Carolyn well enough. Almost certainly, he was in love with her. And on the basis of that, he was prepared to marry her, and even wanted to. The fact that she was pregnant was forcing both their hands in a way which was nearly amusing. Everyone they knew was so amazed —"I never thought it would happen to you!" Grimly, he could have enjoyed the sudden notoriety and muted sympathy. He could have felt superior and thought them all fools for pitying him for getting what he wanted. Almost certainly, nearly, quite, he could.

But for Carolyn. She had betrayed him. When she knew she was pregnant she did not tell him, she kept it secret. They had made love, and it had been so utterly different from his other experiences of sex that he thought something wonderful had happened. He thought it was to do with passion and love. And it turned out to be simply because she knew she was pregnant; a mechanical trick she was turning on him.

The revelation had devastated him, eroding his confidence and his desire for her. It hit at the root of his male pride, but also at the basis of his love for her. What had attracted Alan to Carolyn initially, and reinforced his interest as he got to know her, was her painful honesty. At school he had always found it easy to get women. He was tall and reasonably good-looking, with a slightly sad, very reserved look which could melt into a charming smile, so intimate that it unbalanced almost any girl he cared to direct it at. He was bright and articulate, the son of a successful doctor and a concert cellist. His home was a four-bedroomed house standing in its own large garden on the outskirts of the town. He had the usual run of furtive sexual fumblings and persuaded three of his girlfriends (whom he then held in contempt) to go all the way. Carolyn, who had been in his English class for years, had always been quite insignificant. With the thinning of numbers to an A-level class of fifteen, she was brought to his attention. She had become rather wispishly beautiful, thin with light hair and quick nervous movements. He decided she was as clear and pure as water, against the other girls' coarseness. She also started speaking in class, which she had never done before. Everyone was amazed when she first did, interrupting the teacher with a series of incoherent stammers which seemed to insist on being articulated, against her will. She would blush furiously, her pale complexion flooding red so that he actually imagined her blood flowing in a hot tide to the surface of her flesh; a thought he found exciting. The things she said were always in disagreement, with the teacher or another member of the class, and cost her so much, in terms of physical anguish, that they carried great conviction. Some people laughed at her, but after a while they began to take her seriously. She had an odd, idiosyncratic way of looking at things – he felt she had some standards which he wasn't familiar with, against which she matched the things they said. Often she had to work so hard to overcome her paralysing shyness that what she had to say burst out in a shout, or in a tone of great fierceness. After a term, she was grudgingly admitted by the flyers in the group to be worth reckoning with – though very odd.

Alan's charming smile fell on stony ground with her. She was uncompromisingly hostile to him, which piqued and fascinated him. She was unreceptive to any of the signals he sent out. She moved away when he sat near her, went into town to change her library books instead of going home when he invented a string of excuses that would enable him to *walk in her direction. She displayed no interest in any of the social events he said he was going to and wondered if he might see her at. She was prickly and sharp with him, and only too obviously relieved to make her escape. He sought her out more pointedly, and was rewarded by, "Why are you following me about?"*

The charming smile. He still couldn't quite believe it didn't work with her. "Because I like you." He watched her blush, and imagined he could actually feel a little glow of heat on his own skin, radiating off her warmth.

"I – I – I thought you were laughing at me," she said.

"Why? Why should I laugh at you?"

"You all do, in English, I know you do."

"No we don't." Suddenly he was embarrassed too, and at a loss. They stared at each other for a moment.

"Will you go out with me?" he asked, blushing himself.

"I – I – I – all right."

Alan had his own reasons for liking her desperate honesty; reasons that went beyond his contempt for the other girlfriends of his youth. Trevor and Lucy Blake were slightly unusual parents, although it was years before Alan and his sister Pamela realized this. They thought it normal for Daddy to get them up and dress and breakfast them, before he went down to morning surgery, and for Lucy once she was up to spend ages talking excitedly and gesticulating on the telephone, before consigning them (with a kiss on the head) to Nissy while she disappeared to the study to practise, and the house was filled with the cello's dismal squeaks and groans, which always recovered eventually, into more or less of a tune. They thought it was normal for Lucy (they had never called her Mummy) to fly from room to room looking for her watch, keys, diary, gloves, scarf, and blow a kiss to them from the garden path as the taxi-driver carried her cello out to the car, while Nissy held them up to the window to wave. They thought it normal for tea to come out of the fridge or the oven in a tinfoil box with a peel-back lid, although they did remember for weeks afterwards Lucy's occasional cordon-bleu phases, when the house had been filled with heart-warming smells, and different kinds of food had appeared out of saucepans on top of the oven, and other dishes inside it. She had a repertoire of all-time favourites, culled from these various phases, which the whole family loved, and knew that no one could make better: coq au vin, boeuf Stroganoff, lasagne with home-made pasta, duck with orange, tandoori chicken.

72

Alan loved his mother hopelessly. He loved the way she looked, with her glossy chestnut hair which reached below her waist when she let it loose, and her tinkle of necklaces and trails of silk scarves, and her neat slender legs in their high-heeled shoes, reminding him of gazelles' legs – or gazelles reminded him of her, he supposed, since he must have seen her first. He loved the way she smelt, the atmosphere with which she surrounded you, the way she gestured, the ear-rings that sparkled in the light when she turned her head quickly. He loved the music that she made on her cello, and the way she sat curved around it, seeming to listen to its inner voice as she played.

He hated the way people were always ringing her up, and she was always saying, "How lovely!" and "I'll be there by two, I promise, darling." He hated the way she was always, always, on her way out and late. He hated the way she said to him, "Tell me tomorrow darling, I must fly now," and the way that when she'd waved Bye-bye and got into the taxi, she immediately opened her bag and took out her mirror and comb, and didn't look at you again, even if the taxi didn't move for ages, because the man was changing the meter or talking into his radio.

He longed to please her. At school he laboured to make himself better than all the others. "You clever boy!" she would cry, throwing her arms around him, and sending him into a transport of joy. "Let's have a look at your book then." Quickly she would flick through his exercise books, glancing from page to page as they flew by. "Oh, this is very good, Alan. What a brainbox you are!" A kiss on the head and she was off, leaving him the more deprived for his brief spell in the full sunny glow of her attention. She always had so many places to go and so many people who wanted to see her that he felt cruelly his own stolid boringness, and was not surprised that she did not spend more time with him.

She wanted them to be musicians like her, and both he and Pam were learning instruments, he the violin and Pam the clarinet. But he wasn't very good, and even to please her (which was his only motive for practising) he could not make himself into a musician. Pam was better at it. She seemed to get along quite well.

In the evenings his mother was out, and Dad would read them stories and put them to bed. Sometimes, amid great excitement, his mother was in, with guests who drank wine and laughed loudly and spoiled him and Pam. He was ashamed of the way his father sat in his armchair staring at them without joining in the conversation, or even rudely reading as they talked. Everyone always wanted to talk to Lucy and listen to what she had to say, everyone was always looking at her.

As he grew older his own life began to have more centre to it and he gave up yearning so hungrily after his mother's attention. He began to find his own satisfactions in doing well at school, in his friends, in his drawings. Sometimes Lucy would seize on one and cry, "But darling, this is marvellous! I've bred an artist! This must go up on the wall!" and stick his latest painting up with Sellotape alongside the daubs by the mentally handicapped group she had played for at Christmas, and the postcards from her friends all over the world.

Despite the fact that she seemed rarely to be in it, the house reflected her taste. It had a breathless untidiness, with an underlying stratum of solid good things: expensive carpets and curtains in dark plain colours, antique furniture ranging from valuable to junk, but having in common a charm or whimsicality that had made each piece claim her attention originally. She and Trevor went to auctions together. It was the only pleasure they seemed to share. And there were always flowers. Lucy would laugh and wave her hand when people said, "How lovely they are." "Flowers are my weakness!" she said. "I must have flowers, I can't bear it without them. Flowers are my vice." Trevor bought her a huge bunch every Friday, the florist made it up specially for him, and she often bought them herself as well, when something caught her eye: carnations, roses, freesias, lilies, pockets of scented air in the corners of rooms – and flashes of colour, violet iris, scarlet tulip, golden mimosa shining on the dark polished furniture. Most of her guests brought flowers when they came, knowing how she liked them, and how she loved to arrange them in tall glass vases on the kitchen table while people gathered around her, chatting in a tight excited crowd.

As Alan grew older he noticed that when his mother promised "Tomorrow", she always forgot. And he caught himself thinking, as she spoke sometimes, "She doesn't mean that." When he reached sixteen he was ready to condemn her as superficial and a hypocrite. He judged her the more harshly, and was the more hurt by his judgement, because he still worshipped her. He would have given anything for her unadulterated attention and approval.

It was Pam, much more worldly-wise than he, who told him about the affair.

"I feel sorry for Dad," she said casually one day, as they sat in the kitchen after school, helping themselves to a packet of chocolate digestives.

"Why?" he said crossly, already knowing she was going to say something stupid.

74

"The way Lucy carries on."

"What d'you mean, carries on?"

"You know." She was scraping the chocolate off the biscuit with her top teeth, and pretending to be absorbed in it.

"Stop being so thick!" he shouted angrily.

"I'm not thick, you are."

"Why?"

"Because you don't know."

"What?"

"That she's got a boyfriend."

Alan stared at the noticeboard on the opposite wall, pretending to read something but seeing nothing but a blur of the leaflets, notes, scraps of ribbon and withered buttonholes which Lucy had pegged up there. "Who?" he said finally.

"Jeremy. The double-bass."

"How d'you know?"

"It's obvious, as soon as you start to think about it. But anyway, I saw them."

"When?"

"You're not cross-questioning an enemy spy, you know," she flared, and turned her attention back to her revolting biscuit.

"Go on. Tell me. When?"

"'Please.' You are the rudest person I ever met."

"Please. Tell me."

"Last night. I woke up and it was late – after two. I was starving so I thought I'd come down to the kitchen. When I got downstairs I could see the drawing-room light was on so I thought they must still be up, I'll go and see if they want a snack. Anyway, it was dead quiet and I felt a bit funny as I opened the door –" She stopped.

"And?"

"And there they were."

"What d'you mean?"

"On the sofa. Lucy and Jeremy."

"Doing what?"

"What d'you think?"

"TELL me." He was so angry with the stupid little brat he wanted to smash her face in.

"All right, if you must know every disgusting detail. She was lying on the sofa and he was – I don't know – doing something to her. I couldn't see properly."

"With no clothes on?"

"I don't know. I shut the door quick, before they saw me."

He imagined opening the drawing-room door. The sofa faced the fire, at a slant. You would just see one end of a person lying on it. "How d'you know it was Jeremy?"

"His jacket was on the floor. And his double-bass was in the hall," she said smugly.

Alan stared at Pam, fighting back the tears which welled in his eyes. How could she? How could she?

"Hadn't you guessed?" said Pam in her chirpy voice. "I've known for ages there was something going on. I mean, she's always out, and she's not at that many concerts. She's probably been at it for years."

"Shut up!" Blindly, Alan ran to his room, where he beat and punched his bed and cried aloud in a rage like a child.

Pam was right, of course. He realized afterwards that he had known for years, that there were a hundred fine details that he had chosen to ignore about her behaviour, her phone conversations, the times of her comings and goings. Dad must know. Unless he was wilfully blind too. But if he knew – why did he let it go on? They were obscene, disgusting. He started going out with Carolyn soon after Pam made her announcement. Carolyn, he knew, would never behave like his mother.

Meg was shocked when Carolyn told her about the baby. She couldn't believe that Carolyn had done that. It just wasn't like Carolyn. But she was diverted from her own reaction by Arthur.

"That bloody lad. I'll kill him. I will, I'll kill him. Who does he think he is? I'll bloody kill him."

It was only the second time Meg had seen Arthur really angry. The first was some eight years ago when he'd been accused of shoddy workmanship on a car which had been involved in a crash two days after he'd MOTed it. He had had a fight with the insurance inspector and ended up in court charged with Assault. He was such a quiet, retiring man. "He's never had a cross word for me or Carolyn – never," Meg told Jean ruefully. When he was angry like this he went berserk, she knew. She argued and pleaded with him, and warned Carolyn to keep Alan away from the house.

"He's a nice lad, Arthur, honest he is, a really decent lad. I wouldn't wish for anyone better for our Carolyn, myself. And it's not as if – I mean, he wants to marry her. There's no sense in it now, come on. What's done is done. No use crying over spilt milk."

Arthur could have been deaf, for all the effect this had.

"You can't blame it all on him, anyway. It takes two you know. You can't blame him and not her. You're behind the times, Arthur, you're old-fashioned. They all do it now, look at the papers – look at the telly. It's not like it was when we were young." In the silence in which Arthur received this, Meg reconsidered. "Well, it wasn't so different when we were young, for that matter. Look at our Bertha, she was three months gone with Harry when she married Jim. And you know as well as I do Jim wasn't the father. It happens all the time. It's not as if they've done anything very unusual now, is it?"

He glared at the Cosiglow, ignoring her.

"And she's not a child any more, she's over eighteen. Lots of girls are married by eighteen. And he's a sensible lad, with good prospects, he'll do well enough when he's finished studying at that university. He's going to be an architect, Carolyn tells me. His Dad's a doctor, you know, they live up on Quickedge, in ever such a nice house. Four bedrooms, Carolyn says they've got."

To Jean at work, she said wonderingly, "I know they all do, these days, I know that. But she does seem young. It doesn't seem more than a few months since I was knitting clothes for her dolls – and now –" She held up her needles, speared through the left front of a pearly-white matinée jacket.

Alan's parents were perfectly civilized about the marriage, and Alan took considerable satisfaction in the fact that he knew they were rather shocked. Serve them right. Lucy insisted on not taking it seriously for days.

"It's too absurd, getting married at your age, you're far too young. Come on darling, be sensible. You'll meet thousands of girls before you find the one you like." She ruffled his hair. "You're so romantic and silly – there's nothing to an abortion these days. It'll be awfully sad if you marry her and find you don't like her later."

Like you, Alan said to himself. You hypocrite.

Meg, who thought things ought to be done properly, invited Alan's parents round for tea, just before Christmas. Lucy accepted, but Alan knew they wouldn't go. She rang up on the morning with breathless excuses about having to practise a particularly beastly new piece for a concert tomorrow.

"Why don't you go?" Alan asked her when she put the phone down.

She pulled a face, and ran her outstretched fingers through her long hair, pulling it out sideways from her head to that it fell back softly in the shape of a folding fan. "It's very sweet of them, Alan, but I really think it would be a bit of a disaster."

"Why?"

"Well darling – because I don't think we've got very much in common."

"Isn't your children getting married something in common?" Alan said venomously.

"Why are you so angry, my love? Do you really want us to go? If you really want us to, we will. I don't suppose it'll be that bad!"

He was astonished that she had backed down. She phoned Meg again and told her she was so silly, she'd made a muddle with the dates of two concerts, and it would be perfectly all right for them to come tonight but only if Meg was absolutely sure it wouldn't be too much trouble, it was so sweet of her . . . Alan was repelled by the ease with which she lied.

He had harboured for months the idea of telling her that he and Pam knew about Jeremy. But he knew that he never actually would. He dreaded her reaction: seeing her wriggle and flick her tail and swim away in a sea of lies – or seeing her pop like a burst balloon. Either would be terrible.

Carolyn came round to his house that evening, and told him about her mother's preparations for tea. He realized he hadn't warned them what sort of meal tea was. Lucy took afternoon tea at about four o'clock, and dinner at eight. Carolyn's parents had tea at six p.m.

"Mum was awfully nervous about it. She thinks your parents are terribly posh."

"Huh." He had told her everything about his mother. Her reaction had been quietly puzzled. She had not condemned Lucy, as he half hoped, yet feared she would.

"She thought they'd better have something to drink so she got some sherry, then she was worried because she's only got those little glasses – you know, little tumblers, and she says they're only for whisky."

Carolyn's parents never drank in the house. Occasionally Arthur would go for a pint at the local, but that was it. Alan was pleased. Lucy would find nothing more disgusting than a tumbler of sweet sherry with her dinner. Tea.

"They don't like me, do they?" Carolyn asked, as they sat picking at some smoked ham and coleslaw Alan had found in the fridge.

"Don't know. It doesn't matter." He realized from Carolyn's face that it did.

"Dad does. Lucy's hardly met you, has she?"

78

"But they don't want you to get married."

He shrugged. "None of their business, is it?"

"I feel –" she hesitated, looking round – "I don't know, frightened, when I look round this house. I mean, it's all so – rich and everything."

"It's just junk," he said angrily. "Antique junk."

"No but it's like – like a stately home or something. And all these beautiful flowers. . . ."

"I hate them. It's like living in a chapel of rest."

"Don't you want to live in a house like this when you grow up?"

"When I grow up," he said, smiling at her phrase, "I don't want my life to be anything like theirs. They are a pair of hypocrites. I don't like the games they play."

She got up from the table, the food hardly touched on her plate. "But it is nice. There's so many strange little things –" She was staring at the shelves of the dresser, where various antique plates (prized by Lucy for the colour of their glaze, or the intricacy of their design) vied for attention with two corn dollies, a brass frog, some Victorian bottles and two tall feathery maidenhair ferns. "We haven't got anything like this at our house. These are beautiful, you know." She touched one of the old plates, which was covered in a dense pattern of tiny blue flowers, a brilliant deep Victorian blue. "Really lovely."

Alan made a farting sound through his lips. "Clutter and junk. Don't you like this?" pointing to her untouched coleslaw.

"I don't like the dressing much."

"Shouldn't you eat, for two and all that?"

She shrugged. "I don't know how to cook this sort of stuff either."

"Stop it, Carolyn. I don't care if we live on chips and fish fingers for the rest of our lives. Here, have a bit of cheese."

They went out to the pub, and when Alan came back Trevor and Lucy were at home. He found them, most unusually, sitting either side of the fireplace having a drink together. Pam had been out at a friend's all evening.

"Did you have a nice time?"

His mother giggled. "Have you been into their house? You must have been – isn't it sweet? I don't think I've ever seen so much furniture in one little room. You should have seen our tea: ham, salad, cheese, crackers, potatoes, hard-boiled eggs, bread-and-butter, trifle – all at once, mind you – cream cake, sherry, cups of tea –" She counted them all off on her fingers, smiling innocently as she spoke. "It was perfectly wonderful."

Alan asked his father, "Did you like them?"

"The mother seems a kindly soul. I don't know about the father. He hardly said a word. Is he very shy?"

"He wants to kill me, Carolyn said."

They stared at him in silence. At last Lucy said, "What on earth for?"

"Getting his daughter up the spout."

There was another shocked silence. His father cleared his throat. "I – well, I hadn't realized he felt like that. It was all – it was all very civilized and friendly. There wasn't really any difficulty over it. I wonder if – I wish you'd told me that, Alan. Perhaps I could have had a bit of a chat to him."

Alan shrugged. "Don't think it would make any difference."

His mother took a swig of her brandy. He could see she was recovering.

"The detail in that house really is splendid, isn't it?" She turned to Trevor. "Did you notice what they had above the fireplace?"

"No – horses, something like that."

"Yes," she enthused, "exactly. That famous one from Woolworth's – with the horses charging out of the sea. I've never seen it on a wall in a real house before. It was worth it just for that."

"It's on more walls in more houses than any other picture in the country," Trevor said mildly. "That and Tina."

"And the carpets!" she cried, getting into her stride now. "They are so wonderful! Who on earth designs them? With patterns like – like giant sputniks, and about twenty colours in them." She smiled at Alan. "They positively assault you, don't they? I bet you could keep thieves out with a carpet like that."

"You mean, they'd know there was nothing worth stealing?" said Alan.

His mother looked at him for a moment without an expression on her face, then she smiled and waved her glass at him. "All I can say is, I hope young Pam shows a bit more taste and discernment when she chooses her parents-in-law."

She said it as if it was a joke, but Alan knew perfectly well that she meant it from the bottom of her heart. He went to the door.

"Alan?" she said. "Come on darling, can't you see the funny side? We liked her parents, they were loves. I expect they'd have a giggle about our house, if they came round here."

"Goodnight," he said, and shut the door. He hated her.

Carolyn and Alan did not make love again until they were married. It was Alan's idea. He made a sour kind of joke out of it, that they must wait until their wedding night. Carolyn agreed because she could see he meant it, although she didn't understand why. On their wedding night he was drunk, and she was affectionate and clinging, and it was as hopeless as he had been predicting to himself. He felt, when he woke the next morning, that his life was at an end – a complete disaster.

Alan's term began again on January 20th, and he returned to university with a guilty sense of relief. Carolyn, who still had her job at the 'Craft Basket', stayed at home.

"I do think you're sensible, love, doing it like this," said her mother. "It's far better. He can get on with his studying, without getting distracted, and you can be earning your little bit and putting it away towards a house. And your Dad and I can keep an eye on you and make sure you're not overdoing it, for the sake of the little one."

Carolyn nodded. She had not been given any choice in the matter. Alan had obviously expected to return to university alone, once the fuss was over. And there certainly wasn't any point in her moving out of her Mum's to live alone at a time like this.

It was as if she wasn't married; just as it had been before, going to bed in her pink and white room, setting off for the 'Craft Basket' at half-past eight in the morning, just as she used to set off for school, home by five-thirty, tea, telly, and some needlework to keep herself occupied. She was making a patchwork quilt for the baby's cot. Meg had already knitted a whole drawerful of matinée jackets and bootees, in white, pink and blue. ("I'll put whichever colour it doesn't need in the shop window, love. They'll all get used, don't you worry.")

Alan came back most weekends, and they went out for long drives in his father's car. At Easter Carolyn went to stay with him at university for a week. He was borrowing a house that two of his student friends rented. They had both gone home to their parents'. It was a dingy, poorly furnished little terrace, reminding Carolyn of the old house on Railway Street. But it was the first time they had ever lived privately together. This week was a revelation to both of them. They could do what they liked – go to bed, get up, eat, bath, go back to bed – there were no rules. No one to notice or be offended. It was a week lifted out of real life. Carolyn's pregnancy added to the strangeness. There was a neat solid bulge where her flat belly had been. The baby was kicking, at night Alan lay with his hand on her side and felt the repeated thrusting movements. He found it almost repulsive to think of it in there, kicking at the walls; but it roused

81

him sexually as well. It made her strange. Sex was in the air all the time. Each was constantly aware of the other's movements, the other's body. Even if they were reading or washing up, there seemed to be rays of heat running in the air between them. Pregnancy made Carolyn aware of her body in a way she had never been before; her small breasts had become heavy and almost painfully sensitive, and when Alan stroked her, or breathed close with his hot breath on her nipples, she felt giddy and weak.

"Will it be like this when we live together, do you think?" Carolyn found it suddenly possible to talk about the future, which she had not dared to do before. It was the middle of a dim afternoon. Outside the rain pattered lightly on the window, and in the room there was a great sense of tranquillity. They were lying on the bed after making love, every trace of lust scoured out of them, their bodies clean and abandoned.

"I don't know," Alan said slowly. "I hope so."

"What are we going to do?" she asked. She felt that everything between them was clear now, so that speech was like dropping pebbles into clear water and watching them sink to their resting place. The friction of their bodies had rubbed away all the untidy mess of misunderstanding, and they could speak directly.

"I could rent a place like this next year. In September."

"September," she repeated, and listened to the rain.

"You'll have to stay at home till the baby's born, won't you?"

"Yes. We could move before September, though. We could move in the summer."

"Yes. We'll do that."

They lay quietly, fingers just touching, Carolyn watching the lightshade sway in a slight draught, Alan watching the gentle rise and fall of her ribcage as she breathed.

Chapter 9

Carolyn began to notice the household around her. She came downstairs for all her meals. She was still very quiet and unapproachable, jumping and stammering if a remark was addressed to her, but self-contained. Disciplined. Able to sit, composedly, eating and listening while they talked. She was still an awkward presence because she was never relaxed; there was an unnatural quality of alertness in her posture, in the intent way she stared at you as you spoke, in her sudden jerky movements. They soon gave up trying to draw her into conversation. The first advances she herself made were to Sylvia, Sue's four-year-old daughter. Sylvia was pestering her mother for a story one morning after breakfast. Clare had gone to work, and Bryony was deep in the newspaper. Carolyn was picking up on the movements of the three women, which had seemed so mysteriously random at first. She knew that Sue worked as a nurse four nights a week, going on duty some time after the children had gone to bed in the evening, and returning at seven in the morning. On these mornings her freckled face was blanched, and she sat motionless at the breakfast table, staring sightlessly into a cup of cold, wrinkle-skinned coffee, while her long red hair gradually slithered out of the nest of twists she had knotted it into, and hairgrips pinged out over the floor and the table around her. After she had gone upstairs Carolyn collected them and put them in a jar on the mantelpiece. She was surprised by the extent of Sue's gratitude, when she came looking for them the following evening.

"Shall I read it, Sylvia?"

The little girl leaned back against her mother's knee, staring at Carolyn.

"Let me read it. I don't know that story. Can I have a look – please?"

Dragging her feet reluctantly, as if she was being pushed from behind, Sylvia took her book to Carolyn, standing well back and handing it to her at arm's length. Carolyn opened the book on her knee and studied it.

"This looks interesting. What's it about? The Snow Queen? Who's she?"

Sylvia put her thumb in her mouth.

"Where does she live, Sylvia?"

"In the North Pole."

"Does she? What does she look like?"

Sylvia suddenly moved forwards and grabbed the book. "In a picture –" she riffled the pages "– there!"

"She doesn't look very nice, does she? Shall we find out what she does?"

Sylvia nodded, and leaned her weight against the side of Carolyn's chair. As Carolyn started to read a look of absorption came over the child's face, and her thumb slotted into her mouth. She gazed at the pages as Carolyn read, as if she could see the events unfolding there.

Soon Carolyn was the favourite story reader, both with Sylvia and her older brother Robin. They liked her because she didn't put the book down in the middle to go and do something else, and because she read stories properly, as if she wanted to know what happened too.

Carolyn was cautious about the times when she came downstairs. She knew Sue's movements. She felt all right coming down when Sue and the children were there, or when the kitchen was empty, although the suddenly-abandoned look of the room always gave her a shock. There was always the odd dirty plate or mug on the table, and a tub of margarine (open) and milk (in its bottle) lying around, not put away in the fridge. She tried to avoid Bryony, which was difficult because she could not work out her routine. If their paths crossed Bryony usually ignored her, but with contempt, as if she was behaving stupidly. Carolyn found everything about Bryony so alien that she could not begin to guess what she was doing that Bryony didn't like.

Bryony was squat with a cropped bristly head, reminding Carolyn of a wrestler on television. She wore enormous shapeless skirts which looked as if they were made from old curtains or bedspreads, and baggy sweatshirts which she had dyed herself in dingy shades of rust, snot-green and pale mouldy purple. She described colours which appeared to Carolyn to be faded, dirty, or both, as "subtle", and Carolyn realized that her clothes were not these shades by dismal accident, but by the most painstaking design. She had tie-dyed various instantly recognizable T-shirts and scarves for Sue, Clare and the children too, and was obviously pleased by the blotchy and imperfect (in Carolyn's view) results.

She wore the strangest shoes Carolyn had ever seen. They had thick flat soles, to each side of which was stitched a straight flap of leather. The flaps stood up on either side of her ankle, and were laced together where they met in a stiff ridge over her foot. Through the gap at the end her thick grey sock protruded. Carolyn commented on them, and for once incurred Bryony's pleased attention, as she explained how a friend had made them for her to an ancient design, and that unlike any shoes you could buy, they were made to last a lifetime, were completely healthy and natural, and did not threaten to deform the foot or posture in any way. Bryony also had an enormous bag which she took with her everywhere, a great soft shapeless thing which looked as if (Carolyn's guess was later verified) it had been home-made out of wash-leathers. There were odd jagged seams all over the place, and the pale soft chamois leather had effectively polished dirt off every surface it came into contact with, so that it was now as grimy as the leathers Carolyn's Dad used at the garage. There were things embroidered in red wool on the top flap of the bag; in time Carolyn recognized them as feminist symbols. She thought that by far the most apt symbol of women's liberation was the beautifully simple clenched red fist-in-a-bag, which Clare and Sue also wore in their lapels. When she later read (at Clare's instigation) the Pankhursts' story, with the exhortation to suffragettes to be "an iron fist in a velvet glove", she immediately linked that image with the symbol of "fist-in-a-bag".

Most of the conversation at meal times made little sense to her. She was content to let it wash over her, occasionally noticing, like someone with a different first language, the way they laughed at things she didn't see the humour of, were made angry by perfectly innocent-sounding newspaper articles, discussed people she had never heard of as if they were better known than the Royal Family. She was still concentrating on surviving, each day presenting its own series of obstacles; she was content simply not to appear too odd or ignorant.

She began to piece together what it was that Clare did. There was a house somewhere near, where women who had been beaten up by their husbands stayed. There was a "Refuge Rota" pinned by the house telephone, with six different names filled in for different times in the week. Clare's and Bryony's names were on it, and they were at home at those times (unless the phone rang for them). Otherwise, Clare was mainly out. Carolyn gathered that she spent a lot of time at the Refuge. She always looked in on Carolyn, when she came home; gradually Carolyn came to realize how kind this was, and how many other claims Clare had on her time. Clare was the only one she wasn't nervous of. She liked the way Clare called her "Caro". She began to ask questions, about the other two women, the Refuge, even some of the mysterious topics she had picked up from meal times. Half jokingly, Clare assumed the role of teacher-guide, and fed Carolyn a steady supply of reading material on the Women's Movement, ranging from *Spare Rib* magazine to the lives of suffragettes; from *The Female Eunuch* to pamphlets on Consciousness Raising.

Carolyn was made glaringly aware of her own ignorance, a looming space which grew rather than diminished, as she was able to define its area by reading more. It was as if a balloon was being blown up inside her head, and the space in the balloon needed to be filled with knowledge. She was in turn confused, amused, horrified by the things she read – and sometimes had that closer reaction, recognition of something suddenly true – something she absolutely identified from her own experience, but had never put a name to. The mixture of incomprehensible lunacy and clear truth was as surreal as the life she was living; treading a thin line between the sharks in her room and Bryony, waiting for those times of distant peace, when she could watch the moving clouds through her window in simple tranquillity; descending nightly into drugged black sleep, and carefully, anxiously behaving herself as inconspicuously as possible in front of the inhabitants of the house. Once or twice when she crept down to the turn in the stairs to see if it was safe to go and get something to eat, she was scared back by the murmur of unfamiliar voices, and saw three or four bicycles parked in the hall, leaning together with their pedals tangled in each others' spokes, forming an intricate barrier to outside.

She could not help noticing the untidy grime of the house, and because she wanted to please the women who lived there, she began to clean. She started in the bathroom, where she washed down years of dust from walls and ceiling, scoured the toilet so that it sparkled, and dug out the thick dusty webs behind the pipes and wash-basin, disturbing a colony of frantic spiders. She scrubbed the old lino floor until it revealed a pleasant geometric pattern of tan, brown and yellow diamonds; poured bleach, then caustic soda, and then her own physical energy into the stained hideous bath, succeeding in restoring it in several places to snowy whiteness. With a nail brush she scrubbed persistently at the frosted glass of the small window, where something black (dirt? or some kind of growth?) spread all along the indented patterns on the glass. It was particularly difficult to remove from the corners.

She took her time over it, waiting until she was sure no one wanted to use the bathroom, and going downstairs a couple of times for drinks and stories with Sylvia. The gradual transformation from squalor to cleanliness gave her satisfaction, and she was pleased to think that the others would be pleased too.

She was nearly finished – polishing the taps – when Bryony poked her head around the half-open door.

"Thought it was you," she said contemptuously.

Carolyn put down her cloth. "Sorry – d'you want to come in?"

"No. Haven't you got anything better to do?"

"What?"

"Haven't you got anything better to do with your time?"

"I – I mean, I thought – it was – it could do with a clean so I – "

"Proper little housewife, aren't we."

Bryony withdrew her head and shut the door sharply, leaving Carolyn bewildered. She wondered whether Bryony was offended; perhaps she thought Carolyn was criticizing them for not keeping it cleaner.

That night Clare commented on the bathroom when she brought Carolyn her sleeping pills.

"Looks nice. Take you long?"

"All day, on and off."

Clare nodded. "Rather you than me. Cleaning's quite thera-peutic sometimes though, isn't it? I cleaned the whole apartment when I was pregnant – Jesus, I was at it from morning till night, you could've eaten your breakfast off of the john."

"When were you pregnant?"

Clare hesitated. "Oh – a long time ago. The kid's six now."

"I – wh – I mean, where is he?"

"He lives with his father." Clare bit off a torn fingernail. "In Mexico."

"Mexico?"

"Yeah." She shifted impatiently. "It's a long story. I married a Mexican guy when I was at college. He got a teaching job at the University in Monterrey – huh – and I got pregnant." She made it sound as if the two things should have been similar.

"I – then – what happened?"

"It didn't work out. I had to leave."

"Don't you ever see him?"

"Who? Juan? My son? No." She moved to the window, looked down at the wasteland garden. "No. His Grandma looks after him. It's better for him. More settled." She turned abruptly, holding out her hand. "Here. I'm going to bed."

Carolyn took the two pills. "Why don't you give me the bottle, instead of two-at-a-time? Don't you trust me?"

Clare smiled. "Yeah, I trust you. The goblins'll eat you before you OD." She went to the door. "Gives me an excuse to come and put you to bed, I guess. Thwarted maternal instincts, that's what it is." She laughed. "Now you know. Sleep well." The door shut behind her.

Carolyn sat on her bed and swallowed the sleeping tablets, washing each down with a mouthful of water. She did not understand Clare's sense of humour. It was OK to clean, though. Clare didn't mind it. Whatever Carolyn did wouldn't please Bryony, that was plain, so she might as well get on with it.

She tackled the TV room. It was called the TV room because all it was used for was to watch television. The kids sat in there before they had their tea, and sometimes the women went in there to watch some particular programme, for an hour on a certain night. Otherwise they used the kitchen. This made it an easy room to clean, no one would want to come in while she was working. Bryony might not even notice. It would be nice for the children when it was done, she thought. It was a bare square room with ugly yellow paint, and a sofa and three armchairs all pushed against the walls like a doctor's waiting room. In one corner were three big cardboard boxes full of filthy old jam jars. The open grate was choked with rubbish, and on the mantelpiece stood a stack of unopened mail, election leaflets, circulars and letters for people who'd moved. Gasping at the weight, she staggered out to the dustbin with the jam jars. Then she flopped on the sofa to sort through the letters. The third one was addressed her. "Miss Carolyn Tanner." She stared at it in confusion. Her mother's handwriting. The address was by someone else. "It's for me," she said aloud. Why hadn't they given it to her? She ripped it open and saw the date in her mother's neat childish writing. October 31st.

My dear Carolyn,
    Your father and I are worried sick about you. Please you must ring us up as soon as you get this to tell us if you are alright. I will be waiting by the phone. I was so upset and shocked when I came to the hospital and you were gone I could of died. I did not sleep a wink last night for worrying about you and if you are alright.
    I know you were down when in hospital but you will feel a different girl when you get home again, I know you will feel better. I'm sure it would be better for you to be in your own room in your own home again with your Mum and Dad who love you to look after you, than amongst strangers. Please please please my darling girl come home you are breaking your mother's heart.
                          All our love,
                          Mum & Dad

Carolyn put the letter down on the arm of the chair. What had she done? For days (was it weeks? she had no idea of the date) her mother had been worrying about her. Every time it had crept into Carolyn's head, she had pushed it out again. Night after sleepless night, her mother had been thinking about her, while Carolyn slept deep black sleeps and tried to keep her head empty. She began to cry, both at her own guilt, and at

89

the awful net of her mother's concern which was coming down over her.

"What are you playing at?" the Meg-voice in her head cried. "Living in this dirty house with weird people, with nothing to do, no plans, what are you playing at?"

She didn't know. But her mother's letter introduced into her head again that debilitating pressure she had felt in hospital – the feeling which was the opposite of sitting in her watch-tower and gazing at the sky. Suddenly the door banged open, and Bryony burst in.

"What the fuck are you doing?" she shouted. "What have you done with my jam jars? It's incredible – you didn't even ask me. You can fucking well go and bring them back again."

Keeping her head lowered, Carolyn made for the door, and hurried out to the dustbin. She picked up the first box of jars and went back to the room. Bryony was sitting on the sofa glaring at her.

"Why are you so obsessed with cleaning?" asked Bryony. "And throwing stuff away? Don't you ever stop to think? Why d'you think those jars're here? Doesn't it occur to you that they could be used again? Oh no – throw it away, never mind when the whole of the earth's covered in rusty cars and broken glass as long as my little house is spick and span."

She stamped out of the room. Teeth gritted, Carolyn went and fetched the other two boxes. Then she took her letter up to her room. Bryony had effectively dried her tears.

She stayed in her room all day, going down at quarter-past six to telephone her mother. Over the exclamations and tears at the other end she mechanically repeated her message.

"I'm sorry, I didn't get your letter till today. I'm sorry, I've been ill. I couldn't ring you. I'm better now Mum, I'm fine, don't worry. I'll come and see you on Saturday. I'll come and see you on Saturday, Mum. I'm sorry."

Clare came to her room later that evening.

"Why didn't you come down to supper?"

"I had a letter from my Mum."

"When?"

"I don't know. I found it in the TV room. It came ages ago."

"Oh God – oh Caro, I'm sorry – I don't know how that could've happened." She paused. "Yes I do – I guess one of the others

90

picked it up and it was just an unfamiliar name. I'm terribly sorry. What does she want?"

Carolyn looked down at her hands. "Me to go home."

There was a silence.

"D'you want to?"

"Bryony does."

"Bryony? Why?"

"Because I threw away her jam jars."

Clare started to laugh. Then she said, "Well you could've asked her."

"I didn't know anyone was saving them. They were filthy. They must have been there for years."

Clare nodded. "Bryony recycles them."

"She what?"

"Keeps them to use again."

"What for?"

"Oh – jam, or pickles, something like that."

"Does she make jam?"

"No. Not yet."

"She hates me."

"No she doesn't. She's just – maybe she's jealous."

"Why?"

"Because – I don't know. I don't know why. What are you going to do about your Mum? You don't want to go, do you?"

Carolyn got up and walked to the window. "I don't know. I'm going to see her on Saturday."

Clare didn't speak. Carolyn turned to her. "I mean – what am I doing really? I'm not doing anything here – and it's making her upset that I don't go home. Bryony hates me – I suppose I should go."

Clare shrugged. "Up to you. But you're not going to know what to do at home any more than you do here, except for what your Mum bullies you into. And Bryony'll come round. She's very territorial. She's angry because I didn't consult her before you came."

There was a silence.

"I don't mind what you do. If you stay here, though, you eat. I'm not having an anorexic on my hands. Come down now, and feed."

91

The next morning Carolyn stayed in her room and read, dipping in and out of Clare's books and staring out of the window, feeling surprisingly content. In the evening there seemed to be a lot of noise and excitement downstairs. Carolyn went down to tea slowly, feeling apprehensive. As she went into the kitchen it seemed to be alarmingly full of people and commotion, though when she sat down and worked them out it was only Clare, Bryony, Sue and the kids, and a strange man in a duffle coat. Sue and Bryony were busy cooking, and the kids were chasing each other round the table, squealing and pushing chairs in each other's way. The table was pretty, with a red cloth and a pot of golden chrysanths in the middle, and all the places neatly laid. There were bowls of salad, vegetables, sauces and pickles, and things she did not recognize. Carolyn noticed that there were little green tissue-wrapped parcels by all the places too. She was confused. Was it a day she had forgotten? Not Christmas, yet – what was it? She wished she could go back upstairs.

Clare put a glass of wine into her hand and smiled at her, opening the door to show the strange man out. Carolyn sipped it awkwardly. Sue and Bryony were carrying dishes from the oven to the table, filling the table with steaming food. When Clare came back everyone took their places. The children started to clamour for different kinds of food. Clare was talking to Bryony about the leaflets the printer had brought (that man?).

"Yes, you can start," Sue told Robin. "We'll leave the presents till after, shall we?" she appealed to Clare.

Everyone helped themselves to food. The conversations buzzed on around Carolyn: the new worker at the Refuge, Bryony's dealings with a woman called Margaret. Carolyn kept her face down over her plate, picking over the unfamiliar food. She recognized curry, but not the strange things which accompanied it, a pale beige paste with a dusty yet lemony flavour, and bits of cucumber chopped up in a bitter white sauce.

In the middle of this strange house's celebrations she felt much more of an outsider than she had done sitting on her own in her room. Sue filled her glass.

"OK? You look a bit stunned."

"I'm – I didn't – what's this for?"

"Oh, I thought you knew. It's our house birthday. It's the date Bryony and Clare moved in, but not the same year. Bryony moved in two years ago, then I came with the kids, and a year later to the day, Clare moved in. Bryony thought of a house birthday – to celebrate the household."

Sue filled her mouth with houmus and chewed silently for a moment. Clare and Bryony were arguing excitedly about something.

"Caro?" Carolyn looked up at the quiet tone of Sue's voice. "Clare said you might be thinking of leaving. If you – well, as far as I'm concerned I'd like you to stay. If you want to – " Sue turned back to give Sylvia some unnecessary help with her food.

When everyone had finished the plates were cleared and Clare produced a big chocolate cake with two candles, sending the children wild with excitement. There was much relighting and blowing out of candles, and finally the opening of the presents. The children were first. They each had a big rainbow packet of felt pens, and a Dinky car. They began to race each other around the edge of the table, making loud zooming noises. Carolyn watched Bryony pick up her green parcel and shake it. She tore the tissue paper off and held up a little polythene envelope, with two silver fist-in-a-bag ear-rings inside. Carolyn noticed that everyone was watching Bryony, and Bryony smiled and threaded the ear-rings through the holes in her ears, and they must all have a look and comment. Carolyn shrank from opening hers. Then it was Sue's turn, and she opened up a shimmering square of silk scarf, which had been flattened to the size of an envelope and now expanded and billowed across the table like the sail of a brilliant ship. Clare unwrapped her package quickly, and three small screwdrivers fell out. She burst out laughing, and jumped up and hugged Bryony, who was laughing so much that she couldn't catch her breath and had to be thumped on the back. The noise and excitement in the room was deafening. Carolyn's face ached with smiling, trying to join in. Now Sylvia picked up Carolyn's present and waved it under her nose. Carolyn took it quickly and inserted her index finger under one of the flaps of folded-over, Sellotaped paper. In her nervousness she used too much force, and her hand, released by the tearing of paper, flung out and knocked over the wine. Everyone jumped up and ran about moving things and mopping up. Carolyn was near to panic. Putting the parcel down and making herself breathe calmly, she unpeeled the paper and took out two flat paper envelopes – packets of seeds – and a little wooden block with wire on it. It was a mousetrap. She turned it over in bewilderment. Clare was laughing.

"I – th–thank you," said Carolyn, not knowing what to do.

"I'm sorry about that," said Clare, still laughing, leaning across the table to her. "It's just me being silly. I figured out –you know that noise in your room – that ghost or whatever you thought it was – "

Carolyn sat rigidly still, appalled that Clare was talking about this in front of the others.

"Well it's a mouse – it must be – you know, under the skirting board. I thought you might think it was funny, to catch your spook in a mousetrap – "

Carolyn smiled automatically and ducked her head down to study the seed packets, waiting for them all to start talking again. It was a joke, she realized, they were being kind to her; celebrating, welcoming her. Sue's kindness – Clare's kindness –the meal itself, confused her, sharpening her awareness of the differences between herself and them, but making her want to belong. She envied them the sense of occasion and togetherness that they had.

When she went up to her room that night she sat in her chair not listening for ghostly rustlings, but to the rise and fall of their conversation downstairs, punctuated with bursts of laughter. And finally, as she went to bed, she heard them singing softly, shushing each other and giggling, as one clear voice (Sue's, she recognized) carried on the melody.

Next morning it was Friday. One day till she went home. Outside the sky was cold and steely. The house, after Sue and Sylvia had taken Robin to school, was quiet. She could hear the wind in the chimney. Carolyn paced her room. The sense of pressure was mounting. She should have taken Clare up on her offer of going to work with her one day. She should have done something to keep herself distracted. Idly she picked up her packets of seeds. Wallflowers and Slipper Flower. She turned them over.

"*Calceolaria* (Slipper Flower). Half-hardy. These attractive flowers are generally grown for greenhouse decoration, but *C. Rugosa* is useful for bedding outdoors in the summer. Sow in the greenhouse from December to February, harden off in April."

94

Something in that reminded her of Clare and she stared out of the window, frowning, as she tried to think what it was. Hadn't Clare been repairing a greenhouse when she fell? Where was it? Carolyn leaned to the far side of each window, but there was no greenhouse to be seen. If there was one she could plant these seeds.

She put on her anorak and went down to the TV room. The french windows were damp and warped in their frames, and she had to heave with her shoulder against the door to get one open. She stepped out on to a narrow cement path. There was a biting wind from the right which made all the dead winter stems rattle and rustle feverishly. Shivering, she pulled up her anorak zip and turned to the left. Under and among the brambles was litter of all kinds, half bricks, broken bottles, sodden sweet papers. In front of her was a heap of bottles in the soggy remains of an old cardboard box – presumably also being saved by Bryony. She made her way as best she could along the overgrown path, following the house wall. When she turned left around the corner of the house, a dilapidated building came into view. It was more sheltered on this side. She walked towards it, pulling back and ducking under the prickling runners of a giant bramble that had overspread the path. Close to, she saw that the building had a brick base, up to about three feet, and a metal framework above it. The door faced the path. She pushed it open; it was an old wooden house door drooping on one hinge. It stuck, only a third open, wedged on broken glass on the floor. She eased herself in.

The place was wrecked. Broken glass lay scattered over the cement floor, along with pieces of brick, broken flowerpots, dead leaves. Above her the metal framework of the roof made an unbroken tracery of lines against the grey sky, but many of the panes were cracked or broken, or entirely missing. Where had Clare fallen? She half expected to see bloodstains. Along either side of the glasshouse at waist height ran a wide ledge, littered with broken glass, old flowerpots, a bucket and tins full of slimy green water, clods of dried earth. There were dried sticks and brown leaves everywhere. As she stepped, slivers of glass cracked and crunched beneath her feet. Using a wide piece of wood as a scraper, she cleared the glass and rubbish from a section of ledge, and sat down.

She noticed a pile of yellowed newspapers under the opposite ledge, and a rusty trowel and fork, and a ball of green twine wound in criss-cross pattern around a stick. The lower windows were covered with cobwebs. It was not warm, but it was sheltered from the wind outside, and the stillness and randomness of the tools and litter gave it an almost religious significance, made it seem as if it was waiting. The brambles of the garden had forced their way through one pane, and stretched in over the ledge, curling upwards like long scrawny fingers. How long had it been like this, untouched by people, gradually decaying and changing with the wind and the weather? She picked up a small flowerpot-shaped lump of earth. It retained its pot-shape although the pot was gone. It was dry and light to the touch. Squeezing her fist together she crumbled it into fine powdery dust. In the centre was a small wizened bulb like a tiny onion.

Carolyn worked in the greenhouse for the morning. Awkwardly and delicately, as if her own arms and hands were unfamiliar tools, she gathered flowerpots on a cleared area of ledge, took a bucket outside and poured away the green standing slime. Using the trowel she chipped at the ground outside the door, prising cold earth from among the prickly stems and broken bricks, gathering it with her hands and putting it into the bucket. It was hard to get, and she filled the bucket by crumbling into it some of the clumps of dried earth that were still inside old flowerpots. Then she mixed it up and ladled the soil back into the flowerpots, tore open her seed packets and hastily poked the seeds into the soil. Someone would come home and wonder what she was doing. She didn't want them to know she was out here. She patted down the earth in each pot, watered them from a slimy tin, arranged them in a row on the ledge, and darted back along the path to the house.

That night she couldn't sleep, despite Clare's tablets. Her brain raced over and over what her mother would say, how awful she would feel, what she ought to do, until she felt that the movement in her head would spin her off the bed and send her whirling round the room. Outside it began to rain heavily. The wind was still strong, and the rain lashed against the roof, increasing, with its persistent sound, her sense of frenzy. Dawn came late and sluggishly. When she went downstairs to make herself some toast it was still very dark, although it was eight o'clock and she could hear the children talking in their room. When she'd finished she got her bag and anorak, checking that she had enough in her purse for bus fare, and let herself out the kitchen door. She wasn't taking her suitcase. It would be deciding the issue in advance, if she took it. She did not admit to herself that to leave it was also to decide the issue in advance.

Chapter 10

Carolyn lay on her side, spine curved, head right on the edge of the bed so that she could stare down on the baby in its cot beside her. The cot was a transparent box (like a vegetable compartment in a fridge, she thought) and it was filled with a parcel of neat white blankets. From one end of the parcel emerged the living head and shoulders of her new baby. It was impossible not to stare at him all the time. He was breathtakingly beautiful. Breathtaking, literally; she felt her breaths trembling and coming short in her throat, seeming to make her whole body float and quiver. He was so perfect. His head was long. She knew, before the talkative nurse had told her so, that it would have been squeezed to that shape by her own body giving birth. The shape would change. On his head was a fuzz – a fluff of pale downy hair, almost transparent. Through his translucent skin showed the blue veins, his insides as visible and vulnerable as a tiny transparent shrimp. His face moved continually, different expressions rippling and flowing across it as if he really were a sea creature, moved and swayed by the changing tide and currents in water, in continual motion – flickering from smile to grimace to pain to peace, eyelids half rising to reveal a sea-shell sightless crescent of pearly blue-white, lips parting then closing, breaths shuddering and shivering him as if air were too strong and coarse a medium.

It seemed to Carolyn that there must be a vividly speeded up life flitting through the infant's dreams, as if it skimmed in the air like a bird over the facts of its life and they were reflected as changingly and as unknowingly on its face as the moving bird would be in seas, rivers, lakes, in stagnant puddles on flat roofs, and silted-up canals. Each expression was as swiftly melted into the next as a tiny wave lapped by a faster following. His hands were moving too – constantly, with that same undersea random motion. Open-palmed they waved with no more sense of the use of hands to touch grasp or hold than a water plant; infinitely gentle trailing things, the blind tendrils of a sea-anemone.

Carolyn's eyes swam with tears as she watched the baby, though she could not tell why. Her emotions were as confusingly mingled as the child's expressions laid one over another. She had been quite unprepared for his beauty and his otherness. He was nothing to do with her and Alan. He was a visitor from another, undersea world; an innocent, transparent, perfectly gentle alien. Babies she had seen before had fat fleshy faces that spread from a central dummy. They grinned or bawled, prefiguring the fixed expressions of their adult lives, solid features emerging from rolls of fat to express the hideous fixity of adult character. She had not known they started clear, clear of expression, transparent and mobile. She would protect it. Save it from that coarsening. It would not need to thicken and curdle, and become dully opaque to defend its tender insides from the preying eyes of the world.

But even as she vowed to protect she was filled with terror at the unhappiness the fleeting expressions rehearsed; pulled up against the staggering independence of this creature to experience its own ranges of reaction, its life, quite separate from and un-understood by her. She was faced starkly by the absolute wonder of life, and enfolded in that double-edged knowledge was the taste and imminence of death, which would be quite simply the absence of movement in the baby: stillness. From an infant's fluttering speed it would go through the thickening slowness of adult life to the full stop of a corpse. Because it was alive it would die. She had never understood that fact before.

It was miraculous that so tender and fragile a creature had emerged from the violence of the preceding day. She could believe that this was the creature that had floated inside her – yes, like a starry astronaut in his liquid capsule, attached to his red life-support cable – she had pored over photographs of embryos and imagined him a hundred times. But surely only his perfect oblivious innocence of all evil including pain had enabled him to survive the journey down. The labour had been a nightmare. She remembered it in vivid violent snatches punctuated by haze or darkness. The beginning, a long time ago, was quite clear: sitting up in bed at home, swinging her feet round to the floor, standing up – and a warm flood spilling down her legs so that she cried out in fright. Looking down she expected to see blood, awfulness, something dead. Then her mother was in her room, wrapping her up, sitting her down, kissing her.

"Hush love, it's all right, it's just your waters – you're ready, love."

She sat her on a towel and they had a cup of tea, huddled together like

99

conspirators on the edge of Carolyn's bed.

"I had a feeling when I went to bed last night," her mother told her.

"But it's early," said Carolyn, still shivering with fear and surprise. "It's not due till July the eighth."

"Only two days. It knows when it's ready, don't you worry. Everything's going to be all right. Your father's telephoning Alan."

Through the opened curtain Carolyn saw the dawn dimness light up as the rising sun emerged over the rim of the world and the quiet undertow of bird clatter rose to a crescendo of calls and squawks. "I wish you were coming with me."

Meg looked up, through the window. She could not help thinking of her own first labour. She wanted and did not want to be there, fearing that her very presence would create complications as if they were contagious, but also that if she were not there, there would be no one to control events and protect Carolyn. She had been Carolyn's protector for so long. It was not a role her heart could relinquish.

When they heard the car they went carefully downstairs, and her mother settled her in while her father held the door and Alan put her bag in the boot. Then they drove away and Carolyn carried with her the sight of her mother's tense white face leaning down to look through the window at her. In the car the contractions had started and suddenly she had felt excited. It would be all right.

Then the dim increasingly blotted memories of different doors, different faces peering, being naked, shaved, enemaed, injected, while it went on hurting her repeatedly, relentlessly. They left her alone with a great heavy belt strapped round her belly pressing her and making green and yellow lights wink on the huge machine by the bed, and she couldn't move and her back was aching and they put a tube into her wrist and she couldn't move and she began to panic. Then she was sick, they gave her an injection, they wouldn't let her—
it went to pieces, black fragmented with pain.

At last she felt clear and a kind woman smiled at her among the machines and said, "Nearly ready now."

They wheeled her bed down a corridor, and put her in a huge bare room with blazing lights. She remembered the way the midwife had bent her knee so that Carolyn's calf pressed against her thigh, and held it pinned with her own bare arm. The woman's skin was wonderfully warm and smooth and her hold was completely firm. That touch was one of the clearest sensations. There were a series of impossible pains like knife cuts, but she could also see distantly how the women were

100

skilful and trustworthy. There was a head, they'd been telling her. She felt it splitting her in half, then slipping back. A head, a head. It must be true.

Born, they held it like a long skinned thing and for a moment she stared at it hanging in the air not knowing if it was alive or dead, good or bad, not believing it was over. They wrapped it up and gave it to her, and it did have a head like a baby. It was alive.

And now it was here. It had survived the squeezing and pushing and pulling, the drugs and the pain, protected by its ignorance, it had survived to blink its grey eyes and wave its underwater hands, and turn its small blind mouth instinctively to her nipple, seeking food with the determined accuracy of an animal that intended to live.

Chapter 11

Carolyn did not move back to her mother's, as Bryony (who perhaps would never stop being jealous; Clare's mistakes were as often with women as men) had hoped, and as Clare herself had half expected. She returned from that visit almost sprightly (desperate?) in her attempts to please and to ingratiate herself into the household. Clare watched her listening, taking note, modifying her language and behaviour as carefully as an animal adapts its camouflage to fit into a new environment. She helped Bryony to fold and deliver the January *Women's Paper*. She accompanied Clare herself to the Refuge and looked after the children while the women had a meeting with some councillors. She marched with them on International Women's Day. She came to the C.R. group the three of them belonged to, and looked, and listened, and said nothing. Clare was not fooled by any of this, although Sue certainly was, and Bryony seemed to be coming round. Caro's silences were too deliberate, pregnant with disagreement and criticism. She asked for explanations which she received without comment, as if listening to someone who had just incriminated herself. She was exhausting company, not because she argued but because there was a constant play of restless nervous energy in her. She remained as thin as a rake, although she was eating properly now.

Clare couldn't concentrate on anything else when Caro was there. She found herself self-conscious under Carolyn's exhaustive scrutiny, and caught herself trying to measure and examine the things she said from the girl's point of view. Carolyn made her physically uncomfortable. She wanted to stroke and hold still Caro's skinny nervous arms and legs. She made herself spend less time with Carolyn, monitoring her own contact with her.

Gradually, what Clare had sensed as Carolyn's critical watchfulness began to be apparent in more obvious ways. The first was the February *Women's Paper*. She refused to help with folding again.

"I'm sorry, I don't think I – I don't think that I know enough about some of the issues, to go along with it completely."

Bryony was exasperated. "What don't you know about? That women are badly paid? That there aren't enough nurseries? That abortion should be available on demand?"

"Yes."

"Yes – yes what?"

"Yes, I'm not sure about abortion."

There was a silence.

"What d'you mean?"

"I'm – I'm not sure I agree with abortion."

"What? Any abortion?"

"Yes. I think – I think women should have babies if they get pregnant. I think those children want to be born."

"Jesus Christ." Bryony was genuinely staggered. She appealed to Clare. "You talk to her. I can't cope with this."

Clare looked at Caro, who was bright red and agitated with the effort of arguing.

"You really think a woman should be forced to have a baby if she doesn't want it?"

"Not to keep it – of course not. Have it and give it away. Plenty of people want new babies."

"You think she should be pregnant for nine months and go through all the agonies of giving birth, and then give it away?"

"I – I'm not sure – yes, I think so." Carolyn hesitated. "It seems – to me – the least she can do, really. She's started the child off – it didn't ask to be born. Once she's started it she should let it grow in her – until it can survive on its own."

"For fuck's sake!" screamed Bryony. "What d'you think she is? An incubator? What if she doesn't want to be swollen to the size of an elephant with a bleeding parasite kicking her in the guts day and night? She didn't make it on her own. What about the man?"

Carolyn shrugged. "I don't know. I mean, he can't do anything can he? You can't make him responsible, at that stage."

"If it's aborted early on," said Clare, "you really couldn't call it human. There's hardly anything there."

103

"But – it's – but – " Carolyn stammered and stopped. "But it's got a will to live. That's what's there. A decision to live."

"But Caro – carry that to its logical conclusion and you don't believe in contraception. Because every time someone screws they could make something with a will to live. If you've got a coil you're just making your womb into such an uncomfortable place that the little things with a will to live can't actually live there."

"Yes," said Carolyn simply.

"Yes what?" Bryony was nearly apoplectic.

"Yes, I don't know about contraception. I'm not sure about abortion. I need time to think about it. That's why I don't want – I'd better not fold the paper – until I've worked out my ideas a bit more." And she went out of the room, leaving Clare and Bryony facing one another over two thousand five hundred sheets of paper that had to be folded by Friday. Not only did she not help; in the time when she could have been helping she did things like lining the kitchen cupboards with flowery paper, polishing the brass door knocker, ironing tea-towels and shampooing the TV room carpet. Clare was relieved to be able to share Bryony's anger.

"Caro, for God's sake, if you haven't got anything better to do why don't you help us? There's no point in cleaning that carpet, it's covered in coffee stains – nobody minds it. It won't look any better when you've finished. You're wasting your time."

But Carolyn carried on. Not only doing unnecessary jobs, but actually creating work by transferring cooked food out of saucepans into dishes before serving it, decanting milk into a jug and margarine on to a saucer. She discovered a tablecloth which she started to use. On a Formica table it was so patently stupid that they left the shaking and washing and ironing of it to her in contempt.

The winter was long and hard work. Carolyn tried to get on with them; listened to them, read their magazines, had things explained by Clare. But it was not easy to fit in, as she had hoped.

She was alive. She had survived the accident, and all that mess afterwards. She had made a change in her life, broken away from her mother. She wanted to fit in here more than anything, to be part of their household. But she was not the same as them, she could not pretend to be. As time went by, she seemed to be more and more different. The things they believed – and did – were so complicated: she had to stop, and think, and ask questions – and still she wasn't sure. . . . She saw shades of grey where they seemed to see none – complications, contradictions.

It was exhausting and she did not know enough to analyse each problem properly. And she knew she was annoying them whenever she questioned their assumptions. If she did not do what they wanted then they managed to make her feel wrong or stupid. How was it her point of view was never right? And they were very untidy. The house was always littered with things, papers, books, children's toys, piles of clothing on their way to or from the launderette – it was terrible. They didn't seem to mind at all. Carolyn remembered the way her mother would whizz round the room with a can of spray polish and a duster, after tea, and say, "Well I just can't settle if the place isn't tidy." Here, you were lucky if you could see any surfaces to dust. She didn't know where half the things went, but she tidied them up and put them in piles on the stairs so people could taken them up to their rooms when they went, and the kitchen looked nice and tidy. Sylvia tripped over some clothes as she was coming downstairs one day and Sue went mad.

"Can't you leave our stuff alone? You've made a bloody death trap on the stairs. It's our mess, we live in it. For God's sake stop fussing around and find something sensible to do."

It was always with a sense of relief that Carolyn escaped to the greenhouse to water her seedlings. Nearly all of them had germinated, although it had taken them weeks and weeks to do so. When she had watered them she often sat on the ledge, simply staring at their thin greenness and absorbing the peace of the place. It was secure there. Gradually she came to realize that it was reminding her of her father – her father and the allotment. It wasn't just the smells of dug earth and the friendly shapes of garden implements which she associated with him; it was the sense of escape the place gave her. Patiently she examined her memories. It was years since she had spent time alone with her father. Yes, literally, years. When she was too little to be anything but a nuisance on shopping expeditions, her mother had left her with her father on Saturday mornings. Carolyn had always resented being left behind, and clamoured for the shops with their sweets, toys and new clothes. Her mother talked and instructed and bustled until the minute she left the house. Then suddenly it would be very quiet. It seemed to Carolyn (perhaps her memory exaggerated) that her father never spoke at all. But it was a warm peaceable silence. They would put on their old trousers and wellingtons, and go down to the allotment, to the damp-smelling shed where her father kept his gardening things. She would play in the dark shed, where there were millions of daddy-long-legs, or stand about watching him while he dug. Sometimes he would call her over. "Want to see this worm Carrie? He must be near nine inches long." "Hold this twine for us lass, will you?"

Yes. She would hold the end of the twine while he walked away from her backwards across the freshly dug earth, unwinding the ball of twine slowly and deliberately, crouching at the other end to peg it into the earth, then coming back to stake her end too.

"Thanks lass."

She remembered the smell as he tipped out the bag of manure he got from Tandy's every now and then, and the way she would hold her nose and shout "Pooh!", and he would laugh and call her Miss Dainty Socks. In summer he let her cut a bunch of flowers at the end of the morning, to take home for the table. She was allowed to fetch the scissors herself from the drawer in the shed. She remembered hesitating, choosing, picking the biggest and bluest cornflowers, and him looking up from his planting and saying quietly, "If you pick the ones as aren't quite open yet, they've a chance of lasting longer, maybe." She remembered with strange clarity the concentration she had put into cutting the flowers; how she had hoped her father would think she had chosen the right ones.

Peace. Peace from the frenzied pressure of her mother's attention. She had not valued it. She had leapt joyfully at the chance of going shopping, when she reached the magic age of usefulness.

Sitting in the greenhouse with her seedlings, she was safe from the frantic activity in the house. But it was childish really, she told herself. It was high time for practical things, it was time to get a job. Her mother had had a fit when Carolyn admitted that she was living on social security. "Scrounging off the dole – after all those years of schooling – it's wicked, that's what it is, wicked." It wasn't wicked, Carolyn knew – but she couldn't hide in here forever.

Then Lisa, one of the support group for the Refuge, moved away. The phone rota was redrawn so that the week was divided between five, not six. Clare asked Carolyn, casually, if she was interested in taking on a few hours a week. Carolyn was dismayed; she had found the place very frightening on her previous visits. It was a dilapidated terraced house, the only one in its row that wasn't boarded up. Inside it was overcrowded and primitive, with no hot water and an outside toilet. The seven children there had seemed more like seventeen. Although Clare spoke lightly about it, Carolyn understood that it mattered, and that Clare wanted her to get involved. She had discovered that it wasn't a proper job (as she called it to herself) since none of them was paid for going there or being on the rota. It was only much later that she came to understand that the place was in its infancy. Clare, Bryony and the others had squatted the old council house and campaigned for support for battered women through their *Women's Paper*. The Council had just agreed to rehouse women who stayed there, and had promised larger, more permanent premises for the Refuge itself. The idea was that the women should run the house themselves, but there was a series of crises (husbands discovering the address, a fight between two of the women, harassment from a gang of local kids – and the children themselves to be looked after) which meant that a couple of the support group had to be around most of the time. It would have been difficult for the women to explain their cases to DHSS officials and lawyers, with screaming children in tow.

Carolyn did not want to go, but felt miserably self-critical for her reluctance. On the first morning when she went with Clare the place was very quiet. The older kids were at school and two of the women had taken the younger ones to the park. A new woman with two children had been brought in by Jacky in the night. She was sitting on the sofa holding a baby, with her little daughter beside her. She was thin, with a bony face and bulging, frightened eyes. Clare and Jacky conferred briefly in the kitchen while Carolyn stood awkwardly smiling at the woman. Then she heard Jacky calling goodbye, and Clare came back into the room with some mugs of coffee.

"Hello, Maria," she said to the woman, and "Hello," to the little girl. She handed out the coffee and sat down.

"Would you like to tell us what happened, Maria?" she asked. "Jacky's told me a bit of it – and then we could think about what to do next."

"I'm not going back," said Maria.

"No, all right, you don't have to. Would you like – d'you think your little girl wants to go and play with – "

"No," Maria interrupted her, "she's staying with me." The child, who looked terrified, was clinging on to her mother's arm.

Clare nodded quickly "All right love – look, you don't have to do anything you don't want to do, now. Would you like to tell me about it?"

Clare seemed completely different, motherly and unselfconscious. It was the first time Carolyn had heard her without that note of irony in her voice. Maria glanced around the room with her scared eyes. Carolyn noticed that her thin white legs were bare, and that she had a pair of fluffy pink mules on her feet. The skin above her heels was purple.

"He came home after closing time. He said – he –" Maria stopped.

"Is he your husband?" asked Clare. "Are you married?"

Maria nodded, staring straight at Clare with her bulging eyes. "He gets mad when Gary doesn't sleep, he says it's my fault, he says I make him do it – and –" She stopped again.

"How old's Gary?" asked Clare, after the silence had lasted a little while.

Maria looked down at the baby. "Eleven months. He doesn't – he's never – he doesn't sleep nights, I can't help it. I can't do anything with him, only hold him."

"So what happened?" said Clare gently. "Was Gary awake when your husband came in?"

"He gets pissed and he doesn't – " She started to cry, weakly. "He's all right. He's been good to me. He's a good man. Only when he's been drinking he just – he –"

"Did he ask you to put Gary to bed?"

Maria shook her head convulsively. "He was shouting at me. Calling me. I asked him – I told him 'Shut up or you'll wake Cathy too' and he got madder – he – he thinks – he says I keep them awake so – so – so I don't have to go to bed with him." She

108

stopped speaking abruptly and stared at Clare with a look of fixed terror in her eyes.

"He thinks you don't want to sleep with him, so you keep the kids awake as an excuse?"

Maria nodded. "He – I knew what would happen – last time he – he started – he got Gary off me and left him – in his cot, he was screaming, he were scared – he was rough you see he gets rough when he's drunk, he doesn't think – "

Clare nodded.

"So I was upset I said I didn't want to, I was crying and it made him madder."

She stopped.

"Did he hit you?" asked Clare.

Maria nodded, almost impatiently. "Oh yeah, he hit me. But he – he – "

"Did he force you?"

"Yeah." She turned her face away from Clare, looking down at Gary who was sleeping peacefully enough now. Carolyn could see that she had her right hand clasped around the fingers of her left, and was squeezing so tightly that the finger ends were white and bloodless. She looked up apologetically at Clare.

"I was scared. I never thought he would – would've done that. He was calling me all the time – awful things. He put his hand over my mouth so I couldn't breathe – "

"That was before, did you say? Last time? What happened last night?"

"I didn't want him – I didn't want him to come near me – so I locked myself in the bathroom, with Gary – I didn't know what else to do. He was shouting. I didn't know what to do, he was banging on the door and Gary were crying – then I heard Cathy – " She shook her head desperately. "He started shouting at her, I could hear her crying, so I unlocked the door. I didn't know what to do – I opened the door and he got Gary. He was pulling him, trying to get him off me – he threw him – he just threw him at the bed – I knew he was all right, he were screaming but I couldn't –they were both screaming, Cathy and Gary both, and he got me by the throat. He was shaking me calling me a slut and a whore and saying they weren't his kids – everything, I don't know, I couldn't breathe – he were choking me – "

"And did he let you go? You were afraid he was going to rape you again?"

She nodded quickly. "He were choking me. I must've blacked out. When I looked then at first I couldn't see, it was all – you know – black like inside my eyes, but I knew they were open and I could hear the kids yelling – and when I got up he was lying on the sofa, snoring – he must've just dropped me and let me where I lie – " She stopped and Clare sat quietly waiting. "So I just – I got the kids out of the house – 'n' I rang this number." She gave a shaky little laugh, holding out her skinny forearm to display the number written there in blue biro. "I saw it at the doctor's on the board – an' I wrote it down after last week – I didn't know what else to do. It was two o'clock in the morning."

"And Jacky came to fetch you."

"Yes. I'm not – he can't come here, can he? I'm not going back again."

"It's all right," said Clare. "He can't come here. He can't find out the address. You can stay as long as you need to." She hesitated. "Can I – do you mind, Maria, if I just look at your neck – to see if he's left bruises? You see, we might need a doctor to testify that you've been hurt."

Maria gave the baby to her daughter. She gathered her straggly hair into a bun at the back of her head, holding it with her left hand while she pulled down the polo neck of her thin jumper. Her neck was mottled with bruises: several that Carolyn could see were the exact shape and size of thumb prints, yellow, dark purple and red. The woman sat quite still, displaying her neck without embarrassment. Carolyn felt sick.

"Thank you," said Clare gently. "I think you ought to be examined by a doctor, Maria. Shall I make an appointment for you?" Maria nodded. She seemed limp now – exhausted.

"How old is Cathy?" The little girl was still holding the baby, cradling it and smiling into its face.

"Five."

"Does she go to school?" Maria nodded. "Well we'll get her into school with the children here, for the time being. We'll get her started tomorrow. Have you got enough clothes for them, Maria? What did you bring with you?"

She shook her head. "Nothing. I were afraid of him waking – I didn't bring anything."

110

"Does he work?"

She nodded, yes.

"So he'll be out today? You could get what you need – pack a case. It's all right, I'll come with you–" as Maria started to protest. "You'll need some clothes for you and the children, some things of your own. . . ."

As Clare went on arranging things in her calm quiet voice, Carolyn lost concentration. She heard Clare talking about the DHSS, a lawyer, an injunction, all sorts of different things, while Maria sat silent in front of her, head drooping slightly on her injured neck.

Carolyn found the days at the Refuge terrible. She felt quite inadequate to help anyone there – and almost scared of them, as if the pain and horror of their lives were contagious. It was so ordinary. They all took it for granted; men hitting their wives and children, men raping their wives and trying to kill them. The women lived with it – some of them came here for a week and then went back to it. Often when women rang the beds were full and no more could come in. There was nowhere else for them to go.

Although Carolyn told herself she respected Clare, and the others, for the work they were doing, she was repelled by it. She hadn't known. . . . The women's stories and miseries haunted her, filled her dreams; the desperation of their situations made Carolyn herself feel trapped and frantic, so that she dreaded going to the Refuge and was tongue-tied when her help was most needed. Their injuries seemed to violate her.

She tried to hide her feelings by concentrating, as she had done at the Red House, on the children. The younger ones needed looking after while the mothers were busy, and the distress of the children, although more naked than that of their mothers, was less terrible. Because they could still be comforted or distracted, by a sweet and a story. She could try, with them.

She hated going to the Refuge and she dreaded letting Clare know that. She felt she could no longer trust her own ideas, the disagreements she had had with Clare, Bryony and Sue must be due to her own ignorance. How could she presume to argue with them when she knew nothing – nothing – and they lived and worked in situations like this? She was humiliated by her own ignorance, felt herself losing control completely over the ideas she had begun to hammer out and grasp. Either side of the Refuge, time closed in, with meetings, the children to be looked after, books to be read, until she felt light-headed with the sense of not coming to grips with anything, of being forced to spin like a top.

In between feeling guilty and inferior to the other women, she felt resentful. Her resentment saved her. She had been forced to go to the Refuge. They expected her to do it. She knew she didn't want to. And she *had* made a choice; she had chosen not to go home, she had chosen to live here and cope with sharks between the furniture and Bryony's contempt, in order to purchase a freedom . . . to choose what she would do next. At times this was crystal clear. At others, she despised herself for being selfish, even wicked, for not being able to help people who needed her support so much.

Her discontent came to a head with the beginning of spring. During the winter there had been near-continual snow and rain, then in late March there was a week of mad blustering winds, with racing cloud and fitful sun.

"March showers bring April flowers," Carolyn recited to herself. Or was it April showers that brought May flowers? She was restless, full of ineffectual undirected anger. After being at the Refuge on Saturday she woke early on Sunday morning, head crowded with things that needed thinking about and sorting out. Her windows were rattling in the wind, patches of sunlight and shade sped across the view. Up in the hills it was like a searchlight, like the revolving beam from a lighthouse moving on then reappearing, light, shade, light. The hugeness of the world out there only served to increase her sense of confinement and frustration.

She went down to make a drink, and as she turned the light on in the dingy kitchen a dark thing shot across the floor to disappear under the dresser. Mice. Carolyn froze. Then she stepped quickly on to the nearest chair and stood there, listening. Silence. It was waiting for her to go. She jumped down and ran out of the kitchen, shutting the door carefully behind her. Why should they stay in the kitchen, though? They're probably in all the rooms. Running over our beds at night. She remembered the mousetrap Clare had given her. She'd thought it was a joke! Hurriedly she unbolted the french windows and pushed them open. The sun was shining brilliantly, for a moment, and the wind rushed full in her face. She ran to the hall for her coat, then went out, crossing the poor battered garden. The wind and sun seemed to make everything race, to make her excited about something she didn't know, like a child.

The winter rain and snow had beaten down the weeds to a mulch of sodden brown stems, through which the bricks and rubbish on the ground protruded. Striding away from the house, Carolyn stubbed her toe badly on a brick end and had to sit down to nurse it. There was a log beside the blackened site of an old bonfire. As she sat rubbing her foot a sense of the ground around her intruded on her anger; a sense of the garden as a place, with its own shape and past. How had it got like this? There were bricks and stones everywhere. Something must have been demolished. An old outhouse, perhaps. Bits of broken glass sparkled in the sunlight. She picked up a piece of pottery and turned it over. It was a long sharp fragment of a willow-pattern saucer, three little blue figures crossing the hump-backed bridge. Idly she began to stab at the wet ground with it, but it struck something hard straight away. She scraped the earth back and saw something very dark blue – china or glass, buried there.

The wind in her face was good. As sunlight moved over she closed her eyes and put her head back. What am I going to do? She felt as if she never wanted to go back into the house, as if it had tied her with a million cobweb fine lines, as the Lilliputians had trapped Gulliver, and that she could not get free. The piece of saucer, scratting and scraping, had cleared a length of blue glass. It was an unusually deep blue. Abandoning the saucer, she scrabbled at the moist earth with her fingers. The gritty soil filled the cracks behind her fingernails, and the smell of newly uncovered earth reminded her of her father. It was a bottle, an old-fashioned one. She prised it out of its little grave and wiped it clean. It was very dark blue, quite perfect, about six inches long. The soil clung to one side, stuck in the roughness of the design. Letters. "NOT . . . TO . . . BE . . . TAKEN." She cradled it between her palms with satisfaction. How nice to discover. How long has it been here? Twenty years? Fifty? It was full of earth. She turned it upside-down and shook it. But it was packed. "NOT TO BE

113

TAKEN." Like Alice in Wonderland. Why should they sell bottles of "NOT TO BE TAKEN"? It must be for murderers, she thought, and smiled at the house. Three spoonfuls in everybody's tea. There's probably more under the soil.

She started to scrape again with the shard of pottery. The feeble sun was almost warm when it came out. I'll gouge the soil out of it with a knitting needle, when I go in. I don't want to go in.

The clear day stretched before her; when she walked back into the house her day would be filled. Stay here, then. Stay here. Stay here and dig the garden. Make a place to plant those seedlings. It was such a good idea that she couldn't think anything for a moment – as if someone else had suggested it to her, and she needed to digest it.

I could stay out all day. I'd have an excuse. It's worth doing – it needs doing. I could grow more things. I could stay here. They'll laugh at you.

Well let them. She flung the fragment of saucer as far as she could, watching it spinning against the sky. Then she balanced the bottle on the log, and went to the greenhouse.

Taking up the big garden fork in the corner, she went straight out again. Where to begin? Instinctively she headed for the fence at the far end, wanting to be as far away from the house as possible. Selecting a clear-looking spot she jabbed the fork into the earth and stood on the crossbar. It stuck, shivering in the ground, the prongs buried to a depth of about three inches. Then it wobbled under her weight and tilted forwards. She jumped off and tried again – same effect. It felt as if the prongs were meeting solid stone. Using the fork like a pick she chipped away at the soil. Brick. She scraped away trails of earth to reveal the dark orange rectangle of a whole brick. She knelt and prised it from its bed. In the damp earth its indentation was like a casting mould, clear and sharp-cornered, composed of earth and living things, tiny translucent snails and a pale slug. She threw the brick over to the bonfire site and attacked with the fork again. Again, it struck something solid.

After unearthing four bricks, a milk bottle, and an unidentifiable piece of metal, it was possible to turn over a forkful of earth on that spot. If the whole garden was covered in such a layer of rubbish, she would be mad to dig it. She walked a few feet and stabbed at the earth with the fork. It hit something hard. A few yards further – again. Each random spot she tried was the same. The ground was solid with rubble.

Bitterly disappointed, she sat on the log. It would take weeks of back-breaking work. Crawling round on your hands and knees, prising up brick ends. Mad. There are enough bricks to build a house. And the soil's probably useless anyway. The french windows banged and Clare came out into the garden, holding a piece of toast. She walked quickly over the uneven ground.

"Hello. Nice day. Have you taken leave of your senses?"

Carolyn nodded.

"How long've you been up?"

"Don't know. Since eight."

"Two hours. Well, at that rate – " she indicated the square foot of dug earth, and the fork abandoned beside it, "I guess it'll take you – ooh – three years?"

"Ha ha," said Carolyn sourly. "Look, I found this." She passed the bottle to Clare.

"That's nice. Victorian blue. Lovely. Want some toast?" She handed it to Carolyn, who ate in silence.

"What's the matter?"

"I don't know." Carolyn chewed a mouthful of toast, then said, "There's mice in the kitchen."

"I like mice," said Clare.

"They're dirty. They carry diseases."

"No more than a dog or cat." Clare watched her eating for a moment. "I'm going to clean up this morning. I've been busy."

"I know." Carolyn was consumed with guilt.

Silence. "What's the matter?"

Carolyn gouged some earth out from under her nails. "I don't know what to do."

"I can suggest lots of things."

Suddenly, unaccountably, Clare reminded her of her mother.

"But I don't want to do what you suggest."

Clare blew a raspberry and stood up. "Dig the garden then." She went back into the house.

Carolyn worked in the garden all that day. It was slow, back-breaking work, but it gave her great satisfaction. She enjoyed uncovering a corner of brick enough to insert the trowel blade

115

beneath it and twist, and prise it slowly out of its bed. She enjoyed picking the loosened brick up and weighing it in her right hand before swinging her arm to sling it on to the rubble pile. She liked scraping the dirt away from unknown objects, trying to guess what they would be. She worked like an automaton, and her mind was as drowned out by it as her speech would have been in a noisy factory. Scratch, clear, scrape; stick, twist, heave; lift, weigh, sling. A large blister came on the heel of her right palm, from forcing the trowel handle down to prise bricks up. Her spine, neck and shoulders ached dully, but after a while she could almost relish the aches, as if each physical pain was another blotter for the press of ideas in her head. She worked crouching down, and the infinitesimal pace of her labours made her feel like an ant, toiling away earnestly at a microscopic task. It was satisfying to be an ant. She wasn't thinking at all; hands preoccupied with textures, grainy soil and rough brick, smooth stone, slimy wetness of the odd slug or worm.

By the evening there were two damp heaps of rubble and a cleared row of just over five yards. A sharp cold wind had sprung up with the fading light, removing the sweaty warmth of her exertions and letting her know that she was cold and exhausted. Her back ached, her hand was blistered. She was starving. She felt light-headedly happy. She had escaped – for a whole day she had escaped even the thought of the Refuge.

Next morning she was up at seven. She wasn't expected at the Refuge till lunch time. She could busy herself in the garden till then. She'd been digging for a while when she looked up to swing the stone in her hand on to the pile, and saw Clare standing there.

"Smells nice."

"Yes – it's the soil."

"Aren't you cold?"

Carolyn shook her head. "You get warm working."

"Are you coming to the Refuge today?" Clare asked quietly.

Carolyn watched Clare's feet. It hadn't occurred to her that she had a choice. "Don't you need me?"

"Yes." Clare grimaced. "But if you'd rather do this –"

There was a silence.

"You don't like coming to the Refuge do you." It was a statement.

116

Carolyn shook her head, still not looking up.

"Well–"

"I would rather do this. If you don't mind."

Clare laughed. "You must really hate the Refuge!"

"No – no – I mean–"

"Why are you doing this? Isn't it an awful waste of energy?"

"I – no." Again she felt that stubborn anger. "Perhaps I want to waste energy."

Clare watched her in silence, then asked, "Why?"

"I don't know." She scraped at the earth covering a brick.

"OK," said Clare briskly. "Shall we go for a drink tonight?"

"Who?"

"You and me."

Carolyn just stopped herself from saying why. "I – yes, that would be nice."

"OK. I'm at the Refuge for tea. Meet you at the pub on the corner, at nine?"

Carolyn nodded.

"See you then." Clare walked quickly back to the house.

Carolyn wanted to leap with joy. You don't have to go! You don't have to go to the Refuge! The reprieve had been so quick and sudden and she had been dreading the conversation so much. . . . She was afraid that Clare would try to make her feel guilty that evening. But it was done. She'd told her she didn't like going. She'd escaped.

She worked in the garden every day, from then on, unless the rain was torrential. She cleared the sills in the greenhouse and planted more seeds in flowerpots, repairing the holes in the glass with sheets of polythene. With the bricks she had unearthed she started to build a path around the perimeter of the garden. The slowly growing clear patch, the sprouting seeds in the greenhouse, the peace of the garden and spring unfolding around her were all marvellous.

And the miserable hotchpotch of confused ideas and pressures was quietly buried in the depths of her mind, just as a wilderness of plants dies down and goes underground for the winter.

On July 7th the sun was already hot by seven-thirty, shining through veils of mist rising like steam from the drying earth. Carolyn let herself out of the french windows and made her way along the trodden track to her garden, now a dug rectangle of some eight by twelve yards, backing on to the wall of Keswick's warehouse. The low sun made the street wall cast a long black shadow over half the garden, but it stopped just to the right of her patch. The morning air was vibrant with memories of similar mornings. She stood still, savouring the accumulation of days of her life behind her like beads on a string, something tangible. The wet garden was alive with smells: damp earth, the dry smell of bricks, faint smoke from yesterday's bonfire. Drops of dew shone in the weeds and grass, and sparkled like diamonds in the centres of the dark green upturned palms of her nasturtium leaves. The nasturtiums were flowering, brilliant and ragged across the soil, orange as flames. All their trumpets tilted up from the ground, as if together they were sounding a blast to the sky. She squatted at the edge of the dug soil, experiencing pleasure in her own body's supple movement and the warmth of the sun on her skin, and looked along the rows of plants. Pale lettuce seedlings, dark pansies, sweet peas, hopeless carrots, runner beans showing two blood-bright flowers today. Across the earth between rows shone dry silver trails, sticky to sight, where the slugs had been. Behind the beans, onions, no lupins (it must be two months now – they must be dead) and love-in-a-mists on impossibly frail stems curved and gyrated toward the ground, bearing slender eyelid-blue buds. She had not planted very sensibly, she thought. The tall beans should have gone at the back. Trowel in hand Carolyn stooped over the dense lettuce seedlings and carefully removed a clump of them. The leaves were cool and wet. She picked off two pale sticky little slugs and flicked them away into the weeds, then crouched over a clear patch of soil and started to pull apart their tangled cotton-thread roots. Working quickly, she planted out the lettuces at ten-inch intervals, abandoning the trowel in favour of her fingers for hole boring and soil patting.

Her mousy hair had been bleached by the sun to a more nearly-blonde than it had been since her childhood, and her skin was very brown. Squatting in the soil, knees bent double either side of her head, intent on her hands working between her legs, Carolyn could have been taken for only half her age. She was painfully thin.

The road behind the tall wall was still quiet, but the birds were making up for it, their incessant repeated sounds rising to sudden random crescendos as they all chirped fiercely together. She kept noticing the birds, here; always before she had thought of them as "singing". They didn't sing, they squawked and chattered like a jungle. June had been a lush warm month, drawing her seeds from the ground with charmed fingers, stretching the runner beans a full four feet from their first green sprouts, and winding them neatly up their bamboo canes. Do beans always curl around sticks in the same direction? she wondered. Or are there rebels? And can you fool them, by planting them back to front?

The soil was dark and friable between her fingers. She had commented on its goodness to Clare, who guessed at how many years it had lain fallow; five – six? Long enough to gather fertility from the winters of dead leaves, the rotting vegetation and the passage of cats, birds and dogs, shrews and voles, caterpillars and slugs.

Suddenly she heard Sue calling her name.

"Yes!" she shouted. "Here. At the bottom." She straightened, looking towards the house.

From among the grass and high weeds appeared her father. She was so surprised she couldn't think of anything to say and just stood for a moment staring at him.

"Hello Carolyn."

She put down her trowel and went towards him. He kissed her awkwardly on the head, and patted her shoulder.

"Is Mum –?" She could think of no other reason for his appearance.

"Don't worry." He nodded gravely. "No one's dead."

"Oh. D'you – d'you want to come in and have a cup of tea?"

He glanced back at the house and she wondered who was in the kitchen. Sue and Sylvia – too early for Bryony. How strange the place must look, to him.

"No," he said, "let's stay out here. I'd like to have a little talk with you."

Automatically she turned back towards her garden, and he followed her.

"This is very good," he said, as they stopped at the edge of the bare earth. "Is this your handiwork?"

119

"I – yes. It was an awful job to clear the ground."

He walked along the edge of the plot, naming her plants to himself. "Well done," he said. "Those beans are further on than mine. You've an ideal spot here, haven't you? Sunny and sheltered – ideal." He crouched, and picking up a handful of soil, rubbed it through his fingers.

"Soil's not bad. Did you use anything on it?"

"No – no I didn't. I didn't know what."

"Well, never any harm in a bit of manure. It's not so easy to come by these days though. They're all these chemical things now – I dare say they're just as good really. It's a bit heavy, isn't it? You could do with a spot of sand in it." He stooped over the sweet peas and examined them.

Carolyn watched him, caught between her astonishment at his presence here, and the sudden absolutely natural way they were talking. At home, before the accident, he hadn't said so much to her for years. She hadn't really thought about him, she realized. About him missing her or worrying. It had all been Mum. He came back and crouched by her side, staring at the garden as he spoke.

"I took the liberty of calling," he said.

"Dad!" she interrupted him. "You can come any time. You or Mum –"

"Yes," he said. "It's about your Mum I wanted a word with you. She's taken all this badly, Carolyn." He spoke slowly and deliberately, almost maddeningly slowly. Adjusting her position and half closing her eyes against the sun, she too stared out over the garden, waiting for him to get to the point.

"She's had a lot of disappointments in her life. She lost the first two babies, you know that, and she's always done her best for you. She's always worked hard and thought of you. She's not –" He hesitated. "She's taking it badly now. She doesn't understand, you see, why you've never been home."

"I did," Carolyn said quickly. "I came for that weekend. Then I came, oh, a couple of Saturdays ago."

"Last month," he said. "Yes. But it's a shock, you see, after expecting you home all that time you was in hospital – it's not what she expected, that you would be off somewhere else. She's – well, you're important to her. Girls are, aren't they, to their mothers. I don't want. . . . She's worried about you. Of course

120

she is – it's only natural."

There was silence.

"What do you want me to do?" asked Carolyn.

"Well," he said slowly. "I don't want you living in our pockets. When it's time for you to go, then you must go. But she broods, you see. At the weekends she broods. She sits and thinks about you. It would cheer her up if you came for your tea." He paused. "Children do grow up, I know," he said, staring at the bean poles. "They do grow up."

It seemed inconclusive. He straightened his knees. "You do what you like, lass. I'm glad to see this, you've done well here. You can have some carnation slips next time you come home." He turned to go.

"Dad – Dad – don't you want a drink or–"

"No lass, I'm on my way to pick up a radiator. I'm on garage time already."

He glanced at his watch. Suddenly he looked awkward, she saw his shoulders tense and his head duck slightly as they neared the french windows.

"Here, you can get out this way Dad, there's a side gate." She led him round and past the greenhouse.

"Right then," he said, "Thanks," and hurried away without kissing her goodbye.

She wandered slowly back to the garden. He must remember those days well she thought. Yet he had come here on her mother's account, not on his own. He was content to let it go. Childishly, she wished she could still go gardening with him. She could have asked him about the carrots. Substantial memory melted suddenly to consciousness of present loss. As she grew up, her father had been of no account to her. Whose fault was it? Her mother's? But he had always chosen to stand back; to be busy. He believed that children were the woman's affair. She felt that between them, they had cheated her.

.

Chapter 12

Alan, Carolyn and Christopher moved into a flat the September after he was born. It was the converted first floor of a large terraced house, within walking distance of the university. Alan continued to work hard at his course, and Carolyn looked after the baby and kept house. Christopher was a slight child, with rather too thin arms and legs, and little flat wrists which always gave Carolyn a stab of apprehensive fear when she noticed them. His face was elfin, with wide grey eyes and a fuzz of pale hair, more like the fluff on a duckling than human hair. He was a demanding baby, and rarely slept through the night, even when he was a year old. When she heard him, Carolyn got up quietly, pressing the blankets down again to stop the cold air getting at Alan's back. She crept into Chrissy's room, shutting the door silently behind her. She was usually able to rock him back to sleep quite quickly. He fell asleep with one arm curled around her head, clutching a handful of her hair, his other thumb in his mouth. The only moment of danger was as she laid him in his cot again. Sometimes then he would wake and start to cry.

She dreaded Alan waking up. He would roll over heavily and sigh and say, "Oh that damned child," and then, "I'll go, I'll go – you stay here." He would get up and blunder about falling over shoes and unable to find his dressing gown, until at last the light had to be turned on to sort him out, and Chrissy had worked himself into a frenzy. When he went into Chrissy's room he said, "Well, what's up then?" too loudly. She listened, shrinking under the blankets, for Chrissy's angry wail at the sight of him, and the "Mu – Mu – Mu!" that he chanted when he wanted her. Alan always came back defeated, sooner or later, and then it took her twice as long to settle the child. It was so much better if she could slip out quietly and not let Alan know. Sometimes Alan said, "He didn't wake at all last night, did he?" with such pleased pride that she smiled and shook her head. What did it matter, a little white lie like that? Anyway, Alan needed

122

his sleep, he had books to read, plans to draw, and essays to write. You can't think clearly on four hours' sleep. It was better not to let him know that Chris woke regularly two or three times every night.

When he was twenty months old he became ill. The doctor examined him cursorily and told Carolyn that it was some kind of viral infection.

"Keep him warm and give him plenty to drink. His temperature may well go up before it goes down. Nothing to worry about." He left two prescriptions.

Chris was plagued by a dry ticklish cough which kept him (and Carolyn) awake for the best part of three nights, and on which the cough medicine had little effect. He refused all food and she could hardly get him to drink. Within a few days he was a pitiful sight, white-faced with huge puffy red-rimmed eyes, his thin hair plastered to his head with sweat and the comfortable roundness of his baby tummy melted away. He cried on Carolyn's shoulder, through pure discomfort and weariness, she believed, rocking him automatically and feeling like crying too.

Meg gave lots of good advice down the phone. It was she who suggested feeding drinks by the spoonful, and bathing his poor red eyes in a weak solution of bicarb. of soda. She offered to come down for the weekend to help, and Carolyn wanted her badly enough to hesitate before putting her off. There wasn't a spare bed, for a start – but the main thing was that she knew it would annoy Alan. He was working hard to complete a special project for Friday, and had already told her he would give her a hand at the weekend. He would be angry if she preferred her mother's help to his.

On Thursday night Chris came out in dark red blotches. Carolyn, appalled, called Alan to look. After a moment's shocked silence, he said triumphantly – "Measles!" Of course it was, she realized. Measles, nothing worse. All children caught it. He didn't have meningitis, or scarlet fever. He wouldn't die. She felt light-headed with relief.

"Of course!" cried her mother, on the phone. "I should have realized when you told me about his eyes. I am a fool. I was lucky with you, you didn't get it till you were at school, so you were that much older. But you were bad with your eyes all the same, I remember you were in a darkened room for days. Eh –" she laughed "– I remember, I put a headscarf over the lamp, and your Dad gave me such a telling off. It was singed – you know, scorched, when he took it off. Could have had the whole place up in flames."

When they had finished talking, Carolyn crept into Chrissy's room with two kitchen chairs, and draped her shawl over them like a tent, and put the lamp underneath.

123

On Friday night Alan had met his project deadline, and spent the evening in the pub, celebrating with a few others from his course. When he went to bed he fell into a dead sleep. He woke in the small hours, feeling cold, and moved over to be closer to Carolyn's warm body. But she wasn't there. He groaned, and curled himself into a ball. Then he poked his head out from the covers to listen. He couldn't hear anything. He recurled and waited, for what seemed ages. There was still no sound. Perhaps she'd fallen asleep in Christopher's room. She'd be getting cold. He reached for his watch. Quarter to four. He put on his dressing gown and opened the bedroom door. He could hear her voice talking softly now, from inside Chrissy's room. He moved to stand by the door, his head an inch from the wood. Her voice was clear and light, its pitch was always a shock to him, when he heard her without seeing her. She was crooning to the child. "Chrissy, Chrissy love, bumble-face, listen – just have a spoonful my sweet, just a little taste – open wide, come on love, open wide. . . . Good boy, good boy. That was nice, wasn't it? Oh my lovely, look at your little eyes, they look like bee-stings. Sweetest bird, my sweetest love, oh, oh, it'll soon be better. D'you want a drink? Chrissy? Here, try it, just a little, come on." The child coughed and began to cry half-heartedly. "All right, never mind, hush, hush – listen Chrissy, what sort of a noise does a bee make, hmmn?"

There was a silence, then she laughed. "That's what he does, that's what he does, bzz, bzz. Ooops-a-daisy, up he comes, bzz, bzz, he's coming, he's coming –" The child made a noise which sounded like a mixture of laugh and cry. "Here he comes, no, no Chrissy, hush – listen, what does he do then? Mmmn? Off he goes, bzz, bzz, look – till he comes to the dog's house. And he knocks on the door, tap tap tap with his little feet and he says, Bzz bzz, Mr Dog, have you got any flowers for me to eat? And the dog says – ?"

After a pause Chrissy's high voice sounded pathetically, "Woo, woo."

"Very good! and oh! up jumps the bee and goes buzzing over to the other side – to – to Max's book, and he says to Max, bzz, bzz Mr Max, have you got any flowers for me to eat? and Max says – ssh, can you hear him . . . ?" Her voice trailed off and started up again after a minute, in a whisper. "So the bee picked up his flowers and flew back home to his friend Christopher, and said, night night, Christopher." There was silence.

After a long while Alan opened the door a crack. The room was very dim, he saw that she had suspended a shawl over the light, so that it shone dappled on walls and ceiling above. Although it was so dark, it reminded him of summer, being under thick leafy forest trees in sunlight. She was

124

sitting in the armchair with the baby curled over her left shoulder, his head buried in her neck, and both his hands clasped around her head. Alan saw that her eyes were closed. She had not heard the door as it softly brushed the carpet. Christopher's outstretched right hand was running slowly through her hair, touching her head at the roots and pulling the hair outwards so that it fell back like a fan. Alan saw that she herself stroked the back of the child's head rhythmically with her right hand. Her face was relaxed. He stepped forward, then stopped uselessly. He wanted to tell her to come back to bed, to put the child down now he was quiet. Something in the syncopated rhythmic movement of their two stroking hands stopped him though. In the uneven forest-dappled light, the mother and child were quite self-contained. He stood staring for another minute, then turned and, shutting the door silently behind him, went back to the cold bed.

Alan was having his breakfast when Carolyn came into the kitchen in her dressing gown.

"Want some tea? I was just going to bring you some."

"Please. He's asleep, I don't know how long for." She slumped in a chair and folded her arms across her chest.

"You look awful," Alan observed, pouring boiling water on to a tea-bag.

"So does he. It's horrible – it's really pathetic. His little eyes are completely raw, he can hardly open them." She paused. "Thanks. It's not just the spots, he's all puffed up and swollen with it. I just feel as if there's nothing I can do. He won't drink, hardly at all." She fell silent, sipping at her tea. Alan watched her, noticing the pallor of her face and deep rings under her eyes.

"When did you last go out of the house?" he asked suddenly.

"What?"

"When did you last go out?"

"I don't know."

"You didn't go out yesterday or the day before, I know. Or Wednesday. Did you go out on Tuesday?"

"Alan, I don't know. I don't even know what day it is. Of course I can't go out while he's got a temperature."

"You'll make yourself ill."

"I'm all right. I'm just tired. I wish it was over, that's all."

"Why didn't you wake me?"

"When?"

125

"Last night. When he woke up."

"Alan –" she looked up at him, laughing disbelievingly. "What's the point? He's not sleeping for more than two hours at a time at the moment. I know what he needs. I know where his medicine and his drink are, when I last changed him, everything. There's no point in both of us being awake all night, it's not going to make him get better any quicker."

"In other words, you can do without me."

"Oh for God's sake, Alan. You have to go to college don't you? What am I supposed to do?"

There was silence while Alan turned the pages of the paper mechanically.

"Well I'm at home today. What needs doing?"

"I don't know. Do what you want."

Speechless with weary anger, she cut herself two crooked slices of bread and put them under the grill.

"Why are you so angry?"

"Because – because it's just so unfair. I'm up all night for nights and you don't thank me, you act as if I'm trying to exclude you from something. All you think about is yourself. It's incredible."

"All right!" he shouted, jumping up and slapping the paper down on the table.

"Sssh – shut up, don't wake him!"

Alan sat down again, knotting his legs around one another so that he made a dangerously tight parcel. "All right," he said quietly. "I'm selfish. I go out all day to college having a lovely time while you stay at home making yourself ill. I don't have to go. I don't have to pass exams or get a job, we don't need the money – oh no, I do all this purely for my own amusement."

"I'm not talking to you." She stood by the oven, rubbing one bare foot against the other, glaring at the toast which was already burnt.

"Carolyn! It's on fire!" He jumped up and tipped the flaming toast into the sink. "Sit down. I'll make you some."

When she was eating her toast he said, "What d'you want me to do today, then? Why don't you go and have a sleep for a couple of hours while I keep an eye on Chris?"

"I – no, he's – I want to – can you go to the chemist's for me? He needs some more fruit juice. Delrosa, get the orange and the rose-hip, and some disposable nappies? I'm not – they're all dirty, I didn't do them yesterday, they won't be dry. And something for dinner –"

"OK."

Alan went into the bathroom. Carolyn sat with her eyes closed listening to the water running and the traffic outside. Alan came in again.
"No. You go."

She looked up blankly.

"Look Carolyn, this is ridiculous. You haven't been outside that door for days. Ever since he got ill – for nearly a week, I bet. If I can't look after my own son for a couple of hours while you go shopping, heaven help us."

"But Alan, he'll wake up soon."

"Good. Why can't I give him his breakfast? Get dressed and go, go on."

Carolyn went slowly to the bedroom. When she came back, tears were running down her face.

"What's the matter?"

"I don't want to go. Alan, you go."

"Carolyn, you're becoming unhinged. You know what you want to buy better than I do anyway. What d'you think's going to happen? D'you think I'll let him die? Come on lass, pull yourself together." *Kindly, he dried her face on a tea-towel, helped her on with her coat and shepherded her down the stairs.*

"I haven't looked at him," *she wailed.*

"Carolyn, I'll go and look at him as soon as I shut the door on you. Go on. I'll see you soon."

He stood for a moment listening to her standing still on the other side of the door, then heard her footsteps moving slowly away. Running upstairs to the sitting-room window, he was in time to see her cross the road, staring up and down vaguely like a blind person. It was ridiculous. She was a nervous wreck, and all that was wrong with the child was measles.

He went quietly into Chrissy's room, stopping inside the door for a minute until his eyes adjusted to the dimness. She had rigged up an old green bedspread over the thin cotton curtains, so the room was very dim with a murky greenish light. Chrissy's breathing was fast and rasping in his throat. He slept with his mouth open, lips pouting like a pig's snout. His face was puffy and covered in dark blotches. It looked mishapen in this light, almost as if something was eating away at it. His hair was like streaks of dirt on his head. Alan put his fingertips close, touched the top of the head lightly. Heat was radiating off it.

He crept back into the kitchen and made himself another cup of tea. As he was stirring it he heard Christopher cough and start to cry. Quickly he went to pick him up. "Hello Christopher, hello old mate. Well, what's up then? Would you like a drink, eh?"

He lifted the child gently from the cot. Christopher's feeble complaining cry continued. Alan wrapped one of his cot blankets round his shoulders and took him to the kitchen to make a drink. As they entered the kitchen Christopher let out a wail, ducking his head in towards Alan's body. "What's up? What's the matter?"

The next scream was louder, Christopher's fist gouging at his eye sockets.

"Oh God, the light. I'm sorry Chris, I'm sorry. All right, come on, let's go back."

Alan took him back into his bedroom and walked up and down with him mechanically, trying to soothe him. The crying diminished to a monotonous weary complaining level. Alan sat in the armchair, setting Chrissy on his knees. "Would you like a drink, Christopher, eh?"

"Dink! dink!" The crying stopped a moment.

"Good boy. Good boy. I'll get you one. Look, you'll have to sit here and wait for me, all right? You wait here while Daddy gets you a drink."

"Dink — DINK!"

As Alan sat him in his cot and left the room, Christopher began to howl in earnest again, interrupted by spasms of coughing which left him breathless. Frantically, Alan searched the kitchen for the feeder cup. It wasn't in the cupboard, the sink, on the draining board — was it in his room? "Hush, Christopher, drink's coming, coming in a minute." He found it on the floor by the armchair, rinsed it, poured it half full of milk. "All right Chrissy, here we are, here we are, it's coming now." The child was still crying as Alan sat down with him, but he grasped greedily for the milk.

"Here you are then. Hold it yourself. Steady — steady now —"

Christopher gulped at it and started to choke, spluttering milk all over both of them.

"Oh Christopher! Here, give it to me. Come on, hey, hey, steady now." He patted the little boy gently on the back. Chris started to cry again for the drink. Alan gave it back to him, but when he had had two mouthfuls he let it drop.

"Christopher? Come on, drink up. Don't you like it? Come on old boy." With a peevish cry Christopher pushed it away.

"Well what do you want? What are you going to drink, Chrissy? D'you want some juice?" Christopher wriggled around on his lap, rubbing fiercely at his eyes. Alan remembered that Carolyn had mentioned bathing them.

"Shall we wash your eyes — hmmn?" The blanket was useless, as Christopher wriggled and threshed. "Stop it — look, you'll get chilled.

Better put a jumper on – here, come on." It was a fight to get Christopher into the jumper. He struggled and cried, his arms as bendy as rubber. Alan left him howling in the cot again while he went for a bowl of water.

With water, cotton wool and towel laid ready on the chair arm, he lifted the hot screaming creature out of the cot and sat it on the chair. "Christopher – shush. I'm going to make your eyes better, stop crying." He dipped the cotton wool in the water and dabbed at the livid puffy eyes. The cries changed in tone, rising, terrified. Christopher jerked back and kicked, and the bowl of water spilt into the chair, over his legs and over Alan. Alan dabbed hurriedly at him with the towel and picked him up. "Hey–ey, I'm sorry Chrissy, shush, shush –" He joggled him up and down, but the in-earnest high screams, punctuated with shuddering gasps for breath, continued remorselessly. "Would you like – look, here's your teddy, look, d'you want him to do a dance – Christopher?"

Alan tried in vain for the ensuing limbo of time to distract and comfort Chrissy. The little boy was settled into a continuous breath-jerking crying, his eyes no more than slits now. Alan imagined Carolyn detained; lost, run over. What would he do? Christopher hadn't even had any breakfast. He hadn't been changed or taken his medicine. Alan thought of the little scene he had witnessed the previous night. He even tried repeating the bee. "Bzz, bzz, what did he say to the dog?" But the slit-eyes looked through him as if he did not exist. Which he didn't, he realized sharply, for Chrissy. Chrissy's howls were those of someone abandoned, utterly desolate. Alan could be of no use to him. All he wanted was Carolyn. "Christopher! Stop it! I'm here, what d'you want? A drink? sweet?" The screams continued unchanged. "I'm going to put you back to bed if you don't stop it. D'you hear?"

Alan put him back in his bed and Chris continued to scream hoarsely, with no increase or lessening of force. Alan stood outside the door, arms by his side, fists clenched, listening. Gradually the intensity of sound diminished. There was a moment's silence, broken by sucking noises. He was sucking his thumb. Within a few minutes of shuddering breaths, hiccups, and desperate sucking sounds, silence fell. At last Alan gently pushed the door open, to see that Chris was slumped against the bars of his cot, bent double, his thumb rammed into his mouth. Bitterly Alan pulled the blanket up around him, and went to the kitchen. What had settled his son at last was sheer exhaustion, and Alan's absence.

Chris was still asleep when Carolyn came home, and she was relieved to hear that he had been fine while she was out. Over the next few days he made a remarkably swift recovery. Soon they were laughing over the melodrama of it; how quickly he had seemed to arrive at death's door, and how absurdly soon afterwards he was stuffing his face and bouncing with health.

"It's like a speeded-up version of an adult illness," said Carolyn, who still looked white and exhausted, two weeks after Chris was fully recovered. They were in the kitchen, sitting over cups of coffee, reluctant to move to do the washing up. Chris was asleep, and outside in the dark, snow was falling silently. They found themselves both staring out, at the flakes which fell within the window's patch of illumination, large and white against the blackness.

"It's so soft," Carolyn said after a long silence. "The flakes are almost floating."

Alan moved to the window. "Soft it may be, but it's sticking. It's already covered the lawn. I bet you roads'll be blocked in the morning."

"It seems incredible," she said dreamily, hypnotized by the slow constant motion.

Staring out at the dim white lawn, through the close-up falling lines of black and white, Alan said quietly, "You love him more than me, don't you?"

"Christopher?" She did not seem surprised. "Yes, I suppose I do."

There was a silence.

"He needs me more than you do," she said, as if that was an explanation.

Alan waited. Outside, the snow blotted out the last irregularities in the flowerbed, making it one with the lawn.

"You don't mind, do you?" she said, rousing herself. "Surely it's natural – don't you feel the same? He's completely dependent on us. It's nature's way of making sure we look after him properly, I suppose." She stood up, beginning to stack the plates. "After all, you'd survive if I disappeared, wouldn't you? It would be harder for him."

"Yes," said Alan. "I suppose so."

A snowflake touched the glass, stuck there for a moment then melted. He turned to help her clear the table.

Chapter 13

Caro got off the near-empty Sunday bus and walked quickly through the light drizzle towards her parents' house. She was laden with presents from the garden: lettuce, spring onions, radishes, and a large bunch of sweet peas. There was not a lot of point in bringing these gifts, since her father's allotment kept them well supplied with fresh vegetables (although he did not grow sweet peas, considering them more trouble than they were worth). But she brought them because it salved her conscience to bring something, and she had not been for two weeks now. In the three years since her father had first called so unexpectedly at the Red House, she had made an effort to see her mother most Sundays. It was rare for her to have missed two in a row, as now. She had had to work the first Sunday. There had been the usual final frenzy to get the parks ready for festival week, and various people had been smitten with untimely summer flu. She had ended up, ludicrously enough, supervising the planting out of the county coat of arms in tiny flowering plants. And last Sunday had been Clare's birthday, and Clare's only day off that week. They had got up early and gone for a swim in the reservoir, which was deserted and silk-smooth, with a pearly mist hovering a clear foot above its surface. She had planned to get over to her mother's by the afternoon, but the day had been so rare that neither of them could bear to finish it. Only three or four times, in the whole of the past three years, had they actually had the luxury of a whole day together. Both of them (for different reasons) were anxious about seeming to exclude the rest of the household, each of them still (even after so long) unsure of her claims on the other. Fear, on Clare's part, and a natural fastidiousness on Caro's, kept them from ever spelling out their relationship.

As she flicked over memories of the day – embracing in the cold silken water, under that mysterious layer of white mist which cut off the sky above yet gave clear vision to the other side, a quarter of a mile away – the sense of wicked escape, as they laughed together in the empty lunch-time pub . . . she decided that she would tell her mother she'd been working both Sundays. There were many things it was not possible to discuss with her mother.

The estate seemed small and sad in the rain. How she hated these arid little gardens with their square yard of grass and ugly bare borders, the nasty little brick wall surrounds. The design and planning that had gone into these places was minimal. And yet people were glad to live here. Grateful for "a garden". She would sweep the lot away; if no more land was available, at least knock down all the petty walls and create a line of planting to lead the eye along the (not unpleasing) curve of the road; use shrubs and bushes, plan for mature growth on a large scale. Lined with trees, shaded by trees, how different this road might look. She narrowed her eyes to send the close out of focus, and painted in broad splashes of border colour – a bank of lupins there, clumps of huge red poppies over here.

She sighed as she turned in at her parents' tasteful wrought-iron gate. They wouldn't like it anyway. They were all happy to have their own tiny enclosed plot of garden, and to labour to keep it nice and bare. That was really seen as the crowning achievement, keeping your garden clear of weeds – not what you managed to grow in the space. Even her father, for whose gardening abilities she now had a deep respect, did not deviate from the norm. Although he grew beautiful flowers for competition in his tiny greenhouse on the allotment, he was content for the front garden to consist of a small shaved lawn and empty flower bed with two statutory rose bushes and a border of tedious alyssum.

She caught a glimpse of her mother watching for her through the window, before the net curtain dropped. But she knew Meg would wait for her to knock, and then take her time coming to the door – pretending, of course, that Carolyn's arrival was a complete surprise.

"Hello Mum!"

"Haven't you got an umbrella? Your hair's soaking wet." Meg wished she hadn't said it before it was out of her mouth. "Come in, come in. How are you love? We've missed you these last two weeks."

"I know, I'm sorry Mum. I've been working. It's been really frantic this summer. But things should quieten down a bit now, that's the end of the festival fuss."

Meg nodded. Caro knew she wasn't listening. She handed over her bag of vegetables, which Meg put away in the kitchen without examining. She took them for granted, of course. Arthur brought them every week. But Caro couldn't help feeling snubbed that her mother had not given the lettuce a little squeeze, to see how good and hearty it was, or commented on the size and perfect shape of the radishes. Caro began to arrange the sweet peas in a vase.

"Here, dry your hair, you'll catch your death. Leave those, they can wait."

Meg fussed around her with a towel and hairdryer. "Haven't you got any better shoes than that? They're not very practical for this weather, are they?"

Caro looked down at her battered pumps and wished she'd remembered to change them.

"Take them off and let's get them dry, you can borrow my slippers for the time being. Eeh, I'm beginning to think those legs of yours have disappeared, it's so long since I saw them. Haven't you got any skirts any more?"

Caro had ironed a clean pair of jeans especially for this visit.

"Skirts aren't very practical, in my line of work, Mum."

"No, I don't suppose they are. Funny sort of thing for a girl to be doing. But when you start your course you won't be grubbing about in the soil all the time, will you? Shall I buy you a skirt for the beginning of term? Would you like that?"

Caro turned on the hairdryer and saved her answer for a couple of minutes, which gave her time to make it tactful.

"You know what I'd really like, Mum? Remember that big sloppy jumper you knitted me when I was in the sixth form – that maroon one? Would you make me another?"

Her mother's face lit up. "Well that's easy enough. Of course I will. Just plain? What colour would you like?"

"Oh – the same – or, is there anything nice in green? A sort of deep green, bottle-green?"

133

Meg reflected. "There might be, in the new chunky that's just come in. I'll have a look on Monday. What size are you now?"

Caro repressed a sigh. "I'm just the same size I've always been, Mum. Thirty-two."

Meg shook her head decisively. "You're never a thirty-two now, my girl. I don't know what you eat but it's certainly not very nourishing. You look as if you've been in a concentration camp – you do! and that's the truth. You've never got up to your proper weight again since the – since – since you – you know."

Caro had noticed before the way her mother always avoided referring to the accident and Caro's time in hospital, almost as if it were something obscene.

"Come along now and get some dinner inside you, if that hair's dry. It's on the table waiting."

Caro went into the dining area. "Dad at the allotment?"

"Mmn."

"I'll pop down and see him after dinner."

"He'll be up for his tea." Meg's tone was injured.

But he doesn't say anything when he comes in here, Caro told her mother silently. I like to go to the allotment. We can compare the growth of our peas and beans, and moan about the weather.

"We could both wander down, perhaps, if the rain stops. It'll be nice and fresh."

"Hmph." Her mother put a huge shepherd's pie on the table. It was a bad idea, her mother would complain about the mud and her father would say nothing.

"Now, get some of this inside you and you'll look a bit more like. What do you eat for your dinners?"

"I eat a lot, Mum. Stews, curries, salads, all sorts. Honestly."

Meg said nothing, but continued to ladle more food on to an already impossibly large helping.

"Stop – stop, please, that's enough."

After they had eaten, her mother let Caro make them both a cup of tea.

"Tell me a bit about this course of yours, love. Jean was asking me the other day, and really, you've told me next to nothing. I felt a bit of a fool."

Caro clenched and unclenched her toes in her mother's too warm slippers.

"Well, it's just what it says, landscape architecture. Learning

134

about landscape design, you know – using natural features, hills or rivers or whatever – and improving on it. Like – you've heard of Capability Brown?"

Meg had heard of him, and Caro saw it was what she wanted to hear. Her mother so much wanted her to be doing something prestigious, Caro thought bitterly, something she could boast about to her woolshop cronies, after all that dreadful "grubbing about in the park". She had been appalled by Caro's first job, lowly assistant gardener in Limetree Park, riding across the lawns on a great smelly mower, digging out dead bedding plants and dragging pruned branches to bonfires. "It's no sort of job for a girl," she had complained. She said she wouldn't go in the park any more, she would be too ashamed if she met Carolyn, covered in muck and wearing dirty overalls, doing some filthy job. Caro had been so delighted by the job (spotted by Sue, an advert in the local paper) that she could feel no sympathy for her mother's whinings, and the Sunday visits had been stiff with hostile silences.

Caro supposed her mother had got used to it, as Caro got better at the job and was given a spell of greenhouse work, then offered day release to improve her qualifications. She'd been taken on by Harman almost as – well yes, his protégé really. He'd encouraged her to look with his eyes – a planner's eyes – at the scope of the whole thing; to raise her sights from the individual plant in the bed, to the design of the whole park, and the needs and expectations it must fulfil. So she had applied, at last, for the course. With Harman's blessing they were seconding her. She had been lucky. And at last her mother was coming round, seduced by "landscape" and "architect", nice clean professional words, nothing to do with grubbing around in the earth. Let her enjoy it, Caro told herself; seldom enough you please her.

Outside, the drizzle continued. The afternoon was passing appallingly slowly. Caro washed up and her mother dried, making her usual little jokes about how Carolyn couldn't dry because she must have forgotten where everything went, by now. Then came the routine questions about the household, and "those poor children", by which her mother meant Robin and Sylvia. She had visited the Red House once only, at Caro's invitation. Caro had spent the preceding day cleaning and tidying, but her mother had come determined to disapprove and did so easily. She pretended (Caro was sure it was pretence) to be particularly worried about the two poor fatherless children, and always asked after them. And yet she's jealous if I want to see Dad on my own, Caro thought. She would have been quite happy to have fatherless children. Was that fair? It was certainly hard to see much in her parents' relationship; it seemed to Caro now a sad empty thing. They looked after each other, that was all, as each of them might have cared for a pet and been solicitous for its well-being.

When Caro made her escape after tea it was with all the usual feelings of guilt and frustration; with her mother suggesting brightly, "Just let me measure you for that new jumper before you go, Carolyn," and, "Did I show you the new suite we were thinking of getting, in the catalogue? Just a minute. . . ." and finally, "Well, I expect we'll see you when you've the time," as if she only visited them twice a year.

Her father looked up from the newspaper and nodded. He had not said a word. Her mother came out and stood at the gate waving until Caro had walked out of sight, and Caro had to force herself not to run to escape that imploring cloying gaze.

Sitting in Clare's room late that night, Caro and Clare talked about Caro's mother.

"She always manages to make me feel guilty. Every aspect of me is wrong: the way I look, how I dress, what I eat, what I do . . . I can't do anything right."

"Uh huh," said Clare, who was lying on the floor smoking, with her eyes closed. "That's because she made you. How would you feel if you knitted yourself a nice little doll, out of the most expensive yarn you could buy, and spent the best years of your life working on it to make it as perfect as you could – then it suddenly got up and walked away and turned into something different?"

There was a silence. She had been at a Women's Aid conference in London all weekend, and she was tired and depressed.

"You always oversimplify," Caro said softly. "What a world you live in – all mothers are possessive predators – all men are potential rapists."

"Yeah," said Clare without opening her eyes. "Tell me how the world's different. You missed out that mothers are also oppressed sisters.''

"Well how do you resolve that?' Caro asked innocently.

"I don't know. I don't resolve it. I don't oversimplify. But it helps you make sense of the world, you know, if you have an analysis to hang things on.''

Clare let herself get angry. She sat up.

"It's so easy, isn't it, to condemn us? It's so nice and easy to say we oversimplify, and there are all these examples that disprove this and disprove that – all these nice men, all these women with great careers – isn't it? If it was left to your subtlety and refinement, nothing would change, ever. You'd never get it together to say 'this is unfair', 'this should be changed', because you'd be too busy counting the exceptions. You're not the only person who's noticed that the world's complicated and every-one's different, Caro. But you appear not to have noticed a few glaring facts like that women in general don't rape men, or beat them up, or design weapons or make the laws and enforce them – or hold enough jobs of influence and authority to make an iota of difference to the way this bloody patriarchal shit-heap is run.''

There was a long silence. Clare lit another cigarette and lay down slowly, closing her eyes.

"All right,'' said Caro. "I'm sorry.''

After a long pause Clare opened her eyes and looked at Caro. "No you're not.'' There was an edge of humour in her voice. "You're a self-opinionated self-righteous little turd.''

"Yes,'' said Caro. "I am. Have you stopped being angry? Can I explain about my mother?''

"If you must.'' Clare closed her eyes again.

"Well, what I was going to say is, look at her good points.''

"What are they?''

"There are lots. She is a kind and thoughtful provider – of home comfort, food, clean sheets, ironed shirts, fresh bread – all the things you take for granted at home.''

"Yeah.''

"She cares about me and Dad more than anyone else in the world. She'd do anything for us – and we both know that, which means I suppose that we have a sort of shell of security which goes with us everywhere.''

Clare blew a smoke ring.

"She's prepared to adapt her life to ours in any way."

"Is she? Isn't that bad?"

Caro hesitated. "I don't know." She paused. "What I was thinking about was Mrs Ramsay."

Clare rolled over on her stomach. Always (and she always forgot it) came this moment of poignancy with Caro. She wondered if it was how she would define love. When she was most irritated by Caro's holier-than-thou, most nearly offended by how stupid/insensitive Caro must think her, with her "what a world you live in", and was thinking "How young, how predictable, how *limited* you are," came the twist in the conversation, the unexpected note, that looking back along the line of the conversation, was the note Caro had been heading for all the time. But it almost hurts, she thought, it's sharp like a knife. You can think you know someone as well as yourself, but then you are caught up, surprised, by something they say. You love them because they're different, they say the thing you don't expect. But why is it so poignant? she wondered. Because you see with her eyes for a moment, share her vision, escape yourself – it renews and twists the love, because it reminds you you don't know her, don't own her. So in the moment of escape from self comes the reminder of isolation. All our lives, she thought, we are after union; join me, love me, fuck me. Let us be one. And at each instant of its happening, its bitter-sweet wonder is that you know it can't last. We are all, for nearly always, single. She was very tired; an uncharacteristic wave of sentimentality – of pity, almost, for all living things, brought tears to her eyes and made her want to clasp her arms round Caro. "Mrs Ramsay," she said.

"I thought you'd gone to sleep."

"No. I was just thinking. Tell me about Mrs Ramsay."

"*To the Lighthouse*. You must have read it. You lent it me."

"Yes, I've read it."

"Well – look at her. She comes across as wonderful, doesn't she? She's the heart of the book – her presence brings order and happiness. She's kind to everyone, puts everyone before herself, is all things to all people – mother to James, wife to her husband. . . . And I was thinking, do you remember, the wonderful bit about the sheep's skull in the children's bedroom?"

"Yes," said Clare drily. "She covers it up and tells the little girl it's full of fairies and pretty make-believe so she mustn't be scared, and she tells the boy it's really there, dead, under the shawl."

"I – oh Clare, surely it's to do with the ages they are, not the sexes?"

Clare shrugged. "Little girls can't cope with nasty reality." She was both satisfied and angry with herself for having tripped Caro so neatly.

"Go on, anyway."

"All I wanted to say was – her life is devoted to serving and servicing others – and the book shows that by playing that role – that that role adds more to human happiness and richness than anything else. And what is it – what is it but, to a better degree, the qualities of my mother? Or anyone's mother; loving, giving, selflessly. . . ."

There was a silence. Caro thought Clare had not understood her.

"They're all motherly and wifely things – thinking of others, wanting people to get on together, wanting to provide nice food and pleasant surroundings and calm everyone's fears. . . ."

"Yes, yes, I know." Clare sounded impatient. "Are you sure it's all good? What about Lily Briscoe?"

"I knew you were going to say that," said Caro.

Did you, Clare thought, did you? Don't I ever surprise you, and twist a knife in your heart? She spoke harshly.

"All right: firstly, she survives Mrs Ramsay and paints a picture which catches the whole thing. She's the artist. It's the book. She makes the thing that lasts. What is it she says – 'Time stand still' – something like that –?" She stood, groping along the shelves for the book.

"It's here, at the end. I only put it back on Friday. Yes, you're right."

"But also – she herself loves Mrs Ramsay, doesn't she –"

"Yes."

"But she criticizes her. Doesn't she say – doesn't she imply it's selfish, the way Mrs Ramsay gets everyone to need her so much? Isn't that the heart of it? That those kinds of women make everyone need them and rely on them, so they foster an array of –of emotional cripples around them. Look at her husband. He's an emotional cripple. She bolsters him up and feeds his ego and tells him he's wonderful – is it kind? Is it right?" Clare was turning

139

the pages of the book furiously. "Here," she said at last. "Remember when she's dead? Ramsay's organizing the trip to the lighthouse at last and Lily's trying to paint, and he comes up demanding sympathy. Remember? Listen – Lily thinking: 'That man, she thought, her anger rising in her, never gave; that man took. She, on the other hand, would be forced to give. Mrs Ramsay had given. Giving, giving, giving, she had died – and had left all this. Really, she was angry with Mrs Ramsay.'" She looked up at Caro. "Once she's dead they fall to pieces. She made herself indispensable. Isn't that an amazingly selfish thing to do?"

"But –" Caro stammered. "You twist it Clare. You do –"

"No. I don't think so." Clare was suddenly full of energy again, harsh, intent. She hated Mrs Ramsay and all she stood for. She thumbed the pages quickly, her eyes running up and down over the print.

"Listen – here, she's condemned out of her own mouth – going up the stairs after dinner: 'They would, [Mrs Ramsay] thought, going on again, however long they lived, come back to this night; to this moon; this wind; this house; and to her too. It flattered her, where she was most susceptible of flattery, to think how, wound about in their hearts, however long they lived she would be woven –' See? And anyway –" Clare sat again, holding the book still before her face but looking over it at Caro " – It's all very well isn't it, being the gracious model of womanhood, with a tribe of servants around you. What about the woman who does the cooking? And the one who cleans? And the poor little nanny who spends the whole book upstairs crying for her dying father? Of course Mrs Ramsay can be bloody gracious and beautiful, on the back of everyone else's hard work. What if she had to do it all herself, like your Mum and mine?"

"Then she'd be that much less gracious and beautiful, as they are!" said Caro, with a triumphant laugh. "You've just come out on my side of the argument. All I'm saying is that those motherly qualities are good, and necessary, when you're dealing with children. Maybe with men too, God knows. And it seems a bit much to suddenly turn round when you're grown up and say to the mother, 'No, you shouldn't be like that. You should put yourself first and not care or be possessive about your children, or about making your husband the breadwinner happy, or making the home a nice place to be.'"

Clare seemed to be studying the cover of the book. Then she let it fall open, and began to read immediately, as if she had known it, "'Why, [Mrs Ramsay] asked, pressing her chin on James' head, should they grow up so fast? Why should they go to school? She would have liked always to have had a baby. She was happiest carrying one in her arms.'"

Caro looked down. "I think you have to be like that, to be a good mother," she said. "It comes back to where I started. My Mum. What I hate in her now, I needed then. But why should I expect her to change just because I have?"

Clare laughed shortly. "If I were you, I should provide her immediately with a clutch of grandchildren to look after, and she can go on being happily the same until the day she dies."

"I'd like to have children, I think." Caro was ignoring Clare's tone. She didn't want the conversation to end. "I would like to, I think – but I'm afraid I might be like that – I think I would want to be like that. If you care about changing women's lives you've got to consider that Clare, you can't just throw Mrs Ramsay out –"

"No," said Clare. "I know, Caro. It's complicated."

Her tone was suddenly flat and weary. Looking at her Caro nearly jumped with the shock of remembering that Clare had a child, that Clare had thrown it out.

"Clare?"

"Yes?"

"I'm sorry. I wasn't thinking – I was being awful –"

"No. It's all right. My son, you mean? I think the trouble is, perhaps, people think Mrs Ramsay is *the* way to be a mother. And I'm not really prepared to be that. . . . But –" she said, her voice suddenly bitter, "I'm not in a position to talk, since all I could do was run – eh? You should be talking to Sue. I'm tired, Caro. Are you going to bed?"

"Clare – I'm sorry."

"OK. Goodnight." Clare's voice was light, brittle. When she was hurt she put herself out of reach; Caro knew that by now, and she would have given a lot to undo the conversation. She hesitated on the stairs, knowing it would be difficult to sleep – then went down to the kitchen.

Bryony was there, making toasted cheese under the grill.

"D'you want a bit?"

"OK. Thanks."

"What's the matter?"

"Nothing. What's the time?"

"Half eleven." Bryony took the toast out and began to smear it with tomato chutney. The jars had been recycled at last; Caro's tomatoes had ripened all at once, last September, and she and Bryony had filled sixteen jars with chutney.

"Aren't you working tomorrow? What time d'you start?"

"Six. It's OK. I'm getting good at walking in my sleep."

Bryony had finally found a job she liked, after various bizarre false starts, and months on social security. She was a post-woman, walking on a round that actually included their own street. It seemed to Caro that she had probably discovered the only job in the world which was suited to her strange requirements. She wanted to be out in the open air, but excluded farming and gardening because of the evils of chemical fertilizers, pesticides, and hybrid animals/plants which deviated from nature's intentions. ("Nature intended them all to be small and prickly," Clare had pointed out unkindly in one animated discussion.) She did not want to be responsible for the reckless consumption of any of the earth's resources in the shape of fuel, and so a round on foot suited her perfectly. She did not want to be employed by a private, capitalist firm; the GPO was at least nationalized. She did not want to find herself in a hierarchical situation in relation to others at work, thereby creating false barriers and reinforcing the capitalist class structure. Since she did her round alone, this was not a problem. She wanted to wear what she liked, or at least sensible clothes and her everlasting shoes, which she could do. She wanted to have some measure of control over her own productivity – which she could exercise by walking more quickly or slowly. And she wanted to be doing something manifestly useful. Which it was. There were problems about being the carrier of bills, final demands, and offensive advertising material, but as far as Caro knew Bryony overcame her scruples sufficiently to deliver all mail except for a succession of very obvious plain brown envelopes, which were frequently sent to one particular address on her route. These she threw away, rightly assuming that whoever had requested such filthy pornography would be too embarrassed to complain about its non-arrival.

142

Caro liked Bryony very much, now. It had taken a long time for the initial hostility and suspicion between them to wear off. Bryony was the most definite, dogmatic, and (in the defence of her own ideas) fierce person Caro had ever met at close quarters. She was also absolutely open and honest; her integrity blazed through all the details of cranky behaviour which the execution of her principles in her daily life demanded of her. She was intolerant and contemptuous of the majority of the human race, whom she saw as wasteful, deluded, and politically ignorant. In particular she disliked men, because her political analysis revealed them to be oppressors, and responsible as a sex for many of the worst aspects of our civilization (war, the arms race, the stock exchange, rape, science, motor cars, additives to food, defoliants, hospital management of childbirth, competitions, multinational companies, cosmetics, pornography and vivisection). Because she disliked men, she did not cultivate their friendship. She was intensely loyal and endlessly kind to those (women) she knew well and respected.

They ate their toast in silence. When they had finished Bryony put the kettle on and asked again, "What's up?"

"Oh – I don't know. I've been talking to Clare."

Bryony nodded.

"It was my fault. I was talking about children. I always forget – it just doesn't seem to go with her, having a kid."

"No. It does seem odd."

There was another silence, then Bryony said, "Do you want kids?"

"I don't know. Maybe. Do you?"

"No. Oh no – I wouldn't want to be responsible for landing someone else in this mess."

"Well – it's not – like that, is it? In practice? I mean, you look after it and protect it. . . ."

"For a bit. You're not going to be able to protect it from radiation, are you? or brain damage caused by lead in the atmosphere? or cancer caused by preservatives in food?"

"No. I suppose not."

Bryony busied herself making coffee. Her voice softened.

"In a way I would like to very much. But – what right have we got?"

"None. But people do."

"Yes. People do." She sat down again.

"There are—" Carolyn hesitated "—there have always been external dangers, anyway. I mean, children used to die of diseases which are stamped out now. Children used to have to work in dreadful conditions, in factories and mines. There have always been wars. If everyone had waited until they could promise their children a safe life, the human race would be extinct."

"Yes. But—some situations are worse than others. People stop having children when the future they face is too appalling. Look at the Red Indians. If you have a child, OK, you know it may die of illness or accident—but isn't it different, if you know the whole world might be blown up and poisoned?"

"But you can't be responsible for the world, Bryony."

"Who will be then?"

"I don't know."

"Even on a small scale—all right? Even the things that are within your scope. A child's education—they would teach it things I didn't want it to learn, at school. It would pick up all sorts of violent, sexist ideas from TV—"

"You'd want to control its life."

"Yes."

"But people have to make their own choices."

"It's not a choice, though, is it? If you grew up in a certain kind of society, you adopt its values."

"You didn't."

"No. But I'm a freak."

"Well, you might have a freakish child."

Bryony laughed. "I might. Better not to have one, I think." She put her mug in the sink and said goodnight. Caro waited in the kitchen till she heard Bryony's heavy tread going from the bathroom to her bedroom. Then she went upstairs herself.

Caro dreamed she was driving along a straight empty road. The grassy countryside was flat on either side, stretching away as far as the eye could see. The bare road bisected it like a parting. There were no other cars. She pressed her foot down and the car leapt forwards along the road. She was going faster than the wind but nothing moved, there were no landmarks, simply more of the same scenery. It was like running on the spot. Then there was a

144

dot in the distance, on the left side of the road. It grew bigger with incredible speed, she was whizzing towards it. She must slow down or she'd miss it. She took her foot off the accelerator and put it on the brake, and as the car slowed she could see now that it was a child, a toddler with a red woolly hat on. His back was to her, he was toddling along purposefully in the same direction as her, across that bleak empty landscape. She stopped next to him but he ignored her and kept on walking. She moved on and pulled up in front of him.

"I'll give you a lift," she called, and opened the passenger door. The child looked at her and climbed up on to the seat. He did not say anything. She leaned across to pull the door shut after him and felt his warm breath on her cheek. "Where are you going?" she asked, but he didn't answer. She thought, he's too young, he can't talk yet. He sat leaning against the back of the seat with his legs stretched out straight in front of him. His feet in their little red shoes just reached the edge of the seat. He was tiny. He was wearing blue trousers and little white socks. He stared ahead through the windscreen, his hands clasped in his lap, and she started to drive again. On and on they went, and the scenery never changed. She didn't know if they had been driving for minutes or days. The little boy sat still and never moved. But each time she glanced at him she felt a shock. He was so small. He's getting smaller, she thought, and she tried to watch him as she drove. But she couldn't see him getting smaller, any more than you can watch a plant growing. She was convinced he was shrinking.

He was staring at the glove box now, he was too low to see out of the window. But his clothes must be shrinking too, she thought, that's not possible. His little red hat and shoes still fitted him.

But he was tiny now, his feet only reached to halfway across the seat, he was only about twelve inches tall. What if he vanishes? she thought. Oh no, he couldn't, how silly. How silly I am. She felt relieved and pressed her foot down again. In the distance now she could see a big silvery building. It was the hospital. Not long now, she thought, they'll soon see if there's anything wrong with him. As the hospital grew bigger and nearer, she glanced again at the little boy and saw with horror that he was tiny. He was nestling in the crack at the back of the

145

seat, he was smaller than a doll, he was no more than five inches long. Desperately she pressed on but she knew with an awful certainty that he would vanish before she got there.

She picked him up with her left hand and held him clasped in her palm. She could feel him shrinking by the second. Only one thing to do, she told herself, to make sure he's safe. And she opened her mouth and put him inside, on top of her tongue. He'll be quite safe now. Carefully she turned in through the wide hospital gates. She was so relieved that she had saved him. She jumped out and ran through the swing doors and over to a desk where a nurse in a white uniform sat waiting.

"It's a baby," she said, "he's shrinking but I think he can be saved." She put her fingers into her mouth to take him out – There was nothing there. He'd gone.

She cried and rammed her fingers down her throat. "I've swallowed – I must have swallowed him –" There was a bitter taste in her mouth, a dusty lumpy bitter taste of lemons and ashes dissolving, dissolving. . . .

The nurse looked at her calmly and smiled.

"You've got to get him out!" she screamed, and the nurse smiled and shook her head.

"I'm sorry we can't help you dear," she said.

Caro woke up covered in sweat, the bitter taste still in her throat.

Chapter 14

When Alan and Carolyn had been married for four years, Alan's grandmother (Lucy's mother) died, leaving him and Pamela £20,000 each. Everyone was surprised. Lucy and her mother had fallen out years before, and the children hardly knew her. She had lived alone, with a housekeeper and gardener, ever since her husband died of a heart attack thirty years before. To Lucy, her only child, she left nothing.

Coinciding as it did with Alan's trainee appointment to the firm of Lark and Clarkson, Architects, back in the city where he was born, the money marked the beginning of a new era in Alan and Carolyn's married life. Suddenly they zoomed up the social scale. Or rather, Alan bobbed back, to float again at that level from which (in his family's eyes at least) Carolyn had dragged him down. They bought a house in the wealthy area to the south of the city some twenty miles away from their parents. It was "respectable semi-detached Victorian gothic", according to Alan. A palace, Carolyn told herself, a dream house. The roof sloped steeply, and the front of the house was ornamented with mock-Tudor black and white beams. There were four bedrooms. In the back garden, the oval lawn was surrounded by beautifully tended flowering shrubs and bushes, giving complete privacy.

Alan lay on his back on the grass, hands clasped under his head, eyes closed. The sun was pleasantly warm on his skin. From the garden around him came murmurs of sound which were as soothingly constant as the sunshine. He could hear Carolyn reading a story to Annie, the words coming clear at certain points then fading back to a murmur. "UP jumped the troll . . . I want to eat you up. No! No! mmmm mm mmmm. . . ."

He could hear the constant rapid clicking of Meg's knitting needles, and her erratic conversation with Christopher, who was lying on the grass at her feet, drawing. "What's that, Chrissy?"

"It's a rocket."

Long pause.

"Ninety-two. Is it? That's very good. Will you do me one to take home with me and put on the wall?"

Rustle of paper.

"Of – what?" Christopher's serious childish voice, making that odd little pause between words, as if he still needed to think of them.

"Um – just a minute love – a hundred and ninety-four, good. Um, do one of your Mummy and Daddy for me, will you?"

Further away, intermittent, came the sound of Arthur's clippers. He was having a go at the privet hen. The privet hen had been a joke ever since they moved in; a piece of topiary of which the house's previous owner had been inordinately proud. Very quickly it grew ragged and dishevelled. Carolyn had had a couple of goes at it and made it into – well, more of a privet dodo than a hen. Now at her request Arthur tackled it, serious and silent as ever. Alan was glad he was busy. There was, even now, a strain between the two men.

"We must be going, Carolyn," Meg raised her voice to interrupt.

"You're sure you won't stay for tea?"

"No love, we'd rather get back before it's late. Your Dad'll want to pop down and see his blessed allotment before we go to bed anyway. We've had a lovely day, haven't we Arthur? And I've got a piece of ham that'll spoil if we don't eat it tonight."

"There's plenty of food."

"I know there is love, I know there is."

Annie started to clamour for the story to go on.

"Stand up a minute, Christopher, and let me measure this." The clicking stopped and Meg muttered to herself. "There's a good boy – oh yes, that's plenty long enough. Carolyn – ?"

Carolyn stopped reading again.

"I'll get this finished this week. Will you be coming over next weekend?"

"No, it's all right Mum. He won't need it for a bit if this weather goes on. Anyway, I'll be seeing you before long. I think Alan's got a weekend course coming up. Alan? Oh, is he asleep?"

Alan pretended to be. "I'll find out when it is, anyway. I think it might be the week after next. I'll bring the children over to see you then."

148

"On the train?"

"Yes, if Dad'll meet me at the station—"

"Of course he will. We shall look forward to that. Will you come and stay at Nana's house, Chrissy? Well, let's get ourselves sorted out."

He heard the garden chair squeak and sigh as she heaved herself out of it.

"I'll just give you a lift with these pots before we go."

"Oh no, it's all right Mum, leave them. I'll do them later, it won't take long."

"Well at least I'll get them into the kitchen for you, I can't leave you with all this mess, can I Chrissy?"

Christopher didn't reply, sensibly enough, thought Alan, and he listened to the clink of china and cutlery as the two women cleared the coffee cups and last few lunch things.

"It is nice," Meg was saying, "to sit out here. Like being on holiday, isn't it? It makes a lovely change, it's so nice and private here. You couldn't eat outside on our street, you'd have all the neighbours counting the peas on your fork. . . ."

Her voice and the rattle of pots faded away into the house, and he heard, close to, Annie's uncontrolled chortle as she approached him with some wicked intent. He could hear her becoming still next to him, trying to decide how best to attack, and he grinned in readiness. Then she flung herself on to his stomach, squealing with delight, and he began to tickle her.

At last Meg and Arthur took their leave. Carolyn was just sitting down again, with her "thanks-for-putting-up-with-them-and-that-wasn't-too-bad-was-it?" smile, when the doorbell rang. Alan raised his eyebrows and smiled at her. "What've they forgotten? Knitting needle? Spectacles? False teeth?"

"Alan!" She indicated Chris with a quick nod of the head, and ran up the garden to the house. He hoped they wouldn't come back outside. It would be pleasant to lie and chat now, for a quiet half-hour or so, while the shadows lengthened over the lawn. He felt completely lazy and relaxed.

But then the sound of different voices came to his ears, and Carolyn called him from the french windows. "Alan! Al–an! Come on out," he heard her say, "would you like a drink? Would you like a cup of tea, or something cold?" She stepped into the garden uncertainly, followed by two tall people. Mike and Sarah, he recognized suddenly. Mike and Sarah from the office. He jumped to his feet.

"What a nice surprise!" he cried, hurrying towards them.

Mike was laughing embarrassedly. 'Thought we'd look you up – in your little Garden of Eden – hope we're not intruding."

"Of course not. Carolyn, let me introduce Sarah – and Mike. Mike's the other half of my office, yes? You've heard me talk about him." Mike pulled a face. "And Sarah, well, Sarah has an office all to herself."

Sarah smiled charmingly at Carolyn. "Just shows you how much more important I am than them, doesn't it?" she laughed.

"Come and sit down – come and sit down." Alan ushered them down towards the table. He was surprised and rather flattered that they'd called. When he had found out that Mike lived in a flat he'd invited him to come and enjoy their garden any time, but without really expecting to see him. He was intrigued that Sarah was with Mike. He'd suspected them of having an affair for a while, but they had both kept their tracks well covered. Sarah, he seemed to remember, was married. After the routine admiration of children, garden, and so on, they began to chat about the office.

Carolyn came out and served them tea and cake. When they all had what they needed she turned her attention to Annie. "D'you want to wee, Annie-pod? Come here–" She felt the little girl's knickers. "Annie! Why didn't you ask me for the potty? Eh? Come on, leaky sieve, let's go and find some clean ones." She led her into the house. It wasn't surprising, Carolyn thought, with all this coming and going. On the whole she was pleased with Annie's progress on the potty, she seemed to have got the hang of it much earlier than Christopher had.

Annie trotted obediently beside her, chanting to herself, "Wanta-wee wanta-wee wanta-wee," in a sing-song voice. Carolyn put her on the pot in the downstairs toilet, and laughed at her.

"Come on then, Miss Wanta-wee, get on with it."

"Mummy wee," demanded Annie imperiously, and Carolyn obliged her, listening for Annie's echoing tinkle in the pot. It never failed.

"Good girl – who's Mummy's best girl?" She emptied the pot and gave Annie a hug. It was all so much easier, somehow, than it had been with Christopher. Annie was so solid and content, she was like a shiny red apple. Carolyn never experienced the same sort of anguished worry about her as she had with Chris. Annie buried her face in Carolyn's shoulder. She was tired, Carolyn reflected, she'd missed her sleep that morning because of Mum and Dad. "Early bed for you tonight, my lady." How warm and soft she was – and heavy too! Leaning their combined weight against the wall at the top of the stairs for a moment, Carolyn felt she would be content to stay there always.

150

I must go down, she thought, and meet Alan's friends. She took a pair of pants from Annie's drawer and hurried downstairs. Christopher was coming through the dining room, drawing book dangling from his hand.

"What's the matter Chrissy?"

"Nothing," he said despondently, and threw the book on the floor.

"Hey, hey, hey, what's up, Mr Moody?"

"I'm – sick – of – drawing," he said. The way he paused between words made her smile, it made his speech seem foreign, an inadequate translation of his thoughts. She mimicked him with an Italian accent which always made him laugh.

"Ees–a – seek–a – of–a – drawing, ah? What shall we do?"

He wrapped his arms around her knees, grinning up at her. "Can we watch telly?"

"Can we watch telly please?" she said automatically, glancing out through the windows at Alan. They seemed to be deep in conversation.

"Pease! Pease!" crowed Annie. For Annie, "please" was a magic password, whose sure prospective effectiveness overwhelmed her with delight. As she said it she grinned from ear to ear, physically contorted by her joy into a sort of bow, arms out stiff behind her like someone about to fly. Carolyn laughed. "All right, all right. I'll turn it on for you. But no touching the knobs, do you understand?" She left them side by side on the sofa, intent on a cartoon, and hurried out to the garden.

"Ah! At last," Alan smiled at her. "Come and drink your tea, lass, it'll be stone cold."

Carolyn smiled and nodded to them, sitting down quickly.

"Johnson's another one with his nose in the trough," said the woman, who was talking to Alan. "Haven't you noticed how often he takes his dear friend Councillor Waverly out to lunch?"

Alan smiled and shook his head. "I'm naïve, aren't I?" he said. "Is it the same with all the council contracts we get?"

"Damn near," said the man. "Waverly's chairman of Housing and Benson's chairman of Policy and Resources; and Benson's like this –" he made an expressive gesture "– with Fielding. The whole thing's rank, once you get down to details –" he laughed, "but I'm not selling the story until I've got a job with another firm." He turned to Carolyn. "The corruption goes from top to bottom, like a cheese, you know. Did you know what a nasty business your husband's got himself into?"

Carolyn smiled, sipping at her tea and putting it down because it was, in fact, cold. "I thought he was designing better places for people to live."

They laughed, although she had not meant it as a joke.

151

"Are you going away on holiday this year?" the woman asked her.

Carolyn was aware that the woman was making conversation with her. She stood up.

"Yes, we're going to St Davids. I'm just going to add some hot water to this tea." She made her escape from the table, boiled the kettle and looked in on the children. When she returned with her teapot, Alan waved it aside.

"Why not have a proper drink?" he asked the visitors. "Scotch? Gin and tonic? It's nearly six." He consulted his watch. "In fact, why don't you stay to eat, if you're at a loose end? I don't know what there is but I'm sure we can rustle something up—" He looked at Carolyn.

"Yes — oh yes, why don't you stay?" she said.

They demurred politely, but finally succumbed to Alan's persuasion. Carolyn stood by the table, sipping her new tea and wondering what she could cook. The conversation continued.

"It's not the worst place to work, by any means," said the woman. "Look at Jays — I'm amazed by what they get away with there. You know they did the plans for that community college?"

"Sedgemoor?" asked Alan.

"Yes. And now the roof's leaking so badly they've had to close the gym completely."

"Yes," said the man. "But the council's so embarrassed about that one that they're just leaving them to put it right as quietly as they can. Everyone knows it should never have been passed. It's the most terrible design I've ever seen."

"Some of these councillors are so thick!" said the woman. She turned to Carolyn with a laugh. "Politics, politics, politics — we seem to end up there every time, don't we?"

Carolyn smiled quickly. "I — I — don't pay much attention to politics, I'm afraid," she said. "What would you like to drink?"

"It's all right, Carolyn, I'll get them in a minute."

As if Alan had excused her, Carolyn made her way to the house. What could they eat? The children were watching TV peacefully, but Annie saw her as she bobbed her head around the door, gave a pleased gurgle and started to scramble down.

"No Annie, stay there love, stay with Chrissy. Mummy's got to do some cooking."

They had had a big Sunday lunch, with Mum and Dad being there. She hadn't planned to cook tonight. She opened the fridge and stared inside. There was plenty of salad stuff at least, her father had brought a lot with

152

him. But there's no meat, she thought, and started to unwrap the various packages which she already knew contained cheese, a couple of kippers, some liver pâté. No, there was no meat. Eggs. Yes, there were plenty of eggs. Omelette? Quiche? Soufflé. She was pleased to have remembered it. It was still half a game, this cooking business – learning to make the sort of food they had when they went out to dinner. For years they had eaten the shepherd's pie, cauliflower cheese and Lancashire hot-pot that she had learned from her mother. Alan, who liked buying food, occasionally bought things which she didn't know what to do with (aubergines had stumped her completely) but on the whole he seemed content with his diet. It was when they started being invited out for dinner, or going to restaurants for special occasions, that she remembered he knew about different kinds of food. She made coq au vin on his birthday, painstakingly following a recipe (a thing she'd not done since basic cookery lessons at school) and he was so pleased he bought her a Cordon Bleu cookbook. Sometimes her common sense still told her it was nothing but an invention for dirtying three times as many dishes, this business of frying and parboiling, and moving things from plate to plate. But the results were good; people praised her cooking lavishly, and she began to take a pride in doing it well.

She looked up cheese soufflé. It took longer to cook than she had expected. She had to wash up the lunch things before she could get started. Then she put the salad greens to soak. There was only half a loaf left. Oh, too bad, she decided to cook some new potatoes and they could take them or leave them. Alan would eat them, anyway. She started to grate the cheese. Annie came into the kitchen.

"I dough lak cartoo!" she announced. Carolyn stopped and stared at her.

"Say that again, Annie. What did you say?"

"I dough lak cartoo!"

"Well! Who's a clever creature, eh? You don't like the cartoon–" She abandoned the cheese and picked Annie up, laughing. It was the first complete sentence Annie had said. Carolyn went into the sitting room.

"Chrissy – Chrissy, did you tell Annie this? Listen–"

Obligingly, Annie repeated her triumph. Christopher shook his head and returned his attention to the box. Back in the kitchen, Carolyn gave Annie a saucer of currants to eat (she ate them so beautifully, one by one, held painstakingly pincered between thumb and index finger, *her other fingers cocked like a tea-sipping lady) and carried on with the food. She was stirring milk into the roux over a low heat when Annie finished her currants and announced, "Wanta-wee, wanta-wee."*

"Oh good God, child, you choose your times don't you –"

"Wanta-wee, wanta–"

Carolyn turned off the gas. She still had half the milk to add. It would go lumpy. She hurried Annie to the toilet, but once there Annie didn't seem to want to do anything but giggle at her. After coaxing her and turning on suggestive taps, Carolyn brought the pot back into the kitchen and left Annie knickerless. "Sit on the pot if you want to wee, all right Annie?"

The sauce was thin with a layer of sediment over the bottom of the pan. She stirred it vigorously, but it remained ominously thick in places, as if it would go into lumps as soon as it were heated. Sighing, she held the pan under the tap and rinsed it out. She melted another lump of butter and stirred in the flour. Now the milk –

"Wanta-wee!"

"Then sit on the pot now – go on!"

Annie weed down her leg and started to wipe it up with her hands.

"Annie! No! Stop it now! Chris – Chrissy!" She wouldn't leave the sauce again. Christopher appeared, looking put upon. "Please love, be a good boy, just wipe Annie's hands for her on that flannel and take her to watch telly, will you? I'm trying to cook something."

Chris wiped Annie in a surly, businesslike manner, and dragged her from the kitchen. They left two trails of wet footprints.

Alan appeared in the doorway. "Hello, what's going on?"

"I'm cooking, what does it look like?"

"All right. You've been gone so long I thought someone had run off with you."

"Alan – don't stand there. Look, Annie's just weed."

"Oh –" he tutted with annoyance, and lifted his feet one after the other. "Can't you wipe it up?"

"I can't leave these eggs now."

"Where's the floorcloth?"

"Under the sink." *You've been living here as long as I have,* she thought.

Alan wiped up, leaving the dirty floorcloth in the dishrack, and looked over her shoulder.

"What is it?"

"Soufflé."

"Why's it taking so long?"

"It's not. I just keep getting interrupted."

"Can I do anything?"

"Well, what do you want to do about the kids? They'd better eat before us, hadn't they? This'll take an hour to cook."

"I suppose so. I didn't think it would be a major operation –couldn't we just rustle up something quickly?"

"There isn't anything, Alan. The fridge is nearly empty."

"OK. What shall I do then? Feed the kids? I can't leave Mike and Sarah for too long –"

"No. Tell the kids to wash their hands and come in here when the programme's ended. I'll give them some cheese on toast. You go back out. It's all right."

"Right then." He went to the cupboard. "I'm just getting a refill. What would you like?"

"Um – nothing yet, thanks, I'll wait a bit."

The soufflé was in the oven, potatoes boiling with mint, salad chopped and ready, dressing mixed. She had thought they could have fruit for dessert but the bananas looked a bit black and sorry, and there were only two (bruised) peaches left. She decided to make a fruit salad, and sat peeling and chopping as the children ate their tea. Chris described to her in painstaking detail the story of the cartoon they'd been watching. She smiled at him. He had a quizzical, earnest little face, whose lines moved easily into unhappiness. But he's not unhappy, she told herself, just serious. He loved being read to, and having things explained. He was overjoyed when Alan showed him his plans, and told him what the different symbols meant, so that the lines on the paper became a living world of houses, roads and trees. He leant right across the table now, to push Annie's spoon back to her, and Carolyn put down the apple she was peeling to stroke the hollow in the back of his neck. It was still hardly wider than her finger. The backs of their necks are so vulnerable, she thought. Frail but strong, like the stems of flowers. There weren't really any flowers in the garden that would look good on the table. The sweet williams wouldn't be out for a few days. What about those little pink things on the hedge? The bees think they're marvellous. Yes, and you'll have a tableful of bees if you don't watch out. I should buy some flowers, really. But Alan says he doesn't like them. . . . Annie threw her spoon away again, it landed on the floor this time. Carolyn wiped their hands and faces.

"Right – now you can watch telly again for ten minutes while I lay the table – or you can go out and see Daddy and his friends if you want."

She set the table and checked the soufflé. It seemed all right. Just time to put Annie to bed before they ate. Alan reappeared holding a child's hand in each of his.

"Shouldn't these two be heading for bed?"

"Annie's going in a minute. Chris can stay up till we've eaten, can't he?"

"Well, I'll take her if you want to go out and have a drink."

"I – I –" She rather dreaded it. "No thanks, Alan, I'll do it, because I need to keep an eye on the soufflé anyway. It won't be long now."

He shrugged. He was looking at her oddly, she thought.

"What's the matter? Have I spilt something –?"

"That skirt makes you look dumpy. Middle-aged. It's all bulky round the waist." She looked down at her skirt. He'd never said anything about it before. "It's all right," he said quickly. "It just doesn't suit you very well, that's all. Have a drink this time? I'll leave a gin and tonic on the side here, OK?" He went out quickly. She knew he was embarrassed because he'd criticized her.

She took Annie up and put her to bed, then went to their bedroom to change herself. Her blouse had a splash of egg on it anyway. She put on the black and white dress, hesitating a moment as she looked at herself and thought, it's too smart. She had nothing in-between. She combed her hair, looking at herself in the mirror. She hadn't got many clothes she liked at the moment. It was so impossible taking Annie shopping, it was easier not to bother. The dress really wasn't right, though – Remembering the soufflé, she hurried downstairs. It was dark brown at the back, nearest the gas flames – not exactly burnt, but very crusty. She turned the oven off and went to call them.

A wave of tiredness swept over her once they were served. There were a few minutes of silence as everyone concentrated on their food. The soufflé was hard on top and quite runny underneath, but they said it was delicious. The belt on her dress was too tight.

As if he had read her thoughts, the man turned to her with his glass raised. "Congratulations – Alan tells us you're expecting an addition to the tribe."

She laughed and nodded, embarrassed. Funny, she had forgotten about it all afternoon, even to putting this dress on. She remembered from last time how quickly it got too tight. Good God, how long have I had it? she asked herself. Did I really have it before I was expecting Annie?

156

Alan had noticed the change of dress and was irritated by it. The dress didn't suit her, it was too stiff and smart, it looked as if she was trying too hard. Her clothes never seemed to be quite right. And why had she changed just to please him, anyway? If she liked her skirt, why hadn't she stuck to it?

"Do you look forward to having a baby again?" asked the woman intently, "or do you prefer them when they're older? It's the one thing that puts me off breeding – I love children, but I can't stand babies."

Alan laughed. "They eat, they sleep, they shit, they cry. They wake you at three-hourly intervals all night long. What more can you ask for?"

The woman pulled a face. "Exactly."

"You're right," Carolyn said, "but – I know it's corny – but it is different when it's your own. It does the same tedious things that all the other babies do, but it manages to do them – uniquely–" She laughed with them, at herself. "Really. I never thought I would like babies till I had one. Now it makes me sad to think of them growing up." She hesitated a moment. Sarah and Mike were listening attentively. "They seem pathetic, when you compare them to adult humans, and expect them to do human things – because obviously they can't. They can't do anything much. But I remember with Chris especially – he didn't seem human–" she smiled quickly, forestalling Alan's amused interruption "–but like something from another planet. So you weren't aware of what he couldn't do, so much as what he could do and did do, and how little of it you could understand. Do you see what I mean? That a baby's behaviour and perception are completely other than ours, and that maybe we know less – understand less – than them."

She stopped uncertainly, flushing crimson. Alan felt a wine-tinged surge of affection for her. He was sorry that he had criticized her to himself, for hiding in the kitchen, for not being attractive. He felt as if he had only just remembered, after a long time, why he valued her.

When Mike and Sarah had gone, they flopped on the sofa. It was midnight.

"I haven't ironed your shirt for tomorrow."

"Never mind, I'll do it in the morning. Did you like them?"

Carolyn shrugged, then nodded.

"You didn't say much."

"Alan, I don't know half of what you're talking about – people at work and all that–"

"You could listen, then you'd know."

157

"But I've got other things to do, love, everything doesn't stop, just because your friends come round. The children still need looking after, the meals still have to be made—"

"You're turning into a mousy little housewife." He was half joking. There was a silence.

"Am I?"

"No. I didn't mean it. Only—"

"Yes?"

"Sometimes it seems as if you're only interested in the children."

She considered this seriously. "I am mainly interested in the children. At this stage. But isn't everyone mainly interested in something? Aren't you mainly interested in work? That was what you wanted to talk about."

"Not just work—politics, things that are happening in the world—" He felt the argument slipping away, was conscious of the contradictions in his own feelings. He wanted her to stay at home and look after the children as much as she did; he wanted her to be mainly interested in them. He wanted her to be a real mother, not like Lucy.

"Oh, I don't know." He stood up abruptly and pulled her to her feet. "Can I take your dress off?"

She laughed in his face. "Why take the dress off a middle-aged frump? What poor taste you have – your friends would be shocked."

It was all right. With a leap of joy he saw that she understood, could read his mind and arrive before him. Laughing, she fought him off till he'd got the dress off her by brute force, and wooed her consent with practised skill.

Afterwards they lay on the floor, his head resting on her stomach. She gazed at the ceiling, feeling her heartbeat and breathing slowing to normal, her body quietening. His eyes were closed, and she was surprised when he suddenly said, "Are you happy?"

She laughed and patted him on the head, but he sat up and frowned at her impatiently.

"I don't mean that, I know that."

"Modest."

He ignored her, pursuing his question. "In general, are you happy?"

"I think so." There was a silence. "Yes," she repeated. "Aren't you?"

He sighed. "I don't know. Let's go to bed." He got up and went to the bathroom before she had time to move.

In bed she was vaguely troubled by it, and examined her own answer. Yes. She remembered sitting on the garden step, early that morning, before her parents arrived. Alan was sitting down at the end of the lawn, his back to the house "so you don't distract me", finishing off some work for Monday. Chrissy, on the step beside her, was choosing which story she should read to him, and Annie was in the sandpit, trailing sand through her clenched fist into a yoghurt carton. Carolyn could hear the hissing of the sand as it fell on to the plastic and then, when it had covered the bottom of the carton, the way it fell almost silently, with a whisper of its former sound. She loved the way the children absorbed themselves in activities. They were, in the garden, the points of focus for her own attention; and the fact that they themselves were concentrating intensified her satisfaction.

Alan was concentrating too, his shoulders hunched, his head moving slightly as he read. She remembered looking down the sunny garden and feeling content. Her life was contained like an egg in its shell, within the oval garden; her son, her daughter, her husband. She did not fear that she would lose it, because it was the world – her world, the reality that encased her. She worried that Chris might fall and break his leg, that Annie might swallow a stone and have to go to hospital, that Alan might give himself an ulcer through working too hard. But for the framework, she no more feared nor doubted it than she did the position of the stars in the sky. Looking back on that moment now, she felt it tremble before her, round and perfect as an overfull drip, and she caught her breath at the thought of its transitoriness, its shimmering beauty, and suddenly whispered to herself, "I am happy," as if she feared it might not last forever.

Alan must be happy too. He must be. She would ask him what he had meant tomorrow.

When she fell asleep, she began to dream. She was driving along a motorway. It was a bright sunny day, and there was very little traffic. She drove in the middle lane, skimming past lorries. Her window was open and warm fresh air blew in her face and made her hair stream out behind. She felt light and free. She was happy, but she felt immediately that it was threatened. It was as if menacing music had been played in a film, accompanying a scene of innocent happiness. She wanted to warn herself, who was driving the car without a care in the world, but she couldn't get through. The sun went in, and gradually there were more cars on the road. They kept going just as fast – faster – but there were more and more of them. She was trapped in the middle lane, there was a solid wall of lorries to her left, and to her right a blur of fast cars. Ahead there was space, but her foot was pressed down to the floor and the car wouldn't go any faster. There was a lorry coming up behind her, a huge one, coming

159

fast. It filled up her mirror and made the car dark inside, it was bearing down on her. Closer and closer – it was touching her car, thundering in her ears . . .

There was a gap; blackness. She found that she was driving again. The lorry had gone, but she was tense and nervous. She could feel that the muscles in her stomach were clenched into a tight ball. She glanced down and saw to her horror that her stomach was growing. It was the shape of a football. She tried to concentrate on driving, she got the car into the slow lane and looked down at her stomach again. It was swelling like a balloon being blown up, expanding by the second. She knew she must get out of the car quickly, or it would get stuck behind the steering wheel. Already it was pressing against it, jamming the wheel, making it difficult to steer. She slowly forced the wheel to the left and the car moved on to the hard shoulder and stopped. She was squashed between the seat and the wheel, the seatbelt was cutting into her like a rubber band around a swelling finger. She struggled to free herself, and rolled out of the car and on to the ground. Her belly was growing huge, it overshadowed her. She was suffocating, it was squashing her, pinning her to the ground. She could hear cars and lorries swooshing past and tried desperately to call for help but she had no breath. The belly continued to grow, blocking out the light. She felt the skin on it stretched to bursting point, the pain was awful. She knew she would burst – she was going to burst.

She opened her eyes. It was dark. The belly was gone. She was all right, she was awake. Alan sighed and turned over, and she curled herself around his curved back, and waited for a more friendly sleep to claim her.

Part Three
Five years later

Chapter 15

Early in January Caro and Bryony drove to Heathrow to meet Clare, who was returning from a year in the States. It was a Friday and bitterly cold. The heating in Clare's car was not working; Caro sat in the passenger seat wrapped in a blanket, and Bryony drove in a Balaclava, enormous army surplus gloves and two coats.

Bryony had picked Caro up from work. It was dark, and had been since mid-afternoon.

"It'll snow." Caro peered up to the black sky.

"No. It's too cold."

"Did you check if the flight was on time?"

"Of course. God, I can hear your teeth chattering."

"It's that building. I hate it. They keep the temperature so high you can't adjust when you come out, and everyone gets ill. I'm going to start doing some outside work again next week, thank God."

"The new park?"

"No – oh no. Everything's seized up while the ground's frozen – there won't be much happening there till spring now. No, I'm going to fill in for Jim on the Canal project."

Bryony nodded.

"Did you have a nice day?"

"Mmm. I gave in my notice."

"Did you?"

"Yup."

There was a silence, broken at last by Caro.

"When did you decide?"

"Not until this morning. I was pretty sure I would, but I just needed something to give me an extra push."

"What did?"

"Well – when I was at the camp on Saturday night, we were talking about dreams." Bryony had spent the weekend at the Women's Peace Camp at Greenham Common. "It seemed as if quite a lot of people had had the same dream – or a similar one, at least – there were similar elements in all of them. About after the bomb had dropped – you know, people running about and screaming, great fires and heaps of rubble – looking frantically for children and friends – obvious things, really. I was thinking about it yesterday, I suppose – and then I had a dream last night. It's not – I don't know. I mean, I probably dreamt it because I'd been hearing all their dreams and thinking about them. I don't think it's some great subconscious warning or anything."

Caro nodded. "Was your dream the same?"

"No – no. It was like – almost as if I was trying to answer them, in my mind. I was sitting in a large cinema, with a lot of other people, and there was an American guy talking about the effects of nuclear war. He sounded terribly smarmy and reasuring – you know, a real politician's voice. Telling us all how we would have to adapt in various minor ways to changing circumstances, but that basically our lives would carry on very much as normal – and it was weird, I was wanting them all to believe him, and him to be telling the truth. I kept saying to them all in my mind, 'You see? It'll be all right. There's nothing to panic about. It's under control.' He said, naturally there would be some changes amongst plant and animal life, but species would adapt to suit the changes in climate and atmosphere and so on. The film was black at first then it turned a sort of brownish colour, getting lighter but still weird colours, browny yellow, till we could see it was water, a river or something, and its bank. And there were some birds swimming – floating down towards the camera, they were brown. They were ducks – ordinary mallard ducks. But they didn't have any heads."

After a silence Caro said, "Is that it?"

"Yes, I woke up."

"Headless ducks."

"Yup, maybe I was half awake. But it's a fairly strange thing to invent."

"Yes."

"So there we are. There I am."

"What d'you think will happen?"

"I don't know. Even if they evict us, or break up the camp – or deliver the fucking things – it'll go on. A group of women will go on protesting. That's why it's taken me so long, I think. Because I'll be doing it for the rest of my life now. I mean, it's not like waving a banner at a demo on Sunday afternoon and going back to work on Monday. It's the most important thing –that's what we're saying by being here. The most important thing is to stop them building, storing and using these weapons."

"Was it good at the weekend?"

Bryony laughed. "It was filthy. It was bloody freezing, with a wind like a knife. The sheeting – you know, the polythene – sounded like whips cracking when the wind got into it. It was bloody horrible. I'm going to get a thermal bodystocking before I go back."

"I'll buy you one. I'm glad you're going."

"Why?"

"Because – it's good. It's what you should do."

"You could come too."

"It's not – it's not my sort of thing. I've got my park to do, anyway."

"Your park won't be worth having when the bomb's dropped." Bryony spoke with the contemptuous sharpness which had so alienated Caro at the beginning. She recognized it now as a mark of Bryony's own conviction, rather than an attack upon herself. "You can buy me a bodystocking if you like," Bryony went on after a pause. "Considering your salary."

One of the customs officers decided to do a thorough job on Clare's luggage. She folded her arms and leant back against the rail, watching while he tipped out and examined the contents of her sponge bag, and spread her socks, knickers, T-shirts and jeans across the counter. Everything looked worn and grubby. She tried to remember if she had brought anything illegal. He picked garments up and turned them over with his fingertips, gingerly, as if they were disgusting. What an awful job. For a moment Clare felt like telling him not to bother, just chuck the whole lot away. They were old. She needed new ones.

Glancing up as someone walked out, she recognized Caro waiting out there. It gave her a jolt. She was really here then. Back in England. At last the officer finished. He confiscated two apples that she had in her handbag, and warned her about penalties for importing plant and vegetable matter. She stuffed everything back into her bags, and made for the door.

After the huggings and kisses they stood back.

"Are you all right?" Bryony asked. "You look like death."

"I'm tired. Incredibly tired. You, on the contrary, both look disgustingly healthy." They did. Bryony's cheeks were flushed and her eyes bright and excited. Caro's face was paler, but still fresh and absurdly youthful. Clare noticed that her hair had been cropped shorter than before, so that it was almost like fur on her head.

"And how's Sue?"

"All right," said Bryony shortly.

"I think she's working tonight," Caro explained. "We don't see much of her really. She spends a lot of time at Jack's now – most weekends. The kids are around more than she is."

Clare nodded. Sue had met Jack before Clare left England. He was large and boring. Clare wondered whether Sue would move out.

"Let's go then," said Caro and picked up the big carpet bag. She moved away in front of them. Her face hasn't changed since I met her, Clare thought, as she and Bryony followed. The only thing that's changed in ten years is the way she moves. Caro's stride was long and loose and graceful. Clare remembered how she had seemed at first to be constrained in all her movements – and jerky, almost as if her stammer manifested itself through her body as well. It might have been the accident. But no – she's more confident, that's all, Clare thought. She herself felt old and stiff and unspeakably weary.

Next morning Clare knocked at Caro's door at eight.

"What are you doing? I thought you would sleep for hours."

"I can't. It's lunch time in New York. Are you awake?"

"Well, I am now. Have you had breakfast and everything?"

"Yes. Can we go for a walk? Why don't you show me this wondrous park of yours?"

"It's not mine." Caro sat up in bed. "If it was mine it would be wondrous. As it is, it's a mess. Nothing's been planted yet, anyway. It's all bald."

"Never mind. The rest of the earth isn't exactly verdant at the moment, is it? I need some exercise." Clare stood in the doorway, as if unsure whether to come in or go out. "I'll make you a cup of tea then," she said, and went back downstairs.

It was difficult to talk. There was the solid wall of a year apart standing between them, with not a loose brick in sight. Clare had been an erratic correspondent, and several of Caro's neat, carefully written letters had been delivered to addresses Clare had moved on from. They had covered the easy areas of quick gossip last night, and now they both felt constrained. They walked down the street in silence, each sharply aware of the other's presence, of the cold, of the greyness of the street and the claustrophobically low cloud. As they turned the corner, the first flakes of snow fell. Clare pulled her fur coat more tightly around her (it came frum a jumble sale and lacked any conventional form of fastening) and complained.

"But you had something like two feet of snow in New York, you said!" laughed Caro.

"Their snow is warmer than ours."

"It's because you're tired. You should have stayed in bed."

Clare shook her head. "I'm full of cramp and junk food. I need to move around and get some fresh air inside me."

"Didn't you sleep at all?"

"No. Bryony's looking good."

"Yes, she is. I think she's much happier now."

"Like a nun who's had the call."

"What d'you mean?"

"She's found her mission in life."

"I – I suppose so. Isn't that good?" Caro was surprised by Clare's cynicism. There was no reply.

"Do you know where you are?" Caro asked suddenly.

"Of course I do. We've only been out five minutes." Clare looked up, and realized that the terraced rows either side of the road had disappeared. Ahead, through a high wire-mesh fence, the landscape looked blitzed.

"Sweet Jesus, it's the end of the world! It's so *near –*"

"Yes! Yes!" Caro started dancing on the spot beside her. "Come with me. The canal's over that-a-way, but if we head over towards the old brickworks –" She unlocked a huge padlock which fastened the gates.

"Has that gone too?" asked Clare.

"Yup. There's a bit of a hill so you'll get more of a view – "

"But there's *nothing*," Clare repeated in amazement, as she followed Caro over the raw uneven ground, and looked back at the truncated ends of the streets they were leaving behind them.

"It was all empty. Derelict. You know it was. I think they had a bit of juggling to do, moving people out of the odd house in rows they demolished, and into the empty spots in ones they're keeping – like filling decaying teeth – but most of it was just rotting where it stood. All the factories were derelict. Look, you can see St Thomas's over on the other side now – " They were climbing a fairly steep mound. Gradually the shape of the cleared area began to emerge distinctly.

"The park's at its widest point here," Caro said, stretching her arms to demonstrate. "But it follows the line of the canal right through, gradually getting narrower towards the east. To the west it gets narrow quickly, then there's a big bulge where the river runs in, at Tandown Primary School, then it ends fairly sharply."

"It looks huge," marvelled Clare, revolving slowly on the spot to take in the empty landscape.

"Twenty-eight hectares, not big really – except in so far as it's in a totally built-up area."

"And completely horrible," Clare continued. "It's like the Russian steppes. There's not a *single* tree. Anything less like a rural retreat – "

"Clare – use your imagination! This'll be wooded eventually. They'll grass it this September – and down there – " she pointed to a wide area of churned up ground, where frozen water stood in ruts " – the adventure playground, with swings and slide and all that stuff, but a nice climbing frame and fort too. Over there the leisure centre/sports fields thing. My poor little blind garden, what's left of it, just up over here, near the top gate – and – " she turned in the opposite direction " – down by the river, in the old primary school building, which is in fairly good nick, they're setting up a field study centre, and strips of land for school gardens. They've done the lake – you can see. We planted some trees along the canal in the autumn – as soon as it unfreezes we'll be putting more in, it'll be an avenue. . . ."

168

Clare was nodding and smiling in a half amused, half indulgent manner.

"I know why you do this now, Caro my sweet."

"Why?"

"It's like being God, isn't it? 'Lo, and let there be – water!'" Clare stretched out one regal hand across the whitening wasteland. "'Yea, and let there be also a shady spot, with trees; and let there be small yellow flowers, with crimson centres. Let there be grassy slopes with swings on, and litter bins clearly labelled.'"

Caro shrugged and ran down the hill. At the bottom she turned, her face serious. Clare walked down slowly to meet her.

"It is power – yes."

"You take it so seriously," laughed Clare.

"Yes, I do. Look Clare – look what was here; fil–filthy mean little houses not far enough apart for the wind to blow between them; derelict factories with slates slipping off them and armies of rats – not a blade of grass in sight. And people, leftover people like – like grubs that've been kept in the dark. Now there'll be grass and water and light. The kids from the houses up there–" she waved her arm in the direction of home – "will come and play on the grass – the old people from the council place will come pottering down and sit on the benches by the flowerbeds. Women will bring little kids to the adventure playground and talk to each other instead of screaming over the walls of their backyards – oh, piss off!"

Clare's smile was wide and ironical. She patted Caro on the shoulder. "You'll change the world, my love."

"Yes," said Caro. "I will. Starting with a blind garden and lots of trees in Millside."

"What will you do when kids root it all up and carve obscenities on the trees?"

Councillor Bellamy had asked the same question, Carolyn recalled. They had held a site meeting on Thursday and he had turned up instead of the committee chairman they were expecting. He was the new leader of the Council. He was a broad-chested, powerfully built man, with manners like a bulldozer.

"What happens when kids start breaking in here, eh? What's your security like?"

169

"It – it's not a prison," she replied.

"I'll tell you something, young lady, and I'll tell you straight. If it'd been down to me, this park would never've been sited here. It's a mess – the whole area's a mess. You mark my words – within twelve months of it opening, it'll be a wreck."

"Why?"

He shook his head irritably, as if she was stupid.

"Wrong area for a park. Waste of money, here. They won't appreciate it. A prison'd be more useful, if you want my opinion."

Ron had winked at her and steered Bellamy away, down towards the foundations of the leisure centre.

The answers Caro wished she had given him were still boiling and bubbling inside her.

"P–plant again. When they see the trees come back – and come back again – they'll stop eventually. They haven't lived near anything worth preserving before." She turned round slowly on the spot, critically examining the contours of the park's three little hills (like molehills, Clare told herself) against the grey sky.

"It's not wonderful – I know that – there's hundreds of things wrong. I would have done it differently – OK, you know about the blind garden. But the point is, at least it's here – it's a start. No matter how badly designed it is, it's a thousand times better than what was here before. And I've salvaged some of the blind garden, and I've got the tree planting. And next time I'll have more – and more – till I finally *do* have the power to do something big, make something big."

They walked on across the cleared area in silence. Snow was settling thickly on the raw earth, now, and on the blacker areas which had already been topsoiled. When they reached the canal Caro turned right to walk along it. On the opposite side the canal's former contents, removed by dredger, made a barricade of frozen mud and rubbish six feet high. Bicycle frames, pram wheels, parts of cars, and nameless slimy objects protruded from the frozen mud like the jumbled contents of a newly excavated grave. Clare stopped and folded her arms, facing it.

"Caro, this is wonderful. This makes me glad I flew three thousand miles to see it. Millside's answer to Guggenheim. All the galleries of New York do not contain its equal–"

170

Caro linked her elbow through Clare's arm and turned her homewards.

"Shut up. Tell me what you've been doing, while I've been moving mountains."

"Oh – exercising my cynicism on the American Women's Movement; falling hopelessly in love; visiting my mother; failing to see my son. That sort of thing."

The summary did not invite closer questioning. Caro nodded, consciously slowing herself down to Clare's pace. Clare was more brittle and self-contained than Caro could remember ever having seen her. They walked on home in silence.

Chapter 16

Alan's unhappiness was erratic and Carolyn never really discovered what it was about. She thought that he probably didn't know himself. He was simply moody, he went up and down more than she did. Over time, as that characterization formulated itself and stuck, Carolyn no longer wondered why. It was something to accept about Alan, like his height, his untidiness, his charm. He was moody.

It was irritating – sometimes infuriating. There were rows. Once when she had invited various friends (including two of Alan's people from work) to Sunday dinner, he announced in the morning that he couldn't stand it, and went off for a walk. He rang her at ten-thirty p.m., from a pub twelve miles away, asking for a lift home. Patsy from next door had to come in to babysit. Carolyn had coped with cooking and hostessing and children, and covered for Alan with hints of illness among relatives. She was exhausted, angry and suspicious. Alan, when she found him, was exceedingly drunk. His tale that he had been in the pub since it opened was clearly true.

Gradually she learned not to ask questions about these episodes, because it enraged him and made him turn his venom and misery against her. If she left him to himself he seemed to come round more quickly. She could not stand it when he was angry, and went to great lengths to avoid confrontations. Several times, she had been frightened that he would break something, or hurt somebody. Worse than that, she was frightened in a way she never spelt out to herself: for what might happen, in such a complete loss of control; for what irrevocable thing might be said, for what destruction of things more precious than merely physical might be unleashed.

Music was the clearest signal of his moods. Carolyn hardly ever used the stereo. It was Alan's, as was the growing collection of classical records and tapes. At the beginning he had never listened to music, but since

Cathy's birth he had started buying it. When he was depressed he shut himself in the study and played the same things over and over again, until Carolyn was filled with the kind of anxiety that made her say "Yes" to the children without knowing what they'd asked. Brahms, Symphony No. 2, Bach, Cello Suite No. 2 in D minor. She hated the sound of them. And she knew he knew she didn't understand them. It gave her the same unease she felt on the rare occasions when they visited Lucy and Trevor. But he had played the violin; his mother was a musician, she reminded herself. When he suggested buying a piano for the children, she was relieved. If the children could do it, they would bring it within her world.

It was a long time before she realized how much he was drinking. The Sunday dinner episode seemed a lone instance, and excusable (if it was at all excusable) in that he had been twelve miles from home; a pub was the obvious place to spend the evening. They kept assorted alcohol in the house, and Carolyn replenished stocks whenever guests were coming, but it did not disappear with undue speed. Carolyn knew of course that Alan's job was not the nine-to-five sort. Obviously he spent a lot of evenings (most) working late, and sometimes went for a quick drink before coming home. But he never appeared drunk. Often she was glad he had been for a drink, because then he was more talkative and cheerful, and they were more likely to sit and have a pleasant half-hour over a nip of whisky or a mug of Horlicks, and go to bed and make love. And she was usually relieved when he was late home because she seemed to have things to do, things that just couldn't be fitted into a day of getting breakfast, cleaning up, walking Chris and Annie to school, dawdling for half an hour before taking Cathy to Nursery, rushing home to use the precious hour and a half of Cathy's absence to shop or clean or (delicious luxury) have a cup of coffee and a child-free talk with Patsy next door, collecting Cathy, collecting the others, giving them dinner, walking the older two back to school, preparing the evening meal, doing the washing, playing with Cathy, collecting the children from school again . . . and so on. Often there was ironing, or letting hems up or down, or messy things like making jam or decorating, to be done in the evenings when the children were in bed. If Alan had to work late it seemed fair enough for her to do the same. If he was home she felt that she should sit and relax with him, and he was restless and impatient – or else he watched television in a moronic stupor which she thought excluded her, but then asked in hurt tones why she wasn't sitting with him, when she left the room to get something useful done.

173

Even after that weekend which she saw in retrospect as a milestone, and came to regard (when she knew the end) as the beginning of the end – even after that weekend, she did not think of him as an alcoholic, but rather as someone who was dangerously susceptible to alcohol. An alcoholic, she thought, woke up and reached for the sherry, and kept bottles hidden behind books on the shelves. Alan was simply moody, and liable to drink when he was down. She needed to keep a closer eye on him at such times – as she did with the children when they had colds (which made them more susceptible to nasty ear infections).

That weekend gave her a taste of a fear which she had not experienced before; a metallic, lingering taste which it was impossible to wash from the mouth. He had been moody for some time, and busy every single evening. Then he said he would have to work all the coming weekend, to finish some drawings. Carolyn decided to take the children to visit her parents, because it was something that Alan hated doing anyway. It was easier to go into the city and out again by train, than to drive on her own with all three children. They caught an early train on Saturday morning, and returned at four-thirty on Sunday.

Alan was not at the station to meet them, as he had promised to be. After waiting half an hour, with Cathy refusing to be carried and continually trying to run in front of the taxis, and Chris and Annie repeatedly shouting "He's coming now" when he wasn't, Carolyn telephoned the house. There was no reply. She took a taxi home. The curtains were drawn, although it was not dark. She was scared, and made the children wait in the car while she went and unlocked the house. Alan was asleep on the sofa. There were a lot of bottles on and under the coffee table. There were dozens of beer cans, and he had finished all the alcohol in the house, except for a half-bottle of liqueur. She shepherded the children into the kitchen and gave them their tea. She looked in on him once, but their noise was not having any effect on him. There was vomit in the sink.

"What's wrong with Daddy?"

"He's not very well. He's been working hard, he needs a rest." She was as calm as a sleepwalker. Had he been alone, or had someone else been here? She had to force herself to look in the bedroom, but the bed was neatly made as she had left it. She put the children to bed with automatic calm, and sat hugging her knees on the landing until she was sure they were all asleep.

He was snoring loudly, his mouth open. The room stank of alcohol.

"Alan. ALAN!" She shrank from touching him. There was a bluish stubble on his chin, his posture reminded her of old men on park benches.

174

But she had to shake him to make him wake up. He sat up with a jerk, and stared at her for seconds before he showed any recognition.

"Carolyn –? Lyn! What are you doing – how did you –?"

"I got a taxi."

"Are the kids – ?"

"In bed."

"God – I should've – I'm sorry – I should've met you –"

"What have you done?" she asked quietly, her control wavering.

He stood up unsteadily and waved at the room around him.

"Mike came round and we had a few jars. . . . God . . . I feel as if I've been blackjacked."

"Last night?"

"Mmmm."

"Have you done your drawings?"

"No. Bloody hell, no. What time is it?"

"Quarter-past eight."

"Shit. Let me get some coffee."

She followed him into the kitchen. "Alan?"

"What?"

"Why – why did you drink so much?"

He looked at her and frowned.

"Why not? Mike brought some beer in – we got talking. Why not? I like Mike, he's very funny."

"How did he get home?"

Alan laughed. "He had to get Sarah to come and collect him. She was furious. Absolutely livid!"

He turned his attention to the coffee.

Carolyn watched him trying to get the spoonful of granules out of the coffee jar. It kept knocking against the sides of the jar, and the granules fell back off the spoon. "What time was that?"

"Christ knows." *He turned angrily, and threw down the spoon, spilling coffee over the work surface. She wished she had taken the spoon from him and made him the coffee. But that would have angered him too.* "What is this – an inquisition? Do I have to ask your permission to have a few drinks with a mate, in my own house on a Saturday night?"

She went quietly upstairs, to digest the fact that he did not think he had done anything monstrous or strange.

Carolyn was pleased when Alan got a new job, with the Metropolitan Council that covered the depressed area of town to the east of the city –

Millside. The money was significantly better, and it also removed him from the company of Mike, his most constant drinking companion. She hoped that it might revive some of his idealism and enthusiasm. He was utterly contemptuous of Lark and Clarkson, and often bitter about the way one of the partners would always step in, if he got something interesting to do.

"No matter how long I stay there I'll never be more than office junior — until one of the bastards dies."

When he was a student, Carolyn remembered, he had imagined designing houses and schools, buildings for ordinary people. From time to time he had taken her round newly built council estates and pointed out to her with indignation how shoddy they were, how poorly designed. Perhaps, she thought, he will be happier now he is working on more worthwhile things. When he was happy, they were both happy. There were still enough good days and nights for Carolyn to remain certain that it was the world outside which depressed Alan, and that if all other pressures were removed, they would be perfectly happy together — the children, Alan and herself.

Three months in the new job were enough to convince Alan that it was no better than private practice. Work was done more slowly; procedures were more bureaucratic — and the whole thing, frankly, was more boring. At least at Lark and Clarkson there had been some days that buzzed, when the phone rang all day, when he had meetings with clients, planners, the district surveyor, deadlines crowding in on him. Here he was on the same tedious project all day long. And there were always, always, wrangles over money. It became, if anything, more depressing than his former job — at least there had been a few clients who were interested in a classy finished product rather than the cheapest version possible.

Socially, the Architects' Department was a dismal place. He accompanied them dutifully to the pub at lunch time, and regularly consumed steak sandwich, chips, and two pints of bitter — but he found their company stolid and boring. And the building he had to work in was hateful: a sixties-inspired civic centre, eighteen storeys high and shedding a shower of facing bricks every time the wind blew. They had never had the scaffolding down from it since it was completed. Inside it was cheaply futuristic, with inadequate sound-proofing, hideous pegboard ceilings, and open-plan offices littered with little barricades of filing cabinets, boxes, and plants, behind which people screened themselves in a primitive attempt to gain working privacy. He found it grimly amusing to regard the civic centre as the fruit of centuries of

176

architectural learning and experience – combining as it did an unsafe exterior with maximum interior ugliness and discomfort to users. Those on the higher floors with insufficient kudos to obtain more than one filing cabinet as shelter became neurotically insecure, and the absentee rate on the top floor was a standing joke. The panoramic views of the town (it hardly deserved the name of town any more; it had had an identity a hundred years ago maybe, but now was simply absorbed into the uglier side of the city's sprawl) were appalling. There were vacant vandalized industrial sites interspersed with mean little terraces and the scars left by demolition; flattened blighted acres of car park. On the skyline to the east, like a half-forgotten dream, the outline of the hills. To the west, the assorted and affluent skyscrapers of the city centre gleamed smugly. Millside's ugly civic centre stood forlornly single, pinned to the sky with its scaffolding, in deformed imitation of its city centre cousins. Looking down from its windows Alan felt that its growth from the squalid devastated land around it was as fitting as a blackhead on dirty skin.

The floor containing self-service cafeteria and bar had never been opened, due to problems which had arisen in the construction of the kitchens. It was only by chance that Alan discovered the temporary canteen for council employees. No one from Architects' ever descended to lunch there. It was a ramshackle wooden annexe, tacked on to the side of an old primary school which was now being used as a records store. It was a five-minute walk from the office, along dark terraced streets. Alan went in out of curiosity, and found himself enjoying the school-dinners atmosphere and the cheery buxom ladies who waved ladles and offered "A touch of carrots, love? A nice bit of stew?" and seemed to have running jokes going with (or know the favourite dinners of) everyone in the queue. It was good to feel wooden boards under the feet, and a cold draught down your neck.

He sat alone at first, sizing up the people around him. The square tables dotted round the room seated four, and most people came in with others whom they seemed to know. He sorted them into three categories: the longest serving council employees, who had got into the habit of eating here in their youth and never got out of it; the lower salaried ranks (you could get a three-course meal for under a pound); and those who ate here for convenience or from principles. Convenience because it was quick, principles because it wasn't exclusive. There was a serious dearth of attractive young women, most of whom (he supposed) were on diets and didn't bother with lunch, and of people (young men he meant) in his kind of position. Presumably they were all busy licking superiors' arses and

177

chewing leathery steak sandwiches in pubs. He enjoyed the half-hour or so that he spent there, anonymously eavesdropping and fantasizing, outside the earnest claustrophobia of Architects'. Soon the dinner ladies hailed him as a regular, and didn't need to be told that he liked custard on apple but not on cherry pie. Alan had been, since his youth, a favourite with cleaners and dinner ladies, upon whom he exercised an almost nauseating degree of charm.

When he had become familiar with the regulars at the tables, and concocted backgrounds and occupations for most, a youngish and not unattractive woman started to frequent the canteen. She was often ridiculously dressed, with muddy wellingtons and baggy waterproof boilersuit, and several shapeless jumpers underneath. He watched with interest as she peeled them off. She was transparently thin. Her mouse-blonde hair was cut too short, in one of those butch feminist cuts. Alan took the trouble to imagine her with long silky strands framing her face and brushing her shoulders.

She attracted attention (not his alone) because there were so few women worth looking at in the place. Also, she always stripped off (though she didn't put all the layers on again at the end, he noticed). And then she ate a remarkable quantity: soup and roll, meat and three veg, and apple pie and custard, at speed and without embarrassment. She usually sat alone. There was a washed-out looking woman in her forties (a terribly dependable personal secretary, Alan had decided) who came in a couple of times a week, and the girl sat with her on those days.

Gradually Alan got to know some people from other departments, and found himself on nodding terms with a few of the canteen regulars. There was an overfriendly man called Robinson, a planner, who started to eat there because, as he told Alan repeatedly, the old ulcer was playing him up. He was regretful about his inability to go to the pub and not drink; "I miss the company – but Christ, I couldn't do it – any more than I could disappoint a lady, eh, eh?" He had an embarrassingly loud voice. He took to sitting at Alan's table and complaining loudly about the food and the lack of personable women, and describing the reactions and dimensions of his ulcer. He was such obnoxious company that he drove Alan to lunching at erratic times, in attempts to avoid him. When Alan came in one day, he saw that Robinson was already there – not sitting predatorily alone, but astonishingly accompanied by the boilersuit blonde. Alan sat himself at a distance, where he could watch them and eat in peace. They were arguing. He had not known that Robinson knew her. He noticed that the woman was unusually smart in a silky

178

white blouse and green waistcoat. He wondered again what she did. She was giving Robinson a rough time.

As Alan went across to get some coffee Robinson bellowed at him – "Two more, you anti-social bugger!"

Alan filled two extra cups and took the tray over to join them.

"I thought you were having a private conversation."

"No no," said Robinson hastily – "just work – it's all work here, eh?"

The girl stirred her coffee and ignored him. Alan sat down and Robinson introduced them hurriedly. It was obvious that Alan had been summoned because Robinson was losing the argument. The girl's name was Caro something, and she was in Landscape Design.

"Ah!" Alan smiled his direct and charming smile at her. "That explains it."

She looked up at him coldly. "What?"

"The clothes – the Worzel Gummidge outfit. I thought you must be in Parks and Gardens, but then you looked too elegant today."

She looked at him steadily for a moment, then flushed bright red.

"Wouldn't you think – wouldn't you think I was rather rude, if I suddenly started comm–commenting on your appearance?"

Robinson began to laugh.

"I didn't mean to be rude –" said Alan.

"Yes you did," she said quietly and fiercely. "You wouldn't dream of speaking like that to a man, patronizing him about his appearance."

"Have to watch your step here, old boy," said Robinson joyfully. "You're speaking to one of the original bra-burners. She won't stand for any of your male chauvinist piggery. Isn't that what it's called?" He appealed to Caro. She looked at him with such contempt that Alan felt almost sorry for the man. But he was irritated by the way she classed him with Robinson.

"I wasn't patronizing you, as a matter of fact," he persisted. "I've spent a large number of lunch hours working out the occupations of the people in this room, on the evidence of their clothing. Men and women."

She looked at him and raised her eyebrows briefly, in acceptance of the statement. Then she turned to Robinson. "You will be there tomorrow, then ? Do you want me to call for you? At nine-thirty?"

"No, no," muttered Robinson like a naughty schoolboy who's been caught out. "I'll be there."

"Good. Bring some boots. It's very muddy." She nodded briefly at both of them, picked up her tray and left. Alan noticed that she had thin, rather fragile-looking legs, and was wearing cream-coloured stockings.

179

She moved well, with a long flowing stride.

"You may look," murmured Robinson insinuatingly, "but that's as close as you'll get. She's a les – lives with a load of other women." He sat back in his chair, expansive and relieved now she had gone. "Not my type anyway. Too skinny – not enough on top, eh, eh?"

Alan avoided replying by swallowing his coffee very slowly. Robinson was a nauseating jerk. He was embarrassed that Robinson had noticed him looking at her legs. He made his voice matey and conspiratorial.

"Well what are you up to then, young Robinson, meeting a man-hater at nine-thirty for a muddy tryst?"

Robinson humphed. "I wish she'd get off my back. It's the new park site – she's got some beef about the contractors not finishing off the earth moving properly. Well they've started some demolition work for us, over that side – and now she's going overboard about the thaw and her bloody planting season. I've got to be dragged along to look at some mess they've left, so she can persuade me to send them back. What she needs is a good fuck, in my opinion; that'd give her something else to think about. Bah."

They stood up.

"Why d'you call her a les?" Alan asked casually.

"You are interested aren't you!" Robinson nudged him so that his cup slid off the saucer and spilt coffee dregs over the tray and his jacket.

"Sorry old man. Keep your pecker up, eh, eh!" Robinson departed. Alan told himself that the coffee dregs were divine retribution for the complicity in which he placed himself with Robinson.

A few days later, she was sitting alone at a table near the till, surrounded by her heaps of discarded clothing.

"May I?" He sat opposite her on impulse. She looked up, nodded, and continued to eat.

"You must work out on site a lot," he said, indicating the clothes.

She swallowed her mouthful.

"A–At the moment – I'm doing someone else's job really." She took another mouthful and he waited then saw that she needed prompting.

"What's that?"

"Oh – we got one of these Manpower Services schemes through, to do canal reclamation – so we appointed a Project Officer to look after them. It's a shame, he's been ill on and off since the thing started, and he's a nice bloke –" She took another mouthful.

Alan wondered if she was in a hurry, or just very hungry. He noticed that although she wasn't wearing any make-up the skin around her eyes was dark and purplish, and that her eyelids were full, almost puffy. She looked as if she might have been crying. "So what have you done?"

"Well, we haven't replaced him. They look after themselves pretty well, but I do about three mornings a week with them at the moment."

"On canal reclamation, you said?"

She nodded.

"Where are you working?"

"We're on the stretch between Gorst's Mill and Bailey Hill Railway Station. D'you know where that is?"

Alan nodded. It was close by. "Isn't there going to be a new park round that area?" he asked. "Robinson was saying something about it."

"Yes."

There was a silence.

"D'you only come in here when you've been working outside, then?" asked Alan, realizing that he had only seen her the once in office clothing.

"Usually. It makes me hungry. I don't get hungry in the office." She finished her potatoes and turned immediately to the apple pie and custard. The conversation was beginning to feel like an inquisition. Alan concentrated on his food, and there was another silence. At last she said, "Are you new in Architects'?" and they talked briefly about Lark and Clarkson, and the frustrations of working for the Council. She excused herself as soon as she had finished her food. After she had returned her tray she came back to pick up her boilersuit and jumpers, and smiled at Alan as she left.

Alan didn't have lunch in the canteen for a week or so after that. He had various lunch-time meetings, and spent quite a bit of time on site at a partially built clinic where unforeseen drainage problems were developing. It was a messy job – he had been given it half done and each time one problem was solved another seemed to arise. On the one day when he was heading for the canteen he recognized Robinson entering the building, so he turned back around the corner and went to a pub instead.

He had to call in at an estate management office near Bailey Hill Railway Station, at the end of the week, and found himself leaving there at eleven forty-five. It was a stupid time – too early to go for lunch, but not a long enough stretch to do anything useful in the office. The sun was shining weakly, for the first time that year, it seemed. On the spur of the moment he cut across the railway car park, over the footbridge, crossing both railway and canal, and down on to the canal towpath. He started to

181

walk in the direction of Gorst's Mill. The surface of the canal was clean and silky smooth; the bordering flagstones had been uncovered and a red ash path laid beside them. Small straight saplings had been planted in the mound of raw mud that ran parallel with, and to the right of, the path. He ran up the mound to look over the landscape on the other side. It was behind a tall wire-mesh fence. There was an expanse of featureless muddy ground, running away to a bare hill, some distance to his left. Much nearer, the ground was staked out, and some digging had been done, on what was obviously intended to be the foundations of a fairly large building. Behind the digging rose another naked hill, lopsided in shape. It all looked rather arbitrary and silly. There was a group of people up ahead, clustered around a lock beyond a bend in the canal. He ran down and walked on quickly, slowing as he came within sight of the lock. The narrow space to the right of the path opened out into a sloping area where two stark new picnic tables stood. There were several people standing around the tables, and another group, who were laughing and shouting, on the bridge over the disused lock. The lock had been blocked up. Water cascaded in a steep waterfall from the higher level to the lower, under the near side of the bridge. Three large steps had been built to break the force of the falling water, and low iron railings ran across the edge of the lowest step. The railings were clogged with plastic bags, bits of wood, a tyre, clumps of weed; a mass of rubbish which blocked the whole lower step. Alan saw that Caro was in the centre of the group on the bridge. She said something and there was a burst of laughter. She was holding up a coil of heavy rope and demonstrating something – then she began to wind the rope around the waist of a tall boy, amidst cheers and wolf-whistles. Alan watched her fasten the rope and hand the coil to two others. The boy started to climb down the side of the waterfall steps. She spoke to them again, then ran down over the bridge towards the picnic tables. Alan moved forward quickly.

"Hello."

"Hel–hello, what are you doing here?"

"Just taking a quick breather. I was at the station, so I thought I'd come and see what you were up to."

"Oh." She nodded. "Well – this is it–" She glanced up to the picnic tables. It was obvious that they were waiting for some sort of instructions from her.

One of the lads on the hill wolf-whistled, and a girl shouted, "That your boyfriend, Caro?"

She laughed and turned away from him. "No Kerry – he's all yours, if you fancy him." Under the burst of laughter that came from the kids she turned back to Alan, her face flushed red. "I – I'm sorry," she said, laughing herself. "It's awfully hard not to sink to their level."

"That's all right," said Alan, feeling irrationally pleased. "The same sort of thing happens to me in the company of fat pig Robinson."

She glanced at him with a fleetingly serious expression, then laughed. The kids were calling to her from the lock.

"I must go – look at Kevin! He's showing them his mountain-climbing skills, would you believe – he'll break his silly neck." The tall boy was leaning out at right angles to the stone wall. She moved quickly. "I'll explain the park to you sometime. Have you had a look? Over there–" She waved an arm and ran up to the lock again.

Alan headed back for the station. He found himself in a good mood for the rest of the day.

She joined him at his lunch table a couple of days later, and asked him what he thought of the park.

"Well – it's a very nice field of mud. It hasn't got pretensions to being anything else yet, has it?"

She laughed, tilting her head back quickly as if to duck out of his teasing. Eating and talking with astonishing speed, she began to describe the features of the park, as if they were plain for anyone to see. Her enthusiasm struck Alan as almost eccentric; he poked fun at her for a while, then found himself being drawn into the sort of serious discussion which he had not experienced since he was a student. They were conscious of the canteen emptying around them, but even when they returned their trays and hurried to the doors, it was impossible to stop talking. Afterwards it seemed to Alan that the conversation had been stopped in mid-sentence, literally torn apart, as they had separated at the outer doors, each to go in their own direction.

He thought about her as he drove home that night. She was too serious. Too serious for what? he asked himself. The question made him squirm.

Alan had indulged in several brief sexual adventures since his marriage, but they had all been of the sort Robinson would approve –physical and functional. He did not describe them to himself as infidelities, because they were both different from and irrelevant to his relationship with Carolyn. Naturally he hid them from Carolyn, out of good taste, and because he knew that she would have been upset to a disproportion-

183

ate degree. She would have assumed all sorts of depths and threats which simply did not exist.

He found himself becoming angry as he drove home, angrier and angrier as if he were being squeezed by an invisible fist. When he reached the end of the road he drove past it, went round the next roundabout and took the road for the city. He drove to Lark and Clarkson's. As he had expected, Mike's car was still there. Alan parked beside it, to wait for Mike to come out. He considered telephoning Lyn to tell her he would be late. Better to do it from the pub in an hour or so. It would seem less premeditated. If he rang now he would save her the trouble of preparing an unnecessary meal, but he knew she would be less offended if he rang later, made it sound casual and impetuous. ("Carolyn love, I'm terribly sorry – bumped into Mike out of the blue – went for a drink, you know what it's like – never realized the time. I might as well make a night of it now. Don't worry about food – I'll get some fish and chips on the way.") If he rang now she would say, "Oh, well, I'll have tea with the children then," with that reproachful edge to her voice; "Will you be late?" Knowing, of course he would be late, if he was drinking with Mike. Suggesting that his choice to go drinking with Mike, rather than coming home to her, was a form of treachery. She would forgive him for being forgetful, scatter-brained, not knowing the time – childish faults – but not the adult fault of preferring anyone else's company, however briefly, to hers.

It wasn't that he didn't love her. Often he enjoyed her company, her cooking, her body. It was the way she seemed to be constantly hovering, slightly reproachful, around the perimeters of his days, as if to say, are there any crumbs of time for me? At weekends she offered him the children, as if they were sweets in a box. "Why don't you take Chrissy fishing for the day? He'd love it Alan, he really would. It's ages since you spent any time with him on his own." There was a reproach in the very request. He hated the way she engineered his meetings with his own children. And he sensed that the children agreed to them only because of her insistence. They would all be much happier spending the day together without him, he was sure. Mike suddenly ran down the steps two at a time like a kid escaping from school, and Alan leant on the horn.

He didn't go to the canteen for lunch for a while after that, consciously depriving himself of a chance of meeting Caro, but also holding it in reserve, as something which he could continue to look forward to as long as he didn't let it happen. Then he met her leaving the building one afternoon.

184

"Hello!" she said. "Have you been ill? I haven't seen you for ages."

"No, just busy."

She nodded and they stood awkwardly silent for a moment.

"Well, I'd better go –" she said. Her eyelids, he noticed again, were full, as if they were swollen. Her grey eyes were very clear and open. She was wearing red dungarees.

"Wait – are you busy? Care for a drink before you go home?"

She shook her head. "It would be nice but I've got a meeting at six, I'm sorry –"

"What sort of a meeting?"

"Women's Aid Support Group."

"What's that?"

"For a Refuge. For battered women."

"Oh. Well – I'll see you."

"We could have a drink on Friday after work, if you're free," she offered.

"I'll see," he said ungraciously. "I'll let you know."

It was not what he intended, to arrange a meeting.

But on Friday morning he enquired the way to her office and, finding it empty, left a note on the desk. "Rose & Kettle, 5.30? Alan."

She was sitting there when he arrived, with a pint of beer on the table before her. He apologized and made a crack about women usually being late.

"Rubbish."

"They are. Most women are habitually late."

She shook her head.

"Well all the women I've met are. My mother's always hours late for everything." He was conscious of not mentioning his wife and wondered whether he would.

"Well it's probably because she's got too much to do and doesn't get enough help from her family. Or because she's ner–nervous and insecure, and afraid of having to sit alone or sustain a conversation alone."

"How can you sustain a conversation alone? You mean, like you were doing till I arrived?"

She pulled a face and made the now familiar gesture of shaking her head back, out of his mockery. He told himself that he didn't like her shapeless hairy jumper. But when she picked up her drink her wrist sliding out the wide sleeve looked so slender and fragile that, ridiculous impulse, he wanted to clasp his fingers round it and help her raise the glass.

"Why are you so skinny?"

185

She shrugged. "Why not? Why do you make so many offensive personal comments about me?"

"You can't accuse me of being sexist, anyway; if I was sexist I would try to flatter you. Why do you have your hair cut so short?"

"I like it like this," she said simply, "Why do you wear yours short?"

Gradually the tension between them eased, and the conversation began to spark and flow of its own accord (oiled, perhaps, by beer). He was suddenly curious about everything about her, her house, friends, family, past. He had never met anyone who seemed so singular. When she had described her household she asked him, "Do you live alone?"

There was a fractional silence.

"No. I live with my wife and three children." He watched her face carefully.

"Oh. I didn't know you were married." She said it simply, without any emotion. He could not tell if she was hiding a reaction, or if she simply had none. "How old are your children?"

They started to talk about children. Perhaps it wouldn't matter to her that he was married. Perhaps nothing would happen anyway. Perhaps she hadn't imagined anything would. Perhaps Robinson had been right about her. Alan suddenly felt that he didn't know the rules. He could not predict what was going to happen. He found himself talking about the children in ridiculous detail. She listened with her head bent, the warm furry top of her head tilted towards him. They had had quite a few drinks. Suddenly she looked at her watch.

"God, I've got to go – I said I'd be in for supper."

"Can I give you a lift?"

"Well I'm on my bike."

"I can give your bike a lift too, if you like."

"I – OK – if it fits."

Outside suddenly it was cold and dark and very quiet, and the conversation they had been cocooned in fell away, leaving them naked. Caro ran across the street to the car park, and unlocked her bike from the attendant's hut. The car park was empty.

"It makes it seem ridiculously late, doesn't it?" she said nervously into the silence.

"It's only half-past eight."

There was another cold silence as they manoeuvred the bike to rest in the boot, unlocked the car and got in. He started the engine.

"Which way?"

Caro described the route then sat back in the seat, hugging her jacket round her.

They were each disappointed – almost angry, with the other. They drove to the Red House without speaking again. Alan got out and helped her unload her bike, and she said, "Thanks for the lift."

He nodded curtly, then drove away without smiling.

Caro parked her bike in the hall and leaned against the wall for a minute, before going into the kitchen.

Chapter 17

Clare was in the kitchen, washing up.

"Hello. We'd given you up."

"Is there anything to eat?"

"Of course. Isn't there always, in this haven of domesticity? Sit down."

Caro sat at the table and Clare removed a heaped plate from the oven and placed it in front of her.

"Oh God."

"Well that's nice. Here I am, slaving over a hot stove to provide you with nourishing victuals two hours late, and all you can say is—"

"All right, all right. I'm deeply grateful, Clare. But it is yesterday's cauliflower cheese, warmed up, isn't it?"

"Well, yes. I put some more cheese in it."

"Oh good. Wonderful."

"You're drunk."

"How can you tell?" Caro began to eat, pulling a face as she did so.

"It makes you more caustic."

"Like you, you mean."

"Possibly." Clare emptied the bowl and sat down, drying her hands.

"Well?"

"Well what?"

"Tell me all."

"Nothing to tell. I went for a drink after work."

"With?"

"With a man. An architect. He gave me a lift home."

"You could have invited him in for some warmed-up

188

cauliflower cheese."

"He's got dinner, a wife and three children waiting for him at home."

"Ah."

Caro filled her mouth with cauliflower and chewed stolidly while Clare watched her.

"D'you like him?"

There was a pause.

"Yes." She put down her fork and pushed the plate away. "I don't know. It's stupid. I've met him quite a few times – you know, at work. I didn't – I didn't think – "

"What?"

"I didn't think he would turn up for a drink tonight. And I wanted him to."

"Does he live with his wife?"

"Most married men do, don't they?"

"All right, stupid. I was just hoping it wouldn't be as gruesome as that."

"It won't be. I mean, he told me he was married. He wasn't hiding it. We spent ages talking about his kids. It's not – I'm not – it won't get beyond the odd drink after work."

"How d'you know?"

"Because it won't. How can it?"

"Easily."

"Look Clare – "

"Look yourself, Caro. D'you realize this is a record. This is the first time you have *ever* admitted that you fancy someone?"

"I don't fancy him. And what about Martin, anyway?"

"You didn't fancy him, you felt sorry for him. D'you feel sorry for this one?"

"No."

"All right then."

Caro fetched a packet of biscuits from the cupboard and opened them.

"Is Sue working?"

"Yes. Robin and Sylvie are in."

"They're quiet."

"They're watching telly."

After a pause Caro spoke slowly. "I do like him. It's – it's a strange thing. He's very critical. I mean, he argues with

189

everything I think. But it's as if – it's not an argument exactly, it's more as if he wants to test – I'm not sure, himself or me. He pretends to be – you know, charming, cynical – but there's a – a crack in his shell – not his shell but his manner; underneath he's open-minded, really open to everything – as if he still doesn't know what the world's like."

Clare groaned. "You want to mother him."

"No."

"Well you've just described a child, if he doesn't know what the world's like."

"No – I haven't. You're not listening. It's – it's different because – because he is, he has got that manner – style, whatever you call it, he's developed it and that lets him – be more – I can't explain. . . . It's like a mask. You can be something different behind it, something more real. Instead of if your real face is the one you always have to have on show."

Clare looked as if she was going to reply, for a minute, then she shrugged and ran her fingers through her hair. When she spoke it was with heavy irony.

"So you'll help him to come out, as they say. Out from behind the mask."

Caro's face flushed angry red.

"Why do you – why pretend you want to talk?"

Clare bowed her head till her forehead was resting on the table top. She heard Caro's chair scrape as she stood up.

"If you want to know what I'm going to do, I'll tell you. I'll have infrequent conversations with him over lunch in the canteen, and that's all."

"And be miserable."

"I don't know. I hope not." She went out of the kitchen, closing the door sharply behind her.

Clare sat still with her forehead resting on the table. Caro would be miserable anyway, that was obvious. Either they would have an affair and Caro would be racked with misery and guilt because of the wretched man's family, or they wouldn't, and she would decide he was the love of her life and never see through him.

"You're a ridiculous fucking romantic," she muttered to the floor.

Caro wasn't a romantic, Clare told herself later that night, sitting in her room pretending to read. She still didn't know what Caro was. She was clear, like water. Transparent but unpredictable. Her character isn't – like anything, Clare thought. Some people do wear their characters like make-up; yes, all right, like a mask, telling you exactly how they expect you to react to them. They're full of definites: "I always . . . I never. . . ." There was an actress Clare had seen on a school outing, years ago – at elementary school. After the show the children were allowed to ask the actress questions. Somebody asked her how old she was. The woman's brilliant smile was still vivid in Clare's memory, along with her special-confidential-actress-voice answer: "One thing you'll learn as you grow up, is that we never, *never* ask a lady her age. Now would you like to ask a different question, dear?"

Clare had thought, it will be like that when you grow up. You'll know. She had admired the actress passionately. The memory still niggled her, as did a dozen similar phrases dropped into her consciousness like small pebbles into shoes, since then. Caro was not like that.

Caro was like water, like the taste of water. They had actually been lovers for a very short time only. Clare was aware from the beginning that Caro was still, finally, self-contained. They were close, they could be happy together, but even at the most intimate moments, Caro retained a reserve. It might be (Clare sometimes thought it was) a final, last-ditch unconquerable anxiety about making love with another woman. Or it might just be that she was not in love with Clare. She hadn't seemed to be in love with anyone else either – but maybe now, she was. Who could tell? Clare had been in love with other people. She had been in love with Stephen, in the States. She was sick of being in love. It was always a mess. She would reorganize her life, live celibately, and get the Mad Bitches on their feet again. That was what she had to do. Pity she couldn't raise any enthusiasm, though.

Since she had come back from America Clare had felt old; weighed down by the past, by too many ideas and enthusiasms and loves. It had all coagulated into a great stony mass that she had to drag around with her, wearing herself out. It had all gone wrong. Look at Juan, and the baby; could she really disclaim responsibility? Yes, at the time when it had happened; it may

191

have been a mistake on her part, but it was also a textbook example of women's oppression. It had made her one with a movement. Juan was not an isolated freak; hundreds of thousands of anti-establishment, lefty men who had seemed to accept women as equals and understand the causes of their anger, had turned out like him. Who's going to cook the tea? Who's going to hold the baby? How can I pursue a brilliant and demanding political career which is going to lead to a revolution and the granting of all your feminist demands, if I've got to stay home and wash the fucking nappies? Until, sixteen months after the baby was born, Clare had lifted her head from the sink one morning and understood clearly that both of them had good degrees in political science, and that he spent his days lecturing and his evenings discussing revolution in intellectually stimulating company, while she spent her days feeding and pulling faces at a baby, shopping, cleaning and washing up, and her evenings sitting alone in the house waiting for the kid to cry. And that this caused him to be admired for his ceaseless, selfless work, while her identity was solely defined by his possession of her ("Juan's wife").

It had felt like a victory when she left him: a liberation. The Women's Movement had become the mainspring of Clare's life. They would change the world. The tide had swept through the consciousness of America. Suddenly everyone was talking about women: their employment, their pay, their sexuality, their education, their health, their politics, their feelings. Women were talking to each other – meeting in C.R. groups, identifying their common bonds and desires, writing and reading books and magazines about the movement. The sense of a movement which could reach out and touch the life of every woman in the world had infused all her work; it had been there at the beginning of the Refuge, when they had planned it and set it up, and even in the first year or two of its running. Clare didn't know when it had slipped away. She had pulled out of the Refuge when it was well established at last, independent with its grant assured. It was a success, and the fact that it could function without her was proof of that.

But then she had had time to look around, and take stock of where the movement was going. Where it was going . . . ? Where it had gone. It had shrivelled – dissipated its sweeping force into a handful of loony sidestreams. Suddenly, she was a political dinosaur. The women she had loved and worked with were scattered to the four winds: living on pot and brown rice in self-sufficient Welsh communes (she supposed that Wales was wet enough to grow brown rice, but the climate was hardly ideal for marijuana); or converted to bizarre Eastern religions; turned into successful media-persons who, like *Animal Farm*'s pigs, were suddenly no different at all from the media-men (apart from their mandatory media-woman good looks); or married and terribly busy with children, their CND/Labour Party/SDP membership cards languishing in the depths of their large, safety-pin-filled handbags. These women met her with a gentle incredulity, half superior, half envious: "Are you still keeping up with all that, Clare? I don't know how you find the time."

And those few she could find who still regarded the Women's Movement as the central issue were like a concentrate, a bitter distillation of what had been before. Many of them hated men, even rejecting their own boy-children. Clare was depressed to hopelessness by it, chilled to the marrow. Hadn't the Women's Movement been about changing ordinary women's lives? Ordinary women lived with men, had sex with them, gave birth to sons. The separatists had no more connection with them than Martians. She had not left Juan to be part of a movement that rejected all men. She had thought she was helping to lay the foundations for a new way of living with them.

It was over, it had been thrown away. While she was still angry and disbelieving, Clare had joined Women-in-the-Moon, a feminist theatre group. The group had spent a year tearing itself apart over ideology and material. At last she and two others had left to form the Mad Bitches. The Mad Bitches were not ideologically sound. They were bitter and funny. They could actually play working men's clubs and not get booed off the stage. They did their opening number, "Mad Maggie Blues", in fishnet bodystockings. Bryony had walked out of their first show, and refused to see any others.

Bryony.

Clare appreciated Greenham. It seemed to her the only positive fruit this new, embittered, man-hating movement had borne. It was a symbol the media – and thus the world – could neither distort nor ignore; women united in their stand against the ultimate male obscenity. She appreciated the hardships the peace women suffered: the cold, the mud, the hostility, the occasional corroding sense of futility. She appreciated their courage, their organization, and their imagination. It would have been a relief to be able to join them. But it was no good, she couldn't. She had had a long and terrible argument with Bryony – really it was over the exclusion of men, but somehow it spread to other aspects of Greenham.

"I don't like the things they do!" she had shouted in exasperation.

"What things?" Bryony wanted to know.

"The way they tie things to trees and fences. Photos of their children on the fence, tied up with ribbon. I can't take that sort of crap."

"Why's it crap?"

"I don't know. It's maudlin. It's – it's fey."

"It'll be fucking maudlin when all the kids are dead of radiation, won't it!" shouted Bryony.

"Bryony – I can't. All this mystical stuff – weaving symbolic webs of wool – I'm sorry, I just can't relate to it. I think it's silly."

"So do men," Bryony pointed out. There was no more to be said.

Bryony hadn't argued with Caro. She hadn't expected her to go. Yet she had seen Clare's refusal as a betrayal, and been bitterly upset by it. Caro, Clare reflected, had never aligned herself with anything. She was always on the edge. They had come to accept the fact that she remained a permanent outsider. Often in the past Clare had been enraged by it; called it weakness and cowardice, that Caro would not stand up to be counted or campaign for her beliefs. But her refusal to join groups or attend meetings was absolute. For a long time Clare had thought the whole business of Caro pottering about in the garden, and then pruning bushes in the park, was some kind of evasion; at last she had come to realize that that was what Caro did. That was how she had found her voice. Not that Caro ever described it in those terms. It is only me, Clare thought, who needs to talk about changing the world. Everyone else gets on with living. Why can't I just be one of the Mad Bitches, and do what I do, and be happy? On an impulse, she went to Caro's room, and seeing no light under the door, opened it softly. But Caro was asleep; the sound of her regular breathing was like a whisper in the air. Clare looked at her watch and went downstairs. Sue would be back at half-past twelve; her shift had started at four. Sue had no ridiculous pretensions about changing the world. They would have sardines on toast and a mug of cocoa together. Consolation, Clare told herself grimly. Don't women always console themselves with food?

Chapter 18

Alan and Caro's relationship developed in a stubborn, contorted fashion, sprouting up like a weed in a different place each time it was prevented. Each made a private decision not to seek the other out, and to let the thing die a natural death. Each (at separate times) took positive steps to avoid meeting, by going out rather than to lunch at the canteen. They both persisted in the pretence that all their meetings were accidental – though having coincided by chance at lunch time, they did occasionally arrange to meet for an after-work drink. It was impossible to stop talking: about work, politics, their pasts, friends, houses, holidays, art, books, ideas, fashions, music – everything (except Alan's wife and children).

The park was occupying a lot of Caro's energy and attention. When she described it to Alan, it seemed to him that she was talking about something much more precious than a patch of green for kids to run around in. He was half amused by her fanatical enthusiasm – and slightly shamed by it, because it was a feeling he could not and did not match, in his own work. He caught himself thinking of her as almost childish, at times, for being so single-minded and certain about anything. Her view seemed to him to be naïve, unworldly. He recognized how much easier life would be if he could feel contempt for her at any level. But contempt was impossible to sustain.

She took him to the park site one evening after work. They left at five-thirty on the dot but it was an overcast evening, and by the time they had walked halfway round the area the dusk was thick blue. She described what the area had been like before, and Alan listened in silence, caught up by her intensity, but also slightly embarrassed by it. He was glad of the dark. The park was near her

196

home, a run-down, beaten-up part of town that Alan had never known well. Here, she told him, there had been a football pitch, with troughs of mud and mangy tufts of grass. On sunny days, bits of broken glass sparkled in the mud, and a crowd of close-cropped lads lounged around the goalposts smoking, and chasing away the little kids who came to play. On that side were the ruins of two derelict mills, too far gone for restoration. Over on the other side there was a disused primary school they would keep, it was being converted to a field study centre for local schools. Alan wondered who the conversion had gone to; he found himself thinking that it would be much more interesting than the health clinic lined up for him. Beyond the mills, she continued, were the rows of terraces – mean little houses, with low ceilings and dark cramped rooms, two up two down, with a squalor of makeshift extensions in the tiny backyards; kitchen lean-tos with leaking corrugated iron roofs, or soggy bathrooms running with condensation and blocking all light from the downstairs back rooms. Many of them had stood boarded up for years, waiting for the condition and value of the neighbouring houses to deteriorate sufficiently for their inhabitants to agree to be rehoused. They came to the edge of the river, sleek and black in the dark, its clean surface catching and reflecting glints of distant streetlights. It looked curiously naked, in its banks of empty mud. It used to stink, she told him – flowing like thick soup through the entrails of cars, old prams and bicycles, with a scum of chemical filth and small dead animals. Two little boys had drowned there one summer a few years back, although it was no more than two feet deep. They were probably poisoned by it before they drowned.

They walked on over the uneven muddy ground in silence. Now they had moved away from the river bank Alan was completely disorientated. There were no landmarks in the dark, apart from the streetlights at the edges of the park, which were not always visible because the park seemed to be full of uphills and downhills.

"Are you trying to make a mountain range?" he joked.

"No – just to fit an awful lot into a small space."

The area seemed huge to him. "Who will use it, anyway, now everyone who used to live here has been rehoused and demolished?"

She laughed. "It's the same all around. This bit was no different to what's left on all sides, except that there was no functioning industry left. It'll be used. The primary school on Lawrence Street over there has got seven hundred and fifty kids for a start. They sent the two hundred who were left at Tandown Primary, the field study place, over there, but they didn't get any more space to put them in. They've got an asphalt yard the size of three tennis courts, and wire netting to peer through. You wouldn't keep seven hundred and fifty monkeys in such conditions."

Her incisive accuracy on such matters always gave him a jolt. She knew the area inside and out; she knew the numbers of preschool children who would waddle down to throw crusts at the ducks and fight for the swings, and armed with the figures for the old-age-pensioner population she had waged a private battle for a walled blind garden to be constructed at one end. It would be filled with sweet-scented plants in waist-high beds, with bench seating around them, she said. The suggestion had been clipped and pinched for financial reasons. She explained to him how she and Ron, her section head, had modified the drawings. Her knowledge was too precise to allow his irony scope. He found himself envying her her commitment, that her work was a living thing – almost like a child, he imagined. This area was like a wounded child that she cradled in her brain, imagining and exulting over its development. Her enthusiasm made her magnetic.

When they got back to the road he asked her if she wanted a drink, but she said no. She was going to see a friend.

"Who?"

"You don't know her. A girl called Vicky."

"Well can't you see her later?"

"No. I said I'd be there for seven."

"Oh."

There was a silence.

"Who is she?" he asked, searching for some way round the problem.

"I was at college with her. She's got a stall on the market – she – "

"Caro?"

"Yes?"

"Why don't we go out properly one night? I mean, for the evening – for a meal?"

They were standing beside Alan's car. Caro turned away from him, towards the dark shop window flanking the pavement. It was a butcher's. She studied the empty white trays and plastic tomatoes carefully.

"Is it a good idea?"

"No, it's a terrible idea. I think we'd both be bored stiff. That's why I suggested it."

She was quiet again, then she said slowly, "Not – not in the evening. Why don't we go out in the day – on Saturday or something?"

"What's the difference?" He knew there was one, that she was trying to force something on him.

"I'd prefer it."

"Why?"

"Because –" She hesitated. "Because there are assumptions about how you behave and what happens when you go out for the evening which – which there aren't in the day."

He laughed. "I asked you out for a meal, not an orgy."

"OK." To his surprise, she suddenly laughed. "I wouldn't like anything to happen that you hadn't intended. Better make it lunch. Where shall we meet?"

"I – I'll pick you up. You're a manipulative baggage."

"No I'm not. You were trying to be. I'll see you at twelve." She crossed the road quickly and disappeared in search of her bicycle. Driving home, he found himself still slightly shocked by the way the conversation had gone, the change in direction which he had not reckoned with.

When Alan knocked at the door of the Red House the following morning, Caro answered it and came out immediately, slamming the door behind her. It was a warm morning, but the sky was solid with curdled white cloud, creating an unpleasantly bright glare. She glanced up, shielding her eyes.

"I don't need a mac, do I?"

"No – no, there will be brilliant sunshine this afternoon."

"Really," she said ironically, and smiled.

They got into the car and Alan dangled the keys in his fingers. "Well?"

"Well what?"

She was wearing strange trousers, he thought. They were dark green with a thin gold stripe running through them, and they seemed enormously baggy. As she stretched out her legs in the car he noticed that the full material was gathered into a tight cuff just above each ankle. It made her ankles seem thinner and more fragile than ever. "Why do you wear such silly shoes?"

"Well, why do you wear such silly shoes? Is that the question? Because they're comfortable and I like them." She was wearing flat black pumps. "Why do you think they're silly?"

"They look like a three-year-old's; my daughter wears shoes like that for PE."

"And what d'you think I should wear?"

"Oh – some nice strappy sandals, something like that. Something grown-up."

"You really have the most incredible cheek. Shall I tell you what you look like?"

"Oh please – yes."

She gave a little snort and looked away from him, out of the window. "Most women's shoes are both uncomfortable and physically harmful."

"Ah, but we all know you have to suffer to look beautiful."

She glanced at him and saw that he was smiling. "Oh, piss off."

"Like taking sweets off a baby, isn't it?"

"You haven't seen my feet anyway."

"No. You always keep them in three-year-old's shoes."

She braced her heels against the car floor and slid her feet out of the pumps. There were three toes missing off the right foot, and a shiny mauve scar.

"Oh God – I'm sorry Caro–"

"It's all right," she said, turning the foot and examining it. "It's just not beautiful – although it has suffered, I must say. It's the one that got run over. I don't mind it any more. But it sometimes gives people a funny turn, so I keep it in a shoe rather than on general display." She put her shoes back on.

Alan leaned back in his seat. "Good. Right. Now you've made me feel like a worm, where are we going?"

"If you didn't mind a bit of a drive – we could go out to Gratton Hall. There's a pub there, and they do food."

"Where is it?"

"It's a stately home and garden – out towards the airport. You must have seen it. . . . To be honest, I'd like a look at their gardens. It's somewhere I've always thought I'd go to on a free day, you know, and there never are any."

He started the engine. "And you thought I'd come in handy as chauffeur and porter."

She glanced at him then leaned back in her seat. "That's right."

"You never know when I'm joking, do you?"

"I never know when you're serious, you mean."

The Hall was surrounded by a rolling park with scattered clumps of trees and sheep, like a toy landscape made big. There was no one in sight, although the car park, when they reached it, was half full.

"Where are they all?"

"In the Hall looking at stately treasures? I don't know."

It would be easy enough, Alan reflected, to find a private place in a park that size. Somewhere among the trees and bushes and tall grass. . . . He had told Carolyn he was going out for lunch with a crowd from work. That gave him licence to return early or late. But what was going to happen? He could not imagine at all how the afternoon would develop, and the lack of knowledge manifested itself physically as a hollow in his belly, as if he were about to do or not do something irrevocable – crouching in an aeroplane gazing down through the open hatch at the distant countryside below, and waiting to see if he was capable or not of jumping. Caro seemed very self-contained. When they got out the car she walked over to a map of the grounds that was displayed on the wall, and studied it. He leaned against the car, watching her and waiting. She looked striking, he thought, with her baggy trousers, red shirt, and boyish hair. He liked the way she was standing, with her hands deep in her pockets and her head back looking at the map, and then the way she came walking back, smiling. She looks as if she doesn't care who sees her, he thought. He had noticed that other people stared at her, men especially.

"Why are you smiling?" she wanted to know.

"I was wondering if people stare at you because you're a weirdo or because you're phenomenally attractive."

201

She pulled a face. "Come on." She led the way across the car park.

"You don't like compliments, do you?"

"I – I don't know. I suppose I do. But they embarrass me. There are compliments and compliments, anyway, aren't there?"

"Meaning?"

"Well, when you sit back like that and stare at me as if I was – oh – an exotic animal of some kind, a sex object, rather than a person – it's offensive." She hesitated. "But – "

"But?"

"But then I quite like it if you like to look at me. Which is contradictory, isn't it?"

"You are a sex object to me. I fancy you something rotten."

She laughed.

"Bad, isn't it?" he continued. "I find the trouble with sex is that it's dreadfully sexist. You know, things like the male finding the female body attractive."

"Well if you *only* fancy me – "

"Of course I only fancy you. Can't you tell I'm after your body? Why else would I invite you out for – " he dropped his voice to an outraged whisper " – a meal? Certainly not to have you preach feminism at me."

"Oh, I'm a pale version of a feminist. You should meet Clare."

"I'd rather not."

They stopped at a kiosk and Caro paid for the tickets to go into the gardens. She bought a leaflet and stood just inside the gate reading it, while Alan stared at the rows of ugly houseplants for sale on a display stand. His head was full of banter and quick replies, like flies buzzing around foolishly above the surface of deep water; "What next? and what next? and what next?" – and underneath it a calm deep stillness, like a paralysis, a spot where your life stands still for a moment before it moves on or changes course, beyond the realms of your control, and the buzzing surface flies.

Caro finished her leaflet and began to walk around the side of the building. He caught up with her, and she started to explain the layout of the garden to him. Her words drifted past him lightly. When she stopped there was a silence. They had come out on to a wide lawn, which led down to a view of tree tops. Two giant cedars stood on the lawn, their greenness almost black against the white sky. They both stopped. Alan touched her arm. "Hold hands?"

She nodded without looking at him, and he clasped his hand lightly around her arm then slid it down so that their palms met, and stuck together.

"Your hand is very hot."

"Yes. And yours."

They spoke without looking at each other, standing rigidly still with clasped hands, staring down at the view. At last he said, "Are we going to move?" and in moving it was possible to turn and embrace almost naturally, folding their arms around each other. They separated awkwardly and began to walk towards a pathway that led to the right, between trees, to another lawn.

"Look," she said, pointing to the high wall that ran along to their right.

He looked. It was a red brick wall.

"Yes?"

"It – It's got fireplaces in it – at the end of each section. Those urns on top are chimney pots. To keep the frost off the fruit trees – the gardeners used to cultivate apricots."

"Oh." He didn't know what she was talking about. She had brought them here. She must know what would happen. They walked in silence past the flowerbeds; the flowers were white, then red, then yellow, all of one colour together.

"You're very quiet," she said after a while.

"I'm all right."

"Do you mind if I look at the flowerbeds?"

"I – no. No. I'm going to sit here and look at the view."

"OK."

He sat on the bench by the gravel path and watched her walk quickly along to the end of the beds. She stopped by the last one, bending over and examining the flowers. Then she crouched down, raising the head of a full heavy bloom with her fingers, and inspecting it. The image of her filled his whole head. A blurred crouching figure, with hand outstretched and head down-tilted, absorbed. Like Carolyn with one of the children, he realized. Like Carolyn. In a vision of devastating clarity (hallucination? what was it, that stayed so doggedly vivid through all the flickering joy and anger and despair and drunkenness that followed) he saw that they were the same; Caro and Carolyn. What you see with the right eye when the left is shut, and what you see with the left eye when the right is shut, come together with a jump when you open both eyes: twenty twenty vision. And so (delusion, that he could never be undeluded from, although his rational brain dismissed it on the instant as a dodge to escape guilt) he could not hurt Carolyn. Because in loving Caro he loved her too, the love did not harm her, could not give her cause for jealousy. They were the same.

When she stood up and moved on to the next bed he stood too, to shake himself free of the idiotic thought. He felt suddenly clear and incisive. It would be all right. They would make love. There was no point in worrying any more about what might happen. He walked quickly towards her.

"Well, are they up to standard?"

She smiled and came towards him. "They're beautiful. But look at all those dead heads over there – they should be taken off."

Alan linked his arm through hers. "Come away before you start on them. I came for a romantic interlude, not *Gardener's World*."

"You should choose your company more carefully then," she laughed.

They walked over the grass towards a great yew hedge. A huge bird had been clipped out of the yew, as if it were perched on the bush. Alan thought of the privet hen. It was all right. They went through an archway and into a walled, paved garden. It was full of bright flowers, he noticed, and there was a little summer-house opposite a shallow green pool with tinkling fountain. There was nobody there.

"Shall we sit in the summer-house for a while? It's almost hot here – feel how this stone holds the heat." He held his hand low over the path as if he were warming it at a fire, and looked up at Caro. "What's the matter?"

"It's horrible! I don't want to sit here." She walked quickly around the garden, up the steps on the other side, and out. He followed her.

"It's meant to be a rose garden."

"So?"

"A walled rose garden – a little trap for heat and scent and bees. And what have they planted it with?"

204

Her indignation made him want to laugh. "I don't know. Something pink."

"Begonias! Bloody pot-grown plastic-faced begonias."

"Well it's nice and bright."

"Yes, lovely. I wonder why they don't fill the pool with blue plastic chips and paint the walls Day-Glo orange."

"You're a snob. People enjoy it. It's colourful."

She pulled a face. "They're just lazy. They don't deserve to have a garden like that here, if they can't be bothered to plant it."

In order not to laugh at her absurdity, Alan began to hum quietly. When he'd hummed the tune once, he sang the words.

> "I beg your pardon,
> I never promised you a rose garden.
> Along with the sunshine,
> There's got to be a little begonia sometimes –"

"That's a stupid song," she snapped. Then she began to laugh.

"It's not stupid," he assured her. "Far from it. It has some of the most deeply moving and meaningful lyrics ever written." He placed his hand on his heart and took a deep breath.

> "I can promise you things like big diamond rings
> But you don't find roses growing on stalks of clover,
> So you better think it over.
> When it's sweet talking you could make it come true
> I would give you the world right now on a silver platter
> But what would it matter –
> So smile for a while and let's be jolly
> Love shouldn't be so melancholy. . . ."

"Are those really the words?"

He nodded.

"'You don't find roses growing on stalks of clover'?"

"'So you better think it over–'"

They laughed until Caro could hardly breathe, and had to stop to wipe her eyes.

Heading back for a drink, Alan asked her, "Do you do this often?"

"What?"

"Take strange men to stately homes?"

"No, never."

"Make dates with strange men."

"Well, not with strange ones."

"You're being deliberately obtuse. I want to know about your love life."

"I've never been married."

There was a long silence.

"Are we going to talk about it?" she said.

Suddenly he was furious with her. Was this what she had planned? Did she want to talk about Carolyn, and find out "what was wrong"? Was that what she thought would happen today?

He began to walk more quickly, and she lagged behind. When he got to the big courtyard where the pub was she was out of sight. He drank a pint at the bar, and took two pints outside again. She was sitting at an empty table. He went and sat opposite her.

"Thank you."

They drank in silence.

"Why are you so angry?"

He shrugged. "My wife isn't anything to do with you."

"No. I know."

"It's none of your business."

"Good. I don't want it to be."

She looked at him directly, and he felt so angry and frustrated that he wanted to throw the beer in her face.

"Alan – stop it. I wanted to know – how we stood. I don't want it to be a mess. Now it's clear. All right?"

"What's clear?"

"What our relationship might be. I'm not into wrecking marriages."

He downed his beer and went quickly to get another. When he came back she pushed some coins over the table.

"It was my turn. You were too quick for me." He pushed the coins back angrily, and they fell on to the gravel.

They drove back in a silence more oppressive and explosive than any of those they had come home in in the evenings. When he stopped she turned to him. Her face was flame-red.

"You have a – a filthy temper. Do you ever listen – listen to what p–people say to you?"

He turned away from her and stared directly ahead, over the wheel. She got out quickly and slammed the door.

206

Both Caro and Alan spent the following week in extremely bad tempers. Alan hardly spoke to anyone at all, working grimly through his lunch hours, snapping viciously at Carolyn and the children at home, and watching TV every evening in an irritable trance. On Friday night he went out with Mike and slept on Mike's floor because he was too drunk to get home. On Sunday he and Carolyn took the children to a wildlife park in order to have a pleasant family afternoon. But he was irritated by Carolyn's continuous attempts to please and placate him. Her humility grated on him. She asked him on Sunday evening what was wrong.

"Can't I be depressed without you being offended by it? It's nothing to do with you, surely I'm entitled to my own private moods. You don't own my moods, do you?"

Caro also worked hard all week, but she spent a fair amount of time in the evenings alone in her room, staring out of the window. He was an impossible, bad-tempered, egocentric man. It enraged her that she had butterflies in her stomach when she went to work, and after avoiding the canteen every day for four days she was compelled to go there, and to sit alone with a book (in order to look unconcerned) making her lunch last an unprecedented thirty-five minutes.

When she arrived at work the following Monday morning, he was parked next to the car-park attendant's hut, where she usually left her bike. He leaned out of the window. "Morning."

She dismounted and wheeled her bike over to the car. "You're up early."

He nodded once, and grinned. They both started to laugh. When they had stopped they stood and stared at each other in silence for a minute, then started to laugh again.

"Why's it funny?" gasped Caro.

Alan shook his head. "See you in the Rose and Kettle at five-thirty?"

"Six."

"OK. Till then." He raised his hand in a salute, and accelerated away to park his car nearer to the gate.

By eight o'clock that evening they were both quite drunk, not so much with alcohol as with each other, and relief that the past week had changed nothing. At the end of the silent ride home, Caro said, "Why don't you come in?"

"Into the house?"

"Yes."

"What for?"

"We – we could go to bed together."

Alan hesitated fractionally before saying, "All right."

He followed her into the house but dawdled in the hall as she started to go upstairs.

"May I use the phone?"

"My room's at the top, just keep going till there aren't any more stairs." She disappeared from view.

Carefully, he dialled his own number. It rang nine times before she answered it. "Carolyn? It's me. I'm sorry, were you in the bathroom?"

"Yes; they're in the bath. It's all right, Chrissy's there. Where are you?"

"I'm – I'm at Mike's. We're just going out for a meal. He's – a bit – upset, he's just had a bust up with Sarah. OK? Expect me when you see me."

"All right. Alan?"

"Yes?"

"Don't drive home if – if you've – "

"No. I won't be drinking much, don't worry. I'll see you later on."

He was astonished at how easy it was. He believed the story himself. Poor old Mike. He moved to the bottom of the stairs, then turned quickly back to the phone and dialled Mike's number. But there was no reply.

He ran up the stairs two at a time. The door to her room was open. It was a big shadowy room, there was no light but a small lamp on a box by the bed. She was lighting a candle that stood on a piece of furniture against the wall. He closed the door quietly. She looked up but he could not see her expression. "Well, here we are."

He walked over to the window and looked out; beneath the black sky there were houselights and streetlights. "Don't you ever draw the curtains?"

"No, not often. I like to look out, at night. No one can see in, we're too high up."

The dark room was large and mysterious, all its detail was hidden. He felt very exposed. There was only one chair. He

208

leaned against the wall by the window, hands in his pockets. She came over to him and put her arms around his waist. He felt frighteningly sober. She raised her face and kissed him.

"What's the matter?"

He laughed uneasily. "Nothing. I didn't think – "

Leaning her weight against him she swayed from side to side. "Don't think, kiss me."

They kissed again, and gradually, and then very quickly, it began to seem all right.

Afterwards they lay hugging each other on the floor in silence for a time that neither of them knew the length of. At last Caro said, "Can we lie in the bed? I've been imagining you in my bed. . . ."

In bed they made love again, slowly, with an intensity that each found almost frightening. When they had lain still for a while Caro touched Alan's face with her fingers. It was wet.

"Are you all right?"

His whisper was so low she could hardly catch it. "I don't know. I'm – hold me."

She hugged him, then sat up in a businesslike way and reached for her watch. "It's after midnight. You'd better go."

Obediently he got up and stumbled round the room picking up his clothes. When he was dressed he was able to think more clearly. He walked back over to the bed. "I can't – I can't go home like this. I'll – I've got to have a bath – I – "

"Where are you supposed to be?"

"At Mike's. I sometimes stay there. She won't worry."

"Do you want to phone?"

"No. Better not. I'll go back in the morning before I go to work."

He undressed quickly and got back into bed. He was wrung out like a rag but it was impossible not to touch and stroke her marvellously unfamiliar, private body.

"Are you going to tell her?"

"No."

Her question focused his attention. "Why did you – why last Saturday, wouldn't you – "

"I think you misunderstood me. I just – I wasn't saying let's not sleep together. I don't think we could not, anyway. I mean, we were making it worse by not doing. I just wanted us both to know

209

that you were happily married, and I was a bit on the side, before we started."

"I – do we both know that?"

"Yes."

"All right. It doesn't matter. Anything you say. Are you cold? Can I peel back the cover? I want to look at you."

He dragged himself from the bed at six in the morning and scrubbed himself vigorously in the bath. It seemed impossible to him that the vapours of sweat and lust and all the secret smells of both their bodies could be removed so perfunctorily; he felt they must follow him, blazing, like the trail of a comet, and that Carolyn would only have to look at him to know where he'd been.

He let himself into the house silently and crept up to the bedroom. She was asleep. He went down and made them both cups of tea, then took them upstairs. When she woke up she smiled luxuriously.

"How lovely. I didn't think you'd be back at all."

"I wanted to come back," he said. "We didn't have that much to drink actually, but Mike really needed to talk to someone. And then when he finally keeled over I couldn't sleep at all – so – here I am. Shall I make a cooked breakfast? You stay here. I'll bring you breakfast in bed."

"Oh, lovely."

He kissed her lightly. It was like a dream, it was so easy. He wouldn't hurt her, he would never hurt her. She would never know about this, and she would never be hurt by it.

Chapter 19

Carolyn was brought near to despair by weeks of Alan's evil and erratic moods. None of his "down" phases had ever lasted so long before. His temper was a factor which had to be added to the planning of every activity and speech, constraining and exhausting her. He always came home at unpredictable times, and there were rows if everyone had eaten without him, or if the children had been kept up late waiting for him. So she started giving the children their tea early regularly, and waiting herself to eat with him. She explained it carefully to him in terms of their being able to have a sane adult meal together when the children were in bed. She did it to save the children from his displays of rage. Its main result was that she herself no longer ate a regular evening meal, but picked at small amounts with the children, had a biscuit to stave off her appetite when he wasn't home by eight, and was beyond hunger by the time he finally rolled up. She lived through weekends on her nerve ends, juggling the needs and whims of the children with Alan's, desperately trying to keep the household on an even keel. If Alan went out drinking, or to Mike's (the two were synonymous) she had failed. But it was getting to the point where the failures were a relief.

Then suddenly, when she was ready to scream with frustration, he changed. Suddenly there were cups of tea in bed in the morning, and little presents: a bottle of wine, a bunch of roses. It was the first time he had ever given her flowers. He had always claimed that he hated cut flowers in the house, because of Lucy and her endless flowers. Carolyn didn't remind him, but took the roses gratefully as a symbol of renewed and kinder love. He paid more attention to her when they made love; they even made love in the morning one day, giggling and locking the door against the children.

As their relationship entered what could almost be described (Carolyn thought to herself) as a second honeymoon, the rest of her life became calmer and more spacious. Suddenly, everything seemed to be going well. Chris and Annie were both enjoying school and at the tops of their classes, and Annie was also displaying signs of unusual musical talent. Lucy had undertaken to pay for piano lessons, and Carolyn was doubly pleased for Alan's sake, both that his mother had finally shown interest in one of her grandchildren, and also that the talent he had felt a failure for lacking had passed through him, like a river flowing underground, to surface again in his daughter. Chris's room was a cross between a zoo and a natural science museum. On the window-sill a wormery and cageful of stick insects with an alarming propensity for losing odd legs, vied for space, now it was spring, with endless jars of frog spawn. Geological specimens and rare fossils hidden in lumps of rock (many of them hidden from all eyes but their proud owner's) cluttered every other surface, interspersed with carefully labelled envelopes containing small dead insects. He was pestering for a microscope. Carolyn intended him to have one for his birthday.

At tea times the children's conversation was more entertaining than that of any adults she met – and more particularly enjoyable for being hers alone. While they ate their tea they told her about everything from black holes to Mozart's childhood to the life cycle of the praying mantis and what they had for school dinner. Even Cathy, who had been the spoiled baby (she was so alarmingly beautiful) for far too long, was growing up now she went to nursery every day. The fact that they were all out for at least part of every day lent relish to their tea times together; and so did the unspoken intimacy created by Alan's exclusion. Although he was no longer bad-tempered, Carolyn did not consider shifting back to the old system of a family evening meal. It was impractical anyway; he was late more often than ever.

Now there was space, and calm, Carolyn found herself thinking about another baby. What would she do when Cathy went to school as well? The house would be empty. It would do Cathy the world of good not to be pretty baby any more. The gaps between the others had been too close; it would be marvellous to have a baby she could spend time on. And Alan would be pleased. He always adored them when they were babies, and it was fitting that a new baby should spring out of this new happy phase in their relationship. Carolyn did not articulate to herself, as a reason for getting pregnant again, the fact that on those rare but increasingly frequent occasions when she had to walk down the street alone, without a pushchair to support her or a child holding her hand, she felt as if everyone was staring at her. She wanted a baby, and the most pressing reason was

212

the physical desire to cup her hand around its round soft head, to see it turn its small face blindly towards her nipple. She could find any number of logical reasons, to convince herself and Alan. She would talk to him, when the right time came.

She began to be more aware of her own looks. It was partly to do with feeling so ridiculously unconfident when she had to do anything alone, but also because of Alan. Because he was paying her more attention, she wanted to please him. One morning she tried on all the clothes in her wardrobe, and filled four cardboard boxes for the Oxfam shop. Alan had always given her money for housekeeping and herself all in one lump; whatever was not spent on food, bills, furnishings or the children, she paid into a building society account. For the first time since the account had been started she withdrew money to buy herself clothes, a hundred pounds. All her clothes had been bought on the run, in sales, with a child under either arm, or had come as presents from Alan. Her mother had always kept her in jumpers and cardigans.

Alan's sweet-tempered phase seemed to coincide with a particularly heavy time at work, unfortunately. He was late almost every night, and often out on Saturdays. That made it very difficult for her to shop without the children – and she was determined that she would give herself that much time, for once. When he told her that he had to go to a conference next weekend, she invited Meg down, and, leaving the children in her care, went off in a state of nervous excitement on Saturday morning to spend the whole day buying clothes for herself.

On Sunday she cooked coq au vin, and put the children to bed half an hour early. She was expecting Alan home for dinner. He finally telephoned at half-past eleven, to say the car had broken down and he had not been able to get to a phone. He would stay in the hotel he was ringing from and get to work somehow from there tomorrow morning. After work he would go back to pick up the car which the garage were looking at. He would be in late tomorrow night.

"Will you be in to eat tomorrow?" She was so disappointed she felt like crying.

"I don't know Carolyn – don't hassle me. I've got enough on my plate without that."

"I'm sorry Alan – I'm sorry, you must have had an awful day. Will the car be expensive?"

"I don't know. I'll see you tomorrow night. Bye."

She ate a few vegetables (which were already mushy and spoiled) but left the coq. It would still be good tomorrow, with any luck.

213

He came in at ten the following evening. Everything was ready, and Carolyn was wearing some of her new clothes: a silky white shirt, and dark green flowing trousers (the woman in the shop had called them harem pants).

"What the hell are you wearing?"

"Don't – don't you like them? I bought them on Saturday."

"They look ridiculous. You look like something out of Aladdin's lamp. Aren't you a bit old for them?"

She looked down at the thin gold and green stripes, which suddenly reminded her of tinsel, and left-over Christmas decorations.

"They're the most unflattering garment I've ever seen."

She should have known, of course, she reasoned with herself, that the car breaking down – the delays, the extra travelling – could be guaranteed to ruin his mood again. It was her own fault for building up expectations. They ate in silence, except for Alan pointing out that the chicken was overcooked. Afterwards he went to have a bath and prepare some work for tomorrow, while she cleared away the dishes. Then she sat in an armchair reading a book. He poked his nose in the door at twelve and said he was going to bed. When he was lying in bed she could feel him staring at her as she climbed out of her ridiculous trousers. "Why are you looking so miserable?"

"I'm not." She shook her head. "I'm just – I'm just a bit disappointed. It's silly, it's my own fault. I was so looking forward to you coming home and talking –"

"I've only been away for two days, for Christ's sake. Why are you so dependent on me? Haven't you got anyone else to talk to?"

"Mum was here for the weekend."

"Your mother!" He snorted and turned over, pulling the pillow around his head. He was fast asleep by the time she got into bed.

Alan's weekend had been stunning; marvellous; exhausting. He and Caro had stayed at a pub in the Lake District. They had talked and argued and made love all weekend regardless of the hours of day or night. Stumbling downstairs, starving, in the small hours of Sunday morning, they had found bread and cheese and cold roast beef left out for them, with a tactful little note suggesting that they must have been out for a very long walk, to miss their dinner like that. After they had eaten, half prompted by the note, they let themselves out into the garden. It was cold and damp out there, the long grass drooping with heavy dew, and the bushes and trees sheltering the garden an indistinct black mass. But overhead the clear blue sky looked almost light with coming dawn; stars, tiny pinpricks of light, were fading out. In the absolute silence one bird began to call, experimentally, sounding two notes. As they stood there gradually a cacophony of bird noise built up, filling the air all around them. They walked down the garden and through a gap in the hedge at the bottom, into a field, leaving the centre of the bird noise behind. The field was empty, rising steeply to a clear skyline. It was as if, Alan thought, the surface of the earth had been cleared for them, and they were in control of the disposition of its sounds and sights. Time was a different element here, with her: a vast fluid space with variations of light and dark, at their command. At home a weekend was a narrow tunnel, through which he squeezed sightlessly, opening his eyes to glimpse boredly the fixed stations of children's clamour, breakfast, shopping, lunch, ritual outing, tea, baths, TV, bed. He was riding through his life like a commuter on the underground, while up here, on the surface of the earth, there was this freedom. They stayed out all morning, climbing the new hill that grew up behind the field's skyline as they ascended. The sun was warm by the time they neared the top of it, and they made love in a hollow of short, sheep-cropped grass. Then they lay basking like seals in the clean sunlight, until Caro, laughing, began to pick dried rabbit turds off Alan's back, and hunger drove them down again.

He persuaded her to stay on another night. But she would not agree to going sick on Monday, so they had to drive back in time for work the next morning, leaving the pub with the dawn again.

"What's happening next weekend?"

"I'm busy, Alan – I can't see you next weekend."

"All weekend? What are you doing?"

"Oh – lots of things. The garden's crying out for my attention. And it's Clare's birthday on Sunday. I want to get ready for that and cook a nice meal – there are lots of people coming. . . ." She broke off.

"What?"

"I wondered if you'd like to come. But it's not a good idea. You don't know anyone anyway. You'd be like a – you'd probably feel a bit out of it."

There was a silence.

215

"I think it's a good idea."

"No, I'm sorry, I don't want you to come."

"You don't want me to meet your friends."

"What – what's the point, Alan? Our lives are separate. It's much simpler if we stick to drinks after work and dirty weekends."

"Is that all this is to you? A good fuck from time to time?"

She looked at him and laughed. "You don't fall over them in the street you know."

"Stop pretending to be tough, and look at me – Caro."

"I'm driving."

"Stop then."

She pressed the accelerator fiercely for a moment, then slowed down abruptly, squealing the brakes. "What?"

"Is that all this is to you?"

Colour flamed up her cheeks. "What – what d'you want me to say, Alan? You've been here all weekend as well as me." She waited in silence for a minute, then started the engine again.

She would only see him twice that week; that night, they had already agreed, for a drink after work, and on Thursday evening after eight.

"What are you doing till eight?"

"W–Washing my clothes, changing my sheets, having a bath and sitting staring out of the window for half an hour. I have to leave some time in the week for myself, or I'd go mad. Don't you?"

"You're on your own most nights this week."

"Yes, but I'm asleep, so it doesn't count."

"And then you have all your other lovers to entertain, of course . . ."

Two weeks later Alan told Carolyn that he was going fishing with Mike next weekend.

"D'you want to take Chrissy?" she offered. "He would be so excited. I know he'd be good."

"No. I don't think so. I mean, we'll probably end up in the pub on Saturday night, and what would we do with him?"

She nodded quickly. "Where will you go?"

"Mike's choosing the spot. I just feel as if I need a break."

She nodded again, smiling at him.

He despised her for being easy to deceive.

He got home fairly late on the Sunday evening. Carolyn was watching television.

"Hello!" He bent over the sofa and kissed her.

"Have a good time?" she asked. Her voice was croaky.

"Oh – yes – yes. Very pleasant. Are you getting a cold?"

She shook her head.

"Is there any food?"

"No."

"Oh – well, can I have a sandwich or something? I'm starving."

"Help yourself."

She always made him food when he came in. He suddenly felt panicky. "What's the matter? Are you feeling bad? Sore throat?"

She didn't reply. He walked around the sofa and looked at her. Her face was swollen and blotchy. "What's the matter? Carolyn."

She stared fixedly at the television, speaking so low he could hardly catch what she said. "Annie had a – an accident. She fell off the swing and broke her arm. This morning. I had to take her to hospital."

"Annie? Where is she? Is she all right?"

"Yes. They put a plaster on it. She's in bed upstairs."

"Oh Christ. Is it all right? What on earth happened?"

"I tried to phone you."

There was a silence.

"At Mike's?" he said pointlessly. He had rung Mike twice to tell him but the bastard was always out.

"Yes – I thought Sarah . . . Mike answered the phone. He didn't know anything about it."

"No."

"So I rang your parents."

"My parents?"

"I thought they might know – if you'd had an accident –"

Alan stood up and went to the window. On television a woman was singing a schmaltzy song. Carolyn got up abruptly and turned it off. The silence lasted a long time. He looked at her. She was sitting rigidly on the sofa, leaning forwards, her hands clasped between her thighs.

"I went – I had to go – for work, I had to. . . ."

She didn't move.

He went and knelt down next to her. "Carolyn. Look at me. Look, I didn't want to upset you – when there was no need."

217

She was shaking. He touched her arm. "Carolyn – look at me. It was nothing – nothing serious. All right? I've come back – I'm here. . . ."

He stood up again. "I'm sorry, all right. I went away for the weekend with someone else."

"Did you sleep with her?"

He was astonished by the question. "Yes."

She began to cry, desperately, as if she had just heard the most terrible news. Alan knelt down awkwardly again, trying to embrace her.

"Stop it – please don't cry. You must have guessed – you must have realized when you telephoned –"

She gasped for breath. "I couldn't believe it."

The night was very unpleasant. Alan was not prepared for the strength of her reaction. For himself, he was sorry she had found out, because now it would all be much more complicated and difficult. And he was sorry she was upset. But he could not actually feel that there was any need for her to react so extremely.

After sobbing uncontrollably for what seemed like hours, while he paced around, trying futilely to silence her, she raised a hideously blotchy face to gasp, "You – were with her – that weekend. The car – when you said the car –"

He did not know what proof she had, and kept silent.

"You were!" she screamed, and threw herself at him, pummelling him aimlessly with her fists. When he put her back gently on the sofa she flopped over like a rag doll and went on sobbing hoarsely, covering the cushion in snot and tears.

At last Alan went to bed. There was nothing else he could do. He was dog tired. He didn't wake up till he heard the children banging about in the morning. He got up cautiously and went into the girls' room. Chris was there too. They were all bubbling with excitement over Annie's plaster. Alan sat on her bed and heard the whole story of the fall, the journey to hospital, the X-ray machine, and what the doctors had said and done. Then he told Chris to help Annie dress, shut the door on the three of them, and went quietly downstairs. The sitting room was empty. He was suddenly badly frightened that she might have gone. But she was in the kitchen making toast. Her face was white and her eyes were red, but she had combed her hair and washed her face, and looked relatively normal.

"Did you sleep?"

She turned her back.

"Carolyn – aren't we going to talk?"

"What d'you want to say?"

218

"I don't know."

"Are you going to see her again?"

"Not if it upsets you like this."

"Not if it upsets me? Did you think I would be pleased?"

"Carolyn, people have affairs all the time. Anyone would think I'd murdered someone. I've said I'm sorry. What more can I do?"

She ran out of the room and he heard the toilet door slam, and then, a little later, her voice upstairs in the children's room.

He did not see Caro at work that day. That night he found that Carolyn had moved out of their bedroom into the spare room – not just made up the bed there, but moved all her clothes out of the wardrobe, her make-up and things from the dressing-table, removed every trace of herself from the bedroom. She had already given the children their tea. There was nothing for Alan or herself to eat.

"Well, look – you go and lie down and I'll make something."

"I don't want anything. I'm going to bed." She went upstairs and shut herself in the spare room.

It continued like that, squalidly and remorselessly, every evening. There were a couple of frostily factual conversations about what exactly had happened when, but she used these to refuel her distress, and retreated from them to start crying all over again, in her room. After staying in and listening on Monday night, Alan went out to the pub at nine on Tuesday, and as soon as he had kissed the children goodnight, on Wednesday.

On Thursday he went to the pub straight after work, telling himself he would stay there all evening. He watched the hands of the clock move through all the minutes between half-past seven and eight o'clock, drinking steadily. He made it to eight. The hands moved on, through five past, ten past, quarter past. He had to tell her at least. Tell her what? What was the point of not seeing her, if Carolyn was behaving like this? It couldn't get any worse; he might as well be hung for a sheep as a lamb. Wasn't it a goat? Goat for preference, at least they're lecherous. He drank up, went out to the car, and drove, with exaggerated alcoholic caution, to Caro's house.

Soon after Alan arrived at work the following morning, he was telephoned by his mother. She wanted to know if he could meet her for lunch.

"Today?"

"Yes, why not?"

219

"Where are you?"

"I'm in Grove and Ellisons, actually." It was a large department store. "Don't be so suspicious, darling. I'm in town shopping, and I suddenly thought how nice it would be to meet my long-lost son for lunch."

"I'm not long-lost."

"Sweetheart, I know you're not. I'm offering to buy you lunch. Yea or nay?"

"Yes, please. Thank you. Where?"

"Oh – shall we lash out?" She named a French restaurant in the city centre.

"I'm only supposed to have an hour, you know."

"Well, I'm sure you can wangle it somehow, darling. See you at one."

She was late, of course. He had a drink while he waited. She had never done this before; in fact, he could not remember a time when she had gone out of her way to speak to him. Then he realized what it was. Carolyn had telephoned home after Annie's fall. That was only last Sunday, although it felt more like a year ago. What a joke. His mother – Lucy, of all people – wanted to tell him the error of his ways. He had walked into it as blindly as a kitten. But after another drink he began to anticipate her arrival with pleasure. What on earth could she say? When he had listened to her performance he would say casually, "And how's Jeremy? Randy as ever?"

He bought a cigar and started to smoke it, occasionally glancing at his own reflection in the mirror behind the bar.

Lucy created her usual flurry on arrival, with dramatic embraces, long and implausible excuses for her lateness, and complicated discussions with the waiter on the correct preparation of various items on the menu. At last they had ordered and she was settled with a drink.

"Well. So here we are. It's an absolute delight to see you again. Have you given up visiting your aged parents?"

"We came at Easter."

"Did you? Was I there?"

"Briefly, yes."

"How's that musical daughter of yours? Is the piano right for her? I did wonder about viola."

He told her about Annie's broken arm, and offered her another drink.

"I can't keep up with you, my love. As a matter of fact, you're looking positively dissolute, now I've had a chance to sit and stare. Have you been ill?"

"No." He was contemptuous. Was that the best she could do? He had hoped for more finesse.

"How's Carolyn taking it?"

"Taking what?"

"Your affair, darling. Don't be so coy, for heaven's sake."

"She's – I–" He stopped. "I don't really think it's your business, mother."

There was a pause. She started to ferret in her handbag, and he listened to the sound of her taking out and lighting a cigarette. He couldn't stop himself from blurting out, "That's why you phoned me, isn't it? It's incredible! What d'you think gives you the right, after you–" He stopped. She always did this to him – always. Within minutes, he was a sulky child again. It made him want to roar with frustration.

"Alan, my sweet, it's the last thing to enter my head. I wanted to talk to you about Pamela, as a matter of fact."

"Why?"

"Well, she's getting divorced. And she's written me a very peculiar letter."

The soup arrived, with impeccable timing, bringing with it the opportunity to fiddle with rolls and cutlery. Once they had started to eat, Alan said unconcernedly, "Well, go on."

"It transpires that she's left Anatole, and she's left Nikki with him." Nikki was Pam and Anatole's one-year-old daughter. "Apparently it's my fault."

"Your fault?"

"Yes. Dreary, isn't it? I can see that retribution will be heaped on my head until the day I die." She smiled bleakly. "This soup's a little bland, isn't it? Almost tired. A weary little soup. I should say these mushrooms came out of a tin."

"How is it your fault?"

"Well, as far as I can understand the poor child, she thinks I should never have let her be born. That's what it seems to boil down to – the essence, I suppose you could say, of her complaints."

Alan laughed humourlessly; a noise to encourage her to continue.

"It is harsh, isn't it? Goodness me, if every infant in the world took up the cause – what adult could escape blame, I wonder? Only the cautious, the celibate, and the frightfully ugly. A purge would leave a motley and

221

unproductive – that's to say unreproductive – crew.'' She sipped her soup meditatively. *''It's not as if she was unplanned. Admittedly we didn't ask her, but medicine was less advanced in those days. . . .''* Her smile died away, and her mouth settled into a bitter line that Alan had not noticed before.

''Did she say why? Why you should never have let her be born?''

''Oh, the usual reasons; she's frightfully desperately miserable, and has been since my hostile womb expelled her into the world. Her life is an empty shell – you know the patter. The sort of thing they say in Dallas, all those women with hair and teeth.''

Alan nodded.

''It appears she might have fared better in this vale of tears, had someone else given birth to her. I, according to her psychoanalyst, am eminently unsuited to be a mother. So it's not being born as such, which troubles her, as being born to me. Even a test tube would have been preferable, apparently. She seems to forget that she's twenty-four. Did they have test tubes in the fifties? I suppose we could have lashed out on a jam jar.''

''Why are you unsuited to be her mother?'' He felt afraid, as he asked the question.

''Ah, that's just it. She didn't say. I don't know whether the venerable shrink revealed that or not. The letter ended with various unsavoury descriptions of how she might choose to finish her days.''

''What sort of –'' Alan broke off. Lucy had ducked her face into her hands. ''Lucy?''

She raised her head quickly, smiling. There were tears on her cheeks.

''How silly. Your father's gone down to sort her out, with his little black bag tucked under his arm, just in case.'' She dabbed at her eyes carefully and inspected her face in her compact mirror. The waiter took away their soup and brought their entrées.

''So – there we are. My curiosity was piqued. I wondered if you could give me any answers?''

''To what?''

''Well, have I really been such a dreadful Mama? I always thought you were relatively happy, as such things go. In between the major tragedies like grazed knees and the cat being sick, and having to practise your instruments. I admit I didn't spend many days up to my elbows in chocolate cake mix, or whatever it is that real mothers are supposed to do – but that would have driven me completely batty, and done you no good at all. You were as happy as most children, no?''

222

"Yes. Yes we were."

She flashed her beautiful smile at him; the question was light but steely, like a wire you might use to garotte a man. "Well why does she say that?"

Alan picked over the food on his plate. "I don't know, Lucy." He hesitated, then plunged. "She was upset, I guess – we both were – when she found out about Jeremy. But she was old then, in her teens at least."

Lucy went very still. He looked up. She was staring at him.

"What did she find out?"

"Well – that you were – having an affair."

"But I wasn't."

There was a silence.

"Oh. She thought you were. She told me you were."

"When? Why?"

He laughed nervously. "She said she saw you. She came down late one night – very late – and saw the pair of you in the drawing room –"

Lucy lifted her napkin from her knees, folded it carefully and placed it on the table. She pushed back her plate. "This conversation really doesn't go with food, does it? Shall we give up and go somewhere more squalid?"

"All right." He thought she was angry. He was going to be appallingly late back to work, but he could hardly leave now.

Lucy chose a pub, a huge crowded barn with a loud TV above the bar. She sat at a table in a murky corner, with a look of fastidious distaste.

"This will do. It suits the tone of proceedings better, I feel. You'll have to buy the drinks, sweetheart. I can't go and stand over there."

"I was going to. What d'you want?"

"God knows. Something they can't ruin. A double Scotch."

When he returned she was smoking, leaning back in her chair. Her elegance and composure were as striking as ever. He sat down.

"Cheers, darling. I'll tell you about Jeremy, shall I? For the record. So that you know exactly what to accuse me of, if you ever decide that I've ruined your life too." She drew on her cigarette and exhaled slowly. "I met Jeremy when I was eighteen. He was the great romance of my youth. We played in the town orchestra together, and were wicked tearaways. It was terribly exciting. We lived together, causing your grandmother – my venerable Mama, as was – never to speak to me again. We used to get terribly drunk – once we got thrown out of our rooms for being rowdy late at night, and had to sleep in a bus shelter. It was all quite overpoweringly Bohemian." She smiled wryly.

"But I was a nice conventional girl, at heart – I found it all much more difficult than I liked to admit. And while Jeremy was enjoying himself being terribly gifted and wasting his talents, and taking obscure and nasty-smelling drugs – and going in for stunningly unpleasant fits of temper – I got more and more depressed." She sighed. "It all dragged on unseasonably long. We'd agree to separate, and just when I was getting myself sorted out, he'd turn up and do his seductive bit and convince me that I couldn't live without him again." She drank her whisky and smiled at Alan. "So at last I married your father."

Alan waited for her to continue but she didn't. "It doesn't seem a very good reason," he volunteered.

"For marrying Trevor? Oh, it was. I knew what I wanted. I knew that Jeremy could charm the birds off the trees, but it would be the most frightful mistake to marry him. I thought I wanted children too, which he would never have tolerated."

"Did Dad know – about Jeremy?"

"Yes. Oh yes. It was all above board. And I got what I wanted – a nice solid husband and two lovely children. I was very lucky."

It was no longer possible to tell if she was being ironic.

"And a romantic lover."

"Not at all. I told him that if I married Trevor that would be the end. It had to be, really darling. Human beings are predictable enough, after all, for me to have seen what might have happened. . . . I've – we –" She laughed and he realized she was embarrassed. "Let me marshal the sordid details. Jeremy and I made love precisely twice, after I'd married your father – in the last twenty-nine years, that is. The first time was when I came back from my honeymoon, I don't know why – I just had to . . . and the second and last time was that fateful occasion in the drawing room. It was – I don't know – a mixture of too much to drink, and nostalgia, and curiosity – a dreadful mistake. Which we haven't repeated."

There was a long silence.

"Do you love him?"

"Jeremy? Oh yes. Desperately."

She leaned forward and patted his hand.

"So you can understand, sweetheart, why it's most unlikely that I would want to pry into your affairs. And much less, to offer advice." She looked at her watch. "Don't you do any work at that blessed office of yours?"

"Yes. I'm only an hour and a half late. D'you want to write me a note?"

She laughed. "Give me a lift to somewhere where there are taxis, and I'll let you escape."

He emptied his glass. "What about Pam?"

She shrugged. "I can write and disabuse her of the notion that I've spent twenty-nine years having it away with Jeremy on the family sofa. It does seem a little unfair, after I'd been so scrupulous to protect your delicate little psyches. And Trevor's. And my own. They do say that virtue brings its own rewards. Perhaps I'll win the Inner Wheel raffle this year, or end up in heaven, or something equally appropriate."

He drove her to the station, and she took a taxi from there – although a train would probably have taken her home faster, Alan reflected. He went back to the office, because he couldn't face going anywhere else. Why should he believe her? But he knew she was telling the truth. He remembered how he had felt as he lit that cigar in the restaurant; cynical and hard-bitten as Bogart in Casablanca. And now he was crying, as he had done when Pam first told him. He wiped his face angrily and pushed his papers into a heap. It was five-thirty. The Rose and Kettle would be open.

Chapter 20

The park was beginning to take real shape now; the landscaping and lake were finished, and Caro was delighted to discover, on one site visit, that two ducks had moved in. They went quacking about their business, not in the least deterred by the workmen's huts, the rich black mountains of topsoil that bordered one side of the lake, the constant engine roar of lorries bringing in, and carrying to destinations all over the park, sandstone, brick, red ash, fencing and logs. The young trees they had planted alongside the canal in March, which had looked like bare twigs stuck into the ground, were green and leafy now. The leisure centre was growing too – several feet higher each time she saw it. The vehicle access paths, which in many places would be the eventual park paths, criss-crossed and divided the area, so that Caro could look at a specific patch of ground which up till now had only existed in that shape on the plans, and visualize its final appearance. By the end of June the weather was becoming hot. The contractors worked stripped to the waist, laying foundations, building walls, preparing the ground for autumn planting. The whole place seethed with energy, noise and dust, seeming to Caro like a gigantic workshop where something huge and precious was being forged. The workmen were initially amused by her site visits, and more inclined to whistle at her than take her seriously. But she checked every detail meticulously, and they found themselves having to re-lay one particular section of paved footpath, because she said the joints were too wide.

"What about wheelchairs or prams?" she asked the foreman, trying to make a joke of it. "With joints like that, they'll need a–an army of boy scouts to push them along, and their teeth will be j–jolted out of their heads."

She stammered and flushed bright red when she had anything critical to say. It made the foreman embarrassed. He began to look out more carefully for shoddy workmanship, relieved if he could pick it up before she did.

Despite the occasional awkwardness, Caro loved site visits, loved watching the place take shape and grow under the men's hands and machines. Ron and David, the two on the Planning and Development team who had done the basic park design, were happier working on paper than in mud – and Caro had been responsible for a lot of detail, like the blind garden, and for the planting design. So they were content to leave her the lion's share of site visits.

As the park suddenly began to take off, moving from the conceptual through a birth of deafening noise, fierce energy, stifling heat and dust, to become something tangible and real: so the relationship with Alan moved and changed also, into something much more insistent. Something so close up to her that it touched and blurred all her receptive senses, stunning her mind and her ability to be rational about it. He was there – right there; so close that at times it seemed she could not breathe, see, smell, touch, taste, hear without it being of him. The flavour and sense of him was somehow soaked into all her being. The fear (it was not an idea, it was a sliver of ice which insinuated itself to maximum effect, like an anaesthetist's cold needle, to freeze and numb her) that the relationship must end was often present. But she was incapable of doing anything other than experiencing it and being at its paralysing mercy. Alan told her that his wife had discovered the affair and Caro felt a kind of relief, because surely that fact must precipitate some change. But it did not. At first he told her his wife did not mind, as long as he could preserve enough semblance of their married life to keep the kids happy. A week later he told her that his wife was devastated, that she had done nothing but cry for a week, and he could not stand it. That week he and Caro saw each other every night but one. He was drinking heavily, and they became almost manic together, like passengers on a slowly sinking ship, determined to extract every last ounce of pleasure and sensation from the short time remaining. His drinking affected Caro curiously. Rationally she might have been worried (sometimes experienced the ghost of the thought, fleeting through the outer bloodless reaches of her brain); might have thought that it was not right for him to drink so much, that it could affect his health. But her feeling about it was quite other. She admired it. It was part of what she loved in him. His drinking was a logical extension of that forcing oneself up to the very edges of experience. She saw that it was as necessary to him as, perhaps, all her nightmare visions after the accident had been to her. That people cannot always live neatly within the hygienic confines of sanity, good sense and sobriety. That there must be nightmares, visions, drunkenness, lunacy, a hand stretched out to grab from the blackness whatever it is out there – whatever it is. He made her aware of the edge of normality again, and the huge compelling chaos that lies beyond that edge.

She drank with him, but not as heavily, having neither the practice nor the constitution for it. Being drunk made her sick, which did not happen to him.

Unless they were really late, Caro preferred to ride in to work on her bicycle, rather than get a lift with Alan. Neither of them had any desire for their affair to be made public. One Friday morning, when Caro got into the empty office, it was not quite quarter to nine, and the phone was ringing already. It was Johnny – the Clerk of Works at the park site. He was very agitated. It turned out that someone (kids, Johnny thought) had climbed the fence during the night, and "made a hell of a mess". He was not very clear about what exactly they had done, his description was full of "over there's" and "you can see's". She realized that the police he had called were on the spot already, and he was trying to explain to them and her simultaneously.

"I'll be there in ten minutes," she said, cutting him short, and ran back down to her bike.

She was relieved when she had seen the site for herself. There was very little damage. The sweet chestnut logs, which were cut to length and treated, ready for the construction of the adventure playground, had been pushed out of their neat piles, and lay scattered about like the spilt contents of a giant box of matches. She guessed that someone had been playing at balancing on them, rolling them along under their feet. They were not damaged. Several cans of spray paint had been liberally applied, but mainly to surfaces that did not matter – the walls of the workmen's hut and store, for example. There was a lot of red spray up and down one side of a large stack of engineering bricks, which were to be used in the construction of the blind garden retaining wall and path. But once the bricks were laid only one edge would be visible anyway. The workmen would just have to take care to lay them with the painted side to the earth. Johnny told her there was graffiti sprayed on the half-built wall of the leisure centre. That was more serious, but thankfully not her concern. He led the two policemen off to the leisure centre, and Caro made her way down to the canalside fence, to see where they had got in. It was obvious; the diagonal wire mesh was sagging between two crookedly leaning support posts. They had simply walked up it. Now there would have to be tighter security. Barbed wire, perhaps a guard dog. She was depressed by it. People should feel the place was free and open for them, not that it had to be fenced off and kept secret. Walking slowly along the fence, to see if there had been any other entry point, she felt upset to the point of tears. It was silly. She knew it wasn't just the park. It was Alan. She had to do something about Alan. It was a pressure of emotions that threatened to come pouring out in tears whenever any ir-relevant excuse offered itself. After Alan had told her that his wife was upset – and that he found her distress unbearable – they had simply avoided the subject. Neither of them had referred to her, or to what happened when he went home to her. The thought of her misery haunted Caro, but she did not seem to have any strength to attempt to change the course of events.

Walking back towards the huts – there were no other entry points she could see – she forced herself to grasp the situation. Alan was spending more and more time with her. He was unhappy. All three of them were unhappy. Something must be decided. He must talk to his wife properly. He must decide what he was going to do. Or if he couldn't decide, really couldn't – then she must decide, and refuse to see him. It would be better in the long run, she told herself – though "the long run" seemed as unreal to her as the notion of going to heaven after you're dead. She told Johnny she would write a report, and add security to the agenda for Tuesday's section meeting.

When she got back to the office she wrote the report mechanically, and sat for a long time staring sightlessly at the papers on her desk. At one o'clock she went down to the canteen to meet Alan for lunch.

He was already there, halfway through his roast beef and Yorkshire pudding.

"What's up?" he asked, before she even had time to sit down. She opened her mouth to tell him about the vandalism, then closed it. This was how it went on, from moment to moment, day to day, because neither of them could face the situation squarely. She sat down and picked up her knife and fork.

"I don't think we should see each other this weekend."

He looked at her in silence for some time, then said, "OK."

There was another long silence, in which Caro pushed food around her plate with a fork, then Alan spoke again.

"What good d'you think that will do?"

"I don't know."

"D'you think it will make Carolyn feel any better to hear that you have banished me to her company for the weekend?"

"No – no. But it – it might make her feel better than knowing we're spending the weekend together. You might be able to talk to her at least – make her understand. . . ."

"What? Make her understand what?"

"I don't know."

Caro forced herself to eat a mouthful of meat. It seemed to need a lot of chewing. "Alan – we've got to do something. We're going on like blind people – "

"You choose your times, don't you? Couldn't we talk about this tonight?"

Caro glanced around the room. Now she had started to talk, she could not bear to give up. "No. I want to talk now."

He slotted his hands together, finger by finger, and rested his chin on the platform they made, looking at her with resigned patience.

"You – you've got to talk to her properly."

"I don't like talking to her. She cries. It upsets me."

"But you – you – If you didn't care about her, her unhappiness wouldn't matter to you."

"No. But I never said I didn't care about her."

"I know. So you must tell her – that – that you do care about her."

230

He nodded. "Sure. I must tell her that I do care about her, and then continue to do what makes her most unhappy."

"No."

"No?"

"No. If you – if you do care about her – I mean, I know you care about her – look Alan – we must stop. That's what."

He nodded. "OK."

"I mean it."

"Of course you do. Shall we start now?" He made it sound like a game of hide-and-seek.

"I'm serious. We must stop seeing each other. How can it go on like this? It's got to finish." She couldn't believe it wasn't a game. A game of dares; running across the lines in front of the train; seeing who dared to go nearest to the edge of the cliff.

"Can you?"

"What?"

"Finish."

"I – I – yes. I am doing."

"What if I see you? What if I pass you in the corridor?"

"Just ignore me."

"Ignore you." He stared at her for a moment, then began to laugh. She couldn't stop herself from laughing too. It made her furious. "It's not f–funny. It's not – not – " She couldn't speak for laughing. What was there to laugh at? Were they both completely mad? At last, when he stopped laughing, he smiled and said "Is that it then?" as if she had meant the whole thing for a joke.

"Yes. That's it," she said angrily, biting her lips to stop herself from giggling again.

"It's an unsatisfactory ending, you know. It hasn't got much of a punch to it. Romances don't end like this in films, or books." He was laughing again.

"I – I don't think there's anything else to do." Suddenly she felt adequately serious. This sense of numb irresponsibility would not last much longer; there is no feeling at first in a savage wound to the flesh, but pain creeps up. She pushed back her chair. "I think I'll go now."

"You haven't finished your lunch."

"I – I'm not hungry. Does that make it more romantic?"

He didn't say anything, but she could tell he was trying not to laugh at her.

"I am serious Alan. Goodbye." It sounded ridiculous. She walked as quickly as she could between the tables, feeling absurd and wooden, like a bad actress in a badly written play.

There was light drizzle all weekend, and the warm air was thick with moisture. Caro spent the time gardening. She instructed Sue and Clare that Alan was to be told she was out, and she did not answer the phone or the door once. She drove herself to the limits of exhaustion, planting out endless muddy rows of lettuce, carrot and cabbage seedlings, more than they would ever be able to eat, and prising up all the weeds that had appeared between the bricks in the path. Then she assaulted and cleared the sodden sticky patch of land at the far end of the greenhouse – the only bit of the garden she had never dug.

Although she was exhausted on Sunday evening, it was impossible not to glance questioningly at Sue.

"No phone calls."

"Good," she managed to say.

She hadn't believed he would be able not to. Unless he was drunk. . . . Through the evening she became more and more frightened, convinced that he was drunk or hurt, somewhere. But there was no way of finding out. She tried to persuade herself that he was at home, sitting beside his wife on the sofa, watching television. It was unimaginable.

When Clare asked her if she fancied a drink she accepted just to get out of her own company.

"Who did the dirty deed?"

"I – I did. I told him I didn't want – want to see him again."

"OK. Want to talk about it?"

Caro shook her head, and Clare told her the outline for the Mad Bitches' next show which she'd worked out, explaining the ideas in minute detail.

He turned up at four that morning. He was paralytically drunk. Caro had not been able to sleep, and she heard him coming down the street from a distance. She ran down to the door to get there before he woke everybody up. When she had helped him up the stairs and into her room he cried hopelessly for a while, sprawled on the floor like a heap of washing, and in the middle of crying fell asleep so suddenly and deeply that for a terrified moment she

232

thought he had died. He did not wake up or stir while she attempted to undress him. His inert body was incredibly heavy. She could not get him on to the bed, but rolled him on to the duvet, easing a pillow under his head. In the morning she made them both cups of tea and sat beside him on the floor.

"Are you all right?"

It took him a while to surface. "Yes."

"Tea?"

They both drank.

"What happened?"

He shook his head. She left him to finish his tea, had a wash and dressed.

"You'll have to get up, you know, or you'll be late for work. You haven't got the car have you?"

"No." Pause. "I don't know where it is. I had it when I left the house."

"Well – it's probably at a pub. We'll find it tonight. Are you getting up?"

"No." He lay down again, putting his head under the pillow.

She hesitated, then crouched beside him, her hand on his shoulder under the cover. "Alan?"

"Go away. Leave me alone."

Caro got on her bike and went to work.

When she came home that evening he was dressed, sitting in her chair looking out of the window.

"Have you been here all day?"

"This is a nice room."

"Yes, it is, isn't it? I love it."

"I used to think it was rather bare. . . ."

There was a silence.

"Well," he said.

"Well what?" She sat on the bed and took off her sandals.

"I've left."

"Left – ?"

"Home." His voice was ironical. "My marriage. My wife."

"What do you mean?"

"She told me I had to choose. Between you and her. So here

233

I am." He did not look at her.

Caro sat very still on the bed. "What are you going to do?" she asked at last.

He shrugged. "Live with you."

She realized that he blamed her. She spoke carefully. "We haven't talked about living together. We – we haven't talked about you leaving your wife. I don't want you to leave her."

He smiled at her bitterly. "Well, it is confusing, isn't it? You don't want me to leave her, I don't want to leave her – the only person who wants me to leave her is my wife, and just saying it makes her howl like a baby."

"Stop it Alan, for Christ's sake."

He turned away from her again, hands in pockets, staring out of the window. There was another silence. At last he said, "All right. Let's talk about living together."

"I – I don't want to live with you."

"What do you mean?"

"That. You can't just – we haven't talked about it all, Alan. Even if we do – I'm not – I'm certainly not going to like this."

He was waiting for her to go on.

"Look, things have got to be separate. There are two separate things. If you decide to – to leave your wife, then you make that decision on the basis of things between you and her. It's nothing to do with me."

He laughed hollowly.

"No. I mean it. And if you decide to le–leave her, then you must do that, and find yourself a place – room, flat, whatever, and live there on your own. If, as two single and independent people we then decide that we might want – to be together – then maybe. . . ."

"Where shall I go?"

"I don't know. Have you got a case?"

He shook his head.

"Well you'll have to go home then."

"Can I stay here tonight?"

"I – no."

He picked up his coat from the floor. "I wish you'd told me this before."

"Alan – we've never even talked about it. I didn't imagine you would leave her –"

"No. Of course not. Well – over a little, insignificant affair like this – who can blame you for not taking it seriously?" He stood still for a moment staring at her, his coat dangling from his hand. Then he went out quickly, slamming the door behind him. Caro clasped her arms around her knees, stopping herself from running down the stairs after him.

She could not sleep for hours, and finally drifted into an uneasy doze around dawn. She was aware that she had to wake up and get up, but couldn't. And she knew when she finally did open her eyes and sit up with a jolt, that she had overslept. It was eight-thirty. She didn't get to the office till after nine-thirty. David looked up in surprise as she came in.

"Are you back already?"

"Back – ?"

"Haven't you been to the park?"

She shook her head. "I've only just got up. What's the matter?"

"Oh – haven't you heard? Fun and games last night. A really jolly little do. They've set fire to the bloody place."

"Set fire – ? What – what to?"

"Johnny's hut. The tool store. The logs."

"Oh no – no." Caro sat down on her desk. "How could they?"

He shrugged, choosing to take her literally. "Probably gave it all a good dousing in petrol – "

"Why?"

"Search me."

"Does anyone know – what happened?"

"Someone called the police in the middle of the night. You could see the fire from the road, apparently. They've had fire engines up there, and the lot."

"They don't know who – ?"

"Ha! That's the best of it. Guess who they caught climbing over the fence?"

"I don't know – go on."

"Kevin. Kevin Jackson. One of Jim's canal lads."

"I know – I know him. What was he doing?"

"Well, climbing over the fence. With a bloody great bonfire blazing behind him. Oh, and he'd nicked a sack of topsoil, I believe, for good measure."

"God." Caro rocked backwards and forwards on her perch. "I don't believe it."

"Well, it's true I'm afraid. They're all down there now, sniffing about."

Caro didn't go to the site that day. She couldn't face it. There wasn't anything she could do, anyway. It was all in the hands of the police. The phone rang continuously. She had liked Kevin Jackson. He was a bright, confident boy who had seemed really enthusiastic about the canal project. He had even asked her about the possibility of getting into gardening work, once the project finished.

It was impossible to do any sensible work. All sorts of rumours were flying about: that more than one of the MSC kids were involved, that the project was being suspended immediately, that work on the park would be delayed indefinitely. Ron told her that the police were advising the council to press charges against Kevin: trespass, theft, and suspected arson.

"Is it up to us?" she asked in horror.

He shook his head. "Council. Our elected representatives. There's a meeting on Thursday – they're the ones who'll make the decision. But I suspect it's already been made."

Caro left the office early and went straight home. She was afraid Alan might call for her towards the end of the afternoon, and she felt as if she didn't want to see anyone – anyone at all. But her plans were foiled by Clare, who called out "Hello!" from the kitchen, as she wheeled her bike in the front door.

Caro went unwillingly into the kitchen.

"Have you seen this?" Clare asked. The local evening paper was spread out on the table in front of her. Caro moved round to stand behind her chair. There was a big photo of something burnt. With difficulty Caro recognized the side of the tool store. Johnny's hut must have been reduced to ashes. There were some charred and blackened logs in the foreground. The headline proclaimed: "Vandals threaten future of park."

Clare pulled a chair out beside her and pushed the paper over to Caro. She read it slowly, stopping every now and then to gaze again at the photo. The details were those she had heard repeated all day long. But the reporter had also interviewed Bellamy, the leader of the Council. There was a lot of rant about vandals and people who have no respect for property. Clare laid her finger

alongside one particular paragraph headed "Ill-conceived". "Cllr
Bellamy said that the future development of the park would be
under review at the next meeting of full council. 'As you know,
the decision to site this park in Millside was taken some years
ago, when the Labour Party held the majority on the Council. We
opposed the decision then, because of the unsuitability of the
area. Vandalism on this scale must force us to now reconsider,
very carefully indeed, whether we have the right to waste
ratepayers' money on such an ill-conceived project.'"

"It's rubbish," Caro said immediately.

"Why?"

"It's not ratepayers' money at all. It's not local money. It's from
central government – Inner-City money and Derelict Land Grant.
They only got the money because it was that site. He's a lying bastard
– they haven't paid a penny towards it. The little shit."

"Oh – well that's all right then. I wouldn't like to see your pet
scheme whisked away from under your nose."

Caro shook her head. "Does it say anything about Kevin?" She
read on quickly. The only mention was in the final paragraph.
"Police are being helped in their enquiries by a youth who was
apprehended near the scene of the fire, late last night." She told
Clare who Kevin was.

"Well – what are you going to do? Are you going to see him?"

"What can I do, Clare? The police caught him red-handed.
He'll have made a statement by now. If they decide to take him to
court, then that's what they'll do."

"Well you could talk to him at least – find out what he was
doing. He might have a perfectly good excuse."

"Then he'll tell it to them, won't he?"

"No, not necessarily. You might be able to help him. He's
probably scared out of his wits."

Caro sighed. "Look Clare – I don't – I'm not–"

"What?"

"I'm not going to."

She got up from the table and went upstairs. What good could
she do? It wouldn't make any difference.

The phone rang as she got to the top of the stairs, and Clare
called her down again. It was Alan.

"You left work early."

"Yes."

237

"Shame about the fire."

"Yes."

"Shall we have a drink?"

"I want a bath."

"All right. I'll pick you up at eight."

She hesitated. But she knew she wanted to see him. "Yes. At eight."

In the car she told him the details of the fire, and about the Bellamy interview. He had not seen a paper.

"He's a pillock, that man," Alan said. "He lives near us, in the most bizarre dwelling I ever hope to see."

She laughed. "I didn't think he would live in Millside! What's it like?"

"A bit like a wedding cake. Sort of white and in tiers. I'll show you, sometime."

By unspoken mutual consent they avoided mentioning the previous evening – or anything that touched on themselves – until they were peaceably settled in a pub. Caro left it to Alan to open the subject. It turned out that he had gone back home last night. Things had been calmer, he said. He had told his wife he was moving out temporarily, to sort himself out. She had seemed happier. Caro imagined that the poor woman must feel happy about anything definite happening.

"Where are you – have you found a room?"

"I'm moving in with Mike."

Her heart sank. "But he's only got one bedroom."

"I'll sleep on the sofa."

"But –"

"But what? What don't you like now?"

"Nothing. Nothing." She drained her glass. "Can we go for a walk?"

"Now?"

"Yes. We could walk to another pub, then back for the car. It's lovely outside now, look at that sky." She pointed through the window opposite their table. The lower panes were frosted, but through the upper ones they could see a clear, dark blue sky, which was lemony yellow – almost green, at the lower edge, from the sunset.

"All right."

They walked in silence for a while, and Alan took her hand.

"Why is this such a bloody mess?"

"I don't know."

"Don't you want us to live together?"

She had prepared herself for this question. "It's far too early to say. You've got to be on your own, and be certain about what you're leaving – and why . . . before we can begin to think about it."

"But it's already gone so far. . . . You turn it on to me. I've got to be certain. What do you think?"

She shook her head. "I can't – I can't say. You're not – when you're free it'll be different. I don't know. I can't imagine us living together."

"Why not?"

"I don't know . . . because of your family, I suppose."

"They don't own me." He grabbed at a switch of overhanging weeping willow, but it did not break easily and he was forced to stop and twist the sinewy stem round and round impatiently before he could tear it off. When he had broken it he beat it along the fence. "I really don't think it will make much difference to the kids." His voice sounded as if he was trying to be reasonable.

"Why not?"

"Because – they're much more attached to Carolyn. They tolerate me. They do things with me on her instructions. You can practically feel a collective sigh of relief when I go out."

"Why? Why should it be like that?"

"I don't know. Because of the way Lyn looks after them, I suppose. She does – she – her whole life revolves around them. She knows what they want before they know themselves. I mean, there's no competition; if I ever do anything for them, I simply don't do it as well as she does."

"She has more time with them than you do."

"Of course, I'm out at work all day."

"Well then it's hardly surprising."

"No."

She saw that he was dissatisfied with this conclusion, though, and waited for him to carry on. The silence lengthened until she realized that he had thought better of it. He was lashing at the wall rhythmically with the stick. The noise irritated her. The sky ahead of them was perfect. The last yellow-green tints from the

239

sunset were fading, leaving a pale eggshell-blue wash which darkened gradually and imperceptibly, rising to the deep blue vault of space overhead. Three pale stars were already visible.

"You feel sorry for yourself," she said.

He didn't reply.

"You could have made more time to spend with them. Your father used to look after you and your sister, you said. He had a job."

"Yes. But there was room for him to look after us. There was a gap. Lucy was practising, or at concerts. Lyn doesn't leave any gaps at all."

"You're blaming her, then."

"I don't know – it just happened. You think it's my fault?"

"I don't know. It doesn't seem fair that you should blame her for looking after them too well."

"Well I'm not fair, am I? I'm a rotten selfish adulterous bloody bastard."

"Stop it," she said quietly. He had never criticized his wife before, to her.

When they came to the pub he did not sit with her, but brought her drink then returned to the bar. She watched him drain his pint and buy another. After a few minutes she joined him. "I'd like to go, now."

"Go on then." He did not turn round.

"What are you going to do?"

"Stay here."

"You won't be able to drive."

"That's my business."

She went out. It was quite dark now, but still warm, and the sky was sprinkled with white stars. It would take her about an hour to walk home, she judged. She could get a bus into town and another out. . . . She decided to walk.

It took her longer than she had expected. It was after midnight when she turned into her street. Alan's car was parked outside the house. She had been telling herself he was despicable; childish, self-pitying. But these certainties evaporated into thin air before the fact of him jumping out of the car and running towards her.

"Where on earth have you been? I've been driving up and down looking for you – I've been waiting at bus stops for hours."

"I just walked back."

"All the way?"

She nodded.

"Good grief, you could have been murdered and raped – why didn't you get a taxi?"

She laughed. "I'm all right."

"I know you are. It makes me sick. Open this door."

"Are you coming in?"

"Yes. But not in the street. It's too cold."

Chapter 21

Getting up and dressed in the morning somehow resulted in them making love again, which slowed the whole business down considerably. Caro was persuaded easily into accompanying Alan to work in the car. She would be late again, if she went on the bike. But to her astonishment he started to drive away from town, in the opposite direction.

"What are you doing? Where are you going?"

"I need a clean shirt."

It took her a while to realize that they were going not to Mike's but to Alan's house – the house where his wife and children lived.

"How dare you – what do you think you're doing? God, if I was her I'd throw them all away. You told me you'd moved into Mike's – you liar –"

"Your argument would be more coherent if you knew whether you were angry for yourself or Lyn. And I have moved in to Mike's. It just so happens that all three shirts I have there with me are dirty."

"Well, I'm not washing them for you!"

"Fine. I didn't expect it. Kindly allow me to go home and fetch a clean one."

Caro sat in outraged silence, as they drove past the flow of commuter traffic pouring into town, past the big houses with their tall hedges and deep green gardens. The sun was shining.

"Nice, isn't it?" he said. "Nice part of town."

He turned off the main road, into an avenue lined with lime trees. The houses were all set well back from the road. "Solid investments, houses like these," he said. "Go up by a few thousand every year. Pleasant too – nice class of neighbours. And look at the gardens; roses, wisteria, blossom in the spring –"

242

They drove past a neat modern primary school. "Close to all facilities, schools, transport – "

"What are you talking about?" she shouted furiously. "What are you trying to do?"

"Nothing," he said pleasantly. "Just showing you what a nice neighbourhood I used to live in."

"Used to? Nobody asked you to leave."

He slowed down and drew to a halt outside a big house with mock-Tudor beams on the front. There was a beautiful Japanese maple, she noticed, in the middle of the front lawn. "Pretty, isn't it? I should think it's worth about fifty thousand pounds by now."

Caro realized it was his. "You shit – you – "

"Careful. Someone will see you."

Almost hysterical with rage, Caro folded her arms and bent her head low over them, so that her face could not be seen from the outside. Alan jumped out and strode up the path to the house, whistling. He didn't knock on the door. He's still got his key, she thought. Of course he has. The footsteps came back down the path almost immediately. When he opened the car door he swung in a white shirt on a hanger, before he got in himself.

"How d'you have the nerve – how d'you have the bare-faced cheek – ?"

"Oh it's easy, when you're as wicked as I am." He began to whistle again, a hateful piercing noise. They turned a corner, into a newer, less established street.

"This used to be green belt," he said informatively. "They changed the planning regulations in sixty-eight. Sold it in lots to private builders. Of course, we older residents look down on it all. Rather tasteless, most of it. That's Bellamy's on the left."

The houses here looked raw and naked, lacking the full hedges and trees of the Victorian streets. Bellamy's house was as ugly as Alan had said. Despite her rage, Caro stared at it. The garden was being landscaped. There was a mound of black earth and rubble at one end, and piles of –

"Stop. Alan. Stop."

He glanced at her and stopped the car. Caro jumped out and ran back down the road. He watched her in his mirror. She was staring into Bellamy's garden. Then she came slowly back to the car.

"Well?" he said, as she got in.

"He's – he's got our bricks."

"Our bricks?"

"Yes. Blind garden bricks. Bricks from the park."

Alan glanced in his mirror and drove off from the kerb. "How d'you know?"

"Because they – they're the ones that were painted. Spray-canned. Red. They've got that red paint all over one side."

There was a moment's silence.

"And he's got topsoil – and a heap of paving stones. . . . He must have stolen the lot."

"It wouldn't surprise me."

"What d'you mean?"

"You're such an innocent," Alan said contemptuously. "It happens all the time. Of course people are nicking stuff."

"But he said – in the paper, that interview about vandals – and they're taking Kevin to court over one bag of topsoil. . . ."

Alan shrugged. "That's the way it goes."

"Well I – I – I'll go to the police."

"That would be silly."

"Why?"

"Because you'd lose your job. Look, Caro – how many people are already turning a blind eye? That stuff's been on site once, hasn't it? So the contractors must have brought it out again for him. They're all in on it. The police'll laugh at you."

"But it's not fair."

"That's life."

She subsided into silence. After a while he said, smiling, "You're a ridiculous idealist."

"Don't patronize me."

"I'm not. I think you're silly. But I'm forced to admire your sense of fair play."

"I don't want you to admire me. I don't want you to think I'm silly."

When they got to the car park he said, "Can we stop it now?"

"Stop what?"

"All this bickering. Kiss me."

"What on earth makes you think I want to kiss and be friends?"

He shrugged. "All right. Let's have another forty-eight hours of hostilities, then. Shall I see you tomorrow night, when you've cooled down?"

She was so angry she couldn't speak, and nearly fell out of the car in her haste to get away from him.

Caro was overwhelmed, in the course of the morning, by the sense of the impossibility of changing anything. Realistically, what could she do about Bellamy? It wasn't even – she tried to add up the value of what he must have taken. It couldn't amount to more than fifty pounds' worth, altogether. People wouldn't believe her because it was too ridiculous, for someone like him to have stolen such a paltry amount.

She refused to let herself think about Alan at all; she could not face examining his motives for their morning drive. She passed a deeply frustrating morning telephoning woodyard after woodyard in an attempt to secure a new supply of seasoned sweet chestnut (the construction of the adventure playground was supposed to start in ten days' time), and a depressing afternoon writing yet another internal report on the extent of the damage at the park. Work there had stopped completely, at the moment. There was not even the authorization to start building a new stores hut until the Council had met on Thursday.

Over the next two days Caro found herself becoming almost manic, doing fifteen jobs at once at work, tearing round the house frantically at home. When Clare came in from her rehearsal the following evening, she found Sylvie and some of her friends in the TV room listening to deafeningly loud music, and Caro in the kitchen dismantling the oven.

"What on earth are you doing?"

"It's filthy. Some of these bits haven't been cleaned for years."

"But there's a time – and a place, Caro. Why has it got to be done now, at – " she consulted her watch "– seven-fifteen on a Thursday evening? How can I cook tea?"

"Have something cold. There's some cheese in the fridge."

Clare got her to sit down, by making a pot of tea and a plate of cheese sandwiches. "What's up?"

"Nothing. Everything."

"Are you still – what's happening with Alan?"

"It's a mess. I don't know. I keep thinking it's finished . . . then – He left a note on my desk to meet at the George at nine tonight."

"Are you going?"

Caro shrugged. "I don't know. I don't know. I'm just not in control any more, at all. I don't know what I'm doing."

Someone turned up the music in the next room, and everything in the kitchen began to vibrate to the bass beat, as if a huge heart had suddenly begun to thump under the floorboards.

"That's nice," said Clare sourly, and they both suddenly laughed. "Shall I go in and throw my weight about?"

"No." Caro touched Clare's arm. "Leave it. It's like being in the jungle."

"Like being in the womb, more like. They play noises like that to babies, now, in trendy nurseries – just imagine what decibel level they'll graduate to, when they're Sylvie's age."

"Clare?" Caro had not intended to tell her. But she suddenly craved the shrewd certainty of Clare's response. She knew what it would be; but she wanted to hear it, like a craving for something strong and salty – anchovy, or Danish blue. "You know Bellamy? the councillor they interviewed in the paper the other day? I – I went past his house yesterday morning, and there were some bricks. . . ." She told Clare what she had seen.

"What are you going to do?"

"Well what – what can I do?"

"Expose him! God, you could reduce him to shreds. All that stuff about respecting other people's property, and standing up to be counted – Caro it's brilliant!" Clare leapt up and hugged her.

"But Clare – "

"What?"

"I don't know . . . will anyone believe me? I mean, why should the police take any notice of me? All sorts of people must know about it already. . . ."

Under the assault of Clare's mounting indignation, Caro found herself mouthing all Alan's excuses.

"But what about that boy?" shouted Clare. "What about that boy they're taking to court? For Christ's sake, Caro – what are you saying? Is that what your fucking park boils down to? – free garden materials for the bloody rich councillors, and barbed-wire fences and court cases for the local kids? What are you talking about?"

As always, another person's certainty filled Caro with stubborn awkwardness. Why did Clare think she knew – any more than Alan did? Why did they all know, and think that she would do what they said?

"What do you expect me to do? Be a private detective? Follow lorries? Snoop around gardens taking photos? The stuff he's taken doesn't amount to more than fifty pounds' worth. Is it worth me losing my job for that?"

A record ended and there was suddenly a shocking minute of complete silence, before the racket started up again.

"I don't believe it," Clare screamed. "I don't believe you can say that. For Jesus Christ's sake, Caro – how can you? For years – ever since I met you – you've sat back and been too pernickety to soil your dainty white hands with anything real – but I always thought – I always thought you were – you would –" She shook her head incoherently. "I just don't believe it. How can you carry on working there?"

"Shut up!" yelled Caro. "Shut up! and tell me what the fuck you think I can do, if you're so bloody righteous."

Clare studied her hands on the table top for a short time. When she spoke her voice was calm. "If it was me – I would – I'd find someone who knows about this sort of thing. You don't want the police. You want the media. That's what'll destroy Bellamy. Someone who knows how to chase it up and ask the right questions. I'll ask Jenny." Jenny was a friend of Clare's who worked as a researcher on the local TV news programme. "I'll ring her now."

Clare got up immediately and went into the hall. Caro heard her shouting at Sylvie. The record was turned down. Caro glanced at her watch – eight-thirty. She ran up to her room and changed, and combed her hair. She was in the bathroom cleaning her teeth when Clare came to find her.

"She's out. They'll get her to ring back in half an hour. What are you doing?"

"I'm going to meet Alan in the George."

"Don't you want to talk to Jenny?"

"I don't know – I don't know!" Caro pushed past Clare and ran down into the hall, before she burst out screaming or sobbing, or started throwing things around the room.

She was in the pub by five to nine. Alan wasn't there yet. He

247

wasn't there by nine-fifteen. He wasn't there by nine-thirty. She left at quarter to ten.

There was a long message from Clare on the telephone table – she picked it up quickly, but it wasn't Alan. It was all about what Jenny had said. Caro scrumpled it in her palm. She went heavily up to her room, threw herself on to the bed, and cried.

She was busy again next day. She avoided anywhere where Alan might be. It was the closing date for applications for the post of warden at the park field study centre. She and David spent four hours wading through the two hundred and thirty-nine applications, and attempting to select six to be interviewed. Council yesterday had huffed and puffed, and permitted work on the park to continue, as everyone had known they must do. She went down to the site to work out how long it would take them to clear up the fire mess, and how much of the old huts could be salvaged. It was a hot dry day, with a fitful wind gusting about under the metallic clouds. Although it had been hot, the sun didn't seem to have shown itself for days. In the park, dust and ashes from the fire blew around in flurries and got into her nose, mouth, and eyes.

She didn't get back to the office till six. Alan was sitting at her desk.

"What do you want?" she said.

"You."

"Don't be melodramatic. Go away. I'm tired and dirty."

He did not move.

"Alan – look, it's no good."

"Just come for a quick drink. I need to talk to you. Please. Go and have a wash, and I'll meet you at the main door. Just one drink, honestly – OK?"

She was too tired to argue.

In the pub he was curiously intent and considerate. She wondered whether he had simply forgotten the previous evening.

"What did you do last night?" she asked casually.

"Oh – I don't know. Had too much to drink. That's right – I tried to ring you. I couldn't get through."

"Why did you try to ring me?"

"I don't know. Because I wanted to see you, I suppose – Caro – we can't . . . it can't go on like this."

248

She nodded ironically.

"No. I mean it. I'm sorry I've – I don't know what I've been doing, half the week. I feel as if I'm falling apart. I want us to go somewhere for the weekend, away from everything else, and get ourselves sorted out – really, work out what we're going to do, and then do it."

She sighed. "Who are you trying to kid? Me, or yourself?"

"Well what then? D'you want to go on telling me it's all over every second day, then behaving as if nothing's happened the next time we meet?"

She recognized that that was what she'd been doing, but it didn't seem very fair of him.

"Well what'll be different at the weekend?"

"I've been thinking – I want to talk to you properly, without all these interruptions – and away from work. I want us both to know. . . ."

There was a silence. At last Caro shrugged.

"I'll come. On condition that we both do whatever we agree to over the weekend."

"Yes. That's what I want."

"Right."

"Right."

They went to an empty Indian restaurant, the type that only fills when the pubs close, and had a meal in the cavernous red gloom before setting off. Caro found her mood of despair lifting like a cloud. There was a high-pitched wailing female voice coming through the stereo speakers. Alan began to speculate on what form of torture she was being subjected to. They agreed that she sounded as if she had been physicaly stretched from India to Millside, specifically in order to make that noise here. Caro was almost light-headed with happiness. Why? What had changed since last night? It was still a mess – everything was still a mess. The only difference was that Alan's presence made her drunk enough to ignore it.

"I can't imagine never sleeping with you again," she said suddenly. "I don't think I could bear it."

He laughed. "Will you write me a reference?"

They called back at the Red House to get Caro's things, and to make love, although they had assured each other that they would not get sidetracked.

The weekend continued as it had begun. Very late that night they booked themselves into an empty little pub-cum-hotel, in Chapelmoor, a village twenty miles east of town. It was absurd to think about talking, discussing the future, organizing their lives, when each other's skin and flesh and bones were within grasp.

They surfaced on Sunday morning – "For our statutory walk," as Alan put it. It was a brilliantly sunny windy day, and they walked beside a reservoir that had flooded the valley between two high moors. Fishermen were dotted along the shore, intent on the sparkling surface of the water. They walked in silence for quite a way, arms around each other's waists, bodies moving comfortably in step. At last Alan said, "All right."

Goose-pimples suddenly came up on Caro's skin, although it had not got any colder. She disentangled her arm from him.

"What are you doing?"

"Getting ready to listen to you."

"Well you can still hold me, can't you?"

"I – I – I can listen better if I don't." She put her hands in her pockets, hugging her arms to her sides, and stared at the water. The wind kept its surface ruffled, and the sun was reflected off the moving crest of every little wave. It was so bright it made her eyes ache.

"I don't want this to go on any more," he said.

"No."

"It's a mess."

"Yes."

"I want us to live together. You're right–" he went on more loudly, overriding her interruption "– we can't do it here, I can't just move in with you. We can't suddenly swap round all the bits of our existing lives, like a jigsaw. It's got to change completely. We must go somewhere else."

"Somewhere else?"

"Yes. Move away. Nothing will be any different while we stay here. I can – I can leave Carolyn – but not while she's within reach. I want us to move away."

The water kept moving and shimmering until she could no longer tell which was the surface and which the waves, and the whole reservoir seemed to be seething and moving horribly like a living thing, crawling with insects – ants, or maggots. Something fell into place in Caro's head.

"You were with her on Thursday night."

"Yes." He paused. "It isn't fair – fair to her, Caro, I – she's right. It's not fair."

"No."

She did not let herself follow up the thread of what he had said, about not leaving Carolyn while she was in reach, because to be upset would be irrelevant. Mechanically, as if she had been set a puzzle to do, she began to make a list of the items that would make the scales (as she already knew) weigh down against what he said – "move away". It was simple. Clare. Her friends. The Red House. Work – the park.

"We can get other jobs," he said. "Neither of us will find it difficult."

But in the autumn she would go round nurseries to choose shrubs and perennials for the blind garden, to fill it with scents and leaves that were lovely to the touch. Children would climb on the climbing frame and tower, and throw bread to ducks on the lake. The place would take shape and grow.

"No."

"You care more about – all that – than –"

"Than you? I suppose so." She could feel him staring at her.

"I don't believe you."

"Well it's true. You're not the only thing in my life, Alan." There was a silence. "And you wouldn't want to know me if you were."

After a short while he laughed bitterly. "I – I've left my wife – and kids – completely screwed up my life – and you . . . don't want to give an inch."

"That's right," she said, making her voice light and cold. If that was what he thought; if that was what it all came down to. . . . She stopped, turning to face him, but he carried on walking, ignoring her.

"Alan!"

He stood still, a few yards ahead of her, not looking at her.

"You don't know what you want!" she shouted. "You need a – a mother, not me."

He met her eyes briefly, expressionlessly, then turned and walked on.

Caro sat on the grass by the side of the path and watched him till he went out of sight, following the curving edge of the reservoir. Then she got up and headed back for the hotel. She felt hollow and dull, in her belly and her head, as if she had a hangover. She wanted to explain to him – she could have explained – but there was no point. She gathered her things from the room quickly, and ran downstairs to the bar. There were no buses back towards the city on a Sunday, the publican told her, looking at her curiously. She couldn't think of anything to say, and asked instead for a drink. How would she get home? At last she checked through her purse for change, and telephoned the Red House. Clare answered.

"Clare? Will – will you pick me up? I'm out at Chapelmoor, on the main road. I'll – I'll start walking to meet you."

It was not until they were nearly home that she began to panic badly about what he might do.

Chapter 22

Over that summer Carolyn's ordered existence collapsed into a chaos, of which very little was memorable afterwards. The period of chaos was ended, with the neatness of a full stop, by Alan hitting her. The night that he hit her provided a punctuation point not only to that summer, but to the first eleven years of their relationship. After it, things were different.

When she found out about the woman, there was a long time which happened in bursts of conflicting emotions, rather than days, nights, or weeks. She convinced herself that Alan was unfaithful (the most obvious fact, for some reason, was the hardest to swallow), that he deserved to be hated, that she would be calm and collected for the children's sakes. She imagined ways of putting everything right, scoured her memory for things that had gone wrong, blamed herself, wept uncontrollably and wished she was dead. She wished he was dead. She wished the woman was dead. She wished he would go for good. She wished above all that he would come back. And every time she saw him he said something different. Twice he convinced her that he wouldn't see the woman again, and life would go back to normal. They both cried, and made love, and she knew he meant it. Then he stayed out the following night. At other times he came in late, drunk, either sentimental or foul-tempered, and banged about the house until he managed to wake one of the children. On several occasions he told her he was moving out. She didn't believe him, not only because of the times when he told her he wasn't, but also because he never took any of his clothes or belongings. When she heard him running upstairs to their room – his room – early in the morning, to change his clothes, she was sickened by it. But she found herself clinging to the fact that he came back, that he was leaving this pretext for coming back, as a kind of hope.

Inevitably, it was the children that determined her behaviour. She must get up, make meals, keep the household running, smile and reply to their questions. She could do it, just about, if he kept away. Each time he returned, it fell apart again.

To destroy the tenacious hope in herself, and to make him go – to make it end, so that something, even if it was worse, could begin – she finally packed his suitcase. When it was full she dragged it into the hall and put his drawing-board on top of it. Then she went around the house gathering those of his belongings that she could carry: camera, binoculars, walking boots, the framed prints and drawings from his study, his big architecture books, his alarm clock, his daft hat with a feather in it. Most of them were Christmas and birthday presents from herself. She began to sort through his records. She worked mechanically, as if she were simply tidying up. It's no good, she kept telling herself, it's no good.

Then what she had dreaded most happened; before she had finished, he came back. She had bolted the front door. She heard him turning and twisting his key furiously in the lock, and ran to open the door before he started banging and woke the children.

"Why's it locked?"

"I – why not? You didn't – you told me you'd moved out. I've got every right to lock the door."

He pushed past her into the hall, then stopped, taking in the pathetic heap of possessions. "What's that?"

"I – I've packed your things. You said you'd moved out. You – You've got to take your things."

"My things?" His voice was faint with disbelief. He walked slowly towards the piled suitcase, and Carolyn realized with a flash of terror that she had been right to fear his reaction.

"Alan – " she ran after him, clutching at his arm "– I'm not – it's not –"

He shook her off like an insect. "Fuck off." He stared down at the refugee pile for a moment, then turned to her, laughing bitterly. "So that's me – tidied up and out of the fucking way. That's me –" He kicked the side of the suitcase. "You bitch – you fucking bitch – you can't wait to get rid of me, can you? You – you –" He shook his head.

"That's not fair – it's not. You're the one who wants to go. You're the one who – who –" She was trying desperately not to cry.

"Stop snivelling." He spoke with such contemptuous hatred that she was silenced. "I'll go – don't worry – I'll fucking go. There's not much bloody point in staying here is there?" He stopped, staring at his things as

254

if he had forgotten something.

Carolyn held her breath, so that he would stop – go away – go out of the room –

"Not much, is it?" he said suddenly. "Not much to show for ten years of domestic bliss. You get the house – do you? And the furniture? This is a fair division, you reckon?"

She had not dreamt of dividing things up. Suddenly she foresaw all the wretched detail of divorce, the haggling over cutlery and school holidays. "I didn't – I never thought of dividing –"

"What the fuck did you think, you bloody neat little housewife?"

"I – I – just so you – can go and not – keep coming back for your clothes – in the morning –" She was weeping openly.

"Stop that fucking noise!" He grabbed a picture from the pile and waved it at her. "Do you think I care? D'you think I care about the fucking stupid mindless things?" He hurled the picture at the stair wall. It smashed, and fragments of glass shot across the hall.

"Alan – stop – the children! You'll wake –"

"The fucking children!" he screamed in her face, and pushed her away from him with all his force.

She fell back against the front door, catching the back of her head on the letter box. She felt a sharp pain on her head, then very hot, then cold and sick. She let herself slump down on her side. It was too much effort to sit up.

Something stopped then, as if the blow had finally knocked some sense into her head, knocked something straight so that she could see him for what he was. She watched from a distance his display of remorse and concern, as he tried to help her to the sofa, nearly slipping himself on a piece of broken glass. He dabbed at her head with a soaking wet towel, and she felt the separate cold trickles of water running down her neck and back, then stopping and being absorbed into a warmer dampness by the waistband of her skirt. She touched at the hurt herself. It was sticky. She must go upstairs and use two mirrors, to see if it needed stitches. The sound of his voice ran on – she couldn't look at him, and brushed away his arm unsteadily, making her way out of the room, holding on to the back of the sofa, and then the door-sills. Pulling herself up on the banister, she went upstairs one at a time. She could feel him behind her, watching. It was hard to see because of the wet hair, but the cut did not seem big. She went to her room and lay carefully on her side on the bed.

At dawn she washed her face in the bathroom. It was a dull pain, it would get better. She was thankful the cut was in her hair where the children would not see. She must clear up the glass before they woke. She went downstairs quietly, and was glad to see that he had gone.

That day, Friday, was calm, and so was the weekend. He did not come back. And the clear vision which the blow had given her did not waver. She did not have to be afraid of him, or try to please him again. He knew no more than a child what he should value. After he had hurt her he had cried and babbled. She was embarrassed for him. Her vision of him, the basis of the way she knew him, was changed. He did not know more than her. He did not know what he wanted or what was right, and so he was blundering about breaking and destroying everything, and blubbering like a baby when he saw the damage he'd done. He was pitiful.

She knew he would be back; and it seemed sickeningly appropriate, as it turned out, that he could not even make it back on his own two feet, but had to be handed back like a baby – "Now she's finished with him," she thought bitterly. The phone rang on Sunday evening and a woman who introduced herself as Clare something said that she had been asked to call to tell Carolyn that her husband was at a certain pub, and might need help to get home.

Carolyn received the news in silence.

"Mrs Blake? Mrs Blake?" The voice at the other end was kindly and anxious, with a slight American accent. "Please listen to me. I know you must feel badly – hurt – by what's happened. But I – if it's any help – I don't think they'll see each other – any more. It was Caro who asked me to call you. I'm sorry."

There was another silence.

"Thankyou," said Carolyn automatically. She took the address of the hotel. It was a long way out of town, she would have to get a taxi.

And so she fetched him home, as if he were an incapable child, accepting from a cold distance the fussy help of the publican and his wife. She did not question him about what had happened, or why. She did not care about it. She simply looked after him, with automatic compassion, as she would have done any sick creature placed in her charge.

Chapter 23

On Tuesday of the week after she had broken with Alan, Caro left work early. She had looked up Kevin Jackson's address in the Canal Project file. He lived very near to the south gate of the park; only a few streets away from the Red House, in fact.

The curtains were drawn across the front window, and from the doorstep she could hear the sound of a television. Kevin himself opened the door. When he saw it was her he half shut it again, as if she might try to force her way in. She was taken aback by the sullen hostility in his face.

"What d'you want?"

"I – I've come to see you. I want to have a talk with you, Kevin."

"What about?"

"About the park."

"I've talked to Jim – I've talked to the pigs – I've talked to that sodding Bellamy – I don't want to talk about the fucking park any more."

"I'm not – I haven't come to – I wanted to see if I could be any use."

He didn't speak, leaning out aggressively with his foot against the door. She stood still, not knowing what else to say. After a minute he stepped back, and jerked the door wider open with an angry movement. He walked ahead of her through the passage to the kitchen at the back of the house.

"Me Dad's watching telly." He leant against the sink, leaving her standing awkwardly in the doorway.

"I'm sorry," she said lamely. "I haven't come to get at you, Kevin – honestly. And I haven't – I don't know what you've said to anyone else. I haven't even seen Jim."

There was a silence.

"I'm sorry," she said again. "I know it must be – boring, going

257

over it all again. But I really would like to know what happened. I might be able to help."

He pulled a face, and gave an exaggerated sigh. She fumbled after the friendly ease that had existed between them when they'd worked together; when he'd done his mountaineering act down the side of the lock, and cracked dreadful jokes while they all sheltered in the back of the van, waiting for a shower to pass.

"Have you seen any of the others?" He shook his head. She forced herself to smile. "Done any mountaineering lately?"

He said, "Huh," under his breath, disgustedly, and turned to look out of the small window over the sink.

"Look Kevin – I – I know you didn't light that fire. I want to know what you did do and what you saw. I'm not trying to catch you out. Stop acting like a kid."

He gave another exaggerated sigh, and turned back to her, folding his arms resignedly. She saw that he was going to talk, and pulled out one of the chairs from the table and sat down.

"I went down to the fence about eleven-thirty – after closing time. I wanted some soil – right? So I nipped over the fence, sprinted down to the stores, and filled a bin-liner. I scraped it in with my hands, right, so that's why they were black." He held them up, as if they were still black, for evidence. "When it was full it was fucking heavy, and I went back as quiet as I could. I didn't hear anything or see anything. I wouldn't have noticed if they'd been letting off fucking fireworks. I was concentrating on getting out and not rupturing myself and not ripping the fucking bin-liner. I was pushing it under the fence–"

"Under the fence?" She was surprised.

"Yeah. You don't think I could chuck it over, do you? – when a cop car comes zooming out of nowhere and stops dead in front of me. And that's it."

"Why did you want the soil?"

He stared at her, pressing his lips together, then shrugged.

"I dunno. For a dare. Someone bet me I couldn't."

"Who?"

"I dunno. I've forgotten."

"Is that what you told the police?"

"Yeah. Why not? It's the truth." His voice was full of aggression again.

Caro pulled a face. "I wouldn't believe it. I mean, I don't believe it."

"Well you know what you can do," he said, and turned round to the window again.

"Kevin – if someone did bet you, you wouldn't forget who it was. It doesn't make sense." She watched his narrow back. His shoulders were hunched against her. After a minute he let them drop, and stood up straight.

"All right," he said flatly. He went to the back door, opened it, and stepped out into the yard. Caro followed him to the doorway. The yard was dark and narrow, flanked by the wall of the Jacksons' outdoor toilet and coal hole on the left, and the back wall of next door's toilet and coal hole on the right. Opposite the kitchen door was the yard door, in a high wall, and a dented dustbin. Along the right hand wall were ranged an old-fashioned bathtub, on curling iron feet, and two polythene-lined orange boxes. The orange boxes were full of black soil, and contained rows of newly planted lettuce seedlings. The bath had a thin layer of soil in the bottom of it. Caro glanced at Kevin.

"I got that lot the night before," he said. "I needed some more for the bath, right?"

"Why didn't you tell them?"

He laughed as if she was stupid.

"Tell them I nicked two lots, and make it twice as bad for myself? One of the stupid sods came out here for a piss and never even noticed it!" He laughed again, genuinely amused, and led the way into the kitchen. Caro glanced back at the orange boxes. They looked like boats with their cargo of soil and brave little sails of green leaves.

"Did you grow the lettuce yourself?"

"Yeah, from seed. I grew them in my bedroom in egg boxes. Real *Blue Peter* stuff! I've got some tomatoes for the bath – I grew them too."

"That's good," she said. "I can – I can bring you some good soil. I've got a garden full of it."

"OK. Thanks."

"But – I think you should tell the police."

"Why the fuck should I tell them?"

She was still unnerved by the speed at which he switched from amiability to aggression. "Because it gives you a motive for being

259

there – it sounds true – instead of sounding as if you're covering something up."

"Covering what up?"

"The fire, for heaven's sake. That's the thing they care about. One sack of topsoil's neither here nor there."

"That's not what that cunt Bellamy said. He said he didn't care if I only took a pocketful of soil, he'd still make sure I got the works."

"Well, we'll see. We'll see about Bellamy. When's it going to court?"

"They haven't told me yet."

Caro nodded. "All right. I – I'll be in touch, Kevin." She opened the front door. "I'll bring you that soil – tomorrow."

He came right out on to the doorstep, smiling ruefully. "First time I ever nicked anything I got caught too. Bastards."

"What was that?"

"A car."

"They caught you?"

"Yeah. I'm on probation."

Caro couldn't think of anything to say, and raised her hand in an awkward wave.

"You'd better keep your nose clean, then," she managed at last, and turned to go down the road. The two boxes of frail seedlings in the brick backyard made an image she could not shift from her head.

Clare let herself in at ten that night, after a long day's rehearsing, and found Caro on the phone in the hall. Clare patted her on the head in greeting and went into the kitchen.

"Jenny Williamson gave me your number," she heard Caro say, and stopped just inside the doorway to listen. "I've got – I know about something that she thinks would be a good story for your programme." There was a pause. "Yes – I . . . we need to meet up. . . . Yes, of course. It's, well, I'm working for the Council, on Millside Park, and I've found out – I can prove – that Councillor Bellamy – "

Poking her head back through the doorway, Clare grinned at Caro (who was not looking) and brought her hands together in a mime of silent but heartfelt applause.

Chapter 24

It seemed to Carolyn that time passed very slowly in the weeks after she brought Alan home. The effort of being an efficient machine made her tired. She seemed to have gone numb in the part of her head where emotions live, and to feel nothing but a lead grey heaviness. With this weight pressing down on her – and no anticipation or interest to act as oil – each task became immeasurably slow and heavy, so that the making of the beds filled a morning, the washing of the clothes exhausted her. Everything must carry on, would carry on, because of the children. But she felt as if she had been removed far away from them, so that she could only distantly perceive their laughter and chatter, and hardly feel the solid warmth of their bodies when they hugged her goodnight. It seemed as if it would never end, this going on of time from day to day, and the mindless alternations of light and dark, like the endlessly tedious revolutions of a treadmill.

Alan, she supposed, when she could be bothered to think of him, felt the same. He returned home in time for dinner at seven-thirty every evening, and they told one another briefly about the events of their days. There seemed to be a lot of silence in the house, like something deep and sticky you had to wade through. Even the children were quieter. But he was polite and considerate to her, as she was to him. They even made love, two or three times, without saying a word. It happened late at night, when the light was out, almost as if it was something they could pretend wasn't happening. She was not upset by it, as she had half thought she would be. She didn't know if there were any feelings attached to it – or, if there were, how they might be categorized. It was mechanical, although the initial impulse to turn to one another wordlessly in the dark seemed not to be a need a machine might feel.

On a Sunday morning in October, Carolyn lay in bed late. Alan was making cooked breakfast, something he had done on and off for years. She roused herself and muttered "Thanks" as he brought a mug of tea in to her and placed it silently on the bedside table. He shut the door behind him but the catch did not slot home properly, and the door sprang open a crack as he was going downstairs. Carolyn heard his footsteps on the last few stairs, then the sound of his voice. There was laughter. Carolyn half raised her head, then realized it was Chrissy. Chris must be down there helping him. She lay flat again, inhaling and warming the cold air her movement had let into the bed. She could hear Annie and Cathy giggling in their room over some silly game or other. After a while she found herself listening to their voices, trying to work out what they were playing. Cathy was giggling uncontrollably. It sounded as if Annie was giving her instructions. Cathy often giggled like that, Carolyn realized; as if she was forcing herself to carry on until she became completely helpless, so that she would stagger about and fall over, hiccuping and unable to catch her breath. It was like the way she made herself giddy, spinning round and round until she fell over, often hurting herself. But then she did it again, as if she felt a need to alter or confuse her senses. Why was she doing that? Was it normal?

The anxiety hit Carolyn with surprising force. She should have noticed it before. She heaved herself up on to her elbows, then sat up properly, pushing the pillow against the wall to make a back rest. She pulled her knees up towards her, tucking in the duvet around her bottom and sides. It was beginning to be cold in the mornings now. She must get Chris a new duffle coat this week. She drank her tea slowly, cradling her hands around its heat.

The smells of bacon and fresh coffee crept into the room, along with a little gust of warm air. They must have turned on the fire in the kitchen. Cathy had stopped giggling now. Carolyn listened intently. Suddenly Annie began to sing.

> "Dance, dance, wherever you may be
> I am the lord of the dance said he
> And I'll lead you all to the bottom of the sea
> I'll lead you all in the dance, said he."

Carolyn had heard the song before. Chris used to sing it – it must be a hymn they all did at school. There was a sudden babble of sound then the two girls began to sing together, or rather, Annie sang and Cathy shouted, "Ant, ants, wherever you may be –"

262

Cathy ended with a squeal and an unnaturally long peal of laughter, while Annie's voice continued the tune. Was it normal? Annie sang beautifully. And her piano exam was on Tuesday. I must remind Alan to leave the car, Carolyn told herself. She had an odd sensation of movement in her head, as if a heavy weight was being shifted slightly. Tilted, allowing a crack of light to enter. He must come home early on Thursday too, she remembered – there's that thing of Patsy's in the evening. Patsy had asked her if she had some time to spare now the children were all at school. She was looking for more one-to-one teachers for the adult literacy class she ran in town.

"I can't do that – I can't teach people." Carolyn had panicked.

"You can read, can't you? For heaven's sake, you've got A levels. You're better qualified than I am!"

Looking back on the conversation now, Carolyn realized that Patsy had been trying to help her, as much as to increase her own tutor numbers. Patsy knew that things had gone wrong; Alan's absences, and the screams and crashes late at night would have told her that much, never mind the sudden embarrassed appearances of Carolyn in search of a babysitter, on those occasions when Alan had to be fetched home. But Patsy always behaved as if these things were perfectly normal and required no explanation. Carolyn knew she would never talk about it with anyone. It was a private wound. And that disloyalty to Alan was unthinkable. Once Patsy's quiet kindness had made her burst into tears. She had come back from taking the children to school after lunch, and found Patsy in the back garden on a stool, braced against a biting wind, trying to tie a knot in the washing line.

"It broke after you left," she told her. "I've put your things in my machine to rinse, I'm afraid they got a bit muddy."

Remembering that day, Carolyn again had a sense of things opening up. It was a long time since she had remembered things like that. She had been stuck – up to her neck – in the present, as if she had no past or future. Well, that's silly – you have, she told herself briskly.

She put down her mug and climbed out of bed, snatching her dressing gown from its hook on the door. The smell of coffee was so strong she could almost taste it. As she fastened her gown she moved over to the window and looked out through the crack between the curtains. What was the weather doing? She felt, ridiculously, that she had not known what the weather was for weeks.

The sky was grey. There was a light drizzle falling; so fine that it was hard to see it in the air, but the leaves and grass were shiny with wet. It *was falling softly, as if the air itself were falling, coating everything with moisture.*

Carolyn leaned her forehead against the window pane, staring out. The sensation of cold glass against her skin was like an echo of the lifting and making of space inside her head. She heard Annie shout "Shut up!" In the silence her clear voice began again. "Dance, dance, you jolly little flea. . . ."

Carolyn wiped away the mist her breath had made on the glass, smiling to find herself humming the tune too. She must tell Annie the words Chris had made up for it. They were funnier.

Acknowledgements

Thanks to North West Arts for their Writer's Bursary which helped to make the writing of this novel possible, and to Jo Barnes, Mary Black, Robin Dawes and Dr Wendy Rogers.

For permission to reprint copyright material the author and publisher gratefully acknowledge:

Chappell Music for 'Rose Garden (I never promised you a)' Composer and Author: Joe South. © 1967 Lowery Music Co. Inc. UK Publisher: Lowery Chappell Music. Published by kind permission; Stainer and Bell Limited, for one verse of 'Lord of the Dance' by Sydney Carter.